Night Walker

Janice E.C. Coleman

DEDICATION

Night Walker is dedicated to first and foremost, my family. Thank you especially to my husband, Mike, and daughter, Sofia, for your time, patience, editing skills, and honesty. I could not have written this book without you two. I would also like to thank Serena, Jessica, and Cindy for taking the time to read my book and offer suggestions. And of course, thank you Mom and Dad.

A big thank you to The Damned, The Screaming Trees, and Triumvirat. Your music set the mood for authoring this book, helping me through many, many nights of writing and revision.

And lastly, I want to thank
the great city of London
and its many ghosts.

PROLOGUE

Knock, knock, knock…

The man grumbled as he turned down the television and looked toward the front door. He listened, not sure if he had heard a knock or not. He decided he hadn't, and so he turned back around to his Graham Norton rerun. As his finger was poised to turn up the volume, he was interrupted by the doorbell this time. Cursing while pushing his pudgy body out of the threadbare easy chair, he lumbered to the front door.

"Who's there?"

"I've locked the keys in my car and was wondering if you had something I could use to jimmy the lock. Sorry, I know it's late."

The man inside peered out the window and saw a tall, thin person in a winter cap and heavy coat, a cigarette dangling from his mouth. Or her mouth. He couldn't tell. The voice wasn't clear enough through the door, and shadows obscured the person's face. Regardless, he figured he could handle any row from this person if he had to, and certainly if it were a woman.

"Awright, I'll be out in a second," he yelled through the locked door. He opened the window so the visitor on the outside could hear him better, letting in a blast of cold air. "I'll meet you at the bottom of the steps. I'd invite you in, but, never can be too careful."

The stranger nodded, turned, and walked down the steps to the street level, dropping the cigarette on the ground.

After a few minutes, the man emerged from his house with a thin piece of metal in his hands. He thought he'd be quick, so he didn't bother with a coat. Shivering, he walked down the steps, "Awright… em… bloke… then, which car is it?" he asked as he craned his neck looking down the dark, deserted street. Mistake.

From behind, the stranger wrapped an arm around the man's throat, squeezed, and spoke softly in the victim's ear. "Don't scream and I won't harm you… too much."

The victim could now detect a British accent, and he was certain from the strength that it was a man. Red faced and scared, the victim attempted to fight back. He tried clawing at his assailant's face, but the attacker's head casually moved just out of reach, like a dog who doesn't want to give up its toy. The victim struggled to kick, but he couldn't find his footing since he was being forcibly dragged down the street.

The attacker calmly, quietly said, "Shhh… relax, John. The less you struggle, the less this will hurt."

Hearing his name gave John pause. Confused, he stopped resisting, but only briefly. He desperately needed air and desperately wanted to see his attacker's face.

The assailant dragged John into the small alley next to the house. John kicked some more, finally striking a shin. His attacker didn't even flinch, responding only with an even tighter seal around John's throat. John tried to dig his fingers into the grip, but his attacker's coat was too thick for him to cause any pain. Desperately, John flailed the piece of metal in his other hand, but couldn't see where to strike.

With one arm around John's neck, the stranger's other hand pulled down the hat, or rather, a black, woolen ski mask. The assailant was very adept at this, unfettered by John's feeble attempts to catch a glimpse or retaliate.

With his windpipe drowning, John started making horrible choking noises. But then, just as he thought his eyes were going to pop, relief finally came. The stranger released the boa constrictor-like grip. But John's relief was short lived as a sharp knee to his back sent him careening face-first into a row of trashcans. On his knees, John turned his head slowly to look at the stranger and then quickly raised the metal tool, but before he could do anything, the stranger kicked John in the face, knocking him yet again against the trashcans. Blood pooled on John's face, making him sputter and cough; the metal piece dropped to the ground with a ping. "What do you want from me? I dun't have any money," John cried; blood sputtering from his lips.

"I dun't want your money. But, I do want you to pay." The assailant's angry whisper had a rasp that made it hard to definitively say whether John knew the person or not. Dizzy from the metallic smell and taste of blood, he tried to stand, but couldn't quite muster the strength or coordination to do it.

The attacker, then, crouched down and grabbed John by the hair, pulled back his head, and exposed his neck. The stranger plucked the piece of metal off the ground and held it up to John's watering eye.

"Tell me, John, do you beat your wife?" The masked stranger breathed, face centimeters from John's. "And don't lie. It's really a rhetorical question. Take your time."

The terrified man paused and thought he best not lie. "Yes, I do…I have… I've been arrested for it, but she dropped the charges."

"But she's still with you?"

"Yes," John gasped out.

"How do you beat her," the stranger asked, calmly, metal piece still poised at John's right eye.

"What, do you get off on this?" he dared to ask as he was trying to shift around and break loose, his hair roots screaming for relief.

"Wrong answer," the stranger warned, wrenching the man's hair tighter.

"I dunno, many ways. I've punched her, I've hit her with a belt... are you satisfied?"

"Did you cause any permanent damage?"

"No... just surface... c'mon bloke, please, let me go," John pleaded.

"Bloke? Well, okay, this is what we are going to do. I am going to beat the tar out of you. After that, you are going to stop beating your wife. Are we clear?" The stranger let go of the crying man's hair to allow him to nod *"yes."* The masked person stood up and stepped back.

"Now get up." The voice now changed to a loud, commanding tone. Stunned, John did what he was told and faced the masked stranger. And that's when the attacker made good on the promise, slamming a balled-up fist into John's already bloodied face. The assailant then punched him in the stomach, followed by an elbow to the side of John's face that made a crunching sound on impact. Brutal strikes continued until John fell to the ground, gasping and sobbing. Pummeled and broken, John thought and prayed the stranger was done, but then he heard a belt unbuckle and slowly slide from its loops. There was a long pause, time enough for John to play back in his mind the punishment he had just received, and the similarities to the beatings he had delivered to his wife. Interrupting his thoughts and his quiet sobs, the punishment began again, violent belt lashings raining down without relent, raising welts and then cutting through John's clothes and into his tenderized flesh. Every blow surgically placed upon every inch of the blubbering man's body.

And then abruptly, the beating stopped. The stranger stepped back, put the belt back on, and rubbed swelling left-hand knuckles, now bruised to a lovely shade of purple and red, while leisurely walking away.

CHAPTER 1

"…he punched her repeatedly until her face became almost unrecognizable with bruises. Her four upper front teeth were knocked out. Blood drained out of her mouth onto the wood floor, staining it forever like a scar on skin. To finish what he had started, we can only assume he choked her to death. Bruises the size of fingers were found on her neck. As she gasped for air, possibly, only a wheeze could be heard. She died right there in that corner room," the guide proclaimed as he pointed to the far right, top floor window. "How do we know about the wheeze, you may ask? Well, fine ladies and gentlemen, there have been plenty, including patrons like yourselves on this tour, who have heard the wheeze from Abigail Smalls."

I heard snickering from the front of the group. "Oh, yeah, I'd like to hear that wheeze." Obviously American, the tourist yapped audibly to the woman standing next to him. She, however, gave the man a nasty look and side-stepped away. This guy was yammering about during the whole tour, heckling and making rude jokes. It was really getting old.

The tour guide, obviously a bit irritated after enduring a whole hour of this, smirked and spoke to the man. "We can do that, if you like." I don't think the American had intended for the guide to hear him. "But, I should ask you one question first. Have you ever gone into a place where it's so still and dark, your skin crawls?" He walked closer to the American as he continued. "A place with such a sinister history, you could feel it in your bones?" The American just stared at the guide, mouth agape. Now closer and barely audible, "I assure you, what happened in the Hartford House to Abigail was no made up account. We know she was a prostitute, we know she was strangled to death by Phineas Hall in the late 1800s. You may check the police records." The guide then paused and cocked his head. "We can go up there if you like," he said even more quietly, staring directly at the tourist who nervously rocked back on his feet.

Abruptly, lifting his head and outstretching his arms, the guide spoke, dramatically, "In fact, if anyone in this crowd would like to go up there, I do have a key." A number of people murmured and shuffled around, but no one volunteered.

Except for me. I stepped forward and timidly raised my hand.

"Ah! A brave soul. Anyone else?" He half smiled and raised his eyebrows at the American man who started to shift uncomfortably in his stance, but did not step forward.

The guide walked up to the tall cast iron gate where spikes adorned the tops of the twisted vertical spokes. He produced a skeleton key from the inside of his cloak and unlocked the barred gate, pushing it open slowly. He ascended six uneven, stone steps and then turned around to face me. As he gestured for me to follow, he looked back at the American man over my head and I am pretty sure mouthed the word "pussy."

Yep, that's what he mouthed. The American didn't seem to appreciate that. He pushed through the crowd, barged passed me while crashing into my shoulder, and then started to run up the steps.

Blackness. No walls, no earth, nothing but blackness. A jolt, a flash, a searing pain washed through me. Teeth knocked out, the metallic taste of blood filling my mouth. Crack, crack, crack, an unseen hand pelting my body with a metal rod, everywhere, bruising everywhere, welts popping up all over my skin. Dizziness, nausea, and then, and then, cold steel penetrating my body. Unbearable pain, another wave of nausea, unending pain. And then…

My mouth dry, I tried to swallow and catch my breath. What the fuck was that? Getting my senses back, I saw the American idiot approach the guide. I licked my teeth with my tongue, examined my arms and legs, seeing that everything felt and looked fine. Whoa, that was weird. Wiping my eyes and smearing black lines of mascara on the back of my hands, I casually looked around to see if anyone noticed anything, but everything seemed normal. Did I black out or something? My imagination must be in overdrive from the spooky atmosphere of the ghost tour. I breathed in and shook the whole thing off while slowly walking through the gate and up the first set of steps.

The American got right up into the tour guide's face and said, "Alright, let's go meet some ghosts." He put "ghosts" in exaggerated air quotes.

The guide shrugged, turned back toward the mansard roofed house and walked another ten feet to the bottom of five more stone steps. He then strode up the steps that led to the wooden front door of the house, clad with bars, matching the entry gate's twisted iron. Inserting another key in the door, he turned the knob and slowly, dramatically, swung the door open to the left. I heard a loud, rusty squeak.

"After you," he said to the man, gesturing with a sarcastic flourish of his hand.

The American walked up the second set of steps and as he slid by, he bucked his face at the guide, who did not flinch, and then turned to go in, paused at the creepy staircase looming above, and then quickly started up the steps. As he got closer to the top, his footsteps became less hurried and then eventually stopped. Making my way down the short path, I paused at the bottom of the second set of steps, peering up at the guide.

"We're coming," the tour guide drawled. He turned back to me. "Ready, miss?" he asked in a gentle voice. He then walked down two steps and held out his right hand. Completely confused and a little out of it because of my really weird hallucination, or whatever it was, I hesitated.

"Don't be afraid, I'll protect you," the tour guide winked at me, waiting patiently for me to take his hand. Tentatively, I placed my hand in his and let him help me up to the door. I shivered from his touch, even though he was wearing gloves. He must have detected this because he cocked his head and smiled ever so slightly. I looked away quickly to hide my embarrassment, let go of his hand, and went into the house.

Our guide turned up his lantern, waved to the curious crowd, and then closed the door behind him, shutting in the eerie quiet.

The wooden stairs creaked under our feet as we ascended toward the waiting, impatient American.

When we finally reached the top of the stairwell, the guide directed "angry man" into a room ribbed with moonlight and shadows. We followed the ugly American; actually, I never really got a good look at the guy's face, but he certainly played the role well. Everything was so dark, but from his silhouette, he looked pretty chubby.

The room was pretty much how I pictured it. Small, dimly lit, wooden floors, peeling wall-paper. It did not have a rocking chair or a creepy carriage with a doll in it, to my relief, but other than that, it fit the mold of the standard skin crawling, haunted room. The tour guide pointed to the corner. "There," he said. "There's where it happened." In two long strides, he reached the corner, crouched down, and held the lantern over the darkened floor. The guide paused there, not moving except for the rise and fall of his shoulders from deep inhales and exhales, as if he were meditating, breathing in the surroundings.

I walked over to the corner, but the American stayed put. "See, I don't hear nuthin'."

"Anything," the tour guide muttered under his breath. I had to smile.

We waited a few more minutes in silence. The place was intimidating, especially knowing what had happened there over a hundred years ago.

Blood, nausea, pain.

I winced again, that same vision and odd jolt went through my body. What the hell was that? I thought as I rubbed my face, trying to clear the cobwebs out of my head. I'd never felt something like that before, except maybe during a lucid dream. I hoped it wasn't some kind of seizure or some kind of low blood sugar effect. I realized I hadn't eaten since breakfast. My thoughts, however, were interrupted by the dickhead. I narrowed my eyes at him. I'd really had enough.

"Waste of 18 pounds." As the American started to leave, I put my hand to my throat and started to pant. My breath became louder and louder and I cried out as if my face was going to explode. I heard a wheeze, but the wheeze was coming from me. I saw the American look over at me, obviously frightened, but said in a high-pitched voice, "This is bullshit!" and slammed down the steps, each creak and stomp getting softer as he descended.

The tour guide looked up at me from his crouched position and abruptly stood and placed one hand on my shoulder, holding up the lantern to my face with the other. "Are you alright?" he asked standing close, searching for an answer in my face. I pulled back a little, startled, seeing his eyes close up in the glow of the lantern. I'd never seen eyes like that— predominantly light green and dark blue with gold flecks. A black halo surrounding the iris matched a dark pupil in the center. The color, the depth, the brightness, pierced right through me.

I swallowed hard, regaining my composure and grinned as I raised one eyebrow, "Just fine."

His facial expression turned from concern to confusion, then softened into realization.

"You're a naughty girl, miss." He noted, amused, dropping his hand from my shoulder.

I just shrugged, "Yeah, well, he kind of deserved it, don't you think?"

The guide didn't agree or disagree, but he smiled. "Well," he said, "we had better get back." He led me down the steps, one hand holding onto the lantern, the other lightly touching my back. When we emerged from the house, the American was barking up a storm at the awaiting crowd.

"I'm tellin' you, you all should get your money back. This is a hoax," and off he stormed after seeing us come out of the house.

"I must apologize to each of you. We had a little incident upstairs, but everything is alright now. It's getting late and we should head back to the visitor center. I hope you enjoyed the tour." As the guide ushered me down the outside steps, I heard murmurs of people speculating on what had transpired in the house.

"This way, now," he charged to the crowd, quickening his step. I followed him, but thought back to the weird pain I had and the creepiness of that room. I hugged myself as I shivered.

When we got back to the visitor center, the guide made his concluding statements and collected his tips. As I walked up to give him a 10, he raised his hand, stop-sign-like and shook his head. The crowd had pretty much dispersed and I started to walk away.

Then, I heard a faint, "Excuse me." I turned to look. The tour guide had his hands in his coat pockets and was chewing on his lower lip.

"Em, w… would you like to join me for a cup of tea?" His question came out with such a lack of confidence, I had to pause for a second to make sure the man asking the question was the same man who ran the tour. This was such a sharp contrast from the commanding, deep voice I was witness to not five minutes ago.

Since I was going home to an empty apartment and really, really didn't want to be alone after the ghost tour and the freaky feelings I had, I nodded my head. Besides, as far as I could tell from the lantern light, he was really good looking. He gave me a shy smile and held up one finger, gesturing to give him a moment. He disappeared into the visitor center, where his "moment" turned into fifteen minutes. I started to get a little irritated and contemplated splitting. Who knew if he was coming out anytime soon? But I stuck around because I had become quite curious about this guy. I sat down on the steps and closed my eyes.

Just as I started to assess the weird pain I had endured earlier, I felt a hand on my shoulder, making me jump.

"S..Sorry! I should have announced myself." The tour guide, now out of his garb, looked a little less, well, ghost tour guide-ish. No more hat, cloak, nor gloves, but an olive-green satin or silk oxford shirt with the two top buttons open and tucked into black jeans. He sported a black pea coat, similar to mine, that went down mid-thigh. He wore the same black Chuck Taylor's that stuck out as the only part of his work outfit that didn't match the ghost tour aura. Standing in the light of the visitor center's entrance, I noticed his complexion was ghostly-white, which contrasted heavily with his black wavy hair, all slicked back with gel except a few long strands that escaped, falling over his right eye. And those eyes. What more can I say about them? He had your stereotypical British teeth—a bit crooked, but in a way that gave his mouth character. His canines were a bit longer than average, giving them an almost fang-like appearance. He held his now bare hand out to me with a slight smile on his face. I took it and stood up, my 5'-5" frame reaching up to about his nose level.

"Shall we," he offered, dropping my hand, ever so gently.

Heading away from the visitor center, he asked, "There is a small cafe a few blocks away. Are you too tired to walk?" His voice back to the deeper timbre.

"No, I'm fine. I pretty much walk everywhere."

"Have you been in London long? American or Canadian, I assume?" he asked as we walked down the gas lamp-lit sidewalk. A soft rain started.

"Yes, to being an American, although, I'm not too thrilled to be lumped into the same category with that guy tonight. Um, I've been in London for about three months now. My workplace offered an opportunity to transfer here, so I thought 'why the hell not?' I mean, I'm single with no real attachments, so what's stopping me?" I glanced up to see if he reacted to this, but no such luck.

As the rain fell slightly harder, we quickened our pace, made it to the café, and stepped inside. He put his hand on my upper back and showed me to a small table in the rear of the cool coffee house. I smiled broadly at the décor—the walls and tables were covered in graffiti—totally my kind of place. There were crayons on the table to scrawl your name or draw a picture, or whatever, anywhere you could find an open spot. "This is so cool!" I chirped a little too eagerly, and took a crayon and started drawing on the table.

The tour guide smiled slightly, wrinkled his nose and mocked, "Yes, *cool.*"

"I didn't catch your name," I said, casually laying the crayon down.

"Thomas Hall… Tom."

"Oh, Hall, like the murderer in the Hartford House!" I bellowed a little too loudly, remembering the name from the last stop.

Tom smiled a little and looked around, "Yes, I may bear the last name of an infamous local, but Hall is a pretty common name, if you look it up in the phonebook, you will find a plethora of them." He paused. "And your name?" Tom asked as he slowly leaned back in the booth.

"Anna Pearson."

"I am pleased to meet you, Anna Pearson. I am sorry about your experience tonight, however."

I paused for a second, wondering if he detected my unease from my 'lack of food' trauma, but realized he was talking about the American. I started to ramble and speak quickly as I do when I'm a bit nervous. "Sorry? What, because of that dude? He was an asshole and I had some fun with him. But, regardless, I really love ghost tours—this one was one of the best I've been on."

"Thank you," Tom said, sincerely.

I went on, "But, one weird thing did happen. Before we went into the house, and then again in the creepy room, I felt this horrible pain, like I was being beaten up, but then it was gone. I guess it was probably from all the stories you told. You made them sound so believable. Um, in addition to me forgetting to eat today."

Tom's eyes shifted a little. He leaned forward and said, "Hmmm, I am intrigued."

With Tom so close, my nostrils flared as a hint of cologne wafted toward me. I stared for a moment into his eyes, which were staring right back into mine with an intense curiosity. God, he was good looking.

With goose bumps erupting on my arms, I broke the eye contact abruptly and decided to give him some more details about my experience. "Well, everything was normal, and then when that jerk wad bumped into me, I suddenly saw this flash of teeth and blood and then felt the sharp pain. My head started to swim a little and it was like I was in a dream where you will yourself to wake up, but you can't? But when I snapped out of it, I felt a little dizzy, but that's it." The chills and the goose bumps returned, but not because of Tom's looks.

"Amazing," he whispered. "And I thought I was the only one." He looked down at the table.

"Excuse me? Only one?"

He ignored my question and looked up again, "Do you think Abagail was trying to tell you something?"

I looked at him skeptically, "Are you serious? I'm sure it was just from the power of suggestion, or lack of food." I reiterated. I really wanted to flag down the waiter and get something in my stomach.

Tom laughed. "I should be Prime Minister if my power of suggestion can cause a reaction like that. Let's get you some sustenance." He raised his hand, grabbing the attention of the waiter, who promptly walked over to our table. I ordered a decaf flat white and a vegetable sandwich. Tom asked for a pot of Earl Grey.

"So, do you get, um, feelings, too?'"

Tom hesitated for a minute, staring at the waters that I only half noticed the waiter had brought. "Ah, yes. Sometimes. But, as you experienced, they are usually fleeting. In that room, though, I always get some sort of foreboding sensation. I don't honestly like going up there." He paused for a second and then asked, "Do you believe in ghosts?" He looked at me from under his brow.

I shuddered at the question. Something about the way he said it and the way he looked at me gave me the creeps. He looked back down and picked up a crayon, mindlessly drawing squiggles on the table.

"I think so. I say I do, but then when something happens, I usually try to find some rational explanation. Do you?"

"Do I? You would think I would. I am intrigued by the prospect, I love the history behind it, and as I've said, I've had some, em, experiences, but, em, I don't know. I guess I am like you, trying to find a reasonable explanation."

"Do you often get one of those obnoxious tourists in the crowd?" I asked, sipping the water, hoping my growling stomach wasn't too loud.

"Not as often as you might think, but, yes, every once in a while it happens."

Our conversation was interrupted by the waiter placing a delicious looking sandwich in front of me. He then set down the flat white and teapot.

As I devoured my sandwich, we started chatting about surface stuff like what sites I have seen while in London, and so on. After about an hour, he claimed, "I'm sorry to cut the evening short, but I have some things to attend to at home. Do you mind if we go?"

A little disappointed, I replied "Sure."

He signaled to the waiter for the check. I pulled out my wallet and he shook his head no. I shrugged, put my wallet back, and thanked him as he handed the waiter some cash.

We both walked out into the unseasonably chilly night, glad that the rain had stopped.

"Did you drive to the tour?"

"Ah, no, I don't have a car," I explained.

"Neither do I. May I walk you home or we could share a cab if you are too far?"

"Um… okay, we're close enough to walk. I live in Clerkenwell," I said, wearily. I guess I trusted him, but more so, I liked his company—and I liked looking at him. As we started walking, I remarked, "You really have a great voice for this tour stuff."

"Thank you." He sounded amused.

We passed by the Asian fusion restaurant with the yellow sign where I get my pure watermelon juice. As we walked, dodging all the beautifully dressed people on the crowded sidewalk, I told Tom about the other tour I attended. "Yeah, so this other tour I went on when I first arrived in London, the guide was good, but he wore sandals, cargo shorts and a T-shirt. He didn't really create the atmosphere you want for a ghost tour. Plus, all his stories were a little formulaic."

Tom just nodded, probably not wanting to comment on fellow guides. British politeness, I guess. Sadly, I didn't really have much of that.

We walked another ten or so minutes, making small talk, until we turned down Seward Street and arrived at the steps leading to my red brick building.

"You know, I try to mix up the tours a bit so the stories aren't always the same, and so it doesn't get too boring for me. If you are game, you could be my guest tomorrow night. We'll be covering the Mayfair area, which has a lot of history." He stared down at me, making me step backwards, tripping on the lowest step. He grabbed my elbow before I fell.

"Quick reflexes," I stammered, embarrassed, as he let go of my arm.

Under the glow from the light on my building's glass brick overhang, I saw his eyes widening a little, waiting for an answer.

"Um, sure. That sounds like fun."

He straightened up a bit and gave me directions to the meeting place in front of the Burlington Arcade.

"Good, ah, splendid! I'll see you there at 8:30 tomorrow evening, then." He lingered for a little longer than necessary, as if he wanted to say more, but finally turned and started walking away. I watched him walk down the foggy sidewalk to the corner. He stopped, pulled something out of his pocket and then rolled his shoulders forward. I thought I saw a puff of smoke swirl up and around his head, blending in with the fog. I sighed. A smoker, dammit.

CHAPTER 2

"You know, my dear boy, there is evil in this world? Scourges of the earth? These, em, 'people,' are prostitutes and homosexuals to name just two types. Do you know what those are?"

"Are they the same thing as whores, sir?"

"Mmm… yes, you understand prostitutes are women who parade themselves around on the street, selling themselves to men. They charge men to have sex with them. Do you know what sex is?"

"Yes, sir."

"These whores, they ruin the fabric of our society. Now, do you know what a homosexual is?"

"No sir."

"A man who has sex with another man. Or a woman who has sex with another woman. It's the most unnatural of acts on this earth. It disgusts me. God did not intend for humans to behave as such."

The boy looked up, nodding in agreement.

"So, I'm going to teach you what we do. Do you want to be a hero? To help London become moral and good?"

"Yes sir!"

"Come along now. There's one right over there."

— *Friday, September 5*

"So, what happened last night? Didn't you do that ghost tour? I've been wanting to do that, but you know, when you live your whole life in one place, you don't really do the touristy thing."

Jamie was both my supervisor and my closest friend in London, so I didn't mind when she started to interrogate me while pouring her tea.

I leaned against the fridge in the cafeteria and just shrugged with a slight smile on my face.

Jamie looked up at me, her eyes wide and her smile overtaking her face. When Jamie smiles, her whole face beams. She has very dark skin, large brown almond-shaped eyes, huge dimples, and a new hair style almost every week. We became friends almost instantly when she was assigned as my "mentor/supervisor" for Jaybee and Rowe, a publisher of mainly coffee table books. We both worked as indexers, going through the pictures and finding items in them that should be in the index. I always found it to be fun, like a "Where's Waldo" kind of thing.

"You met someone, didn't you?" She squealed. "Was it scary? Was he cute?" Jamie had a tendency to ask a lot of questions in one breath. I always tried to answer them all.

"Okay, um, yes, I met someone… I guess. Yes, the tour was terrifying, and yes, he was… cute. I mean he was really cute, but mysterious."

"So, who was the guy? Someone in the crowd? Did you go to a pub after?"

"No, it was actually the tour guide."

Jamie wrinkled her nose and frowned a little, "The tour guide? Aren't they supposed to be either ancient, really dorky, or just strange? I think it's in the job description."

"Well, yes, I mean, I've been on quite a few and a lot of them are like that, but this guy was different. I mean, he had a fantastic voice for it, and he wove a great story, but, I don't know. I wouldn't have pegged him for the tour guide type. He was also pretty young, maybe in his early thirties."

"So, did you go out after?"

Wow, just one question. "Ah, yes… we went to a really cool coffee house where you can write on the walls and furniture."

"Oh yeah! 'Graffiti Joes'… I know that place. So, how did it happen? How'd you start talking? Did he ask you to the coffee house? You ask him?"

"Well, he asked me. There was a real dick at the tour who was making jokes the whole time. Anyway, long story short, the three of us went into one of the houses and I pretended to be attacked by a ghost, which freaked the guy out. I think the tour guide, um, Tom, appreciated the gesture."

"That's brilliant!" Jamie beamed.

"He called me 'naughty.'" I grimaced, looking down at my black, chipped nail polish.

"Called it like he saw it. So, what else?" Jamie sipped her tea.

"Well, he did ask me to be his guest tonight."

"OH!" She got so excited, she spilled some of her tea on the floor. I grabbed a cloth and wiped it up.

"Maybe I should come tonight to check him out. I mean, to check out the tour!" She suggested.

"No way! I might get to have tea with him again."

"Relax, I'm just kidding! Get a picture so I can see what he looks like."

"Okay, if I think of it." We walked out of the cafeteria and went to our cubicles.

***

I tried to focus on work, but it just wasn't happening. I got up and went into the bathroom, where I stood looking at myself in the mirror. Pulling off the two hair ties that held up my pig tails, I assessed the condition of my almost black hair. I needed to trim my bangs, that's for sure. Wetting a paper towel, I gently wiped off the dark, thick eyeliner and red lipstick that I mistakenly applied too much of this morning—too much for work, I thought. I started obsessing about what I should wear tonight. Last night, I sported my vegan Doc Martens and ripped jeans, so I'm guessing Tom might like my style--he did ask me out after all, but he seems so proper. Running my fingers through my hair, I bunched up my hair in the back and secured the ponytail, severely. I sighed in the mirror and went back to my desk to see if I could start the new project I'd been assigned, "The Alleys of London." Instead, I mindlessly clicked through the Internet, watched stupid YouTube videos, played Candy Crush Saga (why?) and read a little movie news. I then clicked on one of the London news sites. Some guy was beaten, badly, not too far from my house.

> '…teeth knocked out, bruised face.'

> 'After a long hiatus, it seems likely that the "London Vigilante," has returned. In March, we reported on the brutal attack on John Atherton, who was beaten within an inch of his life. He had bruises all over his body and face. Atherton had been arrested for domestic violence, but his wife had dropped the charges. We can't be sure if the responsible party is the Vigilante in this new attack, but there are similarities between the two cases. Already, social media is connecting the latest victim to a history of domestic violence, but those reports are unsubstantiated at this time. The debate of whether one person has the right to be judge and jury, no matter the crime, is the subject of our latest online poll. And now, the weather.'

"Hey Jamie?" I called over the low cubicle panel.

She popped her head up like a prairie dog, eyes wide.

"What's this about the London Vigilante?"

"Oh, her? Well, we don't know if it's a 'her,' but we like to think so. She seeks out bad people. Some of the victims had been arrested for some sort of violent act, usually against women, but got off on either technicalities or dropped charges. So, men who beat their wives or children. Men who raped women, but got off because they had good lawyers... that type."

"And, what does *she* do to them?" I asked.

"Well, she hurts them... badly. One story I heard, this bobby who took his billy club to his kids and wife whenever he thought they got out of line? He would strategically hit them in places that most people wouldn't notice. The children would go to school with bruises on their backs. The wife would go to work... same thing. She, of course, wouldn't say anything, but the school got wind of it and had the bloke questioned. Somehow, his name was cleared. Having a good lawyer, and being a police officer and all, I suspect, and the family denying he did anything. I still remember seeing his face in the papers. It was a photo of him leaving the courthouse with his family, sporting a shit eating grin, like he definitely thought that he got away with something. Anyway, two days later, that man was found in an alley with bruises all over his body. I mean all over—and some broken bones, too."

"Billy club?"

"You guessed it! The man lived, but barely. I doubt he lays a finger on his wife or kids anymore. You ask me, the gal's a saint!"

"Hmmm... it's just that, you know, does one person have the right to be the judge?"

"I agree with you, Anna, but sometimes people, bad people get away with things they shouldn't. Why are you so inquisitive about this anyway?"

"Just curious. There was an attack last night not too far from my flat. The dude got his teeth knocked out."

"I wouldn't worry too much about being attacked, unless you've beaten your husband or child," she chided.

"Yeah, I guess." But I still felt uneasy. It was such a brutal attack. Thinking about the man's teeth getting knocked out reminded me of what happened to Abagail Smalls.

CHAPTER 3

I stayed late at work since I had wasted so much of my day, but it was still light when I left the building as civil twilight hadn't hit yet. I took the tube from Leicester Square to the Farringdon Station, walking past the same homeless man with a dog I usually give a pound to. Sometimes, I buy him a coffee at the Pret A Manger across the street or bring his dog a treat of some sort. As usual, pub patrons spilled out onto the sidewalks, drinking and smoking, boisterous in their after work revelry. I didn't have that many friends yet, except at work, and none of them lived in Clerkenwell. I made a mental note to try to get out more and meet some people. At least, I was going to hang out with Tom tonight.

As I turned down Seward Street, past my favorite coffee house, Goswell Street Coffee, the street-lamps started to ignite, forecasting the oncoming night.

I arrived at my building and ascended three short steps up to the front entrance. After unlocking the door, I climbed up the three long flights. My workout for the night.

When I entered my flat, I switched on the lights and assessed my mess. I was living like a bachelor and wasn't too proud of it, but I wasn't trying to impress anyone, either.

I went into the kitchen and made myself a small salad topped with some quinoa, chickpeas, and lemon. Then, I showered. It's my favorite way to decompress after a long day, and to clear my mind. But while shampooing, I kept thinking about the weird sensations I had felt at the Hartford House where Abigail Smalls was murdered. I don't know why it bothered me so much. Despite the hot water raining down on me from my oversized rain shower head, I shivered. My thoughts then turned to Tom. I couldn't get a great read on him yet, but I definitely felt a spark. It was a feeling I hadn't had toward someone since Graham, in high school. I hoped to God Tom wasn't like Graham, however.

After the water started to get cold, I stepped out onto the fuzzy, sea foam green bath mat, dried off completely with a minty powder, and put on my outfit. I decided to wear my *Nightmare on Elm Street* shirt; good choice for a ghost tour, I reasoned. I squeezed into my other pair of size four holey jeans and some old sneakers, and I swooped my damp hair up in a ponytail. I reddened my lips and darkened the rims of my eyes, blotting some of the makeup off. I didn't want to look too much like I did in high school and certainly didn't want to scare Tom away. I pushed some medium sized hoop earrings through my lobes and then waited for the clock to make its rounds.

7:30… I wore a hole in the floor, pacing, waiting for 7:45 to roll around so I could leave for the tour. I was too antsy, so I sat down on my lumpy sofa and switched on the television to BBC News.

> *'More on Richard T. Brown, the American tourist found beaten in a London alley, when we come back…'*

I turned the volume up and left the room to grab a soda. As the news show came back on, I heard that the victim was from North Carolina. I got to the room just in time to catch a quick glimpse of a photo of the poor guy. He looked pasty, with a red, blotchy complexion.

> *'Brown had won a trip to London for being the top used car salesman at the "We Sell 'em Good" car lot in North Carolina. We spoke to his supervisor who declined to comment on his character, but did say he felt sorry for the man's parents. He had no wife or children. Locally, people are speculating that this could be the work of the London Vigilante. Police, however, have indicated that there is no evidence of a connection at this time. More at 2300. And now the weather. Bring a jacket tonight, as temperatures will hit another unseasonable low of 8 degrees Celsius.'*

I turned off the television, grabbed my pleather jacket, locked up the flat, and galloped down the three flights of steps. I stepped out into the chilly September night.

My walk to the tube station felt uneasy; I was alone, and a little unsure of myself. But after the ride to the Green Park Station and walk back to the Burlington Arcade, I started to get a little more confident and excited. When I arrived, a bunch of people already had their tickets and were milling around inside. I figured I didn't need a ticket since Tom told me I would be his guest.

Right around 8:30, we went outside. Out of the night and cutting through the haze, Tom walked toward us. No hat tonight, but he still wore the cloak and carried the lantern. He walked over to me first.

"Thank you for coming, Anna," he expressed as he stood in front of me and kissed me on the cheek. As he pulled away, his brow furrowed and he cocked his head. He lightly took the lapel of my jacket, opened it up to the right, stared at my shirt and then let go, the lapel folding back into place.

He half smiled. "Hmmm, well, I hope you enjoy tonight's tour. Off to work." He winked at me and then abruptly turned and started speaking to the awaiting crowd.

I casually zipped up my jacket.

The tour went on much like last night, but the stories and places were different. The tales were interesting enough, but the eerie mood was set because of Tom's baritone voice and knack for recounting the tales with emotion and drama. I've not encountered a story teller with such an infectious manner of speaking.

"And now we shall take a stroll to one of the most haunted places in all of London. And lucky for you, I have a key to get us inside," he professed as he dangled the silver key in front of the crowd. The group reacted to this enticing announcement with mild gasps and clapping. Since I've been on many other ghost tours in various cities throughout the United States, I was impressed that this tour company had access to some of the interiors of the houses. Almost always, tours are limited to outside the sites.

"It's a few blocks away, so on we go." Tom commanded.

He was ignoring me a bit tonight, but it was probably because he was at work. During the walk, he finally looked back over his shoulder at me and gestured with his head in a way that encouraged me to catch up.

"So, how are you finding tonight's tour thus far?" He asked, leaning into me, our shoulders touching.

"It's cool. I really enjoy this stuff."

"Mmm... *stuff.*"

Wrinkling my nose, I decided to ignore his jab at my choice of words.

Another person from the tour caught up to Tom and started asking a bunch of questions about ghosts and hauntings. The woman started telling her own accounts of strange happenings. I started to fall back into the crowd, slowing my steps, when Tom, without looking at me and while talking to the tourist, reached back and took my hand. We walked that way for a few minutes, with Tom still talking to the tourist and not acknowledging me, except for his firm grip on my hand.

We stopped outside a blue row house across from Berkeley Square Park. The lower level seemed to be a bookstore while three rows of three windows each sat above. The highest windows were a bit unsettling for some reason. Crowding on the sidewalk in front of the door, Tom released his grasp and turned to face the group. He started to weave his story with his colorful language, haunting voice, and dramatic pauses.

Tolerance. What does this word mean? Acceptance? A willingness to accept a belief, a way of life, a culture, that is not your own? As a society, we have come a long way. And yet, still we see violence against those who we deem lesser than ourselves. Ladies and gentlemen, I am about to tell you the story of one such account of intolerance that was met with dire consequences. I give you 50 Berkeley Square, one of the most haunted houses in London. Legend has it that back in the 1800s, a man was found dead in the attic, hanging from a beam. The owner of the house, Niles Thompson, was a columnist known for his harsh words against homosexuals. He wanted to clean the streets of London of, in his words, the scourge of the earth. Every good story needs a twist, ladies and gentlemen, and in this story, we learn that Niles Thompson was a homosexual himself. That is why he invited Christian Miller back to 50 Berkeley Square. Repulsed by his own true urges, he lashed out against poor Christian and others who mirrored his own secret nature. He coerced Mr. Miller to follow him to the attic. It was a deadly mistake, for Niles Thompson locked Mr. Miller in that attic room, tied him up and savagely beat him with sticks, starved him, and maimed him, trying to torture the homosexuality out of him, hoping against hope that this would cure his own wretched nature. But of course, we cannot run away from our true nature, and when Niles Thompson realized his actions were fruitless, he bound Mr. Miller to a chair and castrated him. The victim's blood curdling screams were heard echoing off the walls of the house. Mr. Miller died of blood loss that day, but the deafening shrieks were heard far into the night, along with the scraping, scraping, scraping of the wooden chair legs against the floor boards from Mr. Miller's futile attempts to escape. Even after he disposed of the body, Thompson revealed in his journal that he could still hear the horrible screams and scratching when he would try to sleep, night after night. If only Niles Thompson exhibited tolerance, not only for others, but for himself, he may have lived a long and happy life.

Tom's voice cracked a little on that sentence. After a brief silence, Tom composed himself and continued.

However, driven to the point of insanity, Niles Thompson could take no more and so he stood on that same chair, slipped a noose around his neck, kicked the chair away, and hanged himself. And to this day, ladies and gentleman, if the time and the conditions are right, you too can here the horrific screams, the scraping and scratching of Mr. Miller's chair, and the crack... of Niles Thompson's neck.

"Now, I can take three or four at a time to the attic. Who's game?" He challenged as he opened his arms for dramatic effect.

To my surprise, only a couple of people raised their hands. Everyone's chicken.

"Okay, shall we enter?" Tom looked over at me and widened his eyes, encouraging me to join him. I started forward when some ass from the crowd pushed me aside and barged up to the front door, two nights in a row now!

"Well," the rude man began, "let's see what you got!"

Tom's eyes narrowed, holding the man's gaze while inserting the key precisely in the lock. He turned the knob, gently pushed open the door and finally turned his head away from the man. Tom went in first, followed by the boisterous man, two other men holding hands, and then me.

The guy who pushed me mumbled under his breath, "faggots." Tom, who had started up the stairs, stopped briefly. He gripped the banister a little too tightly and then continued on up until we reached the attic.

"It was here," Tom began softly, "where Niles Thompson and Mr. Miller died—both lives taken by the same hand."

Aside from the light coming through the very small window high up on one wall, the room was dark. Tom shined his lantern around for everyone to see, making shadows dance along the walls and corners of the attic. The floorboards creaked when we walked on them, echoing off the walls around us. The chill in the room was a bit unsettling, so I placed my hand on Tom's arm, who in turn, patted my hand.

The two men gripped each other a little tighter and the obnoxious man just looked around and laughed.

"And what, pray tell, is so amusing?" Tom asked the man. Uh-oh. Tom held his lantern up to get a better view of the man.

Squinting in the light, the man shrugged and retorted, "You ask me, they got what they deserved," he glanced at the two men, who, I think, were too scared to notice or contemplate what the man just opined.

Tom just stared, but it was one of the most frightening stares I've ever seen. The lighting in the room from the lantern cast an eerie glow on his face, changing his brilliant eyes to black. I shivered.

Tom turned to the couple and told them that if they wanted to explore a little, they could as long as they didn't disturb anything. One of the men nodded, the other shook his head, but they went anyway, Tom giving them a flashlight he kept in his coat.

After they left the attic, Tom spoke in a commanding, but quiet voice. "You should go, I'm sure you can find your way out."

"Look bloke, I didn't like your speech... this was supposed to be a ghost story, not a lesson on morality." He stepped towards Tom and hounded, "You're probably one yourself."

Tom closed his eyes and audibly whispered, "Please go."

The man finally shrugged and started downstairs, mumbling "faggot," under his breath. Tom stiffened.

"Tom," I warned.

He held his hand up, took two steps back to the wall and leaned against it. He still held the lantern, but his head tipped forward and his left hand slowly came up and covered his face. I didn't know what to do. He just stayed in that position, breathing heavily. I started to get a little weirded out.

"Tom?" I weakly called out in the dark.

The blackness of the room enveloped me as the lantern started to dim. Tom's body started to blend in with the backdrop of the room. I froze where I was, scared and helpless, when Tom finally spoke in a hushed tone. "Do you feel it?"

"Do I feel what?" I questioned, my heart starting to beat even faster.

"Do you feel the suffering? The pain? Do you hear the name?"

"I... I don't. I don't feel or hear anything in here... last night was the first time I've ever felt something like this. Look, I'm really scared, can we go, please?" I whimpered.

After another minute, he nodded and walked toward me. He wiped his eyes and smiled sheepishly, "Sorry, I... I don't know what came over me, my head started to spin and I just felt... I can't explain."

"Are you okay now?" I asked, really freaked.

"Yes, yes, I'm fine now, I'm afraid I almost passed out from an intense wave of vertigo. Sorry, I didn't mean to frighten you. I assure you this rarely happens."

I didn't say anything. I just wanted to get out of there. I felt his hand grasp mine and lead me to the steps. He practically dragged me down them, but I was relieved to be leaving that room. I looked back up the steps and trembled.

Right before Tom swung open the door to the night and awaiting crowd, he dropped my hand. A few people started asking if we heard anything.

"Nothing really." Tom scanned the group for the homophobe and he must have found him because he cocked his head, slowly blinked and then looked away.

After a minute, the couple came out of the house, looking pretty white. "That was the creepiest place I've ever seen! We kept thinking we saw wisps and heard things… crazy." One of the men gulped.

Tom nodded in agreement. "Well, back to our starting point. I hope you enjoyed the tour. Please do not hesitate to ask me any questions."

This time, I did fall back into the crowd a little. I didn't know what to think. This was all too weird and cryptic, even for my liking. He's mysterious, alright. I undid my ponytail, letting my hair fall onto my shoulders, and secured the scrunchie to my wrist.

On the way back, Tom was in the front, walking at a pretty good clip, taking longer strides than necessary. I was a few people behind him. And then, I saw the homophobe, weaving his way to the front, bumping into me and a bunch of others, trying to catch up to Tom. When he reached him, I could tell the man was goading him. I caught a few words here and there. "Faggots." "Got what they deserved." Tom was trying to ignore him, as far as I could tell.

And then, it happened. The most excruciating pain I've ever felt. "AHHH!" I screamed and doubled over.

My stomach and face felt like they were on fire. Bile welled up in my throat as I gasped for air. I fell to the ground, clutching my stomach, but the trauma didn't end there. My whole body started to feel like it got the wind knocked out of it. My jaw felt like it became unhinged and then everything started to get blurry and eventual fade to black. Images of a horribly beaten body were replaying in my head like a slide show.

"Let me through," I heard someone say. "Anna?! Anna, are you alright?"

I felt a hand on my shoulder. The pain that flowed through me started ebbing away. I opened my eyes and saw a bunch of shoes and boots, then, Tom's face. "Can you sit up?" Tom gently put an arm around me and helped me to a sitting position.

Embarrassed, I saw the crowd all staring down at me. "Just a sec," he whispered and winked at me.

Tom stood up, "Please, everyone, if you could find your way back to the Burlington Arcade, it is right down the road, straight ahead, go on, I'll be there in a minute."

I saw some people trying to give Tom some tips, but he waved them away, thanking them anyway. When the last of the crowd left, Tom crouched back down. "You aren't faking this time are you?"

I shook my head.

"I think we should go to hospital." He implored.

"Ah, no, nope. I'm… okay. I think I can stand." He gently moved the hair strands that were stuck to my mouth behind my ear and then helped me to my feet.

"Are you sure you are alright? What happened? Was it similar to last night?"

"Ah, this was… worse. Much more intense."

"And then, it just vanished, just like that?" Tom asked.

"Yes, although I'm feeling a little worn."

"Of course. How about if I escort you home?" It was more of a statement than an offer, but there was a tender concern in his voice.

I shook my head, "That won't be necess…"

"Please," he interrupted. "I insist."

I sighed and nodded okay. He helped me walk back to the Burlington Arcade. His arm was wrapped around my waist, holding me close, and more importantly, holding me up. The pain wasn't there anymore, but the residual effect of it sure was. My whole body throbbed with a dull ache. When we arrived, the tour group had already dispersed. Tom sat me down on a bench inside and told me he'd be right back. Unlike the night before, he only took about five minutes. He emerged in a slightly more casual outfit, black jeans and Chuck Taylors, but also a starched ecru oxford shirt and black pea coat. He reached out both his hands to help me up.

I noticed a nasty cut on his left hand. "What's that on your hand?" I inquired.

"Hmmm? Oh, that. I cut myself on a tree branch." He claimed as he looked outside.

"Tree branch? That's pretty deep for a tree branch. Looks pretty bad… you might want to get it checked out."

He looked down at me and raised one eyebrow. "Who's the patient here now? If you must know, I was in a cab with my arm out the window and we drove passed a tree. It sliced my hand up. I've put disinfectant on it and I'm fine. Now, let's get you home and into bed."

My eyes narrowed a bit, but I think he was totally clueless about the double meaning. He held out his hand again—this time, the right one—and I took it to stand.

Tom hailed a cab. I was a little unsteady on my feet, so I was glad not to take the tube home, although I wasn't happy about paying the fare. Inside the cab, we hardly spoke; however, he had his arm around me the whole time. I welcomed the warmth and stability, especially since I was starting to feel a little dizzy.

Tom paid the cab driver despite my protests, and then helped me out. "Would you like me to walk you up?" he asked, genuine concern in his voice. "I am not sure you should be alone right now."

I thought about my wrecked flat. The dishes in the sink, the clothes all over the floor. No way.

"I'll be fine, thanks. But, are you alright? You were pretty out of it in the attic."

"Em, of course, I'm fine, just a little vertigo I think. Well, if you're sure you're okay, em, good night then," he turned and started walking away to find another cab, but stopped after a few strides and looked over his left shoulder. "Would you like to have dinner with me? Tomorrow night?" he asked with a little nervous twinge.

"You don't have to work on a Saturday night?"

"My night off," he declared as he fully turned toward me, then took one step backward, hands in his pockets. He was obviously uncomfortable. It was kind of cute.

Despite the oddness of what happened earlier in the attic, I accepted without much hesitation. "Yes, that would be nice."

He nodded once, turned away and started down the sidewalk. I watched him go as he held up his hand to hail a cab since the other one had picked up a new fare. Almost right away, however, a black cab stopped for Tom. He opened the back door, turned back to me and waved. He got into the cab and it drove off, fading into the night.

I walked up the steps to my outside front door. After opening it, I peered up the three flights. The long three flights. I started to feel a little queasy, so I bolted up the steps, taking two at a time. I tripped on the first landing, but caught myself on my hands. Cursing, while righting myself, I ran to the top floor and shoved the key into the lock, slamming the door open. The contents of my open purse scattered all over the floor when I accidently dropped it as the nausea intensified. Barely making it to the bathroom, I retched into the toilet. "Dammit" I snarled out loud. I gripped the toilet seat with both hands waiting for the next wave, but luckily, after a few minutes of heavy breathing and waiting, the nausea subsided. I stood up, flushed the toilet and then washed my hands and face.

I took my jacket off, collected my wallet, makeup and various junk from the floor, and closed and locked the front door. I then went into my room to get changed into my oversized *Jaws* shirt. Old and worn, it was the most comfortable night shirt I had.

I went back to my jacket to get my cell phone out of the pocket, knowing that I needed to charge it. I noticed a text. *Well, how was it?* Jamie. I'd get back to her later.

I flipped on the television and flopped down on the sofa. More on the attack.

> *"...named Richard T. Brown. Sources in America told us he served time for molesting and raping his live-in girlfriend. (A woman in her 40s flashed on the screen.) 'Yes, he abused me while I lived with him. I don't know why I stayed. I'd be lying if I said I was sad he got so badly hurt. He got what he deserved.'*

The photo changed to Brown's face, the same picture I saw earlier. This time, I got a good look at him. He looked vaguely familiar, but I couldn't place him exactly.

I knew this would nag at me, but I decided to go to bed. I put on my favorite band, The Damned, to calm my nerves. I brushed my teeth, rinsed, and brushed them again, trying to get the bad taste out of my mouth and then I crawled under the sheets. I tried to sleep, but I had a really restless night, constantly tossing and turning, changing positions, taking off the covers, and putting them back on. My mind was whirling with worry about the pain I experienced the last two nights, especially the excruciating episode from tonight. I also thought about Tom, torn because I found him incredibly attractive and extremely enigmatic, but also a bit scary. Quite a bit, really. I mean what the hell was that in the attic? But given my slate of boyfriends, that's probably why I'm so drawn to him. Mysterious and scary, just my type. And just the type that gets me in trouble.

Finally, after over-analyzing almost every aspect of my encounters with Tom, I drifted off to sleep.

***

The large basement room of my old high school was bleak and vacant except for the candles flicking light onto an object in the center of the room. The bleachers lining the walls were dark. I was alone sitting on them, observing… something. A ceremony? In the middle of the room, people wearing black hoods surrounded a table where a shirtless man was lying on his back. He had a tattoo on his chest, or maybe a scar. Black jeans. I couldn't quite see his face, but he had dark hair. He seemed to be drugged or in some kind of stupor. The figures in the hoods loomed around him and stared.

In a flash, I found myself in Hallway B. A cold, dark figure, a woman, pulled off her hood, revealing a pale, worn face with deep, charcoal circles under her intense blue eyes. As sinister as she looked, she didn't frighten me, at least at first. Instead, she enveloped me with warmth, but her eyes were pleading, imploring me. Then, she reached out a blue veined hand and touched me.

I awoke abruptly, my heart beating out of my chest and my forehead drenched in sweat. Breathing in through my nose and out through my mouth, I tried to calm myself down, the CD ironically playing "Is it a Dream."

CHAPTER 4

"Yes, that's it, that's it! Push in a little more with the blade… right, right! You are a natural! Now, circle it around… okay, yes, you can go that way. Let's get a big hole, expose the intestines. Yes! Okay, time to pull them out."

— *Saturday, September 6*

I had a pretty mundane day, which was welcome after last night's craziness and restless sleep. Trying to get my mind off it all, especially the disturbing dream, I decided to do a little shopping to prepare for my date. After grazing on some carrots and hummus, I ventured out. A new outfit and new shoes should make me feel better. I trotted down to Farringdon, smacked my Oyster Card on the yellow entry reader and hopped down the steps toward platform 2. I had one stop to Kings Cross Station and then a transfer to the Piccadilly Line, which would take me to Soho.

As the train screeched to a stop, the doors opened and I squeezed my way in. Standing room only, today. Over the loudspeaker, the all too familiar "mind the gap between the train and the platform" politely reminded the riders. I used to think this phrase was so funny since in New York, there is a pictograph showing a man getting stuck in the gap. It always made me laugh, but now it has just become the normal sound of the city. Once I reached my stop, I walked through Soho, checking out different stores and watching the people. In my sneakers, jeans and T-shirt, I felt a little out of place because Londoners tend to dress impeccably well. I didn't care that much, but every once in a while, I felt a little self-conscious.

After grabbing a soy flat white at Pret, I walked to Element, one of my favorite clothes stores, and found a funky red dress with thick straps that went over the shoulders. The waistline cinched in just in the right place and the hem came to right above my knees. I then shopped for some shoes and found a pair that were a little higher than I would usually get, but they were too cool to pass up—black with a closed toe and silver nail heads around the tip and the sides with an ironic small red bow over my middle toes. I found a black punkish belt with silver studs that surprisingly went well with the dress and absolutely with the shoes.

A successful shopping trip with bags in hand, I headed to the tube station, but there were some issues on the lines I usually take. I didn't want to take a cab or deal with the crowds, so I decided to walk the mile and a half back to my flat. I rolled my eyes after the long walk, looking at the three flights. I really wish my flat had a lift, sometimes. I took a breath and ran up the steps, my bags bumping into the stairwell walls. My cell phone started to ring as I entered the flat.

"Hello, Jamie."

"Hi… are you ready for tonight?" I had texted her earlier telling her I was going out again.

"Yeah, I just bought a new outfit."

"When are you going?"

I paused. "You know what? It just dawned on me that he didn't tell me. In fact, I don't even know where we are meeting." Damn.

"I'm sure he'll get in touch with you somehow, maybe through a psychic brainwave," she moaned in a lousy ghoulish voice.

"Very funny."

"Well, call me tomorrow and let me know how it goes. And please be careful; you hardly know this bloke."

"I will, *Mom*… bye."

I hung up the phone and rolled my eyes. Tom hadn't given me a time or place. I figured if he didn't contact me by 7:00, I'd go out myself. I didn't want to waste my outfit sitting at home. I decided to get ready anyway. I showered and then threw on my oversized *Jaws* T-shirt. It was too raggedy to wear out anymore, so it doubled as a nightshirt and a smock.

At 5:00, I decided to look Tom up in the phone book online. Yup, a *plethora* of Thomas Halls. I tried the tour office, but no one was answering. 5:30 rolled around, then 5:32. This was agony! In a huff, I flopped down on the sofa and tried to keep myself occupied while reading Time Out London. My eyes started to get a bit heavy….

"ring ring" "ring ring"

I woke with a start. In a bit of a groggy daze, I looked up at the clock and saw it was 7:15.

"rinnnnggg.." I staggered to the intercom. "Hello?"

"Anna, it's…"

"Shit! S..sorry Tom, um, come on up." Willing myself out of my funk, I buzzed him in, took a quick look at the flat and cleaned the best I could in the 10 seconds I had. Still in my *Jaws* shirt and underwear, I ran and threw on a pair of sweats lying on the floor. Two birds, I thought.

I heard faint, then gradually louder footsteps until they stopped at my door.

Knock, knock….

I unhooked the chain, unbolted the dead bolt, and opened the door. There stood Tom in all his grandeur. Charcoal fitted pants, ecru shirt open at the top, black lace-up shoes, and a tailored charcoal blazer. He had slicked back his dark hair as much as he could, but because of the length of his bangs, a strand of hair fell over his right eye, just like at the tour. On one arm, his coat was draped and in his other hand, a single red rose complimented the outfit. Wow, I thought.

Unfortunately, he didn't have quite the same reaction to me. I invited him in, his eyes widening a bit when he saw me and my trashed flat. He handed me the rose and bowed his head, despite the surroundings.

"Thank you," I muttered and hurried to the sink to put it in a glass and water.

"You have interesting choices in T-shirts," he stated as he gazed around the flat.

Embarrassed, I shrugged and asked him if he wanted anything to drink.

"I'll pass, but thank you."

"Well, sorry I'm not ready. I didn't know what time or where we were meeting and I kind of fell asleep on the sofa. Rough night last night."

He raised one eyebrow.

"Um, trying to sleep," I explained. He also seemed to be a little oblivious to my passive aggressive comment.

"Have a seat, if you like," I shoved the clothes, mail and my book aside, clearing a space on the sofa. "I'll be ready in 15 minutes."

"Take your time." He strode over to my CD collection… great.

I went into my room, closed the pocket door and then, quickly, tore off my sloppy clothes. I snatched my new red dress off the bed and tore the tags off a little too quickly, putting a slight tear in the hem.

"Shit!" I exclaimed, I guess a little too loudly. I started to throw the dress on and heard a knock on the door.

"Everything alright in there?"

"Y..yes," I stuttered, my voice muffled by the fabric of the dress as I was trying to get it over my head without tearing it further.

I went to the mirror on my bureau and brushed my hair quickly, put it up in a high pony tail, then took it out letting my hair fall back down, deciding on a green head band... no, too Christmassy... red head band instead... no, too Snow White! A tan one, yes. I went into the bathroom, which still smelled slightly of vomit, and quickly put on some red lipstick. I grabbed my black eyeliner, and noticed it was too blunt. Rummaging through the vanity drawer, I found the sharpener and shoved the eyeliner into the hole, forcibly twisting the pencil. I then started to apply the eyeliner, but too hastily "DAMMIT!" I yelled as I stabbed my eyeball with the pencil.

Another knock; this one I ignored. I splashed some perfume on, smoothed my dress out, roughly buckled my belt, and walked out of the bathroom. I snatched my shoes and then hurriedly flung the pocket door into its shell. "Ouch!" I yelled, and put my hand to my head. Tom must have been in mid-knock when I threw open the door, but his head was turned so he didn't see me soon enough to stop his fist from landing on my forehead.

"Oh, Anna, I'm sorry," he laughed as he cupped my face with his hands and kissed my forehead. He abruptly dropped his hands, looking embarrassed.

"Sorry, I don't know why I did that. Em... is it better?" He asked, softly.

"Ah, no, not really." I forcibly pushed passed him and sat on the sofa to put my shoes on. My irritation was coming to a hilt. I stood up quickly, quite a bit taller, now, almost even with Tom.

Noticing my mood, Tom confessed, "Anna, I am sorry I didn't make firmer plans with you. I was in a bit of a state last night... and... and by the way, you look beautiful," just noticing my outfit and makeup. "But your eye, why is it watering?" he questioned as he gently brushed a tear away with his thumb.

Geez, he's forward, I thought. I pulled back and rolled my eyes again. "It's nothing. Can we just go?" I located my purse after a whirlwind search. He smirked, seemingly amused at my annoyance.

"So, you like the Sex Pistols? Interesting," and we walked out the door.

***

Tom was taking me to a restaurant about a 20-minute walk from my flat. I insisted we walk as I needed to burn off some steam. Of course, my feet hurt five minutes into the trek. Damned new shoes.

"Wait a sec," I called as I paused and stripped off my shoes, placing my stocking-feet on the pavement.

Tom watched me with a puzzled look and that slight smirk again. "We can still call a cab," he suggested.

"No, no, I like to walk barefoot," I sputtered as I looked down at the ground so I wouldn't step on anything sharp or wet. The pavement was really cold even though the temperature wasn't too bad.

"You know, where we are going, you will need shoes," he drawled.

"I know," rolling my eyes for the hundredth time this evening. Tom looked away from me and I could tell he was trying to stifle a laugh. Is he effing with me?

Tom graciously took the shoes out of my hand to carry them in his right and tried to hold my hand with his left. My petulance was getting the best of me and I put my hands in my jacket pockets.

"So, what kind of music do *you* like?" I asked. Classical, I'll bet.

"I usually listen to Progressive Rock or Classical," yup-figures, "but, I occasionally like to hear something…obnoxious." His mouth turned up ever so slightly. Definitely effing with me.

"I could make you a mixture recording, if you like, with obnoxious music. I have plenty of that."

"Ah… the mixture tape… I had a girlfriend in secondary school who made one of those for me," he needled.

He was being more obnoxious than my music, so I quickened my pace and reached a cross street. I looked the wrong way, still trying to squelch years and years of a reversed traffic pattern. Abruptly, a hand grasped my shoulder, yanking me back out of harm's way while a horn blared.

"Thanks," I said under my breath, highly embarrassed.

"You do realize there is verbiage on the street telling you which way to look," he chided, stating the obvious.

Alright, I had enough. "What the fuck?" I barked. He winced at my brusqueness; his smile evaporating quickly.

"What do you mean? What's wrong?" He asked, concerned.

"It's just that, you're really uppity and disparaging. It's really annoying." I chastised as we walked safely across the street.

I continued my tirade. "I mean, I feel as if you are judging my music, my clothes, my maturity… and who asks someone out on a date and doesn't give a Goddamn time or place? I mean you are obviously interested in me, otherwise, you wouldn't have asked me out, again. So, yeah, what the fuck?"

Tom, let out a breath, obviously surprised by my candor. A broad smile erupted on his face, exposing his fangs, and he started to laugh. "Anna, please." He reached for my hand, but I wouldn't give it up, so he came around to face me, placing his hands on my shoulders, stopping me in my tracks.

"I am truly sorry—I've been ghastly. I would love to hear your mixture tape and see all your T-shirts. You are… different."

I narrowed my eyes.

"In a good way," he quickly recovered, "and have I told you tonight how lovely you look, especially in bare feet?"

I sighed and kept my hands in my pockets as we continued on. My mood was starting to lift ever so slightly. His charisma was hard to resist.

When we arrived at the restaurant, he handed me my shoes. I used his shoulder for leverage and strapped on the horrible foot binding. A hundred pounds down the drain.

"Reservation for Hall, please," Tom told the host.

"Right this way," the host directed as he plucked two menus from behind the station and led us to a quiet table by the window. The host helped me off with my jacket and then held the chair out for me. Tom politely waited to sit until I sat down. I'm not used to this kind of courtesy; it's a little haughty, but kind of nice. The restaurant had a rustic feel to it with an old fireplace by our table, the marble mantel displaying old colorful bottles. My view outside the window overlooked, I believe, the St. Bart's Church graveyard across the street. An elderly man was sitting on a bench in the graveyard with his dog.

"Do you like wine?" Tom asked as he scanned the menu.

"Yes, but generally red. You choose, though, I'm no connoisseur."

The waiter came over, "We'll have a bottle of… Shhhiraz?" he questioned, looking over to me for my approval.

I nodded quickly; he had picked my favorite. I started to settle into a better state of mind, happy to be out, eating at a pretty restaurant with an attractive guy, no matter how obnoxious he was at the beginning of the date.

"Are we okay now? Again, I am sorry for teasing you, but you are very cute when you are incensed."

I smiled, "Yes, Tom, we are okay."

His facial expression became a little more serious. "Was everything alright last night? I was rather concerned and felt I should have insisted on staying with you, at least for a while."

"Um, yeah, I was okay. I was a bit nauseous, but it passed." I didn't really want to go into detail, so I switched the conversation back on him. "I really have no idea what happened. I just hope it doesn't happen again. I feel fine now; all day, in fact. But, what about you? I mean, last night in the Berkeley Square house, you seemed really upset."

I noticed a small eye twitch. "Actually, I don't quite remember. As I explained before, I sometimes get certain... ah... feelings, but they're usually fleeting. I've had this happen to me ever since I started working for the tour company. But, honestly Anna, I'd really like to put last night behind us. It was a frightful evening for both of us. You intrigue me and I'd very much like to find out more about *you*."

"Okay, what do you want to know?" I asked, a little self-consciously. The clatter of a dropped tray echoed through the restaurant, causing a brief halt to all the conversations. The din of people talking began after a moment. Tom raised a brow and started.

"Well, I know you are from Maryland, you work at a publishing company, you have interesting choices in music, you are drawn to scary... stuff (he half smiled at that), and quite frankly, you are a bit, ah, more than a bit of a slob, but a radiant one. So, what else?"

I grinned and almost laughed at the compliment, well, back-handed compliment. I'd never been called radiant before. Who says that, anyway.

"Ah, let's see. I'm 28, never been married, went to high school and then college in New York City and majored in publishing, got a job, and then transferred to here. I like scary movies, I'd like to marry Jack Skellington, I love music, and I played bass a little in high school."

"So, I am in competition with a spider-like skeleton? "

"Honestly, I'm surprised you got the reference."

Tom looked a little slightly put off, "I don't live in a hole, Anna."

"Well, what other music do you like, besides Classical?"

"Truthfully, Progressive Rock is my passion and I do like some alternative."

"Oh, really?" I giggled, "Like who? I'm curious to know what you consider alt-rock. Yanni?"

Tom gave me half-eyes and pursed his lips, "No, not Yanni. My favorite band of that genre would be The The. And I really enjoy the whole Madchester era."

"Wow, I'm impressed," I confessed with surprise in my voice.

"How old do you think I am, Anna?"

"Well, you look my age, but you're pretty uppity, so I'd guess around 60?" I teased.

"Mmmm, uppity, that's the second time you've called me that," he retorted. "You don't know me quite yet. Patience. And I assure you I am not 60. I will be 32 in March."

The waiter interrupted our conversation by uncorking the wine bottle and pouring a taste into Tom's glass. Tom swirled the wine around in his glass, closed his eyes and inhaled the aroma. He then opened his eyes, sipped it, savored it a little in his mouth and nodded. The waiter poured the Shiraz in our glasses one quarter full and left us alone to talk and peruse the menu. Wide-eyed, I stared at Tom in disbelief and inwardly laughed at the irony of it all. I never, ever, dated a guy so pretentious and proper.

"You're 31? Wow, okay." I shook my head in jest. I mean, after that display.

Tom sighed, "Thanks."

I felt a familiar buzzing in my purse. I pulled out my phone and saw the text from Jamie: "Take a picture, dammit!!!"

I tried not to laugh and put my phone back. Tom was busy looking at the menu, so he didn't notice anything.

"And, what about you? Where did you grow up? Happy childhood?" I probed, sounding a little too much like Jamie.

He glanced up briefly from the menu with just his eyes. "No," he pointedly remarked, and looked back down at the menu.

"Okaaay." I shook my head and peered at the appetizers, surprised by his tone. I unwittingly struck some kind of nerve.

We sat in silence, each deciding on what to eat, but glad to have the menus to hide the awkwardness, until the waiter came over to take our order.

The waiter looked at me first, "I'll have the kale pasta marinara, please, and a side salad with balsamic vinegar, um, no cheese, please."

"And I'll have… I'll try the same… sounds good," Tom nodded as the waiter took our menus.

I looked up at him, a little surprised, "Are you a vegan, too?"

"Oh, I didn't realize you were vegan. Em, for me? Food doesn't really matter. I like good food, but I'm willing to try or not try anything. I could give up meat in a snap, if say someone convinced me. It wouldn't take much, honestly, I just haven't thought about it that much."

"Hmm. Well, maybe I'll try to convince you later."

"I look forward to it," Tom nodded his head once, raised his glass to me and took a small sip of wine.

The waiter, as if on cue, came by and refreshed our wine glasses.

Tom sat back in his chair and ran his fingers through his hair, making more of it fall in his face. He pushed his hair aside and started, "Okay, let me get this over with, but please, don't ask any questions. I don't like talking about myself; I'm afraid I'm a bit of a private person. But, you make me feel… comfortable. But, no questions." I nodded.

"So, in a nutshell, I grew up in London with my father and my sister, four years my senior. Mum passed on when I was rather young. My father is still alive, but has ailments, and out of obligation, but nothing more, I go over there at least once a week to check on him. I do have a grandfather I adore who lives in Scotland. I work as a tour guide, as you know, but only because I have nothing better to do and thought it would be a kick to go into the haunted houses. I don't need to work because my grandfather set up a rather sizable trust for me. I like mainly classical, progressive rock and some alt-rock, as I've stated before, and above all, American women who buy expensive shoes, but cannot wear them." He grinned at his own joke.

"So, your fath…" I started, but he interrupted me by holding up a palm and shaking his head, "Anna, no questions. I don't want to spoil a lovely evening with a beautiful woman talking about my father."

"Okay." I assented, slightly embarrassed. These compliments! "Um, I've got to run to the bathroom, I'll be right back."

I took my purse with me so I could reapply my lipstick. I had to walk through the bar to find the bathroom and I caught the picture of the assaulted

American on the TV screen. I shook my head, found the ladies room, peed, washed my hands, and reapplied my makeup.

When I got back to the table, our salads had arrived.

"You didn't have to wait for me." I said as he stood up, waiting for me to sit first, again.

I heard a small chuckle and he shook his head as he sat back down. "Is politeness dead in America?"

"Pretty much, yeah."

We started on our salads consisting of arugula, or rather rocket as it's called here, with cut cherry tomatoes, red onions, and a sweet balsamic dressing.

"So, what do you think of this 'London Vigilante'? Every time I turn on the TV, the newscasters are going on and on about it." The restaurant tables were now at full capacity and so the clinks of forks on plates and conversational noise started to pick up. The smell of the fresh baguettes that were placed on the table pleasantly assaulted my nose. I picked a piece up and dipped it into the oil and vinegar concoction the waiter made for us.

Tom sighed. "I think 'London Vigilante' is a grossly sensationalized name for someone who goes around and beats people up. The news gets an erection—sorry—over these kind of tabloid stories. It's really quite disgusting."

"So, are you more upset at the news coverage or the Vigilante herself?"

"Well, the news. As far as the victims go, they got what they deserved, I guess, assuming they are guilty." He looked out the window on the other side of the restaurant.

"Hmmm. Where have I heard that before? Homophobe, last night?"

"Are you always this direct and sarcastic?" He criticized as he turned his head to stare at me. I couldn't get a read on his reaction. Mad? Playful?

Either way, I challenged, "Why yes, I am," as I held his gaze. He broke the stare by a quick rolling of his eyes, but looked slightly entertained.

A pause, and then, "Her."

"Huh?"

"You said, 'her.' Why do you think the Vigilante is a female?"

"My friend, Jamie, at work told me that a lot of women apparently root for the Vigilante. They like to think it's a woman who is avenging other abused women and children."

Tom seemed charmed by this, "It's an interesting theory."

"What, you don't think a woman can beat the crap out of someone?" I bristled.

"Not at all. My sister and I used to fight all the time as children. She definitely had the upper hand."

The conversation ceased when our food came. The waiter removed our salad plates and then placed our food in front of each of us. The vibrant green in the kale complimented the ruby red marinara sauce on the shiny white plate. I've never seen food so colorful. We changed the subject and in between bites, we talked about books we'd read, our travels, and pets we, or rather, I had owned. Tom would, every once in a while, touch my hand or pay me a nice compliment. While I was speaking, he would lean slightly in and stare at me with a slight smile. Dinner was delicious and I really was starting to like this guy, a lot. I've never met someone so engaging and, to be frank, so interested in me. I chalked the earlier part of the evening up to nerves and quickly forgot about it. The wine, of course, helped.

After we finished eating and the busboy cleared our plates, the waiter came over and enticed us with a tray of decadent sweets. "We have a wonderful dessert selection," and he proceeded to explain each dessert in the finest detail.

Tom looked at me, questioning, and although tempted, I was rather full, so I shook my head. Besides, I doubted anything was vegan on the tray.

"No, just the bill, please, thank you." And then he looked at me again, "Would you like to take a stroll along the Thames? It's quite beautiful at night, all the lights reflecting on the water. We can take a cab there and then walk off dinner."

I lifted my foot under the table and placed it on his knee. He looked down, smiled, and started tenderly rubbing my shoeless foot.

"Ah, yes, the form over function shoes. Well, how about a pint? I'm sure we will happen upon a pub close by."

"Sure!" I reacted, a little too enthusiastically, glad that the evening was not coming to an end. He cocked his head, a mannerism that seems to have many different meanings from what I've seen so far. My cell buzzed again. I laughed out loud this time; Jamie typed in PHOTO about a thousand times.

"Something funny?" He asked.

I sighed. "My friend, Jamie, wants me to take a picture of you and send it to her."

He squinted at me and asked why.

"She's just curious. I told her a little about you. So, to get her to stop texting me all night, can we take a selfie together?"

He shrugged, "I don't think I've ever taken a *selfie*, but alright." Moving behind his chair, I positioned my head so it was right next to his, centered us in the picture, and snapped it. He really smelled good. His cologne must have some kind of pheromone in it, because I just wanted to make out with him right there. Instead, I looked at the photo and thought we looked pretty awesome together. I replied to Jamie to leave me alone, but attached the picture.

Tom paid the bill, looking rather insulted when I offered to treat. We left the restaurant, me hesitating to put on my shoes, but doing it anyway.

We started to walk—well, I hobbled—down the sidewalk. Unfortunately, it started to rain, so I wasn't going to walk barefoot and risk getting my stockings wet. I hate that feeling.

"Would you like me to carry you?" He offered when he saw me stumbling around. I wanted to say, yes, definitely, but I felt a little self-conscious, so I declined. "Look, there's one right there." I said as I pointed to a hole in the wall type pub.

Tom grimaced a little as it was probably not the type of place he frequented, but we headed toward it anyway. He pushed open the worn golden-handled door, letting me in first. The pub was loud and somewhat crowded, so we had to push our way through until we found a vacant high-top table near the window. Tom pulled the stool out for me and I climbed up and had a seat. He leaned into me. I tensed for a second, thinking he was going to kiss me, but instead, he asked in my ear, "More wine? Beer?" I guess he didn't want to shout.

"Yes, I'll have a lager, please. But, may I buy?" I asked, loudly.

He furrowed his brow, pursed his lips, turned, and walked to the bar, completely ignoring my question. My phone buzzed again with just "OMG!!!" What a goofball.

As Tom was ordering the drinks, a man that I kind of recognized came over to me. "Do I know you from somewhere?" He asked in a thick British accent. He reeked of alcohol and cigarette smoke. The bar was a little dark, and I didn't really want to look at him that closely. And, besides, his sewage breath made me recoil and look away.

"Ah, I don't know," I shifted, uncomfortable on my barstool. "My date will be back in a second." Hoping he'd get the hint and leave. He was hovering a little too close for my liking. And his breath!

I saw Tom turn around with two pints in his hand, look at us, briefly pause, and then stride over. He set the pints down a little louder than necessary and sat down. "Is everything alright, Anna?" Tom asked, not taking his eyes off the stranger, who stepped back slightly away from me.

"Yeah, Yeah, Anna… and you," the drunk man sputtered, pointing a finger at Tom, "you're that bloke from the tour last night." He turned to me. "And you're that gal who had her stomach cramps, probably from your period, and fell to the ground." He turned back to Tom," Yeah, you told me to leave, remember?" he looked back at me, "so what are the likes of you doing with a faggot like 'im?" pointing his thumb in Tom's direction. I saw Tom stiffen.

I put my hand on Tom's arm to calm him down. "It's alright, Tom, just ignore him."

Tom turned to stare at me. He was far from happy. I could tell something was about to happen and it wasn't good.

"Aw, did I hit a sore spot?" He then put his mouth an inch away from Tom's ear, whispered "faggot," and grabbed quickly at Tom's crotch.

And with that, it started. I saw a shift. I can't explain it, but some kind of change in Tom's eyes and demeanor. He slowly turned his head away from me, stood up, face to face with the guy and stared right into his eyes.

"Oh… I'm scared… is the *scary* faggot going to hurt me?" The man chortled.

"Right," Tom concurred. He pushed the drunk with both hands and then kicked him right in the stomach. The drunk doubled over, but miraculously, didn't fall. Tom then hook punched the guy in the jaw, re-splitting the cut on his hand he supposedly got from the tree. When the man fell to the ground, Tom swiftly jumped on him, straddling his torso, and started to punch him repeatedly, causing sickening *thwack thwack thwack* sounds. I was terrified, screaming for Tom to stop, as I saw blood start to spatter from the blows. Out of the corner of my eye, I saw movement.

The bartender scrambled over the bar with a bat in his hand while a couple of large men who had been drinking their beers, ran over as well. One of the burly men grabbed Tom around his chest with one arm and around Tom's neck with the other. He yanked Tom off the bloody, now motionless man on the ground, standing Tom upright. Tom was trying hard to tear the hulking man's arms off him, but it was pointless. Two other men flanked Tom's sides, grabbing each arm to subdue him further and hooking their legs around his. Then, I noticed a change in Tom's face. He looked confused and scared, like he didn't know where he was. Helplessly, but screaming my head off, I watched the bartender, a stocky, but built man, rear back and jab the hilt of the bat into Tom's stomach, hard. Tom gasped loudly for air and would have doubled over were it not for the hulks behind him keeping him standing. I ran at the bartender, but another person, who I couldn't see, grabbed me and pulled me back, holding my arms behind me as I stared in horror. The bar crowd gathered and cheered as the bartender dropped the bat and used his fists, landing blow after blow into Tom's ribs and stomach. I could almost hear the bones cracking inside his body. The bartender was relentless. He slammed his elbow into the side of Tom's mouth and nose; blood exploding all over Tom's face and the bartender's white shirt. The bartender continued his punishment, landing a right hook punch squarely onto Tom's beautiful face, splitting open his skin at his cheekbone, the red contrasting horribly with his alabaster coloring. Tom's head lulled to the side as the bartender picked up the bat again and rocketed it into Tom's groin. Tom screamed in agony as the large men holding him finally let go, allowing him to crumble to the floor.

"Now get out! Both of you!" Commanded the bartender to me and Tom. The guy holding me finally dropped my arms.

"He started it, you asshole," I roared, hoarse from screaming during the attack, and pointed to the other guy, who seemed to be knocked out cold.

"I don't care. Just get out; we'll help you." And with that, two of the guys grabbed Tom under his arms and dragged him into the street, Tom wailing in pain all the while. The bartender approached me, but before he could touch me, I grabbed my purse and a cloth napkin from the table and ran out the door. I twisted my ankle trying to run in the Goddamn shoes.

"Tom!" I screamed, limping over to find a curled up, moaning and writhing ball on the wet sidewalk. The rain falling gently on his form.

Eyes closed, cheek to the pavement, he whispered after a raspy inhale, "I'm sorry, Anna."

"Never mind that, we've got to get you out of here in case they come back... and get you to the hospital."

"No, no hospital." He wheezed.

"But,"

"No, please Anna, God no." He panted, clawing at my arm.

I hesitated, not really sure of the best thing to do. "Okay, but you're going to have to get up and get into a cab. Can you manage that?"

And without answering, he tried to push himself up to a seated position with a loud grunt, but fell right back down, barely catching himself.

"Let me get a cab first, don't move." I noticed people looking out the windows and doors of the pub and I started to get worried, especially if the man Tom attacked regained his strength. Tom would be no match for him now. I turned to the street and waited impatiently a few minutes and then found one. I waved my hand vigorously. The cab stopped and rolled down the window, grimacing at the body on the ground. Obviously, the cabbie really didn't want to give Tom a ride, but agreed only if we would double the fare and clean his face up first. Frustrated, I agreed as long as he helped me lift Tom. I wiped his face, hastily but gently, with the cloth napkin I stole.

We pulled Tom up the best we could; the cabbie manhandling him a little too much. Tom in turn let out very audible cries, but miraculously, we got him into the cab.

"5 Seward Street in Clerkenwell, please," I told the cab driver who kept glancing at us in his rear-view mirror.

"I can't walk your steps," Tom whispered, eyes closed. "My place has a lift... Harley Street in Marylebone."

I repeated this to the cab driver so he could hear it and off we went. During the ride, I applied the napkin to his cheek, nose and lower lip as best I could. His labored breathing subsided somewhat during the ride, but it was raspy. I think he was falling in and out of consciousness. I flexed and pointed my ankle, turning it this way and that until it started to feel a little better.

When we turned down Harley Street, my eyes widened. The street lamps revealed ultra-ornate row houses lining both sides of the street. Some had carvings, some had wrought iron balconies and all had elaborate doors. He wasn't lying when he said he had money.

When we arrived at his building, I reluctantly paid the cab driver two times the fare, and he at least helped me get Tom out of the car, but roughly. Tom stumbled over to the street lamp and laid one hand on it as he doubled over, head down in pain. "Right coat pocket," he breathed. I was concerned he was going to throw up, possibly causing more damage and definitely more pain to his ribs. But, fortunately he didn't.

I reached into his pocket, fetching his keys. My heals clicked as I walked up two black and white marble steps that led to a black door flanked with columns. After unlocking the door, I kicked off my shoes and wedged one of them between the door and the jamb to keep the door from shutting. The cool marble felt wonderful on my aching feet. Shoeless, I went back to assist Tom, allowing him to lean on me. His weight, combined with my sore feet and relatively sore ankle, made getting him up the short steps extremely difficult, but somehow I managed. Once inside, I bent down, swooped up my shoes and let the door close. We staggered over to the elevator, I pushed the button, and we waited until the doors opened. Two people came out, giving Tom a squinty-eyed look, and walked on. "Thanks for the help," I muttered.

We got in the elevator and I gently pushed Tom against the back corner for stability. If he had fallen, I don't think I'd have had the strength to lift him back up.

"What floor?"

"Third… flat C." While we waited for the excruciatingly slow elevator to make its ascent, Tom's eyes started to roll back and his body started to slouch. I caught him by pressing my whole body against him to keep him up. He came to again with a grunt and tried to regain his balance. He then put his head down, brought his hand to his face and started to cry softly.

"It's okay, Tom, we're almost there." I gently moved away from him, but kept one hand on his chest.

Finally, the doors opened and I helped him to flat C. Dropping my shoes, I tried a couple of keys, found the right one and unlocked the plain green door adorned with a gold and silver dragon door knocker. I pushed it open while Tom leaned on my shoulder.

I felt for the light, and upon turning it on, saw an absolutely beautiful home. It could not have been more opposite from my flat. Hand scraped hard wood floors, thick egg and dart white crown molding. Columns separated the burgundy wine-colored foyer and living room, creating a dramatic entrance. The word "pristine" would be an understatement; immaculate would be more appropriate.

Still stumbling, we made our way into the living room. The fireplace, the focal point of the room, had the most fantastic green tiles with some sort of design I couldn't quite see just yet. Above the mantle, a white gargoyle smiled playfully down at us. The furnishings were rather modern, but looked pretty comfortable. I led Tom to the sofa perpendicular to the fireplace. With much effort and a lot of complaining and wincing, I was able to remove Tom's coat and blazer, which I spread out on the white sofa. I helped him lay down on top of them as tears were slowly rolling over his cheeks, making the blood on his face glisten, reminding me of a morbid modern art piece.

"I'm going to get something for your cuts," I said, worriedly. I ran back to get my shoes and then dumped them next to the sofa.

I could either go left or right from the living room, where columns next to a wall separated each wing. I went to the right, down an orange painted hall. The first door I came to was a small bathroom with black and white tiles on the floor and partway up the walls. There was a small, white pedestal sink with a mirrored medicine cabinet above. I opened it up and found some gauze, rubbing alcohol, and tape. I wet a washcloth half-way and took the medical supplies back over to Tom. His crying had subsided, but he looked terrible.

His outerwear didn't fully cover the sofa so I asked, "Okay, Tom, can you sit up? I don't want you to get blood all over your gorgeous furniture. See, I told you we should have gone to my flat." He laughed a little, then a pained expression crossed his face. A barely perceptible, 'ouch' escaped his lips as he breathed out. "Please, don't make me laugh."

"Okay, here we go," I grabbed him under his arms and helped him to a sitting position while Tom held his breath to control his pain.

I gently applied the damp part of the washcloth to his cheek, lower lip, and nose, and wiped the rest of the blood off his face. Then I cleaned the blood off his knuckles. I delicately inspected his shaking hands; the knuckles and the whole back were badly bruised and swollen. "God," I murmured under my breath.

"Okay, now brace yourself, this is going to sting." I poured some alcohol on the dry part of the washcloth and dabbed it on his cheek. He inhaled, and slowly exhaling, stifled a scream. Then I moved to his lower lip. He abruptly pulled away, yelling "ouch!!!" as tears pricked his eyes.

"Sorry," I said, "but you don't want an infection."

I took the same care with his hands, but bandaged up the left with the gash. That cut was a bit deeper.

"I'm going to get you some ice for your ribs and hands, and um, elsewhere, okay? My guess is your ribs are broken by the way the dude was hitting you. We should tape them, but first, the ice." I didn't wait for an answer.

The kitchen was off to the left. I went past the other partial wall with half column where a flat screen television hung, leading to a small dining room, and then to the kitchen. It wasn't huge, but it was fantastic. Grey quartz countertops, dark cabinets with curly-cue pulls, stainless steel appliances, and a white and grey striated rock backsplash.

"Cool," I uttered out loud. I went to the freezer and grabbed some small ice packs for his hands and two bags of frozen peas, and two bags of frozen blueberries for his ribs, eye and groin. I heard a loud "oh God!" from the living room and ran back in, toting the ice packs and frozen food after snatching the two neatly draped dish towels from the oven handle.

Tom was lying down on the sofa. He had somehow managed to take his shoes and socks off.

"Let me help you with your shirt so I can look at your ribs," I insisted.

"Anna, please take some money out of my wallet, get a cab and go home. You don't have to do this." He implored, quietly, adjusting his position on the sofa.

"Tom, I'm not going to leave you alone."

He closed his eyes and shook his head slightly.

I gingerly unbuttoned his shirt and pulled it open, revealing a hairless, fit chest and stomach with a little bit of muscle definition. His labored breathing was made more evident by the unnatural rise and fall of his stomach.

On his left shoulder, I noticed some scarring. I started to touch it when Tom gently grabbed my hand. "Please don't," he begged.

So, I didn't. Instead, I laid the dish towels down and then the frozen bags of food on each side of his badly bruised ribs. He inhaled suddenly from the cold but then settled into it. I tenderly lifted his right hand and positioned it palm down on his stomach. I did the same with the other hand and laid the ice packs on them. I hesitated a second and laid another bag of frozen peas on his crotch, making him shudder. I placed the last one on his eye.

After a bit, he started to fall asleep. The rasp in his breath made me worry that a fractured rib might have punctured a lung. I also worried he had a concussion.

I stared at him for a minute. I couldn't help but feel compassion for the man in his current state, but his anger and violence really scared me tonight. It would be relatively easy to just walk out the door. I mean, I just met him. But something about him kept me planted in his flat. I could picture Jamie seething.

I brushed his hair away from his face and then went to the kitchen to fetch some water for myself, and then to decompress.

I walked back into the living room and took a seat in the oversized plush, white swivel chair across from the sofa where Tom was deeply asleep. Moonlight illuminating his pure white face from the floor to ceiling windows that flanked the fireplace, I stared at his closed eyes, one covered by blueberries. Eyes open, his eyes shine brilliantly with bright green and deep blue with flecks of gold around the pupil as well as some aubergine. They reveal so much and so little at the same time. Yes, intelligence, depth, soulfulness, but also mystery. There is something hiding behind them. Not quite sinister, but definitely troubled. Even when smiling, that hint of a 'tortured soul' is apparent. Eyes closed, he looks more peaceful. As I watched him sleep, I noticed his brow would twitch or furrow every once in a while, like he was trying to sort out some internal conflict. I looked up at the clock. 12:30 AM. I really didn't want to leave him here in case he needed my help or if he took a turn for the worse, regardless of what he wanted me to do. Plus, the thought of going back to my flat at this time of night, especially with what had happened in the last couple of days and tonight, I didn't want to be alone.

I definitely *did* want to get out of this dress, however. I went further down the hall, passed the bathroom and found one more door on the left. I peered in and found a combination study and guest room. At the end of the hall was one more door standing ajar, which I opened fully to find his bedroom. Another elegant and charming room. Large enough, but in no way immense, it was tastefully decorated. The wood floors extended into this room as well. A dark wood sleigh bed stood in the middle of the room and a few more white and grey gargoyles adorned the deep blue walls. Two doors flanked the bed. I opened the left door to find another small, but exquisite bathroom. A modern glass-enclosed shower with stone tile and copper accents sat in one corner. A matching copper bowl sink sat atop a distressed wood vanity to the right. I noticed a similar looking raised pattern, just like the fireplace, on the accent tiles. Hmmm, paisleys… cute.

I came out of the bathroom and opened the other door, revealing a very orderly walk-in closet. I grabbed a white button-down shirt, took off my dress and laid it neatly on the bed. I then took off my stockings and bra and pulled the partially buttoned shirt over my head. Since Tom was a bit taller than I, the shirt covered half of my thighs. This would do.

I went back to the living room and looked more closely at the fireplace. Yup, paisleys. He must have a thing for them. I loved how the flat exuded old charm, but also included some fun modern touches. I turned back to the sofa where Tom was lying motionless, except for his slightly labored breathing. I took the frozen food and ice packs off of his injuries, and put them back in the freezer.

I was practically sleeping on my feet. I decided not to use the bed, feeling it would be too presumptuous, so I curled up on the chair across from the sofa and fell into a deep, thankfully dreamless sleep.

CHAPTER 5

— *Sunday, September 7*

I awoke to the end of the Doppler effect from a police siren. 3:00 AM. I looked over at Tom on the sofa, who had turned during the night, so that his bare back was facing me. He must have managed to take off his shirt in his sleep. The shirt lay crumpled on the ground, something I doubted Tom would do consciously, judging from his impeccably tidy and orderly flat. I pushed myself out of the chair and leaned into him to be sure he was breathing okay. I heard a slight rasp with every inhale. This position was probably bad for his ribs, but I didn't want to disturb him. There was an eerie glow in the room cast by an outside light. And that's when I saw them. Criss-crossed, diagonal, long and short scars all over his back, down, and I assume, beyond his waist band. I discovered some discolored, raised circles, about a quarter inch in diameter, right around his kidney area. Squinting, I noticed the circles formed some kind of pattern. Hesitantly, I pulled the waist band down slightly on his suit pants to reveal the rest. Together, these individual small circles formed a smiley face. I gently let go of his waist band and sat back down in the chair in shock. "My God, Tom, what happened to you?" I spoke aloud softly as my eyes began to water. Who could have done this to him?

I contemplated leaving again. As much as I liked him, I did not want another complicated, baggage-laden relationship. But, of course I couldn't leave. Not only would my conscience weigh heavily on me, but I felt for him, much as I would for an innocent wounded animal. And I liked him, despite what he did to that guy. So I stayed. I stood back up and covered his bare back, scars and all, with a paisley patterned throw that I found hanging on the side of the sofa. Then I curled back into the plush chair, hugging my knees in tight, and fell back asleep.

***

The smell of coffee and the sound of piano music woke me up. 9:35 AM, Sunday. Thank God. I couldn't even fathom going to work now. The paisley throw was now wrapped around me instead of Tom, and his shirt was no longer on the floor. I stretched out my legs and arms, stood up and plodded into the kitchen, wrapping the paisley blanket around my waist. I wished I had had my glasses as my contacts were bugging me.

"Oh, hello," Tom smiled, "would you like some coffee or tea? I made both."

"Coffee, please."

He was much more casually dressed this morning, wearing a faded blue button down long-sleeved shirt, mostly open revealing his bare chest. His jeans were slightly baggy and hung low around his hips. His hair was messy, but cool. His face, however, was a different story altogether. The start of a 5 o'clock shadow surrounded his mouth and chin, framing his swollen lower lip—the cut was still raw, of course, as well as the laceration on his cheekbone, which sat on top of a deep purple bruise. His left eye sported a nasty black and blue color that almost sealed his eye shut. He handed me the coffee with some effort; his hands were shaking and swollen.

"How the hell are you even moving?" I asked.

"Em… I'm trying to put on a brave face?" He reasoned. "I must look ghastly."

"Um, let's just call it rugged," I offered, as I gratefully took a sip of coffee. Ah… the elixir of life!

"I am glad you made yourself at home last night," taking in what I was wearing. "I'm sorry I wasn't a better host."

A little chagrined, I explained, "Sorry, I just didn't want to sleep in that dress. I wasn't snooping; I just grabbed the first thing I saw in your closet."

"It's quite alright. Let me fetch you something to wear besides the blanket." He hobbled, slowly, to his bedroom, panting the whole way, and emerged a few minutes later with a pair of sweat pants, trying to catch his breath.

"What are we listening to? I like it."

"Ironically, it's called 'The School of Instant Pain.' It's by Triumvirat, a progressive rock band from Germany that echoes bands like Emerson, Lake and Palmer and Yes."

"Oh! I know some Yes. My father was in to them. Didn't they do that "Roundabout" song?"

Tom's eyebrows went up and he stared at me for a second, bewildered. "Em, yes. And a lot more than that. They are one of my favorite bands. I was lucky enough to see them in 2004 at Wembley Stadium. I believe that was their last tour with Jon Anderson."

"Who?"

Tom shook his head, almost disgusted. "Never mind," he handed me the sweat pants.

I thanked him and went down the hall to change in the bathroom. A little long, I rolled the sweats up to my ankles and rolled them down some at the waist where they loosely hung. I came out and found Tom sitting at the table, shakily pouring tea into a light blue teacup. He then took a sip, wincing. Looking up at me, he said, "Yes, very cute."

God, he confused me. I sat down and concentrated on my coffee, but I could tell he was staring at me.

"Thank you, Anna," he said with the utmost sincerity. He took my hand with his bandaged right hand and gently squeezed. "I cannot tell you all the emotions I have rattling around in my head." He closed his eyes, "On the one hand, I am deeply, deeply ashamed at my behavior last night, but on the other, I'm happy, for I believe I've met an angel." He popped his eyes open, the right eye much more than the left, and beamed, then immediately recoiled from the pain of stretching the gash on his lip, it seemed.

I squeezed his swollen hand back, forgetting about his injuries. He let out a soft whimper and abruptly pulled his hand away.

"Oh my God, I'm so sorry, I forgot for a second," I quickly explained.

"It's okay, Anna. My whole body and face are throbbing, so a little more pain won't matter. I can't even smile without feeling a pang." He didn't take my hand again.

"I must say, I was pretty surprised to find you still here after I woke up. I guess plan C worked," he joked.

"I think I would have preferred plan A or B." I paused, "I couldn't just leave you alone. Since you refused to go to the hospital, I felt I had to stay. For all I know, you have internal injuries."

"Well, regardless of why you stayed, I can't tell you enough how much I appreciate it. I... I guess I owe you something. At the least, I owe you some explanations, if you are interested."

"What do you mean by explanations?" I feigned ignorance.

"I know you have questions from last night, so go ahead and ask. But if you would rather, I can call you a cab—I would completely understand," he offered.

I paused, shook my head, and then it all poured out, "Well, what the hell came over you last night? Do you often get into fights? I mean, my God, I thought you were going to kill that guy. You were so angry."

I started to shiver. "I mean, geez, blood went everywhere and you wouldn't stop, even when he clearly had enough. I get he was an asshole, but did you really have to go that far?" I took a breath and composed myself. "Sorry, I have no right to lecture you, but you made me a part of this. I can't figure you out. You're so gentle and nice and proper, but then…"

He looked away from me. "Honestly, Anna, I don't really remember much of what I did in the fight. I recall the insults and the feelings, but it's all a blur. What exactly did I do to him?" Turning his head back to me.

"Really? You don't remember? You maimed the guy. You probably broke his nose and knocked out some teeth. That's why your hands are so swollen."

He looked at me, somewhat confused. "I just can't recall any of that. I do, however, remember almost every blow when getting attacked by the bartender." He paused and stared at me with sad eyes. "Oh, Anna, I am so appalled at myself, horrified that you had to witness this part of me. I assure you, this is the first time in a long time I've been in a skirmish."

I nodded and sighed, "Skirmish is putting it a bit lightly." Then an uncomfortable silence ensued until Tom broke it.

"Any other questions? I think there is an elephant in the room."

I started to look around and stopped myself. "Okay, you sure?" I cautioned.

Looking a bit uneasy, knowing what was coming, Tom nodded his head.

I breathed out and quietly asked, "Okay. How did you get all those scars? I mean, you have a happy face drawn in what, cigarette burns?"

Tom closed his eyes and took in a deep breath. "You saw that too?" Opening his eyes back up and raising his eyebrows he jested, "I thought you weren't snooping," a sad smile crossing his lips.

Ruefully, I didn't answer and did a quick shrug.

"You really want to hear this? This is not the way I try to impress a girl."

"We're a little past that, don't you think?"

"Right." He took another deep breath and told his story.

'Get your bloody arse over here Thomas. 'Ow many times have I told you to empty my ashtrays. Go on, get it.' I went to the closet where he kept the riding crop he used to use to beat the shit out of horses in order to make them move… one, two, three and then all the way to twelve blows to my back, backside, and legs. I always tried not to cry, but I was only a boy. He was, ah, gentler, when I was really

young. He didn't use a riding crop, but you know, a hand or a ruler, whatever. And the punishment never fit the crime. I would innocently look at him and he would assume I was being disrespectful. Maybe I didn't move fast enough to fetch him his beer. 'Thomas, go get it,' were the scariest words in the Queen's English, as far as I was concerned.

Tom's eyes started to well up. A single tear slowly ran down the contours of his face, wetting the cut on his cheek. He flinched from the sting, wiped it away and continued his horror story:

I was about fourteen. My friend Robbie and I used to play basketball after school at a neighbor's house where a net had been erected for the children on the street. I remember the day. White puffy clouds, beautiful blue skies, but hot. Unseasonably hot. Robbie, and only Robbie, took his shirt off and we continued to play. Eventually, we became tired and thirsty, so we went into my house for some water and decided we had had enough of the heat, so we went upstairs to my room to chat, as mates do.

Tom paused, looked down into his lap as he shook his head. Just as the silence was starting to get uncomfortable, he looked up, clasped his hands and rested them on the table. He then continued after another deep breath.

I don't know why, but my father came home early from work that day or rather, early from the pub. He opened the door to my room without knocking, something he always did, and saw Robbie, shirtless, sitting next to me on the bed. I remember the look on his face. Sinister. Chewing his gum like a cow chews her cud, eyes narrowed and a darkened smile. 'Hi, mate,' eyeing Robbie. 'You need to go now, Tom's got some chores to do. Off you go.' So, Robbie got up and left.

When we heard the click of the front door my father approached me. He stared and chewed for an eternity. His eyes looked, em, how can I describe this, em, there was pure hatred in them, but also a giddiness. Finally, he ordered me to stand up, so I obeyed. Then he started in on me: 'I always knew you were a sniveling li'l faggot. Always crying, still sleeping with that paisley bear.' He spit his gum on the floor and stepped toward me, opened his hand and slapped me firmly across my face. I mean it was so hard it could have been a punch. Scared out of my mind, I just stood there, willing myself not to cry.

He noticed this and sneered. 'Well, no tears yet, is that faggot boyfriend of yours teaching you to be a man?' Then he slapped my other cheek. I stood my ground and warned, 'if you touch me again, I am going to hurt you.' I'd never, ever spoken that way to my father. My dad was a large man; not only in weight, but muscle. I was skinny, and had never thrown a successful punch in my life. I knew that fighting back would not be a great option for me, but I had to do something.

Enough was enough. He took one more swing at me, but I dodged it and kneed him, aiming for his groin, but I missed and contacted his thigh instead, barely making an impact. I remember him roaring with laughter, shaming me at my failed attempt.

Then his expression changed again, his smile turning into a wicked grin, 'Well, finally hitting back, eh? But, I won't be havin' ya disrespectin' your old man.' And with that he punched me hard in the stomach, which caused me to double over. As I tried to catch my breath, he placed his hand on the back of my head and slammed my face into the hard floor. I recall hearing a sickening crunch as my nose hit first, feeling and I assume, looking like it exploded. Blood pooled around my face and into my mouth, the metallic taste making me want to vomit.

And that still wasn't the end of it. I felt him straddle my legs using his weight to immobilize my lower half.

I heard some rustling and then a match being struck, followed by the rasp of a deep inhale and slow exhale. My ears, head and face were throbbing, but I remember him uttering the words 'faggots like art, right? So, I'll make my little faggot a piece of art with me fag.' He laid his forearm on my upper back and then I felt the most excruciating pain I've ever felt. A white hot, searing pain right around the right side of my lower back. Again and again and again. He was humming some tune I didn't recognize while 'painting' his picture. He then pulled the waistband of my loose jeans down a bit to complete his masterpiece. Five more burns.

Tom ran his hands through his thick hair and closed his eyes.

I remember the putrid smell, the skin singeing, the humming and the claustrophobic feeling of not being able to move. I had never felt so much fear or pain in my life—all the belts, fists, riding crops, didn't compare to this. When he was done, he slapped my bum once and said, "Beautiful, I'm a regular Van Gogh," got up, and left me there.

He took a shuddered breath, opened his watery eyes and placed his hands back on the table. I sat frozen in my chair.

I must have been in shock because I cannot remember how I got into bed, nor how all the blood got cleaned up. I was in and out of a dreamlike state. I'd come to and with my paisley bear in my arms and then I'd fall back into a haze. I vaguely remember shouting and screaming in the hall. Through the thick fog in my head, I heard my sister. Noises followed, and I dreamed of a bowling ball, bouncing down our steps.

I was passed out until the next afternoon, missing school. My father finally was able to rouse me and told me there had been an awful accident. He made no mention of what he did to me. My sister had died when she allegedly tripped and fell down the stairs.

Tears started to creep down Tom's face as he continued.

Of course the police investigated, asking me about how I broke my nose, but I told them I fell while playing basketball. I was so afraid that my father would kill me next, so I didn't say a word about the beatings or the burns. To this day, my father claims he is not responsible, that he did not push her. But, whether he physically did the act or not, he created the circumstances for it to happen. I lost a piece of me that day—my sister. And the little dignity I once had, evaporated. It's taken me a long time to get it back.

Tom leaned back in the chair and sighed, wiping his face. "So, that's the story of the smiley face and a few of my scars. Now four living people know how they got there."

"You've never told anyone else?" I whispered.

He shook his head and then put his face in his hands; his body started to tremble as he was trying to hold back his emotions. The CD switched to another prog rock song with an acoustic guitar intro followed by the lead singer singing something about a lucky girl.

I sat in utter horror and disbelief. Tears were now streaming down my face as I reached out and touched his arm. "My God, Tom, I am so sorry."

I moved my chair to sit closer to him and gently put my arm around him. He turned and grabbed me in a full embrace, both of us sobbing, me out of feeling so sorry for the life this poor boy had to endure; and Tom, I think it was cathartic for him, especially after last night. We sat like that for several minutes until Tom was able to compose himself.

He pressed on his eyes and then looked up at me. The skin under his eyes was rimmed with red and the water from his tears magnified the green in his irises and the black in his eyelashes.

"I am so sorry, Anna. I believe I've made a fool out of myself, yet again. I am not prone to weeping, but it seems I've been doing that quite a bit around you." He seemed humiliated.

"I'd think you were a robot if you didn't have some kind of reaction after telling me all that. You've never talked to a therapist or told your grandfather?"

"Actually, I told my grandfather just recently, although why I didn't earlier, I don't know. I suppose I was frightened when I was younger. And yes, I did see a therapist, but it's all a big blur and he certainly didn't help me. So, I withdrew into my own misery. When I was 18, I was able to finally leave home and attend University where I was able to come out of my shell, reinvent myself if you will. I tried to push the memories down in the recesses of my mind and I did a pretty good job of it, too. Experimenting with drugs helped for a bit in my first year, but I saw my grades start to suffer, so I stopped. I made some friends, got on with a couple of girls, and life went on."

"What happened to your mom?"

"She died in a car accident. I was very young when it happened, so I really grew up without a mother, and of course, had almost no relationship with my father. When I went to University, I decided to completely write him out of my life. But one day, a number of years later, he found me. He was like a caricature of his former self. Still big, but more fat than muscle; still lines on his face, but far deeper. His eyes were cavernous and his mouth had been set in an exaggerated frown. He carried himself differently, too; more shrunken and subdued, not quite like the pompous arse I knew and loved," he said sarcastically.

My empathy turned more into anger, and I started my lecture. "I don't understand, Tom. Why on earth do you take care of this man? I mean, Jesus, he wasn't a father to you! A real father doesn't abuse his son and ruin his childhood. You should let the fucker rot away in his own shame."

Tom grimaced at my candor, pursed his lips and stated, a little annoyed, "Anna, *nothing* is that simple."

"Sorry, Tom, I guess it's easy for me to say, but…"

"You're right, it is easy for you to say," he interrupted. "Look. The man has emphysema. He came to me out of loneliness and asked—no begged me—to visit him. He professed his sorrow and regret and said that I am the only person alive he cared about, that he had no one left. He actually cried like a little child. If you've never seen your own father cry, you can't imagine how hard it is to reconcile. So, I don't know, out of guilt or obligation or whatever, I do it. I visit him. It's who I am, Anna."

I drummed my fingers on the table and sat back in the chair.

"Look," he said taking my hand, "it's Sunday and it's supposed to be sunny. Let's go for a walk in the park. I need to get some air in my lungs and I think moving around a bit might help me heal. I mean, if you are still interested in being with me. I'm sorry if I'm being presumptuous."

I softened a bit and asked, "Are you okay to walk around with your ribs like that, and your—um—other parts?"

He held his hands up, "I don't know, but I'd like to try. I would very much like you to join me if I haven't frightened you off. And I can also understand you not wanting to be seen in public with a face like mine."

"No, you haven't frightened me off, and no I'm not embarrassed about your face. But I'll need to go home and change, obviously."

I noticed a small tugging upward of his mouth. "If you insist."

***

As I left Tom's flat, he insisted, rather belligerently, that I take money for the cab fare. There really wasn't any point in arguing with him, so I took his notes, crumpled them up in my hand and traipsed down the steps in my bare feet. I was not going to put those shoes on again. As I rode in the cab Tom had called for me, I took in the neighborhood. The houses were even more elegant in the daylight. Statuary in nooks, Greek columns, and marble adorned many of the houses—opulence in every crevice. We passed a quaint park and then chic department stores and shops. I had never been in this area of town and doubted I would ever be able to do more than just window shop here. About twenty minutes later, we arrived at my flat. I smoothed out the notes before handing them to the driver, telling him he could keep the change. Scrambling out of the cab, I typed in the door code and then ambled up the stairs. I passed a blackened banana peel and grimaced, wondering what grossness I might be stepping in. I desperately wanted a shower. Tom was going to be meeting me here around 2:00 PM, um 1300 hours, rather? No, no, 1400. Three months in London and I can't get used to the 24-hour clock.

When I entered my flat, I sighed, knowing I had to clean before I could shower. I didn't want Tom to think that I always live like a slob, even though I kind of do. I flipped on the CD player, already turned up to "eleven." "Democracy" by The Damned blasted through the speakers as I started on the dirty dishes. Contrasting with the sunny day outside, but mirroring my mood, the music's minor chords and dark lyrics put me in a zone. Hating to clean, the music helped distract me while I continued my chores: gathering my clothes strewn about the flat, stacking extraneous papers, mail and books on the small kitchen table, and making the bed. After vacuuming, I was pretty satisfied with the state of my home, so I stepped into the shower, letting my mind go blank as the hot water eased the tenseness in my body. I stayed under the water for a while, not wanting to get out. The water pressure and the heat felt so good after the absolutely insane evening and morning I had.

I finally stepped out of the shower. The CD had stopped, but I heard the door buzzer. I didn't think Tom would be here just yet; it was too early. Wrapping a towel around my hair and then hastily tying my robe, I pushed the button on the intercom, "Hello?"

"Open this damn door and let me in." It was Jamie.

When I unlocked the door, I found Jamie standing there, hands on her hips, and a scowl on her face.

"I know, I know, I forgot to text you back," I fretted, apologetically, as she stepped past me, not waiting for an invitation.

"I texted and called a thousand times. You on a date with a bloke you had just met. I was worried about you. And, wait, something is wrong around here. Very, very wrong."

I opened my hands up saying "What?"

"Your flat is relatively clean!"

"Haha. Look, a bunch of shit happened last night, so stifle your sarcasm, have a seat, and I'll make you some tea."

Jamie plopped herself down at the table. Once the kettle boiled, I placed a bag of Earl Grey into two cream colored mugs, poured in the hot water, and placed a mug in front of Jamie. Joining her at the table, I recounted all the events of last night and this morning. I left out the part about Tom's scars and how he got them. Jamie listened intently with her mouth agape, hardly touching her tea. She was speechless, almost.

"Anna, this is crazy. He sounds like nothing but trouble. After the earful you gave me about your high school boyfriend, I'm really concerned about you."

"Oh my God. He's nothing like Graham! We talked, a lot! I really, really like him, Jamie. He is very sweet and polite, despite ripping the homophobe a new one. Thinking back, it's kind of badass." I widened my eyes.

"This isn't a movie, Anna, this is real."

"I know, look, I'll be careful, okay. In fact, just stick around, he'll be here soon, so you can meet him." Jamie shook her head and started sipping her tea as I got up and went to the bedroom to get dressed into comfortable jeans and a Franz Ferdinand concert shirt. I brushed my hair and decided to just let it air dry. I then heard the buzzer.

"It's him!" I squawked, a little less cool than I would have liked.

"Hi, Anna, it's.."

"Yup, come on up."

"Em, I may need a little help. I'm hurting a bit more than I anticipated."

"Yeah, I was worried about that, should I just meet you downstairs?"

With that, Jamie got up quickly, ran past me and offered, "I'll help him." She pushed open the door and ran down the three flights of steps with me following.

"You must be Tom," Jamie chirped, way too brightly. "I recognize you from your picture, although your face looked a bit nicer last night."

Tom raised one eyebrow and looked up at me over Jamie's head. I was at the top of the first flight of stairs. His black hair was slicked back, out of his face. The bruises and cuts cleaned, but of course still very noticeable. It looks like he somehow shaved; I couldn't imagine how he had endured that pain. Both eyes seemed open all the way at least. He had on a pair of casual jeans, a pressed white, fitted oxford with blue pin stripes, a black belt, and a light weight black jacket. And in one hand, two roses.

"Tom, this is my friend Jamie," I introduced as I descended further down the steps.

"Ah, Jamie, a pleasure. Anna speaks very highly of you," Tom complemented, extending a hand.

Jamie pumped his hand a little too hard, making Tom recoil and hold on to his ribs with his other hand, breathing out a very soft gasp. Jamie either didn't notice or didn't care.

"I'll help you up, mate. I'm stronger than Anna." Without waiting for a response, she sidled up next to him and yanked his arm up and around her shoulder; forcing a loud gasp from Tom. He gritted his teeth with each step as Jamie hauled him up, giving him encouraging words all the way.

"We should have just met downstairs and left from there," I reiterated, walking backward up the steps.

"Yes," Tom nodded as he noisily breathed out. "Oh God," he protested, sucking back in his breath.

They finally reached the top landing and entered my flat. She guided him to the now cleaned off sofa, helped him with his jacket, and let him down easier than I had expected.

"So, now I see why you cleaned up your flat," Jamie said loud enough for Tom to hear. "I would too if I had a date who looked like him—despite the cuts and bruises." Jamie pointed her thumb towards Tom, giddily. "Smells nice, too!"

"JAMIE!" I exclaimed, embarrassed as hell.

She ignored me, "Cleaned her flat right up, she did!" Tom was laughing, but visibly uncomfortable from it. He held out his hand to Jamie offering her the two roses. "Please, keep one for yourself and give one to Anna," he offered, breathlessly.

Jamie's face lit up. She took both flowers, put one in the glass with the one from last night and held onto the other.

Jamie whispered in my ear, "Okay, I get it… He's even hotter than in his picture, and a bit dashing, but please be careful," she implored, "You don't know him." I bobbed my head in slight agreement.

Jamie then announced, "Well, off I go, unless you need help down the steps."

"I think we'll manage, Jamie," I said, a little irritated.

Tom tried to stand up, presumably to see Jamie out, but was struggling quite a bit.

"Oh, don't get up, Tom. You just rest there. Thank you for the rose. This will make Seamus so jealous!" she noted, devilishly. "Well, you two have fun today!" And she flitted out of the flat.

I closed the door behind her. "Um, yeah, so that was Jamie."

"Charming! She was a bit rough, but I quite like her."

"Whatever you say," I was still a little incensed at Jamie's antics.

"So, your flat looks nice," he noted, sincerely, "I hope you didn't clean up just for me."

Still embarrassed, I muttered my thanks.

"Would you like anything to drink?" I offered.

"Em, yes, water would be lovely, thank you."

I filled a clean glass with ice water and brought it over to him. Tom took a sip and thanked me again. Then he took a long drink before asking, "Have you been to Hyde Park yet?"

"No, I haven't gotten over there. Is that where you want to go?"

"Yes, the park is large, but along the Serpentine, there are plenty of places to sit and watch the waterfowl. I don't know how much walking I'll be able to do."

"Isn't that back your way? I could have met you back at your flat."

"Oh, I don't mind coming out here. And this way, I can be sure to pay the fare," he smiled.

I sighed, "Have you taped your ribs?"

"No, I couldn't reach. In fact, I barely got my shirt on."

I went to the medicine cabinet and found some tape.

I plucked the glass out of his hand and moved it to the coffee table. Standing in between his legs, I started unbuttoning his shirt.

"That's a little forward, now isn't it?"

I ignored him while continuing to unbutton and untuck his shirt. I opened it up wide to see his ribs. I lightly touched the bruises… they really looked bad. He flinched a little from my cold hands.

"Now look, I'm no expert at this, but I was a girl scout and earned a merit badge in first aid. Now, raise one arm."

"You were a girl scout?" He looked at me quizzically.

"Yes, Tom, I was a girl scout," I said, pointedly.

"Did you go door to door and sell cookies—in your uniform?"

"Yes, Tom. It was prior to my punk rock years, okay?" He smiled, but knitted his eyebrows together. He was trying to figure me out, I think.

Carefully, I taped his ribs in a crisscross pattern on one side, then the other. Tom sat quietly and patiently, letting me work. When I was done, I started to re-button his shirt when he delicately grasped one of my wrists. He stared intensely into my eyes while taking his other hand and caressed my face. His hands were shaking again. "You are so beautiful, Anna." He whispered. He started to pull me in closer, but I lost my footing and caught myself by placing my hand out, right on his side. "AHHHHH!" He yelled.

"My God, woman, are you trying to kill me?" He reprimanded a little loudly.

"I'm so sorry, Tom," I giggled.

He shook his head and uttered, quietly, looking down, "It's not funny."

I rolled my eyes as I straddled his legs, my knees resting on the sofa, and chided, "Don't be such a baby." And then I kissed him softly on his lips. He withdrew a little, I assume, because of the cut on his mouth, but then he placed his hands on the sides of my face and through my hair and then continued to kiss me, quite a bit more eagerly. He smelled and tasted so good, I could have devoured him all day, but after about half a minute, I pulled away when I tasted blood.

"We seemed to have reopened your wound," I remarked, sympathetically. I wiped my mouth with the back of my hand and showed him the red streak. He slowly closed his eyes and shook his head. He then touched his palm to his cut to stop the bleeding. "Well, ah, it was well worth it," he said with a quick raise and lowering of his eyebrows.

I gently got off his legs and fetched some ice and gauze. He applied the ice to his sore and then the gauze. After the bleeding stopped, he said, "Okay, give me one more minute to wallow in my pain and then we can go. You don't want me to become a permanent fixture on your sofa."

Um, well....

***

We took a cab to Hyde Park instead of the tube. With Tom's condition, we wanted the least stressful mode of transportation. Besides, he prefers cabs over the Underground, but he didn't really expound upon that. We arrived at the Queen Mother Gate on the Southeast corner of the park. Tom paid the cabbie as I quickly stepped out and ran around to the other side to help him out. I held my hand out to him and he took it, standing with an "umpf."

"Shall we," he offered, keeping hold of my hand. I was very careful not to squeeze too hard.

And we walked on. I smiled brightly seeing the Boy and Dolphin fountain, although I thought the Dolphin looked more like a fish. I took out my phone and took a picture of it, capturing the bright blue sky and puffy clouds in the background. I wanted a picture of Tom, but he protested because of his face.

We then leisurely walked through some of the most beautiful flowers and greenery I have ever seen.

"There are a few things I want to show you in the park. One is right over here." He led me to a wide tree that looked like a huge mound of green hair. The branches grew out from the center and then down to the ground. Tom smiled at me and ducked through a couple of branches, gently pulling me in with him.

"Wow," I said, quietly. There was plenty of room under the branches. Although it was cooler and darker than outside, being under the canopy made me feel warm and safe.

"Isn't it beautiful?" Tom asked, wistfully, looking up at the green "ceiling."

"I love it," I said, leaning back against the trunk.

Tom looked left and then right, gingerly rested a hand above my head on the trunk, leaned in and kissed me, slowly, more carefully this time. He proceeded to kiss me for quite some time until a few kids came clambering in. He then pulled away, smiled, took my hand and then led me out into the sunlight. My God, he was amazing. I started to feel a bit giddy—I think the infatuation was starting to hit.

After walking past more highly manicured and exquisite flora, we came to The Serpentine, a manmade lake that snakes through the center of the park. Families and couples in paddle boats and row boats dotted the water, while swans, Canada geese, and different duck species swam in the water or sauntered around the banks. Tom was starting to look pretty worn, so we took a seat on one of the benches overlooking the water. A curious swan waddled up to us, looked up pleadingly, and then wandered off when it realized we didn't have any food. The pigeons, however, hovered around our feet.

"So, what do you think?" Tom asked.

"I love it! I've really been missing out."

"You've only been here three months, love. London has much to offer and it takes a lot of time to see it all. I've lived here all my life and haven't seen everything."

He then braved putting his arm around me, gasping mildly, while drawing me in close. I hoped I wasn't squishing his side.

"So, Anna, please, tell me about your childhood. I'm afraid, you know far more about me than I you."

"What would you like to know? I already told you it was pretty standard. I grew up in Maryland. My parents tried, sometimes too hard, to be good parents. I mean, they were incredibly generous and gave me pretty much anything I wanted. Um, but my mom can be, well, a bit demanding and nosy, however. I love her, but she's a little hard to deal with. My dad's pretty cool and laid back, though. Um. Let's see. In high school, I was a decent student, but got in with the punk crowd. We didn't do drugs or steal or anything, we would just dress a little weird, spike our hair, and listen to music. I was really into the music. It was so angry, so direct. Something that I wasn't really used to. So, I got pretty obsessed with it. I would spend hours and hours listening in the dark with my headphones on."

Tom eyed me quizzically, "Hmmm, I wonder what you would look like with a Mohawk."

"I never actually got a Mohawk, but I did spike my hair with lots of gel. I colored it also, depending on my mood. My parents kind of freaked out when I started this new look, but then they finally let it go, figuring this was allowing me to 'express' myself. But, that was pretty much the worst thing I did. Um, besides the various areas I had pierced."

Tom shifted a little on the bench. I continued.

"I didn't smoke or drink or do drugs; I would have felt too guilty. So, I just put my 'bad' side into something less harmful—the music."

"And the piercings," Tom reinforced.

"Right."

"Did you go to a lot of concerts?" He asked

"Oh, tons. The Tubes, PIL, The Cramps, and my very favorite, The Damned. Oh, and the Circle Jerks."

Tom laughed a little at that. "I had not heard of the Circle Jerks; couldn't say I'd want to see that in concert."

"Haha, and who have you seen? Let me guess, The British Symphony Orchestra."

"Yes, of course! A number of times, they are extraordinary," Tom mused. "But, I'll have you know when I was around 13, I did see Nine Inch Nails."

"No WAY!" I was so intrigued, I pushed away from him a little too abruptly and stared at him with wide eyes.

"Ouch, watch it… yes I saw them. I take it you didn't." He grumbled, not replacing his arm around me, but rather placing it in front of his ribcage, obviously a little annoyed.

Sheepishly, I apologized and grouched, "No, I didn't." I paused and then said, "I cannot envision you at a Nine Inch Nails concert. "

"My sister—this was a little before she died—took me. She was always getting on me to stand up to my father. She told me the concert would help me get the anger out, let off some steam, and she was right. Watching from the side of the stage, I recall Trent Reznor exhibiting incredible strength. He grabbed the bass player, who looked to be twice Reznor's height, and threw him into the audience. He then took one of the large stage lights by the cord and started whirling it around his head. I was afraid he was going to toss it into the crowd and hurt someone. And then, my sister, she threw me right into the mix of the mosh pit. I remember a sea of black and leather, combat boots, dramatic hair styles and colors swarming all around me. The smell of sweat and leather filled my nose. I really didn't know what to do. It was madness! I got pushed, stomped upon, kicked, and then something magical happened. I started to fight back; I started to push, stomp and kick. I came out of there with one or two bruises, but I felt so exhilarated afterwards, so alive. And then," he sighed, "we went home. Escaping reality can be wonderful, but it is a fantasy; it is fleeting."

Grinning at Tom, I blared zealously, "That... is so awesomely cool!"

"Anna, you are a funny girl. Your vernacular truly amuses me," he needled, nudging me with his shoulder.

"You know," with a slight irritation in my voice, "I don't tease you about your stodgy *vernacular*," I stressed in a British accent.

"Touché," he retorted. "Well, let's move on. There is a lot more to this park, but I am afraid we will only be able to experience a small part of it. We can come back when I am a bit more spry."

I inwardly smiled at the prospect of seeing him again. We stood up and walked along the Serpentine, my arm looped through his.

"So, what made you become vegan?" He asked.

"Um... I really don't like to talk about it, but, when I was 14, one of my friends invited me to her grandfather's farm. They had chickens and cows and pigs. It was fun, because we played with all the animals during the day. But, when it came time for dinner, I saw her grandfather take a chicken named Chloe, and chop off her head." I opened my mouth to elaborate more, but closed it back up, trying to shut out the memory.

Tom didn't press. He merely nodded his head and said, "I applaud you for your convictions. I should probably have more than I do. After all, I am quite fond of animals."

"Maybe I'll be able to convert you."

"It's not out of the realm of possibilities."

We walked along in silence for a minute, while Tom guided me away from The Serpentine.

"Are you peckish, em, hungry?" He asked.

"Yeah, a little."

"There is something else I want to show you and then we can find somewhere to eat. I know you will appreciate this."

I looked at him curiously, but didn't ask where we were going. After walking down more incredible paths lined with beautiful trees and plants, we finally came to the end of the park. Right outside the exit stood a memorial, the Animals in War Memorial. I stopped in my tracks. A white, stone, curved wall stood festooned with animal carvings. The wall had a gap in the middle. On one side of the gap, two bronze mules laden with equipment struggled through the opening. They had the saddest look in their eyes. The other side of the gap displayed a dog looking back at a downtrodden horse. The inscription on the wall said:

"This monument is dedicated to all the animals that served and died alongside British and Allied forces in wars and campaigns throughout time."

And another inscription said: "They had no choice."

I walked up to one of the mules and placed my hand on its head. I started to tear up. This memorial touched me so much.

"Oh, Anna, I didn't mean to make you cry," Tom said as he came over and wrapped his arms around me from behind.

"No, no. Thank you for taking me to this. I had no idea," I said as I wiped my tears away. After a minute of contemplative silence, I said, "Well, let's go, okay?"

Tom held me for a little longer, kissed the top of my head, and then released me.

Tom pulled out his phone and searched for something. "Okay, there is a vegetarian/vegan pub in Soho. Would you like have some tea and a snack there?"

"Yeah, that would be fantastic." So off we went in yet another cab and rode to Soho.

After about 15 minutes, the cab dropped us off at Neal's Coach and Horses. It looked like your standard pub when we first walked in, but when Tom inquired about tea, the bartender opened a waist high door at the bar and directed us up a narrow, almost hidden set of stairs. Tom was a little slower than I, but when we reached the top, we came into a very unexpected, very charming tea room. Blue draped windows were all around, overlooking the street, and tea pots were displayed around the pink room. We took a seat next to one of the windows, adorned by a flower box. The waitress brought us a tea menu and, after asking, let us know what desserts were vegan. I chose a pot of mint tea while Tom opted for Earl Grey. We decided to share a vegan carrot cake.

"So, you played the bass?" Tom asked.

"Yeah, I was in the jazz band in high school and in a punk rock band, but we sucked. It was fun, though. My jazz band teacher? He was a trip. We all thought he did coke because he was always picking his nose. In fact, one time, he actually picked his nose to the beat of the music! He was so weird, but, he made us better musicians." I rambled on about playing at one or two school sponsored coffee houses and how I almost got into a fight because I gave someone the finger. He smiled at me, listening patiently. His bad eye was pretty much open fully now, but the discoloration still surrounded it.

The waitress set two teapots down and turned over a sand timer. She let us know the tea will finish steeping when the sand runs out. I gave some quick, quiet claps at the cuteness of the presentation.

Tom beamed at me. "Anna, I like you. I mean I really, really like you."

I nodded my head and shyly responded, "I like you, too."

Tom took my hand, once again. "Anna, I want to ask you something, and I hope this is not too forward of me." I raised one eyebrow… okaaay.

He seemed a bit nervous, but his words poured out all at once, "Em, would you, em, would you please stay with me for a few days? I absolutely love your company and when you stayed last night, regardless of the circumstance, having you there felt so natural. I am embarrassed to say I had an extremely hard time this morning with the things we all take for granted. It took me 20 minutes to get my shirt on. And, my God, attempting to shave my face…I suppose I could hire a nurse, but I figured I'd much rather have you there and it would be closer to your work and it would be, ah, cleaner," he coaxed with a timid grin. "And, you could always leave if it didn't work for you. Besides, you have to come back as you left your dress and shoes there." Then leaning back,

"There, I said it." He stared at me with those nebulous-colored eyes with the most pathetic look of pleading I'd ever seen.

I blurted out before I had time to think, "Wow, um, yeah, yes, that sounds like fun." Jamie's lecture played in my head.

Tom clapped his hands once, "Stupendous! This calls for a celebration!"

The waitress set the carrot cake down right on cue.

CHAPTER 6

"Now, dear boy, no trace can be left. No one can know it was you. You wouldn't last very long in jail, would you? Always be stealthy. Pick your timing right. Make sure no one is around. Move in the dark. Dress like a shadow. In fact, be a shadow. When you are ready to strike make sure they cannot scream. If they scream, you could be caught and more important, your goal will not have been met. Hand covers mouth first, then drag the knife across the throat. If it's quiet and no one is around, you can prolong the agony. That is most gratifying. Good night, my boy."

***

Back at my flat, Tom waited in the cab so he didn't have to make yet another painful ascent. I gathered work, casual, and night clothes, plus some toiletries for my few days away. I figured I'd pack for two or three days and come back if he needed me to stay longer. I was pretty excited, but something in the back of my mind kept nagging at me that this wasn't a good idea, that I just met the guy, that he has a lot of baggage from childhood; he's got to be at least a little affected, right? I mean, who wouldn't be after what he had to endure. And then the weirdness at the ghost tours. And especially the violent fight. But, I pushed that all aside and thought more of his beautiful eyes and face, his deep voice, his charm, the sexual tension at least I was feeling, and mainly, his obvious interest in me. I've not had this kind of relationship before, and I was liking it. Maybe so much, it was clouding my judgment. Oh well.

So, with my things gathered, lights out, and door locked, I flitted down the stairs to the waiting cab.

Tom smiled broadly when I opened the door, his fang-like canines showing, "You were quick."

"I didn't want to keep you waiting." Translate, I didn't want to wait to see you again. The thought of work tomorrow was killing me.

The cab driver got out and opened the trunk to store my belongings for the 20-minute drive to Tom's flat. With so much back and forth today, the cab fares were adding up. We would have reached our cap on the Oyster Card and saved a lot of money had we taken the tube. But, he didn't really seem to bat an eye, handing out 20-pound notes over and over again.

When we got there, I once again helped him out of the cab. It started to rain, this time, a little heavier than the typical London drizzle. The cab driver got out and retrieved my bag, turned, and handed it to Tom. He grunted at the weight of it and the pull on his ribs.

"More impractical shoes, I presume?" he droned.

I frowned, "No," and snatched the bag from him. Tom paid the driver and we went inside, up the elevator and into Tom's flat.

"Please, make yourself at home. Anything you want to eat, use, play with, I'm all yours... em... the flat is all yours." He looked away quickly in embarrassment and led the way to the guest room, me trying to hide a laugh.

"I hope this suits you," he said, opening the door with a flourish. I noticed his hands trembling a little.

Stuttering his words a bit and speaking a little quicker than normal, Tom explained, "M..my office has a number of tidbits about, but the bed is comfortable and you may use the bureau for your clothes. Em, the... bathroom can be yours. I... I have my own, but I guess you already knew that. Em...."

"Tom, it's alright, relax," I soothed, placing my hand on his arm. "Are you nervous or something?"

Tom smiled and sniffed, "Frankly, it's been a while, a long, *long* while since I had a girl over here, besides last night, so yes, I suppose I am."

"Well, it's just me, so don't worry about it."

He placed the tips of his right hand tenderly on my cheek, "Yes, *just* you."

And then he timidly pulled his hand away. "Well, I'll give you some privacy to get settled." And with that he left the room. I then heard down the hall a kind of muffled "Would you like a proper supper? I can fix something or we can order for take away."

"Anything is fine with me, Tom." I yelled.

I took in the room. There was that same beautiful egg and dart crown molding bordering the ceiling. Straight ahead, a large window sat centered on the wall, overlooking some trees and flats across the street. An ornate wood desk with a laptop and external monitor was off to the left with an old swivel writer's chair pushed neatly underneath. A bureau sat on the wall to the right of the door. The bed, a sleigh similar to Tom's only not as large, sat in the center of the wall catty corner to the window. I took off my shoes, put my suitcase on the floor, pulled back the white comforter, and lay upon the pressed white sheets, which crinkled a little under my weight. The bed was far more comfortable than mine. I breathed in the fresh scent of the room and smiled. After a few moments rest, I jumped back up and started to unpack. I pulled out my messily folded T-shirts and camisoles and refolded them a little nicer, placing them in the bureau. I then brought out my work clothes to hang in the closet that was to the left of the bed. There were some coats in there that I pushed aside so I could fit the few outfits I had brought. I hung them on the wooden hangers, and then threw my comfortable shoes into the closet, but instead of hearing a whump on the floor, I didn't really hear anything. I must have hit something soft so I got on my hands and knees and pushed my head in to retrieve my shoes and to see what I hit. The closet was dark so I felt around for the object and once I found it, I grabbed the soft thing and pulled it out. I sat in the light examining the stuffed animal in my hands. A plush blue bear; the paisley colors were faded, but it still looked like a sweet stuffed animal that a little boy or girl would cherish.

"So, you're the one that kept him company," I whispered, sitting on the floor. I hugged the bear as if saying "thank you."

"What are you doing on the flo…" I turned my head around to see Tom staring at me, noticing what was in my arms. His facial expression changed in an instant from curiosity to troubled.

"I'm sorry, Tom, I was just putting my shoes away and I found him in the back of your closet," I recovered quickly, while standing up and putting the bear to my side.

He shook his head to rid his confusion and smiled, "Please," he held his hand out to take the bear, which I handed over.

He held the paisley bear outstretched with two arms, like one would do to admire the whole of a baby.

"I had forgotten he was in there. It's been so long," he whispered, then kissed the bear, and put him on my pillow.

He then looked up at me and briskly said, "Well, I ordered Chinese. I hope you like pineapple fried rice." And he left the room, the bear staring at me from the pillow. What a sweet man, I thought.

***

Tom felt extremely tired and wanted to just get in his night clothes and watch the evening news prior to dinner. I followed him to his room and helped him take his shirt off. We had to go slowly so I wouldn't cause him more pain. Once he was shirtless, I saw more scars up and down his arms. They were much thinner than the ones on his back. I decided not to question him about it as he went to fetch a nightshirt. He grabbed a light green "Life is Good" tee shirt out of his dresser, decided against it, and then took out a dark blue button-down pajama shirt. I helped him guide his arms through as gently as possible. I could see why doing this solo would be difficult.

He went to his dresser and pulled out matching dark blue pajama bottoms and motioned for me to turn around.

"I can do this one."

"Ah, I'll just go get changed myself," and I went to my room and got into my Jack Skellington nite-shirt and shorts and brushed out my hair.

I came out of the room and down the hall and found Tom on the sofa, patting the seat next to him for me to sit down. Eyeing my shirt, obviously entertained he mocked, "Ah, I don't know too many who wear their fiancés on their shirts."

"Jealous?" I took my seat, sidling up close to him.

He tilted his head to the side, "A little," he said, and placed his hand on my knee and gently squeezed.

With his left his hand on my leg, he used the other to click the remote, turning to the news. Normal news features came on, but then the Richard T. Brown story started and the same picture flashed as before. It was really bothering me where I had seen this guy. He looked not completely familiar, but vaguely.

> *'And now, an exclusive interview with Richard T. Brown, the latest supposed victim of the London Vigilante.' Flash to Richard sitting in a hospital bed, pasty face, greasy hair, very bruised, his hand covering his mouth as he spoke his muffled account.*
>
> *'So, what did your assailant do?"*
>
> *'Well, he attacked me from behind, choking me. I was walking back to my hotel after having a beer at a local pub when he struck. I didn't see him, but I figured he was tall from the angle he grabbed me from. He threw me up against the brick wall where my forehead hit, nearly knocking me out, but I tried to stand my ground. I remember turning to try to see him. My vision was a little blurry, but I thought the guy was in all black and wearing a mask."*
>
> *"Guy? There are a lot of people out there, women in general, who think this person is a woman."*

"Well, I don't know about that. She would have to be pretty strong and tall, like an amazon woman."

"Oh, please," I remarked.

"What makes you think it's this alleged Vigilante anyway, could have been anyone." Richard T. Brown stated.

"Is it true you were arrested and sent to jail for domestic violence, using a lead pipe to knock the teeth out of your girlfriend's mouth and then raping her?"

"I SERVED my time for that, didn't I? 10 years in jail – I pled guilty and cooperated. I did my time. I learned my lesson."

Changing the subject back, "So, the assailant, what did he… or she (the anchor smiled into the camera at this) do next?"

"It's all a big blur. I saw the guy holding something metal. I think like a copper pipe. And then he swung at my body. He kept swinging and swinging. He hit me everywhere, eventually knocking me to the ground. Then, the next thing he did, I really don't want to say it."

The camera panned to the anchor, patiently waiting, then panned back to a watery-eyed Brown.

"Well, I was on my hands and knees, gasping for air, when I heard him walk behind me and then, and then, he shoved the pipe…." And with that the man started blubbering and shaking. "I've never been so humiliated in my life!" After a minute, he composed himself and continued his story, "and then he whispered in my ear, 'a tooth for a tooth you (bleep)' and slammed his foot right in my face, knocking out my teeth (he moved his hand and showed the audience for dramatic effect).

During the report, Tom had abruptly removed his hand from my leg and sat staring at the TV with his arms crossed, one leg pumping up and down very agitatedly, shaking the whole sofa. I looked at Tom, then the TV, then back to Tom when something clicked. "That's it!" I exclaimed and stood up, pointing at the TV. "That's the guy from the ghost tour, the first night!!! I knew he looked familiar."

Tom clicked off the TV and looked up at me, leg still pumping up and down and obviously not too pleased, "And?" he asked, curtly.

"No 'and,' I just think it's a weird coincidence, don't you?"

He took a breath, stopped his shaking leg, and uncrossed his arms. Running his hand through his hair, he leaned forward with his elbows resting on his knees and nodded. "Yes, I suppose it is an odd coincidence. No matter, I can't really say I am going to cry over his misfortune." And then the doorbell rang, interrupting the conversation. The Chinese food.

Tom was about to stand, but I told him to stay put.

I scurried down the hall to my room to get my wallet and then ran back to the front door.

When I opened the door, a small, black-haired man smiled up at me and handed me the food. Before I took it, I handed him 20 pounds, but he declined.

"Already paid for, ma'am. Over the phone. Big tip, too!"

I sighed and thanked the delivery man.

"Geez, let me get one for a change."

"Nope," he proclaimed, popping the "p".

I walked over to the sofa with the food, set it on the coffee table, and started to take out the containers. I felt Tom staring at me and looked over to find one raised, judging eyebrow.

"Something wrong?" I asked innocently.

He started to chew on his lower lip, but grimaced when his sharp tooth grazed his wound.

Then it dawned on me, "Oooh, I guess you don't eat out of the container... um or on the sofa... or in front of the TV. What. Was. I. Thinking." My sarcasm dripped out of my mouth.

"It's fine," he retorted. A little annoyed at his pretentiousness, I forcibly handed him his container of the pineapple fried rice. Then I tossed him some chopsticks as I flopped back down on the sofa. He turned the TV back on, the news now featuring a story about the cosmos or something.

Trying to lighten the mood, Tom asked softly, "Aren't you going to eat?"

I shrugged and took the other container and started digging in. I was pretty hungry. A few pieces of rice fell onto the sofa.

Tom set his container down, plucked up the rice, and looked over at me, "Sorry, Anna, I've lived alone for a long, long time and I am a bit set in my ways as I am sure you are. We will just have to adjust to each other."

Feeling a little guilty about my tone, I said, "That's fine… if you don't like to eat on the sofa, it's no big deal. I mean, it is your house, so I'll play by your rules. Sorry, I was rude."

"It's okay. You are doing me a favor, so eat on the sofa whenever you like."

I took a few more bites. The food was really good.

"Um… why did you get so defensive about Richard Brown? You seemed really angry."

He paused for a second, probably weighing his answer, "First of all, he was a class A prick at the ghost tour that night, so shoot me if I have a tinge of pleasure from his misfortune, albeit extreme. Second, and more so, you did not grow up in an abusive home, so you can't know the absolute satisfaction one gets from seeing such abhorrent scum get his justice, no matter how harsh."

I bit my lip and just nodded.

Softening a bit, Tom started to slowly stroke my thigh with one finger, back and forth.

"Anna, I'm sorry if I've sounded curt this evening. I am utterly exhausted and I get a bit cranky when I don't get enough sleep."

He stopped and rested his hand on my knee.

"I think I may have pushed myself too much with the walking today, even though I thoroughly enjoyed your company. So, if you don't mind, would you be so kind to help me re-tape my sides and then I'm going to collapse in bed."

"Yes, of course, I'll get the tape." I stood up, quite exhilarated by his touch.

Tom took his unfinished meal and stored it in the refrigerator and then took my portion and placed it on the kitchen counter. He ambled down the hall to his room while I fetched the tape. I heard him brushing his teeth and when he came out, his shirt was already opened. I helped him take the shirt all the way off and then instructed him to lay down on his side. Ignoring the scars on his back as much as I could, I removed the old tape and replaced it with new tape. He rolled over, gasping, and I repeated the exercise on his other side. He then rested on his back and stroked my arm up and down, which made me shiver.

"Thank you. I very much appreciate you being here."

"You know, Tom, I am no nurse, so if it's okay, I'm going to check online to find out if this is the correct treatment or not since you won't see a doctor."

"Yes, of course." He slurred, sleepily, "My password is paisley."

I kissed Tom on the left side of his mouth to avoid his cut, which still looked raw. All the kissing today could not have helped with the healing process.

"Good night, Tom." And he was fast asleep before he could respond.

After watching him sleep for a minute, I went to the guest room and turned on his computer, typed in "paisley," and searched around for broken rib treatment. I found out all sorts of problems that could happen. Like the ribs affecting the lungs and that sort of stuff. And then I read a few more blurbs on why you shouldn't tape the ribs. All of them talked about pain relievers, obviously, but I'm not sure he took any. I got worried that the tape was restricting his breathing, so I went back to his room to peel it off. I tried to be quiet and deft as I lifted up the blanket and started removing the tape.

"What are you doing?" Tom slurred in a drowsy voice, lying on his stomach.

"I just read you aren't supposed to tape the ribs after all and that you need to breathe deeply and take pain relievers."

He softly groaned and told me to leave it alone, rolling on his side. I decided it wasn't worth it and that I'd remove it in the morning. I wished he would just go to a doctor. I sat next to him on the bed and watched him for a bit. He looked so innocent and peaceful lying there. I crawled to the other side of him and lay down, my chest pressed to his back, arm around his shoulder, and hand touching his hand. Half asleep, Tom lightly clutched my hand and sighed.

***

"Oh, Shit!!!" I yelled out loud when I woke up and realized the time. 8:30?! I needed to shower, get dressed, and be at work, now!

Tom wasn't in the room anymore. I found him in the kitchen making crepes.

"Hi, Anna," very cheerily, and he came over and kissed my cheek. "I took a pain reliever this morning, masking the ache enough for me to make crepes. Em, I found a vegan recipe. What flavor would you like? I can offer you strawberry, blueb…"

"Tom!" I interrupted, "why didn't you get me up? You knew I had to work today."

Tom looked genuinely surprised, "Sorry, you just looked so cute lying there, I didn't want to disturb you, I guess I forgot."

Exasperated, "Tom, I have to work for a living! Look, I hate being late, so I am just going to call in sick today and I'll go in tomorrow."

"I… I didn't mean to make you shirk your responsibilities. I guess I was not thinking."

"It's okay. I set my alarm on my cell phone, but left it in the guest room, so it's really my fault."

I went to call Jamie.

"Sick? Bollocks, you're sick in love," Jamie teased on the phone.

"Oh, please, I just met him Thursday."

"Right, and you've spent every day or night with him since then. Next thing I know, you'll be moving into his flat."

"Weeellll…"

"Anna, you didn't!"

"Just for a few days, he needs help with everyday stuff because of his injuries. He asked and I agreed."

"Oh, Anna, you really don't understand men, do you? Don't get me wrong, he is extremely charming and he has those brilliant eyes, but, please just be careful."

"It's not like I've sublet my apartment. It's just for a few days. Besides, it's closer to work."

"Well, that didn't help you today, did it?" Jamie sighed, "Alright Anna, enjoy your 'sick' time today, but please come in tomorrow. We have a deadline."

"Thanks, Jamie. You are the most awesome boss ever!"

"Yeah, yeah, I know."

I hung up the phone and came over to the beautifully set table with orange juice in champagne flutes, cappuccinos dusted with cinnamon and cocoa, and three crepes on each plate. One crepe was made with strawberries, one with blueberries, and the other dark chocolate and banana.

"Everything alright at work?" Tom asked, timidly.

"Yes, I'm lucky that my boss is also my friend. Anyway, you have me all day, but I have to go in tomorrow, okay?"

"Of course. I'm really sorry. But, selfishly, I'm glad I get to spend more time with you. Now, please have a seat and let's see if you enjoy my cooking."

I sat down and first tasted the soy cappuccino, which was rather strong, just the way I like it. Then I took a bite of the strawberry crepe. "Are you trying to get me to move in here permanently?"

Tom's eyes got big and then gave me a huge smile. "I take it you like the breakfast?"

"Yes. I can't cook like this. I mean, I can make rice and spaghetti and I make a mean salad, but I'm too impatient for something like this." I then tasted the chocolate and banana crepe. I usually don't like dessert for breakfast, but this crepe was not overly sweet. Rather, Tom somehow was able to extract a slight bitterness from the chocolate, which, combined with the banana and the hint of cinnamon I tasted, was incredible. As I savored the blueberry crepe next, Tom looked at me a little more gravely.

"So, Anna, I have to go to my father's today. What would you like to do? You could come with me, stay here or whatever."

"You want me to meet your father?"

"Em, do I want you to meet my father," he copied while tapping his fingers on the table. "I don't really know how to answer that. I wouldn't want to subject anyone to meeting my father, but, em…."

I took a deep breath. "Alright, I'm just not sure how I'm going to react after what you told me, you know."

"Just don't react… treat him as a cantankerous, miserable, old client."

A little unsure about this, I still agreed. So, we went to our own separate rooms to get ready. I pulled on jeans and a plain black shirt. I heard Tom ask me to come into his room for some help. When I pushed open the door, he had on army colored cargo pants, something I would not have expected him to wear, and he was shirtless. "Would you, please?" he asked, handing me a white button-down shirt.

I gathered he had taken a shower while I was asleep this morning, as he had somehow pulled the tape off and his sides were not sticky at all.

"Do you work out?" I asked admiring his chest.

"Not for a few days now, obviously, but yes, I go to a gym around the corner, why?"

"Um, you just have a nice, um, physique," I said, a little embarrassed.

"I think I'm too thin, but thank you." He said, obviously flattered.

I eased him into his sleeves and then he took over fastening the buttons, leaving the top two open. He undid his fly, tucked his shirt in, zipped it back up, then slid on his black belt. He took a breath and cautiously leaned over to put his socks on, but recoiled and sat back up. I took the socks and put them on his feet and then squeezed his feet into his Chuck Taylors and laced them up. He gave me a shy smile. "I feel like a child."

After making our way downstairs, we hailed a cab on the street and rode close to an hour to Kent. In the cab, Tom gave me a thousand rules as to what to say and not to say, about how to ignore his lewd comments and to remember that he is sick.

"I'm not an idiot, Tom."

"That's not the word I was going for."

I ignored him the remaining five minutes of the cab ride. Tom managed to get out of the cab himself; the pain relievers, I guess. I started to wonder if he really needed that much help. I could hear Jamie in my head, reminding me how naïve I am. Too late, now. Besides, I really liked being with Tom. And looking at him.

Our feet crunched on the little rocky path that led to a covered porch. The floorboards squeaked as we walked up to the front door. The white paint on the house was chipping a bit, but I thought it gave the place a little character. I mentioned this to Tom, but he just shuddered, took out his key, and opened the door.

We walked through a small foyer where, just to the left of the door, a worn patchwork of carpeted steps led upstairs, and to the right, a small living room where his dad sat in front of a very loud television. The place smelled of stale cigarettes, spilled beer, and 1970s shag carpet.

"Dad, I brought a friend with me today, so please, be on your best behavior," he warned as he peered into the living room.

"Don't tell me how to behave. Who's the parent round here?" Then he saw me. "Well! Would you look at tha'. A girl, and a pretty one, too."

He looked nothing like Tom. He was overweight where Tom was healthy and fit. His father had a grizzled complexion with deep lines cutting through his face, whereas Tom's skin, before getting bruised and cut two nights ago, was smooth and flawless. Thomas Hall's pudgy face contrasted greatly with Tom's chiseled bone structure. They didn't even share the same color eyes or hair.

Thomas had light brown hair that was graying around the ears and brown eyes. I guess Tom got his looks from his mother.

"Dad, this is Anna," Tom motioned.

Thomas extended out his hand, but did not bother to get up. His oxygen tank sat next to him.

I reluctantly took his clammy hand, really wanting to dig my fingernails into his skin after what Tom had told me.

"Nice to meet you, Anna. Have a seat," he said politely.

I tentatively sat down across from him on the worn, brown and tan, striped chair. Tom remained standing, leaning on the doorframe, half in and half out of the room, with his arms crossed.

"Where are you from?" Thomas asked, eyeing me up and down.

"America," I stated. His gaze really unsettled me. In fact, the whole vibe between Tom and his father was suffocating. Even though I was only here a few minutes, the tension between the two of them was plainly obvious.

"Ah, an American. Interesting." He turned his head to Tom. "So are you two an item or just friends, as they say?"

I said a little curtly, "We're getting to know each other right now."

"Mmm... so, a girl. When did that change come about?" he asked, in a matter-of-fact tone. My eyes narrowed. What did that mean?

Tom let out an exasperated sigh and dropped his arms to his side. "Dad, I asked you to behave. Now, did you pay your bills like I asked you to?"

Thomas looked at both of us, contemplating something, and said, "I di'nt mean any disrespect, Tom. I've not seen you with a girl before. You were always messing around with that faggot friend of yours, Robbie."

Tom rolled his eyes. "My God, we were never 'messing around' as you so eloquently put it. As I've told you before, you misconstrued situations. And, besides, you were usually drunk, so you didn't know what you saw." Tom took a step forward into the room and stood next to my chair.

"Whatever you say, son. Well, at least you've steered yourself straight now. Maybe I had a hand in that." Thomas glared up at Tom from under his brow, almost confrontational, as he wickedly grinned and cracked his knuckles.

My face contorted and my mouth dropped open. I knew Tom's father was awful, but hearing about him and actually experiencing him were two very different things. Digging my painted black nails into the arms of the chair, I contemplated lunging at the man. I hadn't even been there two minutes and I just couldn't contain myself. The family dynamic was not only uncomfortable and disquieting, but ridiculous as well. My fight response took over and I started to rise from my seat. "Listen, asshole, you…"

"Anna," Tom warned through gritted teeth as he gripped my shoulder, keeping me from standing, "please, just ignore him. Come help me in the kitchen." He clutched my hand, pulled me out of the chair and almost forcibly led me to the outdated room. I tripped a little on the peeling vinyl flooring. Yellowed cabinets hung on the wall, stained with years of cooking exhaust, with doors either missing or askance. Avocado green laminate countertops desperately needed an upgrade as well. A round wooden table sat in the middle of the room with four slat-backed wooden chairs all around. And the cushions, once probably a vibrant floral pattern, were now faded and threadbare.

"Let go," I demanded, whispering. Tom released my hand without hesitation.

"How can you stand him, Tom? He's horrible! He was basically threatening you!" I whispered, loudly, pointing toward the living room.

"I know, I know. He can be a bit frightful, but it would weigh very heavily on my conscience if I didn't help him. He's sick."

"He's sick in the head."

"Don't you remember the advice I gave you in the cab?"

"Hmm, if a litany of rules constitutes advice."

"Okay, Anna, enough. This was a mistake to bring you here. After all, we just met. I appreciate you wanting to defend me, but I'm quite capable. I've had a lifetime of this, remember?"

"And what's with the whole gay thing? Is there something you aren't telling me?"

"Well, one situation, I already told you about. The other, I'll tell you later, but the short of it is that he misread what happened. So no, I am not gay, obviously." He kissed my cheek, filled a glass, and brought his father some water. I reluctantly followed him back into the room and stood as far back as I could with my arms crossed.

"So, did you pay the bills, Dad?" Tom asked, irritated.

"No, I thought you'd take care of 'em this month. By the way, what happened to your face? Did your girlfriend beat you up? She into that kind of stuff?" He chuckled at his own lewd joke.

Tom closed his eyes and, I assume counted to five, because he opened them after I counted five in my head. "No, Dad, wrong, as usual. I got into a bit of a row in a pub. Now, look, this is the last time I'm going to take care of your bills. You have an addiction to Amazon that I don't feel I should enable anymore."

Thomas ignored his son and went on. "Lost, eh? Black eye, cut lip. You're walking funny, too."

I stepped forward and said, "He didn't lose. He beat the crap out of a homophobe." I continued, under my breath, "Too bad it wasn't you."

Thomas looked at me suspiciously, paused and said, "Pardon?"

I didn't answer. I figure I'd let him wonder exactly what I said.

"He only got hurt when three people from the pub jumped him." I said, almost proudly, jutting my chin at Thomas.

"Tha' right? Well, I'm proud of you son. I must have taught you well."

"Yeah, Dad, you sure taught me. And you sure taught Elizabeth and Mum." What the hell did I get myself involved in? I just met Tom and here I am at his insane father's house, wondering if a fight was going to break out between the two of them. It certainly seemed like it was escalating to that. Thomas's eyes narrowed, "Now, how many times have I told you, boy, she fell down the steps." His dad turned to look at me. "He told you I did it, I'm sure. No, she came out into the hall screamin' her 'ead off as teenagers do, 'fuck this and fuck that' she says—she had a mouth on her, that one—then she tries to swing at me, misses, and falls down the steps." He bowed his head for a second.

Exasperated, Tom scowled and went into the kitchen. I was about to follow him, but Thomas cleared his throat loudly. I stopped and looked right in his smarmy face. Thomas, trying to redirect the conversation, asked, "So, why did you leave America for London?"

I paused for a second and then said, "I had an opportunity with work and I took it."

"Well, I'm glad to see Tom has gotten his *priorities* in line. Can't be having a homosexual in my family."

"Look, I don't really know what you are talking about. I believe you are mistaken, but in any event, being homosexual is as natural as being heterosexual. Despite your home décor, this is the 21st century, you know."

Thomas licked his lips and softly said, "Mmmm, you shag him yet? I can't imagine he would know what to do with a girl's pu…"

"Alright, *Thomas*, that's enough. We're going." Thomas clearly did not realize Tom was standing in the doorframe. "Come on, Anna, I am sorry I had to subject you to this. You were right not to want to come; in fact, maybe I shouldn't come back."

And then his father's smug face changed to worry and remorse. He started to beg, "Please, son, Anna, I'm sorry, I don't know what came over me." Blah, blah, blah. If you ask me, Tom was being played.

"Alright, Dad. Just a few more minutes. I'll take care of your bills and then we are off."

***

We were pretty silent on the way home. What was I getting myself into? Hearing the stories was bad enough, but actually seeing what he grew up with kind of freaked me out a bit. Well, Tom certainly wasn't his father, but still. That was one of the most uncomfortable situations I've ever been exposed to. I can't imagine day in and day out growing up in such a household.

Once inside the flat, Tom took me in his arms and held me. "I'm so sorry, Anna. That was… bad. I thought he'd be less like himself with you there. No such luck." He held me for a little while longer and then kissed my head.

"Soooo, um, are you bi or something?"

Tom sighed, "No, I am not bisexual nor a homosexual. Certainly, just like most of us I presume, I questioned my sexual preferences when I was a teen, but no, I assure you, I fancy the female gender. My father, however, misinterpreted a couple of situations. I think he was looking for an excuse to belittle me. Have a seat and I'll tell you the story, but it's not pretty." I sat on the sofa, Tom in the chair across from me leaning forward with elbows on knees and hands clasped.

> *After my sister died, and my horrible beating when my father gave me the cigarette burns, I withdrew into myself. I was depressed, and didn't really engage in school very much anymore. I was interested in virtually nothing. Girls, friends, music— nothing piqued my interest in the slightest. I was confused and at a loss as to the*

purpose of my life. I contemplated suicide, but it was too rash. I was scared and so I couldn't go through with it.

One day, late after school, Robbie caught up with me and asked what was wrong, why I wasn't hanging with him after school anymore. I told him I was just sad about my sister and that I wasn't really in any mood to play ball or get together. He pleaded with me, 'Come on, mate, I miss you. You're my best friend.' I succumbed to his sensitivity and told him I would play some ball with him. It was getting late, but the sun hadn't set yet. I knew my father was at home and that I should tell him what I was doing, but I decided to just play for a bit longer and then go home. We went to the neighbors who owned the basketball net and got pretty into the game. It had been a while since I played hard and it felt good. Robbie and I were bashing into each other a lot during the game, knocking each other over a few times. And then, at the worst possible time, Robbie and I tripped over each other's feet and he landed on top of me. But, instead of getting off, he stared at me and then kissed me full on the mouth. I was so shocked, I just lay there—I didn't really know how to react. Then, just like that, I saw Robbie's face abruptly get smaller for he was yanked off of me. My father. He had come out looking for me. Of all the fucking times he could have come that night, he chose that exact moment. It was as if the Gods were against me. I sat up and I saw my dad push Robbie. I scrambled up and tried to pull him off, but he was way too strong. Robbie got his footing and finally ran away, fast, in fact, I never saw him run like that. Then Dad turned to me and told me to get home straightaway. So, I ran, ran upstairs, into my room and locked the door. I thought he would follow me, but he didn't. I think he knew the waiting was going to be more torture than anything else. Anyway, after a long while, I started to relax a little and contemplate what happened. I never realized Robbie had a thing for blokes, least of all me. I was quite confused by it and didn't really know how to handle it. I was only just 15, after all. The hours went by and I was ravenous, but I didn't dare go downstairs. I decided to just sleep it off. So, I got into my night clothes and went to bed. Next thing I knew, I was hearing my father talking in my ear. He must have jimmied the lock open. He was obviously drunk; he reeked of whiskey and was mumbling away about no relation of his is going to be a faggot, and that he would beat it out of me if necessary.

Tom sniffed and looked straight at me.

"And that's what he did. I told you the beatings lessened after my sister died, but they didn't entirely stop. He hit me with his belt, endlessly. So many times, I lost count. I took it, but didn't shed a tear. I willed myself to not give him the satisfaction. But, I could feel the welts forming all over my back and bum. And then, he left me alone. I lay very still that night, not able to move, just wanting to melt into the bed and never come out. However, later that night, something extraordinary happened. My father came back, knelt by my bed, and wept, 'I'm sorry, boy. I didn't mean to hurt you. I don't know what came over me. Please forgive me.' That was the first time I really witnessed remorse from him, except at my sister's funeral. But, I just lay there. Too shocked, hurt, and confused to do much of anything."

Tom leaned back in his chair and stared, expressionless, at the fireplace.

"Holy shit, Tom. How often did this happen?" I asked quietly.

"Oh, I don't know. Prior to my sister's passing, a few times a month when the punishments were really bad, but pretty much daily he'd get a slap, push or punch in, or some kind of verbal abuse."

"How did you turn out so... so good and well adjusted?"

He shrugged. "I have a wonderful grandfather. And, I'm not so sure I'm all that well adjusted, if I'm being honest." I wondered what he meant by that, but I didn't ask. Instead, I tried to sound a little more reassuring.

"You seem like it. I mean you are nothing like him, as far as I can tell. But, I don't understand how you can stand to be in the same room with him. He's not your father! Only in the dictionary definition, but not in the real sense."

"I know, I know. I guess I've learned to take the high road."

***

We pretty much stayed in the rest of the day and just became a little more used to each other's presence. Besides a few differences in the way we live (slob versus obsessive neat-freak), we seemed to be very compatible. We even brought up religion and politics. To my relief, Tom didn't really ascribe to any religion per se. Also, he was very liberal minded and supported the Labour party. I couldn't imagine having a relationship with a Conservative. Tom decided he was well enough to make pasta with pesto for dinner. I prepared a salad with loads of greens, beets, onions, avocado, and carrots. I also concocted a nice balsamic dressing with a little olive oil and tarragon. He seemed to be okay with my veganism, partaking in the diet.

Tom ran to a local bakery to buy a baguette while I monitored the meal, giving me some time to think some more. I was torn. I had compassion for Tom, and in fact, I was now fully infatuated with him. He had some kind of magnetic pull on me and I found myself starting to fall for him, fall very hard. But, I also feared his past and how it was impacting him. He'd told me two horrific stories about his childhood and his father was still abusing him, at least verbally, yet he takes it and even helps his father. I don't like doormats, I just can't wrap my brain around that behavior. I didn't think he had truly come to terms with his past and I was concerned it was going to creep up more. The bar fight was directly caused by being called a faggot. I thought about Graham, my messy, horrible high school relationship. I remember my obsession with him. Your typical punk—Mohawk, piercings, tattoos, leather—but also a destructive sociopath. Tom was in no way like Graham, at least outwardly, but I feared there was quite a bit more underneath the surface.

Tom entered the flat, interrupting my thoughts. He took off his coat with a bit of effort, hung it up, and brought the baguette to me.

"How did you do at the store by yourself?"

"Fine. The pain relievers are a Godsend. I think I will be fine for work on Friday. Although, I may need to borrow some of your makeup." He winked.

I nodded. After cutting the bread, we sat down at the table and started on dinner. The pasta and salad were terrific and the fresh baked sour dough tasted and smelled amazing.

Finishing up, Tom asked, "Do you want to come to the tour on Friday and maybe invite Jamie?"

"Um, probably not Friday. I know she has a regular date with her boyfriend on Fridays, so maybe Saturday."

"Ah, yes, she has a boyfriend. Maybe we should all have dinner together."

My head finally controlled my feelings and I said to him, "That would be fine, I'll set it up. But, Tom, I think I'm going to go back home tomorrow. "

He started to protest.

"Tom, I think you are managing okay with the pain relievers, and, don't get me wrong, I really love being with you. I mean a lot. And I really like you, a lot. But, I just think things are moving really, really fast. I want to make sure this is right. So, let me get a little distance and see."

Even though his face barely changed expression, the slightest crease formed between his eyebrows, clearly telling me he was heartbroken. "Oh. Okay. We can slow it down a bit. Em, is it my history? My father?" he asked quietly.

"No, I mean, not really. I just need some space to think."

"Am I allowed to call you?"

"Of course, Tom. I want you to. I've had some bad experiences in the past with guys where I rushed into things and it was bad news. I'm just trying to be a little cautious."

"Alright, I understand. Well, you should get to bed since you have work tomorrow." Obviously, hurt.

"Yeah." I got up and went to the bedroom and changed into my *Never Mind the Bollocks, It's the Sex Pistols* night shirt. Tom was doing the dishes when I came back in.

"You want me to clean up?" I asked. He gave me a "yeah right" look and continued cleaning.

"Well okay, then good night." I placed my hand on Tom's back, but he didn't turn around.

"Good night, Anna," he said into the sink.

***

Albeit a little early for me, I got under the sheets and hugged the paisley bear. It was nice to be alone in the dark with my thoughts. I really didn't want to leave, but thought it was for the best. I replayed in my head the interaction with his father today and the story he told me. I wanted to hurt his dad. I really, really, wanted to, but knew that wouldn't be possible. And why am I so protective of someone I barely know? I have fallen hard and fast before, but never like this. It kind of scared me.

Tom knocked and then tentatively came in the room and sat on the edge of the bed, resting a hand on my shoulder. "Anna, I hope I haven't scared you off. That's the last thing I wanted to do. I regret taking you to my father's house. But, you can't know how much these few days have meant to me. I think I'm, em, well I know, I'm rather smitten with you."

I sat up on my elbows, "You haven't scared me off, Tom. Not really, at least. It's just that these past few days have been just so intense. From your past, to your father, to the fight in the bar, to the weirdness at the ghost tours, it's a lot to take in. But, believe me, I'm still really interested in seeing where this might lead. I really like you and want to keep seeing you. So don't worry that this is goodbye, okay? I promise." I lightly touched his hand. We briefly kissed and then, abruptly, he bid me good night and went to his own bed.

CHAPTER 7

"You've done well, my boy, with the whores. You're bigger now, so I think you can handle a man. But, the man isn't your ordinary man. He's a homosexual, a faggot. What else do we call them?"

"The scourge of the earth, sir?"

"Yes, yes! And it's our mission to...?"

"To rid of them this earth?"

"Yes. Now let's get started."

"We have to get back, we're having dinner with the Stepneys."

"This won't take but fifteen minutes."

— *Tuesday, September 9*

"So you're going back home after work today?" Jamie asked quizzically after eyeing my suitcase.

"Yeah, I was only supposed to stay a couple of days, plus Tom seems to be managing okay on his own. And, besides, I want to be sure this isn't just an infatuation and that I'm thinking straight. I'm 28 and have a school girl crush—what's wrong with me? I can't stop thinking about him."

"Well, I do think it's probably good you are getting a little distance, but try not to overthink this too much. So what if you are infatuated with him. You're supposed to be in the beginning. There's nothing like it. Like your first kiss, it only happens once."

"Yeah, I know. But, Jamie, he's so fucking intense; he can be a little scary even. He's just such a presence, filling up the room. And I like it, but it's just a lot to take in."

"Oh, Anna. Please, relax and enjoy this. You are the first person I've met who meets someone extraordinary in personality and looks and is fretting about it."

"Yeah, I guess you're right," I said, but she didn't know everything and I didn't feel right telling her.

I then went back to my cube and tried to concentrate on work. We had a big deadline coming up and I needed to focus.

The day went by pretty quickly. After work, I toted my bag to the tube. On my walk home from Farringdon Station, my bag started to get a little heavy, so I was constantly switching it from shoulder to shoulder. By the time I arrived home and trudged up the steps, I had a pretty bad crick in my neck. Once inside and comfortable in my Peter Murphy T-shirt, I looked at my phone; no calls from Tom yet.

I made myself a quick dinner, watched some TV, and then crawled into bed, a little pissed he didn't phone. I put on some Muse and turned off the light. My thoughts of Tom lulled me to sleep.

> *Blackness. So pitch black, I couldn't see my hands in front of my face. It surrounded me and swallowed me, spitting me out into some even darker void. A plane of nothingness. Delirious, confused, not knowing which way was up or down, left or right. I wanted to throw up, scream, something, anything to wake me from this dream. But, I couldn't. I was paralyzed, shackled by my own fear. But, then, I felt it. A small glimmer of sense, of feeling in my limbs. I willed myself to move, move forward, break through the blackness. But, as I started to inch forward, I felt my knee buckle. And then, landing hard on the stone surface below me, I felt my knee crack, pop and crumble, then burst wide open, sending blood, skin and bone fragments outward. I tried to scream, but nothing came out of my mouth. Then crack, crack, crack, crack, four toes broken, one at a time, into tiny pieces, flattened beyond comprehension. Shards of broken bone scraped the underside of my skin as I tried to get up, wake up, WAKE UP! The dream had a hold on me, imprisoning me in my sleep. Oh, God! Would I ever wake up! And then, I saw a small glimmer of light, a beacon of hope. But, I realized it was the gleam of a metal object, hovering before me, then shooting directly into me like a bullet. My shoulder shifted back and further back and further back, yet again, until my skin tore, blood spurting out in pulses. The void was opening its cavernous mouth at me, sharp teeth and tongues licking me, tasting my blood and bones. I fell, fell further and further into the void, spinning, spinning, spinning until I was flung right back onto the bed.*

I awoke, sweating and breathing heavily. My knee, toes and shoulder were throbbing. The pain was so intense, I cried out, gasping for air. And then everything got dizzy. I knew I was awake now and in my room. I knew I could regain control. I started to take deep, cleansing breaths, until my heart rate slowed, my vertigo subsiding.

Slowly, I came out of my stupor. I felt no pain. It stopped as abruptly as it started. What in the hell was that? Realizing fully the extent of the trauma I just experienced, but knowing it didn't actually happen, I started to panic. I was losing it, going crazy. That's the only explanation. I tried to breathe deeply again, but it wasn't working. My lips trembled, my body an earthquake. I shakily reached for the phone on my nightstand and dialed Tom's number. No answer. He probably was asleep. I swung my legs over the bed and found my footing. I needed water, desperately. In the kitchen, I grabbed a glass out of the cabinet, but I almost dropped it, I was trembling so badly. I succeeded in filling the glass half-way and downed the cold liquid in one gulp. I started to calm down, refilled my glass and took it to the table. I sat heavily on the chair, calming myself down further. Wiggling my toes and rubbing my shoulder and knee, I realized everything was fine. No blood, no broken bones. I laughed silently and started to rationalize that my dream was so vivid, it manifested into actual pain. Unless it was a dream within a dream, but that didn't seem right. The first dream was pretty weird. Random faces kept popping up: Tom's, his father's, Jamie's, the scary lady from the dream the other night. And someone I didn't recognize. Blond hair, brown eyes, but that's all I remember. It wasn't so much the visions, but the extremely unsettling feelings that came with it. Chills swam up my back into my neck. I drank some more water, wiped the sweat off my forehead with my arm and then went back to bed. I changed the CD to Elbow, something more soothing, and fell back asleep.

***

— *Thursday, September 11, 6:30 AM*

Breaking news. The London Vigilante strikes again.

The ticker at the bottom of the screen scrolled over and over again.

A rash of hate crimes targeting homosexuals and prostitutes is also plaguing the city. More after the break.

I sat glued to the television. I didn't have to leave for work for another hour, so I figured I had time. Drinking my coffee, I waited impatiently for the report.

The man assaulted early last night, Stephen Wainwright, endured a long night of torture before he was found whimpering behind St. Marylebone Parish Church. Sources told the BBC that the man succumbed to a hammer wielded by a figure all in black with a black mask. The assailant took his—or her—time with Wainwright. The assailant had grabbed the victim as he was stumbling out of a bar. Wainwright believes he was choked and passed out, because when he came around, his arms were tied to a railing behind the church and his feet were bound together. The alleged London Vigilante first smashed the man's left knee and then

*methodically broke each one of the man's toes on his left foot, one by one. The
assailant slammed into the man's left shoulder repeatedly until it became
dislocated.*

I felt all the blood drain from my body and onto the floor. I froze in disbelief,
my mouth agape and my eyes watering. What… the… hell?

*Police do not know why the assailant targeted Mr. Wainwright. He does not fit
the profile of the other London Vigilante victims. The man has no record.*

*"We're talking now to criminal psychologist Dr. Triston Fields. Dr. Fields, what
are your thoughts on the latest attack? Do you think it is our Vigilante?"*

*"Well, it doesn't really fit, let's just say 'her' since that's the popular thought, her
modus operandi. The Vigilante probably has had a traumatic past, and now uses
that negative experience to fuel a drive to impact society in a positive way. This is a
form of post-traumatic stress syndrome referred to as post-traumatic growth. It's
important to understand, however, that the 'positive' impact is viewed from the
Vigilante's perspective, which can be skewed based on one's morality. Picture this:
You are a child and you are bullied in school. You try to fight back, but you are
no match. The bullying continues much of your childhood and neither the teachers
nor parents seem to do anything. So, you grow up, and what do you do? Either
start an organization to try and stop bullying or you seek out bullies and get your
revenge," Dr. Fields explained.*

*"So, what you are saying," the reporter asked, "is that the London Vigilante was
possibly bullied or harmed in some way long ago, and now uses this as 'positive
growth'? In her mind, she is taking down the bullies?"*

*"Precisely!" answered Dr. Fields. "However, the attack from last night could have
been a copycat, or the Vigilante made a mistake. We are currently aware of twenty
attacks over the course of two years with the same pattern. However, there also has
been a rash of crime against homosexuals and prostitutes, reminiscent of Jack the
Ripper. And let's not forget the rash of assaults in the 1960s. There are a lot of
misguided people out there. Just be careful, as sensationalizing an attacker can be
interpreted by the Vigilante as validation that she is doing something positive."*

*"Thank you, Dr. Fields. We will update you on this brutal attack when further
details are available."*

*"Our next story finds us in the grips of the antithesis of the Vigilante. There has
been a rash of hate crimes against homosexuals and prostitutes. In fact, three
prostitutes were found strangled last night in the Docklands…."*

OhmyGod, ohmyGod, ohmyGod. My pain, my dream! It was all the fucking same! What is happening to me?

Then a buzz from the intercom made me jump out of my seat. Who could that be at 6:45 AM?

I hurriedly got up and pressed the button. A very excited deep voice came over the intercom.

"Hi Anna! I wanted to see if we could grab some tea before you headed off to work."

It was Tom. Tom who hadn't called me for two days. Tom, who didn't answer the phone last night. My head was spinning, so I buzzed him up without saying a word.

When I opened the door, he practically charged at me, almost knocking me down. He grabbed the sides of my face and kissed me. First hard and earnestly, making me stumble more, then a bit slower. And in that moment, my fear and doubts vanished. In fact, all thoughts were expelled from my head. The only things that existed were his soft lips on mine and his tongue inside my mouth. Slowly, he pulled away and then encircled me in his arms. "God I missed you," he breathed.

I had to catch my breath. I was not expecting that.

He unfurled his arms, held my shoulders at arm's length, and offered, "Shall we go?"

"That was… ah, wow," I stammered.

"I'm sorry, I don't know what came over me. I purposely didn't call you to give you some space, but it was sheer agony," he explained as he dropped his hands to his side. I noticed his face was clearing up quite nicely. The swelling was way down and the cuts were starting to heal well.

"I told you that you could call me. In fact, I was kind of pissed you didn't." I started to well up as the effects of the kiss started to wear off.

"Oh, I'm so sorry, but, you wanted to… Is something wrong? Did I hurt you?" he asked as he touched my face, clearly concerned.

I turned away from his fingers and then in Jamie-esque style I started, "Well, yes, I am a little freaked out. I actually did try to call you the other night because I had a really crazy dream, but you didn't answer."

He furrowed his brow and tilted his head sideways. "I was home all night, both last night and the night before."

"It was late when I called you. You were probably asleep or in the bathroom."

"What time did you call?"

"I don't know, maybe around 1:30 AM."

"I was up sitting at my computer both nights pretty late, but maybe not that late. Sorry I wasn't there for you."

I shrugged. He looked at me with sympathetic eyes, which helped me to calm down a bit. "Anyway," I began, "Tuesday night, I had the most vivid dream. That I was being tortured—someone or something pulverized my knee, broke my toes and ripped my shoulder out of its socket. But when I woke up from the dream, my left toes, my left shoulder, and knee were killing me. I was in agony for a couple minutes, and then, just like that, it abruptly stopped, just like last week. So, here I am just a tinge freaked as you can imagine. So, I try to push it aside and carry on. Well, I just turned on the news this morning and guess what?"

Tom shook his head and shrugged, perplexed.

"A man was attacked… broken toes, dislodged knee cap, and a fucking dislocated shoulder… I mean, what the fuck!!!" I started to go into hysterics. "What is happening here? This isn't normal at all. I think I'm going nuts!"

"Anna, calm down. Let's sit." He placed his arm around my shoulder and guided me to the sofa, moved the clothes sitting on it to the arm, and sat down with me. "Maybe you heard about this last night, like in the background, and you didn't realize it. And then you had the dream and then the dream—"

"I know, manifested itself into real pain. I've already thought of that, but dreams don't do that, do they? I mean, maybe for a split second, like when you feel yourself falling and still have that sensation, but this is *nothing* like that. And this isn't the first time. It keeps happening. Why? How do I make it stop? I mean, is there some kind of doctor I can see about this?" I tried to calm myself down a little by taking a couple of deep breaths through my nose, but it wasn't working. "Look, the night of the first tour, when we first met? The dude that got assaulted by the Vigilante? My teeth hurt, a lot, when he rushed passed me. And then, remember, his teeth were knocked out."

"Anna, you had an odd coincidence or two, that's all. But, my concern is that you've experienced this fleeting pain three times now and I think you should see someone. We just need to figure out who. Let's get you something at Goswell Coffee before you have to go into work. I'll bet a soy latte will make you feel better."

Another bout of emotions swept over me and I cried into Tom's armpit while he held me, stroking my hair and telling me in his soothing way that everything was going to be all right. Once I regained my composure, I washed my face and we left the flat.

Goswell Coffee was on the corner of my street and only a two-minute walk. Tom was correct; the soy latte helped, along with the vegan blueberry scone. Tom then hailed a cab for us. It only took us about twenty minutes to get to Piccadilly Circus where my office was located. Tom escorted me in and up the elevator.

"Are you going to be alright," asked Tom, a troubled look on his face.

"I'm kinda freaking out," I cried. My eyes started to feel wet again.

"Yes, I can see that. Come here," he instructed as he took me in his arms. "We will work through this, love. Em, how about I retrieve you after work and we'll have tea and figure it out," he proposed. "If you're ready to see me again, that is."

Jamie caught site of us, "Well, hello!" she sang sarcastically, eyeing me up and down, looking at Tom, then back at me. Tom unfolded me from his arms. Great, this is all I need now. I quickly wiped my eyes so I wouldn't endure a barrage of questions I had no answers to.

"It's not what you think," I informed her. Tom just looked confused at Jamie's insinuation.

"Oh, okay, whatever you say."

"Miss Jamie, a pleasure," Tom nodded in her direction. "Did Anna talk to you about Saturday night?"

"No, what's happening Saturday?"

"Sorry, I forgot," I mumbled.

Tom gave me a quick reprimanding look. "I invited you and your boyfriend to be my guests, at my tour. I thought we could, em, double date."

Now Jamie gave me a squinty-eyed look and touched his arm. "Tom, that would be fantastic. I've been dying to go on one of these ghosty tours. I'll ask Seamus; I'm sure he'd love it."

"I need to get started on finalizing my project," I said. "I'll see you here tonight." As I walked away, I glanced back over my shoulder and saw Tom and Jamie conversing. Then, Tom looked over Jamie's shoulder at me and held up his hand and gave me a short-wave goodbye. He looked really concerned, which scared me even more.

I sat in a daze at my computer. I had to get this project done and missing a day this week didn't help. I couldn't afford to get more behind, but I felt compelled to surf the net just a little to see if I came up with anything about my, um, condition.

> *Search: premonitions, feeling pain*

> Links to: *psychic premonition, manifestations*

'*... could predict what was going to happen to a loved one... premonitions were so vivid, she actually could physically feel the pain... felt her hands burning... fire later took the life of her brother.*

... considered to be psychic... using more of your brain capacity.

... manifested pain throughout one man's life... PTSD was thought to cause painful occurrences...

I tapped my fingers on the desk. These websites were probably just a bunch of hoaxes. There has to be a reasonable explanation.

"Eff this," I hissed and abruptly got back to work.

— *Lunch time*

"So, Anna's got a hot new boyfriend," Jamie announced, exposing my personal life to the coworkers we usually ate lunch with.

"Jamie, do you not understand privacy?" I rebuked.

She smiled her big ass smile.

"What's he like?" asked Andrea, "Is he nice? I assume he's the guy you walked in with today." She winked at me.

"What guy?" Asked Steven with a mouthful of food, sounding a little jealous.

I rolled my eyes, "Yes, he's nice. He's not my boyfriend, just someone I started to date, okay? No big deal. He met me for breakfast this morning, that's all."

"Anna! No one was insinuating anything!" Jamie sarcastically remarked, "I mean, I always walk into work with Seamus and hadn't slept with him the night before."

"Oh my God, Jamie, did you actually just say that?" I asked, exasperated.

Tapping his foot, shaking the table, Steven asked, "So what's the big deal?"

"Exac.." I started to say, but Jamie interrupted.

"Oh… he's a big deal alright. Caring, polite. He's a bit formal from what I can tell, but bad-ass, and sexy as 'ell."

Steven shifted uncomfortably in his seat.

"When I met him, it was after Anna and he had a date. He was all rugged looking with bruises and cuts and all because he got into a barroom brawl with some man who called him faggot." She looked up at Jack and innocently shrugged. "Tom kicked the shit out of him," Jamie professed a little too excitedly.

Jamie continued as I stared at her with my mouth agape. "Yeah, and then he was thrown out of the pub, beaten up pretty badly, but it took three large men to do it. Like I said, bad-ass and sexy!"

I felt my nostrils flaring. I chastised, "Jamie, I'm so glad you find one of the worst nights in my life entertaining. And when I said that he was bad-ass to you, you lectured me that life isn't a movie and I need to be careful. Remember? What changed?"

"I met him, obviously."

"That's not bad ass. That's psychopathic. It's also against the law to attack someone—the bloke he beat up should sue," Steven said, angrily.

I looked over at Steven, a little taken aback by his reaction, "Um, the other guy started it, Steven," I said.

"Gee Steven, aren't we a little judgey today? "Jack said, as he rolled his eyes. He was not a fan of Steven's. He then turned to me and asked, "What's he do, Anna?"

I started to answer, but Jamie interrupted again. "He's a ghost tour guide, but doesn't really need to work because he's loaded." She finally stopped gabbing when she stuffed her sandwich in her mouth, making her shut the hell up.

"Jamie, you are really starting to piss me off. I told you all this in confidence."

Swallowing hard, she innocently explained, "It's the truth, in'it? There's nothing to be ashamed about."

I sighed. "Fine. Yes, he is a ghost tour guide, he tells stories on most weekend nights and he lives in a flat in Marylebone," I admitted, offering as few details as I thought I could get away with. I left out that he's also pretty pretentious and that he's crazy intense. But that intensity is what draws me in. When I look at him, I get so lost in his face, his eyes, his expressions. He's like a vampire, but instead of drinking and draining all the blood in my body, he sucks out all my reason and doubt, replacing them with impulses I can't control.

"What does he look like?" Andrea implored with wide eyes, "I didn't get a great look at him."

I opened my mouth to speak, but Jamie, once again, interjected. "Well, he's what, about 180, maybe 185 centimeters, pretty lean, em, very white skin, but not unhealthy. He's got black shaggy hair; could use a haircut, mind, but I kind of like the look. And his best feature," Jamie swooned, "are those blue, green, and yellow eyes. Did I get everything, Anna? Oh yeah, Anna likes his teeth. She says he's got fangs like Ricky Gervais," Jamie beamed. Goddamn her! I felt red hot fire ants start to crawl up my neck and fill in my cheeks.

Before I could call her what I really wanted to call her, a delivery man entered with a bunch of roses. "Anna Pearson?" Oh no. I tilted my head up to stare at the ceiling. I'll never hear the end of it.

Jamie stood up and signed for the flowers, took out the card, and offered me the roses.

"DON'T, you dare open that. Boss or no boss, I'll have your head," I fumed. This was all a bit much. I thought Brits were supposed to be more reserved. Not this lot.

Jamie harrumphed and reluctantly handed the card to me. I opened it up and read it silently, "One rose for the eight days we've known each other. I've never been so happy. P.S. the ninth is for Jamie." I tried to stifle a smile, but I couldn't help it.

They noticed, of course, Jamie snapping her fingers, "Come on, let me see the card."

I tentatively handed her the card and she read it out loud, smiling broadly at the postscript. "I'll just take this one," and she plucked the fattest flower out of the bouquet. What a bitch!

Andrea and Jack were squealing about Tom while Steven remained silent, finishing his food. Jamie got up to fill two glasses with water for the roses when an obnoxious 'screeeech' broke the excitement. Steven had loudly, violently, pushed his chair back, scowled, and left the room.

"What's wrong with him?" I asked, pointing my thumb in the direction Steven left.

"Are you daft?" asked Jack rhetorically. "He's been crushing on you ever since you started working here."

"Really? I never really noticed."

"Oh come on, Anna," Andrea chimed in. "He's always hanging around your cube and he never used to eat lunch with us until you started up."

"Well, now that you mention it, he does seem to try to create reasons to talk to me. Always saying he lost his stapler or needs a paper clip." I mused. "Hmm."

"He's not really your type, Anna," Jack confirmed.

"Yeah, well, I still don't want him to be sad. I mean, he is nice, but…"

"But he's no Tom," Jamie purred, inhaling her rose.

***

The rest of the day went better than I had expected. Even though lunch was absolutely ridiculous, it at least got my mind off the insanity of my predicament. And of course, the roses helped, too.

When 5:00 hit, the intercom came on announcing to the entire office I had a visitor. I started to the front and the whole entourage—Jamie, Andrea, Jack and Steven—trailed behind me and followed me to the front. "Come on guys, you are embarrassing me." But, they kept following.

Tom saw me and widely grinned, his charmingly crooked teeth and fangs showing. He came forward and gave me a big kiss on the cheek.

"Thank you for the roses. They are beautiful," I smiled back.

"It's the least I could do." Tom went over to Jamie and kissed her cheek as well. If she weren't so dark, I would have seen a blush by her reaction. She introduced Tom to Andrea, Jack, and Steven.

"Pleased to meet you all," he said as he shook Andrea and Jack's hands. Steven kept his hands in his pockets and just nodded tersely at Tom. He looked back at me, "Are you ready to go, love?"

"Mmmm," I heard from Jack. I shook my head at how juvenile all of them were being. They probably held a secret meeting to see who could embarrass me the most.

"Yes. Let me grab my purse and coat." As I left to go back to my cube, Andrea, Jack and Jamie surrounded Tom, and I heard him laughing at something one of them said.

Steven followed me back to my cube. "Okay, Steven, well good night."

"Good night, Anna," and he shuffled away. Poor guy—he sounded so dejected. I'm not used to being the object of someone's affections. Especially not from two men.

With my self-confidence up a notch, I came back to the group. "… so I'll have Anna arrange a time and date with all of you to be my guests, and then we can go out for drinks afterward."

Everyone said their goodbyes, Andrea giving me the thumbs up and Jack whispering I hit the jackpot. If only they knew.

On the elevator, I apologized to Tom for my office mates' behavior. "Sorry about that, they all saw the roses you had sent and it started a commotion. Plus, Jamie's antics."

"Really?"

"Well, a swooning type of commotion. Three of my co-workers are all in love with you."

Tom looked at me quizzically. "Em, okaaay. Steven didn't seem all that pleasant."

"Ah, you noticed that. Well, apparently, he's into me. I didn't know until today when the rest of the group informed me. He's not really my type."

"And what is your type?" Tom drawled, giving me a sideways glance.

I just looked up at him and smiled.

Exiting the elevator Tom asked, "Are you feeling better?"

I shrugged, "A little, I guess."

He started to detail what he arranged for me. "So, we are going to meet a good friend of mine at the café around the corner. I hope you don't think it too odd, but, based on your experiences, I think she might be the best person to talk to right now. Em, she is a professor at University who teaches parapsychology. I've helped her with a variety of circumstances, both professional and personal. I've known her for years."

"There's such a class?" I asked.

"Yes, and in fact you can major in the discipline. Anyway, Holly was quite interested in your, em… predicament." He paused. "I hope I did not overstep my bounds."

We started walking out of the building into the cool night air. "No, no, I'm grateful you found someone. Maybe she can help."

He held out his arm for me to take while we walked along Vigo Street and onto Regent. Bright, colorful lights created a subtler Times Square atmosphere. We then turned down Heddon Street, a pedestrian only street, with restaurants, beautiful plants, and a ceiling of blue lights strung from building to building. Tom seemed to be taking me to Tibits, a haven for vegans and vegetarians in London. I had discovered this restaurant and coffee bar when I first moved here. Looking up vegan restaurants online, I was pleased to see it was so close to my work. As a rule, I try not to go out too much because of the cost, but when I do, I like to come here and indulge.

We went up to the counter and ordered our drinks.

"One English Breakfast and one… coffee?" He asked, looking in my direction.

"No, I'll have tea tonight. Um, the fresh mint, please." I clarified.

Not long after we took our seats at a table close to the window, I spotted a very attractive fifty-something woman walking in the front door. Her blond hair was pulled back in a bun with wisps sprouting out, and she wore a black pencil skirt with a cream-colored blouse and an orange silk scarf, revealed when she opened her stylish, tan raincoat. Tall and lithe on her feet, she continued to take off her coat and approached our table.

"Ah, Holly!" Tom sang, standing up.

"Tom!" They kissed each other on both cheeks. She gave Tom a curious look, but didn't ask anything.

"Dr. Holly Gaines, this is my, em… girlfriend, Anna." Goosebumps sprouted on my arm. I didn't realize we were official, but I rolled with it, anyway.

"Nice to meet you." I extended my hand, Holly taking it lightly.

The waiter came by with the teas and took Holly's order.

"Thank you so much for meeting with us, Holly. How is Jonathan doing?"

"Oh, he's just fine, thank you. He's been working in the woodshop, recently, building birdhouses."

"A new hobby?"

"Yes, another one," Holly said, turning to me. "Jonathon is my husband. He had a heart attack last year and ever since then, he's wanted to experience as much from life as he can, so it's a new hobby every week! It's a little maddening, but I allow him to indulge. How could I not? But, we're not here to talk about him. Tell me what's been going on."

Tom started, "As I explained on the phone, Anna has had some odd experiences in the past week and we're hoping you could sort some things out."

So, I started to detail my experiences. I started with the first night of the ghost tour and the brief vision I saw, and the pain I felt that night in the Hartford House, relating that to the Richard Brown story on the news. I then told Holly about the next night of the tour, at Berkeley place. I described my dream of the woman, then the dream that manifested into all the pain in my toes, knee and shoulder, and finally, I detailed the connections to the Stephen Wainwright news account.

"And that's it in a nutshell." I said. I tried to relax my clenched jaw; I was so worried about all this.

After listening intently, Holly leaned back in her chair and pondered. "Very interesting. So, let me ask you a few questions," she said, leaning back in, "have you ever had these kinds of experiences, particularly the pain, before?"

"I don't think so."

"And when you got to England, did you have these feelings?"

"No, it just started last week at the ghost tour."

"Okay, and did anything happen after the ghost tour?"

"Tom and I went out, but that was it."

"And the next time it happened, it was at the ghost tour again?"

"Yes, well, I felt that intense pain that made me pass out, but I didn't see any kind of attack afterwards on the news, but… well, wait… Tom got into a big fight with this awful guy from Friday night's tour when we went out on our date the next night… and I mean, I guess I felt similar injuries of the guy Tom beat up or maybe it was Tom's pain I felt."

"Thomas Hall! Is that what happened to your face?" Holly scolded.

Tom hung his head in mock shame and gave a nervous smile. "Em, the guy had it coming."

Holly shook her head and looked at me.

I continued, "But, the Wainwright assault had nothing to do with the tour. I was at home in bed."

"By yourself?" She glanced up quickly at Tom.

"Yes, by myself."

Holly tapped her fingers on the table, furrowing her brow, contemplating. Then, she nodded her head and soothingly explained her interpretations. "I don't believe much in coincidences. It seems that your painful premonitions only started after you went to places where there are accounts of paranormal activity. I believe these places can be kind of like a glass doorway to the other side. Not all, but some people have the ability to look through the doorway and see things, while others can actually open that door, walk through and physically experience this otherworldly place. Think of it like a radio station or a cellular phone signal… the further you are away from the tower, the worse your reception, but the closer you are… clear as a bell, but also, now that you've had that strong reception, it stayed with you and that's why you had such strong feelings at home. Mind, I am just theorizing here; we can't know for sure.

"So, what I think you should do is write everything down. Write what you just told me, along with any new insights, and especially if anything like this happens again. Let's hope it doesn't, but if it does, I want you to not only write down the exact feelings you have, but also, anything surrounding those feelings—who you were with, what you were doing, anything that might be pertinent, even if it seems not pertinent. I've heard of this type of thing before. It's basically a psychic premonition, but as to why and how it relates to others, I don't know yet. However, I don't think you are in danger. I mean, I can't be sure, but it seems your pain is not internal, even though it feels that way. Kind of like tracing paper; you can draw all over it, but the picture beneath stays perfect."

"Unless you press too hard," Tom noted, solemnly.

I looked up at Tom and then back to Holly. I wanted to scream! My voice went up an octave, "But, what does it all mean? I mean, premonitions? Really? I'm no psychic. I've never had any kind of weird experiences like this before. I'm not sure I really even believe in psychics!"

"Whether you believe in psychic premonitions or not, does not mean you don't have the ability. There is a lot we don't know about the brain, about death, about other dimensions. I assume since you attended two ghost tours, you must have a tinge of belief or at least curiosity—or a willingness to at least believe in the possibility." Holly explained.

"I guess. Maybe." I shrugged. "But let's say what you are saying is possible. Why then, am I getting them about strangers?" I paused and then blurted out, "And then I keep thinking it's tied to the Vigilante."

Tom laughed out loud, "You think this is tied to the Vigilante?"

"Maybe, Tom, you have a better explanation?" I spat back, a little too belligerently. Tom held up his hands in mock surrender, raising his eyebrows. "I mean, I felt the same pain that Brown felt from the Vigilante and we aren't sure about Wainwright yet, but I guess not the night of the bar fight," trailing my voice off as my theory started to lose its strength. When I said it out loud, I really sounded ridiculous.

Holly interjected, "The fact is, we don't know why. There may not be a why or a direct connection, but please heed my advice and write your experiences down. We'll figure out what to do from there." She reached into her bag and pulled out a black business card and handed it to me. "If it happens again, please call me. We *will* resolve this, love," Holly assured me while patting my hand. "Keep an open mind. I've experienced and researched too much through my career to discount anything."

A buzzing interrupted our talk. Holly took her phone out of her purse, looked at it, smiled and shook her head. "Another effect of Jonathon's heart attack. He's been just a love to me. More so than before. I think he's preparing a candlelight dinner, so I must be off, now. But, please, do call me, and write everything down," she chirped as she stood up.

Tom arose and helped her on with her raincoat. "Thank you for taking the time," he sincerely expressed.

"My pleasure. But, no more fights, Tom. Marring that gorgeous face of yours is a sin!" And then she walked out of the café.

Tom sat back down at the table. "I didn't mean to insult your interpretation. I just thought it a bit extreme and well, dramatic." He tried to suppress a smile, but it didn't work.

I didn't say anything; I just stirred my tea.

"Well, let's give it some time. What did you think about Holly? Did she make you feel a little less uneasy?"

"Yeah, she did, in some ways and some ways not. I mean, premonitions? Me? It's kind of scary and a bit unbelievable, but it doesn't necessarily sound dangerous, I hope."

"Perhaps we should cancel with Jamie. The further away you are from the 'reception,' maybe the better."

"Oh no, I want to go and get to the bottom of this. I've got to find out, now."

Tom reluctantly assented.

"Do you want to eat here? I specifically chose this place as they are vegan friendly."

"Yeah, I've eaten lunch here before, and I love it." So, we went to the buffet and piled our plates with different salads, pastas, and tofu dishes. I was most excited about the vegan mac and cheese. Tom, of course, paid when we went to weigh our food at the bar. We then ate a leisurely meal, staying off ethereal topics.

***

Tom escorted me home via taxi. As we stood at the bottom of my steps, Tom shyly spoke with his hands in his coat pockets, the taxi idling behind us. "So, here we are."

"You want to come up?" I suggested, nonchalantly.

Tom looked up at me, a bit surprised. "Didn't you want some space?"

I shrugged. "Space is overrated. But, seriously, I don't want to be alone right now. I'm…"

"Freaking out," Tom interjected in a terrible attempt at a valley girl accent. I playfully punched him in his ribs. Oops.

"Dammit, Anna, you've got to stop doing that," and he slowly walked over to the cab, holding his side, and paid the driver.

"Sorry," I muttered in a small voice when he came back to me, "but, you're making light of a pretty intense situation."

"I'm trying not to be so… uppity," he mumbled as we walked up the steps.

I opened the door to my apartment.

"How? How does it happen?" he asked, astonished at the mess in the flat. "I didn't want to mention it this morning, but I am flummoxed. How can one person make such a mess so quickly?"

"Y' know, I might be inclined to reopen that cut on your lip," I threatened, taking off my coat and dropping it and my purse on the floor.

Tom paused before he spoke, looking at me, slowly, from under his eyebrows, and challenged, "I'd like to see you try." And then, he stepped toward me, took my hand and led me to my bedroom. We started to kiss as his hands gently went under my shirt and fumbled with my bra hooks. I lifted my shirt over my head and slid my bra completely off. He stood staring at me, and breathed out, "You are flawless, Anna." I thought he seemed a little nervous, maybe slightly out of his element, but, I was wrong, way wrong.

"Won't this hurt your ribs?" I asked, as he took off his coat and laid it neatly on the end of the bed.

"Ask me if I care," he said, quietly. And then he attacked me.

***

— *3:00 Friday morning, September 12*

I awoke with a start to scratching in the walls. I started to stiffen, my heart picking up speed, when I realized it was probably mice. Maybe I should listen to Tom and keep the place a little cleaner.

Tom....

I looked to my left, seeing him asleep next to me, lying on his stomach. The street light from outside shone in, illuminating his scarred back. I traced my fingers over the raised patterns, my mind's eye perceiving letters and faces and numbers. It was a trick of the mind, but the happy face was no trick. I touched my pointer finger on each dot, imagining the scar would stick to my finger, so I could just flick it away. A tear started to well as I thought about this amazing person who endured and overcame so much in his life.

His lovemaking had been manic at first. The intensity mirroring his personality. But then, he was gentle, yet earnest, even desperate at times, but honest. Honest and fantastic. It had been a while for me, but even longer for him, he confessed earlier. Through it all, he was obviously in a lot of pain, but he didn't let that stop him. All of our emotions from this last week poured out of us and into each other. It may have been the most exhilarating experience I've ever had.

I started to reflect on the last week and how much my life has changed, both from the paranormal experiences and by meeting Tom.

Interrupting my thoughts, he rolled over in his sleep so he was on his back. I put my head in the crook of his shoulder and placed my arm around his chest. Half asleep, he faintly sighed and folded his arms around me.

***

— *6:00 Friday morning*

"… going to be a nice night, temperatures around 17 degrees." I awoke to my clock radio and mentally converted the temperature to Fahrenheit. Tom, who seemed not to notice me stirring, lay on his side, with a rasp in his breath. My *Jaws* shirt was lying on the floor, so I swung my legs off the bed and pulled it over my head. I turned off the radio to let him sleep and then went to the kitchen to start my daily ritual of making coffee. I remembered the mice and decided to clean the dishes. 20 minutes later, I was in the shower with lathering gardenia soap, coconut shampoo and conditioner, the warm water washing away premonitions, weird dreams, and pain. Then, I thought more about last night. What a crazy mixture of experiences and emotions.

I stepped out of the shower, towel dried my hair the best I could, and wrapped it up tightly in the towel. I put another around my chest and walked back into the bedroom. Getting dressed, I continued with my usual morning schedule of breakfast, coffee, and today, I decided NOT to watch the news.

I went to get a second cup of coffee when I saw Tom silhouetted in the doorway to the kitchen; barefoot, shirt off, hair going every which way, and his suit pants on from yesterday hanging low on his hips. I couldn't help notice the faint scarring on his arms that I have yet to ask him about. I also glimpsed one that actually looked kind of fresh right around his bicep.

"Good morning, love," he sang and gave me a huge kiss on my lips. He pulled away and touched my cheek lightly with his fingertips. "Last night was… well, I would not be lying if I said it was the best night of my life."

"Um, I wouldn't necessarily disagree," I smiled, slightly embarrassed.

"I see you've cleaned the dishes. Very good! This keeps the mice away, you know," he mocked, winking at me. I guess he was woken up at some point, too.

"Hey, were did you get this from?" I probed, tracing the red line on his upper arm.

He looked at where I touched and made an 'I don't know' face, "I guess I scraped it on something the other day. It seems to be healing."

I nodded. "I've gotta get to work, but stay as long as you want. I made enough coffee for you or if you want some tea, it's in the cupboard. Just lock the door behind you," I explained as I grabbed my purse and keys.

"Alright. I have to work tonight, but may I come by after?"

Setting my keys and purse back down, I walked right up to him, threw my arms around his neck and gave him a long kiss goodbye. Moving back away from him toward the door I said, "Yes, please."

CHAPTER 8

"Use the skills I taught you. When I am gone, out of your life, someone must continue. It's in our blood; that's why we are so good at it. We don't get caught. And we don't get caught because God is looking out for us, you see, because we are doing God's work. You are practically an adult now, so I expect big things from you, big things indeed."

"You did it!"

"Did what, Jamie?"

"You shagged him last night."

"Jamie! Why do you have to be so lewd?"

"It's true. I see it in your face, your walk. You look more confident."

"You see what in her face?" asked Jack.

"Shut up, Jamie," I interrupted as Jamie started to speak. She stopped and Jack just shrugged.

She took my arm and pulled me aside to the corner of the pantry. "So, how was it?"

"Come on, Jamie, you're embarrassing me, again. I don't see how this is appropriate for the workplace, especially from my boss."

"Look, I've got to live vicariously through someone. Look at who I've got."

"What's wrong with Seamus?"

"You have a year? Ah, he's alright, but, new love," she pondered, "there's nothing like it."

"Love? Isn't that rushing this a bit?" I said, playing devil's advocate. But, it sure felt that way.

"What, you don't believe in love at first sight? Happens all the time. You've known him for over a week now; that's plenty of time. I'll take him if you don't want him. You may have Seamus." She had a dreamy look in her eyes.

I sighed and shook my head, but couldn't stop a smile from escaping.

"There you go, see? It's not so hard to enjoy things, is it?" She put her arm around me and talked about tomorrow night, escorting me to my desk. The computer loomed in front of me.

***

— *5:00 Friday evening*

I took the tube home since the taxis were just a little too pricey. I ascended the steps and opened my door. My flat! It was spotless. Everything was in its place, the floors gleamed, the countertops sparkled. Even my books were righted in perfect perpendicular orientation. The only thing out of place was a man lying on my sofa, rag in his hand, fast asleep with some stubble starting to show on his pale skin. I didn't know if I should be angry or grateful. I figured I'd wing it.

"Tom," I said while touching his face.

"Tom, wake up, you've got to get to work soon." Suddenly, he grabbed my hand and woke with a start.

Breathing out, "Anna, I'm sorry, you startled me. What time is it?" He asked, letting go of his grip, sitting up, looking a little disoriented.

"5:45. You cleaned my flat?"

He rubbed his eyes and yawned, "Yes, I meant it to be a surprise. My plan was to leave here around 1600. I wanted it to seem like the mice did it," he smiled. "See, I even started a note." He handed me a piece of paper with a child-like drawing of a fat mouse holding a bottle of cleaning fluid.

I sighed. "You're cute. But, to be honest with you, I'm not sure what to make of this."

"What to make of it? I just spent all day cleaning your flat and there were some pretty unsavory things, I assure you. Let me guess, you think there's some hidden agenda. Me judging you the way you live?"

"Well... a little," I confessed, starting to feel slightly ridiculous.

"I just wanted to do something nice for you. But, if you'd rather have some furry friends as flat mates, I can always turn a rubbish can over onto your floor." Tom said, obviously a little offended. "Look, can't someone do something nice for an American without the conspiracy theory?"

"Okay, okay, you're right. I'm sorry. Really, thank you for cleaning. I could never have gotten it like this," I said as I took my coat off.

He leaned back into the sofa and stretched his arms over his head. "I've got to get home, shower, and get to work. I've really got to go." He still had a slight edge.

"Will you come back after?"

He stood up, looked at me and said, "Yes, but if this place is a mess when I get back, I'm going to take you over my knee."

I looked right back at him and purposely dropped my coat on the floor. "Oops," I said, innocently.

He closed his eyes, and feigned exasperation, but I glimpsed a slight smile. He put on his coat, quickly kissed me goodbye and told me he should be back around 2230.

***

I ate some dinner, and this time washed the dishes. I decided to pass the time and watch some television. Unfortunately, the news was on.

A man was found shot to death last night on Ropemaker street. Julius Thompson was found with a gunshot wound to his heart. He was presumed dead when a passerby found him. Mr. Thompson was out on bail awaiting trial for allegedly harming his girlfriend's baby. The circumstances have some asking if this was the work of the Vigilante. Our field reporter, Samantha Brent, sat down with expert Dr. Triston Fields, who thinks otherwise.

"This really isn't the m.o. of the Vigilante. She would have harmed Mr. Thompson in the same way he allegedly harmed his girlfriend's baby. There were no bruises found on his body, only the gunshot wound that killed him. Also, the Vigilante does not kill her victims."

"Isn't it possible that the Vigilante decided to kill Mr. Thompson due to the fact that he harmed such an innocent being?"

"It's possible, yes, but unlikely from what we know about serial criminal patterns of behavior."

"So you think this is a copycat, much like the Wainwright case?"

"We can't rule out the Wainwright case as a copycat crime, yet. But let us not forget, there is more than one baddie out there. The Vigilante is just one in many. I think the hype from this stems from us wanting to make connections to the city's history with Jack the Ripper and Phineas Hall. However, people are romanticizing the Vigilante because of who she targets. So, let's not get ahead of ourselves thinking the Vigilante—

and indeed if there is only one—is responsible for all violent crime in the
city. If you recall, three prostitutes were found dead in the Docklands
area a short time ago. We've also had a large number of homosexuals
being attacked. We cannot ascribe all crime to the Vigilante. We need to
be realistic and not let her become more legend than real. I've even seen
T-shirts supporting her."

I turned off the television. The sensationalizing of the news is as bad here as it
is in the States.

I put on the Screaming Trees album, *Sweet Oblivion,* and cranked it up.
Grabbing my journal, I started to write down details of all my weird
occurrences: who I was with, when, and where. I even made a circle diagram
to see how any of this at all could be related to the Vigilante. After going in
circles, literally, I put down the journal and got lost in the music until I buzzed
Tom in at 10:45.

***

— *Saturday, September 13*

I awoke to music. A muffled flute, bass, and piano played through the closed
door. Then, the drums started to accompany the other instruments in a
march-like beat, gradually getting louder. I opened the door to Jethro Tull's
"Cross Eyed Mary" blaring mouthwateringly loud. And much to my
amazement, Tom singing along while making breakfast. He had a good voice,
ah, a great voice. I just stood in the doorway and listened and watched.

He abruptly stopped when he saw me smiling in the doorway.

"Oh, good morning," he grimaced and walked over to the CD player, turning
it down, not making eye contact with me.

"Don't stop, Tom. Your voice is pretty awesome."

"I thought you were asleep," he said, quite embarrassed. He continued with
whatever he was cooking in the kitchen. "Em, I was surprised you had Jethro
Tull."

"Yeah, my dad got me into them. But, Tom, your voice!"

"I guess I stay on tune," he muttered into the pan.

"This gets better every day." I said under my breath.

"Pardon?"

"Nothing," I smiled.

He shrugged, "What do you want to do today, love?" he asked. The aroma of French toast wafted into my nose.

"I don't know, I haven't been to that Ferris Wheel yet, I mean, the London Eye."

"The *Coca-Cola* London Eye?" He said sarcastically while shuddering. "I suppose we could do that. I'm not sure how I feel about contributing to that monstrosity; however, it is a good way to see the city. Keep in mind, it will be crowded with bloody tourists."

"Well, I think it's cool. And besides, those 'bloody tourists' attend your ghost tours, don't they?"

Tom paused for a few seconds, then nodded his head and gave me a wry smile. "Okay, you make a fair point."

Tom then cocked his head, contemplating, "So, two days and no painful experiences."

"Yeah, let's hope it stays that way."

"Are you sure you want to put yourself in a situation tonight that could possibly cause you more pain?"

"Yes, definitely. I told you, I want to see this through." Changing the subject, I asked, "Don't you have to tend to your father?"

He sighed, "Yes, but I'll go tomorrow. I'm rather enjoying not seeing him."

***

We took a cab to the London Eye. It was a lot taller and a little bit intimidating up close. I read online that it sits 135 meters above the Thames. I'm not really one for heights, but really wanted to see the views.

"Shall we have a private capsule?" Tom asked.

"Um, no Tom, it's already outrageously expensive. I can only imagine how much that would cost. And besides, you didn't want to contribute any money towards it anyway."

"I know, but you are worth sacrificing my principles," he said, smiling at me while pulling out his wallet.

"Come on. You make me a little uncomfortable spending money so frivolously, especially on me, so can we just get the regular tickets?"

He protested a little, but gave in. He did, however, get the fast track tickets, also crazy expensive. But, at least we didn't have to wait in line too long. I felt a little guilty as it seemed like we were butting in line. We even got a couple of dirty looks.

We entered the clear capsule pretty quickly and went right up to the glass, leaning our faces forward.

The Eye started its slow ascent. "These views are awesome!" I giddily exclaimed as we rode higher. Although not thrilling for its speed, my legs were a little wobbly from the fear of being up so high and pressed right against the glass.

"Yes, they are," Tom agreed with a soothing tone as he stood behind me and wrapped his arms around my waist in a firm, gentle bear hug, his chin hovering right above my shoulder.

"So, there's Big Ben, of course." I said, pointing to the left.

"Well, yes and no, love. Actually, the bell inside the clock tower is called Big Ben. A lot of tourists have it wrong. In fact, everyone seems to think London Bridge is the iconic bridge far over there to the right."

"It's not?"

"No, that's Tower Bridge. One of our comedy shows showed how the American commentators for the Olympics even got it wrong."

I nodded. Tom pointed out Westminster Abbey, Piccadilly Circus, Trafalgar Square, among other sites I've never even heard of.

"Oh, what's that egg building?"

"That would be the Gherkin," he said as he kissed my neck. In fact, the whole thirty-minute journey, he either was kissing me, squeezing me or touching his cheek to my cheek. Never have I experienced this with a guy before and I really liked the feeling. When the ride was complete, we exited and walked along the Thames, holding hands. Although I loved it and would do it again, I felt a little boneless from the ride, so I was glad to be on solid ground.

I was a little bewildered about Tom's affections. You generally don't see a lot of "PDA" in London. Plus, he's so proper.

"You're pretty outwardly affectionate, Tom."

He looked over toward me; a cute vertical crease forming in between his eyebrows. "I'm sorry, did I make you uncomfortable?"

"Oh, God no. I love it. It's just so—unexpected."

"Anna, I am over the moon to have found you. All I want to do is be close to you." He nodded, as if agreeing with his own sentiment. A warmness flooded through me, like a relaxing hot bath.

We strolled along the Thames, weaving our way through hordes of people crowding the embankment. River boats were out in droves, crammed to capacity with tourists. Nice days will do that.

Tom nudged me and asked, "Looking forward to tonight?"

"Yes, I am. I halfway hope something does happen so we can assess my experience better. Then again, I hope it never happens again. Oh, and I started the journal Holly suggested and I may have realized a few things when I wrote everything down. I did one of those circle diagrams to find out some connections."

He slightly laughed as he said, "Go on."

I shot him a look from the corner of my eye. "Look, don't start again, just listen to my thoughts, because I didn't tell you everything. When I look back to the first time I had an incident, it was with Richard Brown, at the ghost tour, right? Well, the pain I felt that night was not just in my teeth, but somewhere… else. It really dawned on me when I wrote it out."

"How do you mean? If you are talking about feeling it in your neck, you were acting that night, if I recall."

"Yes, I was in the house, but remember, right before I went in, I told you I felt this weird jolt of pain through my body and I saw a flash of teeth and blood. And that jolt of pain? I felt it in a real specific place, not my neck."

"Specific place?" Tom looked perplexed.

"This is so embarrassing." I muttered.

"What is?"

I looked away, remaining silent.

Tom coaxed quietly, leaning in, "Anna, I've seen and explored *all* parts of your body, I think you can trust me."

I sighed, "Do you remember the report on Brown? I mean, where he was hit and harmed?"

"Yes, I remember the report."

I stopped walking and turned toward him, the Thames off to my right, now. "His teeth were knocked out and," lowering my voice, "he had a metal pipe shoved up his ass, remember?"

Tom let out a loud guffaw, "And that's where you felt pain that night?"

Annoyed, I pursed my lips and nodded, "Yeah. I did. So glad I could *trust* you. See, I told you it was embarrassing. Thanks a fucking lot."

We started walking again, me a little quicker. "Sorry. Look, are you sure you aren't remembering incorrectly? You didn't tell me anything about that. I assure you, I would have remembered." He tried to stifle a laugh.

I rolled my eyes, "Right, I'm going to tell an incredibly hot guy I just met that my asshole is on fire."

Tom winced at my words, "Do you have to be so crass, all the time?"

"Do you have to be such a fucking prig all the time?" I said, still annoyed.

Tom slowly closed and opened his eyes. I don't think he knew what to do with me. So, he just let it go.

Softly, he asked, "So, what are your thoughts? You think you are somehow attached to this Vigilante? That you feel the pain men endure by the hands of, let's say, the female assailant?"

"Well, let's think about this for a second. So, we have Richard Brown. Pretty sure I had the same pain and let's assume it was the Vigilante who struck. And then…"

"And then you had feelings the second night, your stomach, face, ribs. But, that didn't fit with a vigilante attack, or one that we know about at least," Tom pondered.

"Yes, but you got hurt that night with those same injuries and so did the homophobe. So, could that asshole be the Vigilante?"

Tom shook his head and smiled, "You've got a wild imagination. For that matter, maybe it's me."

"Yeah right, besides, it's a woman, so he couldn't be the Vigilante." I looked up at Tom with a snarky smile and added, "And neither could you."

"Allegedly a woman. We don't know that for certain. And then there is Wainwright, who may have been harmed by the hands of a copycat, but you still felt his pain."

"And the guy who got shot the other night, the one who harmed the baby. I didn't feel a thing related to that one."

"So, really, all we have is possibly Richard Brown. Maybe you just get feelings from people being harmed in your niche. You were close in proximity to Brown, close to Mr. Homophobe, close to me, and for all you know, you passed Wainwright on the street." Tom reasoned.

I took a deep breath and let it out slowly, "That's a pretty good theory, I'll admit. In any event, it's creepy."

We walked along, me pondering Tom's theory, and thinking it could be right. Interrupting my thoughts, Tom asked, "Mmmm... so 'incredibly hot'?" He looked at me disbelieving.

I looked up at him, puzzled. "Uh, yeah. Do you not realize how attractive you are?"

"Em, no, not at all. Have you seen my teeth and ghostly complexion? And let's not forget what's under my shirt."

I just laughed, "You, Tom, are hilarious."

"Okay," he seemed confused.

We passed by a couple of smokers whose carcinogenic puffs accosted us. We both started coughing. "What a nasty habit," sneered Tom. "I do love walking through London, but there are far too many smokers."

"Huh? I thought you smoked?"

Tom looked taken aback. "Me? Whatever gave you that impression? After my experience with cigarettes, I try to stay clear. And besides, when have you seen me smoke?"

"The night we met, I swore I saw you smoking, I mean, your back was turned and you kind of hunched forward as if lighting a cigarette and I thought I saw smoke..."

"It was pretty foggy that night, as I recall, and I probably was checking my phone. I assure you, *I don't smoke*," he proclaimed, enunciating the last three words.

Relieved, "Okay, well good."

Tom nodded in agreement, then changing the subject, asked, "Well, what would you like to do next? The Globe? Tower Bridge?"

"Well, do you want to go to the Tate Modern since it's right here? I've heard it's pretty good."

Tom looked astonished, almost insulted, "Who told you that?"

"Steven asked me if I wanted to go with him to it the other day. He thought I would really like it because I was so alternative." I laughed out loud.

Tom raised one eyebrow and even got a little testy. "I don't care for the Tate Modern. A few pieces in there are fine, like works from Dali and Picasso, but some of the pieces displayed, I hardly can call art. They have not one, but three white paintings. They even have a large drape of fabric on the floor wrapped around a barrel. And to top it off, they have a whole room full of Rothko's," he said with venom.

"Boy, this really irks you. Um, I kind of like Rothko."

He sighed. "You can *like* Rothko, you can want his painting on your bedroom wall, but in no way should it be hanging in an art museum." Softening, he continued, "If you want to see real art, I'll take you to the Courtauld Gallery at Somerset House where they display Van Gogh, Degas, and Seurat."

And so, that's what we did. We walked over Millennium Bridge, me finally getting some pictures of Tom without too much protesting, and made our way to the small, but extraordinary gallery. They only had a couple of Van Gogh's, but there were no ropes, so I was able to get super close to them. I could see his thick, colorful brush strokes, even spots where the canvas showed through. I stood there in awe, staring at the topography of the painting for a really long time. I never felt this emotional toward a piece of art. Music, yes, but not a painting. I think it was the realization that this was not a print, that Van Gogh truly put his brush to this canvas. I heard footsteps behind me and felt Tom's whisper, "It's amazing, isn't it?" Still looking at the painting and nodding, I thought Tom was amazing. The things he's shown me and the way he's treated me, I think my infatuation was turning into something much more.

***

After a long, fun day downtown, we decided to go our separate ways and meet at the tour. We couldn't get a cab, so Tom, the gentleman he is, rode the tube with me to my stop, although he was pretty uncomfortable in it the whole way. He walked me the rest of the way home, kissed me goodbye and successfully hailed a cab.

I went inside to my very clean flat, which I told myself I would at least try to keep that way. Collapsing on the sofa, I turned on the television, but quickly changed the news channel to something less depressing and watched 'Top Gear' for a bit. It was 5:00 PM and I thought I had enough time to take a quick nap. I set my phone alarm to wake me up in an hour and a half and I fell asleep right away.

***

The alarm woke me up at 6:30. I hopped in the shower, excited about tonight. I wanted to see if the tour gave me any more premonitions. Conflicted, I was eager to go out with another couple, but a little anxious in that I hadn't told Jamie about my weird feelings yet. A couple—I grinned at that. After getting clean, I went through my closet to see what would be appropriate for tonight. I opted for dark jeans, burgundy pleather Doc Martens, a white camisole and a pale green blouse. I wore my hair up in pig tails, picked some upside-down cross earrings and a skull pendant necklace. At 7:30, I munched quickly on a banana and ran out the door. Half-way down the steps, I decided to go back up and grab my small backpack I kept travel stuff in, just in case I wasn't coming home tonight.

Since the Underground makes me a little nervous at night now, I decided to hail a cab. Even though the cab was a little more expensive, it gave me a little more peace of mind.

I arrived a little early. We were meeting at 8:30, but thought I'd surprise Tom. I walked up to the visitor center and asked the person at the main desk if he was in.

"You can go to the back office, right this way." The woman stated. She was elderly, maybe in her 70s.

I opened the door to the small, non-descript office and Tom was at the computer, looking very intent, wearing black rimmed hipster glasses. He looked up, squinted, and his whole face brightened when he saw me.

"Hello, love, you're here early!" He bolted out of the chair and gave me a huge hug.

"I kind of wanted to see the inner sanctum of the ghost tour."

"Well, this is it. We share the office. It's mainly just for us to change our clothes, check things on the computer, and kiss our girlfriends." Which he did. "You look lovely tonight. I especially like the fancy blouse juxtaposed with Doc Martens and 'sign o' the devil' earrings." He grinned.

I narrowed my eyes, "Okay, Mr. Chuck Taylor's paired with a suit."

"Stop that, Anna, I'm being serious. I quite like your style."

"I didn't know you wore glasses."

"I don't, really, just when I am at the computer and sometimes when I am reading, but I can get by without them, too. Nerdy, right?" He took them off, placing them on the desk.

"Well, I think you look adorable in them. Nerdy is in now, isn't it?"

Tom cocked his head and looked at me questioningly.

Looking down at the floor, I gathered up some courage to broach the relationship topic. "Sooo, this is the second time you've called me your girlfriend. We never really talked about our status," I noted, sitting on the small guest chair.

Tom sighed and leaned against the edge of the desk, our legs almost touching in the small office, "Okay. Em, I think it's rather obvious, but, let's talk. I'll go first. I'm not seeing anyone else, nor am I going to. I think about you all day and night and want to basically spend every waking and sleeping moment with you. Em, you know more about me than anyone else, except for my father and grandfather. I've never enjoyed making love to someone as much as I have with you. And… and, you took a liking to my paisley bear. So, yes, I would define you as 'girlfriend'."

"O… Okay," I stammered. I wasn't expecting such a response.

"Okay… what?" He crouched down so he was eye level with me and leaned in, but the woman from the front desk opened the door without knocking.

"Oh, I am sorry Mr. Tom. But, your tour is starting in 15 minutes." Tom abruptly stood up and thanked her.

"So, is our status established or would you like to refute anything?" He inquired while taking his shirt off with a slight exhale. He changed into a white button-down oxford, put on a thin black tie, tucked his shirt into his black pants, and shrugged on his coat. "If you don't feel the same way, please tell me," he said as he checked himself out in the full-length mirror on the back of the door.

"No, no… I… I feel the same." I managed to cough out.

He then opened his mouth and touched the tip of his thumb to the bottom of one of his canines, then the other, "My, my these are getting sharper," he said quietly, giving me a sly look.

I flushed. "I am going to kill Jamie."

A chuckle in his voice, "Okay, let's go." We walked out of the office to the front desk to find Jamie and Seamus waiting.

"Hello, Jamie," Tom greeted as he gave her a kiss on the cheek.

"Tom, this is Seamus, my boyfriend." Seamus looked like a Seamus. Very Irish, very pale skin, sandy brown hair that was cut close to his head, blue eyes, and big. Not fat at all; just tall and bulky.

Tom held out his hand and Seamus took it. He must have squeezed Tom's hand a bit too hard because I heard a faint gasp escape from Tom's mouth.

"Nice to meet you, mate. Jamie has told me all about you. Incessantly." Seamus spoke slowly while holding onto Tom's hand much longer than needed, staring, rather intimidatingly, into Tom's eyes.

Tom glanced over at Jamie, perplexed, as did I. Seamus finally let go of Tom's hand. Tom flexed and extended his fingers to, I presume, get his circulation back.

She shrugged, "Seamus doesn't like it when I compare him to another man. How a boyfriend should behave. He's never given me flowers."

"See what I have to listen to, mate?" And in a mocking woman's voice, 'Tom gave me not one flower, but two. Tom won't let Anna pay for anything,' and on and on."

Tom laughed, "I'm sorry, Seamus. How about, I won't hold the door for them when we walk outside."

"It's a start," Seamus mumbled.

Unable to resist, Tom wound up holding the door for us anyway as we exited the visitor center into the cool September air. Seamus shook his head at Tom who in turn uttered, "Sorry, habit." He then turned up the charisma a notch and started to greet the crowd.

"Greetings fair ladies and gentlemen. I hope you are prepared for a night of history and frights. I will be taking you on a journey back in time, to when London was plagued by disease, the River Thames a cesspool of human waste. It'll be delightful. We will start with a walk to Charterhouse Square in Clerkenwell, where we will be standing on… well, I'll tell you when we arrive." Tom held his lantern and started to lead the crowd, Seamus following close behind.

"What are we going to be standing on?" he asked, giddily.

"You'll see," Tom uttered in a deeper than usual voice.

Even though it was dark, I could see Seamus's face lighting up. "He really likes this stuff, doesn't he," I asked Jamie.

"Yea, he wants to play the Ouija Board in front of one of the haunted houses," Jamie said.

We walked down Charterhouse Street until we arrived at Charterhouse Square; a grassy gated area surrounded by buildings and an old monastery. "Gather around everyone; please, come in close," Tom commanded.

A soft breeze blew, pushing leaves around Tom and the crowd, creating an ominous effect. Everyone quieted down, listening to Tom's engaging tone.

"London. Our beloved city. With its historic architecture, some of the most beautiful parks in the world, the fantastic restaurants and pubs. A city so rich in diversity, more than 300 languages are spoken here. But, London has not been without strife. From the Great Fire in 1666 to the 7/7 bombings, we have had our challenges, but Londoners always persevere. One event, however, was so heinous, it killed half the city's population. Imagine, half of London gone. Go back. Go back to the mid thirteen hundreds where Londoners suffered from a terrible outbreak of a disease. That disease was the Black Death, the Bubonic Plague, carried by rats and spread by fleas. This disease caused whole families to be eradicated."

Tom softened his voice and continued, "Children lost their mothers, fathers, brothers and sisters. Mothers lost their babies. All due to something that barely fit on a pin head. The disease caused so many to die, there wasn't any room in the cemeteries. Mass graves had to be dug to accommodate all the bodies."

He started to pace back and forth, "People were laid on top of each other, children interspersed among the adults. Families separated not only in life from the disease, but in death as well. 'Bring out your dead,' the death cart drivers would call through the streets. Picking up bodies and depositing them… elsewhere."

A dramatic pause, and then, "Ladies and Gentlemen, I invite you to place yourself back in that time. Think about what it must have felt like to live in such circumstances. We take so much for granted now, don't we?"

He took a deep breath, another pause to allow the gravity of the thought to set in. "Such sadness, and helplessness," Tom said in a quieter voice, bowing his head. He had captivated everyone in the tour. Crouching down, he continued, motioning with his finger for the audience to come closer, for which we all obeyed, crowding in around him.

He looked up at us, an ominous shadow crossing his face. Softly, he said, "Now, listen, listen very closely. If you put your ear to the ground, it is said that you can hear the chilling moans and screams of those who succumbed to the Plague. For right below your feet, ladies and gentlemen," he stood up, opened his arms, and with a booming voice, said, "you are standing on top of 50,000 dead!"

Many of us took a small startled step back, some stood quiet in a silent prayer, taking in the death that laid beneath us. The wind kicked up a bit, blowing back Tom's hair slightly, the lantern light casting a sinister glow on his face, which only intensified the eeriness of the square. A chill ran up my body and I shivered. My, oh my, could Tom create an effect. I loved it.

"Did you hear tha'?" Seamus whispered to me.

"No, what did you hear?"

"I thought I heard a groan?" Seamus's eyes widened.

"It was your stomach, Seamus," Jamie loudly whispered.

After allowing the unsettling thoughts to sink in, Tom announced, "Alright ladies and gentlemen, let's walk on to Farrington Tube Station."

"What's at the tube station?" Seamus asked Tom.

"Just wait and see, Seamus," Jamie spat, irritated.

We walked down Cowcross Street to the outside of the station, the crowd staying a little closer together than before.

"In the mid-18th century," Tom began, "The Underground did not exist. Houses used to line these streets prior to the Underground. However, with progress, someone usually has to suffer. The houses were eventually torn down to make way for the Farrington Station in the mid-1800s. But, prior to the destruction, there was a house where inside, horrendous, sinister acts occurred. The story begins with a girl named Anne Naylor. She and her sister were brought to this home, the home of Sarah Metyard, a milliner, a hat maker. Metyard would use children as apprentices to help with her work. However, Anne was not a strong child. She couldn't do a lot of the work Metyard tasked her with. And because of that, Anne incurred the wrath of Sarah Metyard, who was the definition of a sadist. Metyard would inflict harsh punishments on Anne, punishments that, of course, never fit the crime. And we have to recognize, no matter how heinous the infraction, child abuse is never the answer." Tom flicked his eyes up at me quickly and then back to the crowd, for his voice had waivered a little.

He continued, "Anne tried to escape a couple of times, only to be brought back where the beatings became more severe. So severe, Metyard and her daughter together once held Anne down while beating her with a broom handle. Anne was then confined to a room upstairs where she was bound and starved. Starved for three days. Then, on the fourth day, she was found lifeless—her poor body just couldn't handle it anymore. Metyard tried to hide this murderous act by locking the girl's body in a trunk. The daft woman obviously didn't think of the inevitable smell. Eventually, they had to do away with the evidence. They dismembered the poor child's corpse, burned part of her and scattered the remains on Chick Lane. Will you be the one to hear it?" Asked Tom, pointing at an engrossed tourist. "What about you?" he said, gesturing to Seamus. "It is believed that Anne haunts the Farrington Platform near where the house she was tortured in used to stand. So, I ask again, will you be the one to hear it? The screams? The shear agony of the tortured innocent little girl? Countless people, including myself, have heard the screams, believed to be from Anne Naylor."

"Did you here tha' one, Jamie?" Asked Seamus.

"No, Seamus, I didn't hear anything," Jamie said, sounding annoyed as she shook her head.

As we walked to the next stop, the tourists chattered about the stories they've heard, singing Tom's praises. I smiled inwardly, happy about our status, pumped that the guy leading this tour was mine. I quickened my pace to catch up to Tom, waiting patiently for an elderly woman to finish questioning him. He gave me a sideways glance and smiled.

"Doing alright?" He asked quietly.

"Yes, how about you?"

"I'm fine. I do get slightly emotional telling the story of Anne Naylor, for obvious reasons," he softly spoke. As we continued down the dark street, a very skanky woman approached to chat with Tom. I stepped to the side.

"Have you really heard her scream?" The early twenty something, very provocatively dressed woman asked, taking my place next to Tom.

"Well, yes, I have. It was night, no one was around the area and I could hear a blood-curdling scream coming from the platform. I suppose it could have been someone else, but it was the scream of someone being tortured."

The woman clutched Tom's arm, as if she were scared. I saw Tom glance down at her, presumably caught an eyeful of her cleavage, and then quickly looked away.

"Frightened?" Tom asked, and obviously a little uncomfortable, for his voice went up an octave and then he cleared his throat.

"Well, a little. I'm Kitty, by the way. You're a really good storyteller."

"Em, thank you."

She paused for a second and then asked, "Hey, would you like to get a drink after the tour?" My eyes got wide.

Tom got a little flustered, patted Kitty's arm that still clutched his and stuttered his sentence. "Em, oh, ah… well, I'm flattered, em, K..Kitty, but I'm afraid I have a girlfriend."

Kitty didn't really seem to care too much. "Well, I can give you my number on your cell phone in case things don't work out. Or if you get bored."

"Ah, th..thank you? But that won't be necessary. I'm quite involved with my *girlfriend*," he emphasized through gritted teeth, looking over at me. I suppose I should have helped him, but I just smiled and shrugged. This was fun. He looked exasperated at me.

"Em, oh here we are at the next stop." Tom informed Kitty as he pulled his arm out of her grip.

Obviously still flustered, he started out a little rushed, but then got back into his groove. He took us to a few more places, weaving more tales of murder, torture, sadness and haunts. Other than the woman, we completed the tour without incident and went back to the visitor center. Tom made his final remarks, nodded to us, and quickly went back into his office, avoiding Kitty's further advances. During the remainder of the tour, she had been relentlessly trying to talk to him, and she kept touching his arm or shoulder or back. Once I noticed her hand start to explore lower down his back, but Tom quickly turned to avoid her target.

"He's just going to change," I told Jamie and Seamus. "So, what did you guys think of the chick hanging all over him?"

"Prostitute," Jamie said.

"Oh definitely," I agreed.

Seamus, oblivious of our conversation proclaimed, "I know I heard somethin'."

"You thought you heard something at every single stop, Seamus," Jamie remarked. "I swear you are mental!"

"I did hear something. Tom told us he's heard things, so why is this so hard to believe?" Seamus challenged.

Tom came walking out. Blue Jeans with a black belt and a black button-down shirt, first two buttons open, Chuck Taylors, and his pea coat. He scanned the crowd, looking a little weary, and then came over to us quickly. Kitty had left.

Jamie nudged me. "So hot."

"Cut it out, Jamie, you've got a boyfriend, so stop trying to steal mine." We both looked over at Seamus, who was recounting what he had heard and seen to some tourist. Jamie and I burst out laughing.

"Something funny, ladies?" Tom inquired.

We heard Seamus saying, "…and it was a loud groan, I tell you."

"You know, Anna, you could have helped me with that girl. She was relentless. Her hands were all over me. I mean she tried to grab my… anyway, she slipped this into my coat pocket," he handed me a card. It was red with black curly queue writing. 'Kitty' was stamped on the front and a phone number on the back.

"Yeah, Jamie and I were right, she's a prostitute."

Tom looked completely flummoxed. "She was not a prostitute."

"Yes, Tom, she was," laughed Jamie. "Maybe a higher class, um, like an escort service, but you were being solicited by a prostitute."

Tom huffed. "Well, then more so thank you so much for getting me out of that situation." He sarcastically stated.

That, coupled with Seamus's account of the evening, made Jamie and me double over with laughter.

Tom's irritation furthered, "Alright, alright, can you two *biotches* cut it out."

Tears in Jamie's eyes, she said, "Look, it's not just you Tom, but Seamus's stomach was growling the whole time. I could hear it, it was so loud, and that's what he was hearing, too, thinking it was a ghost." Jamie roared even louder, and I gasped, trying to catch my breath.

Tom pursed his lips, walked over to Seamus, and put his arm around him, guiding him away from the thankful tourist, "You hungry, mate?"

"I'm starving," Seamus exclaimed. I could tell Tom was holding back a laugh.

***

We started walking back toward Clerkenwell to find a pub with food.

"Mate, you were great. Not only were the stories good, but you have a way of telling them that really creates a horrorshow." Seamus beamed. I guess he was over his initial wariness of Tom.

"Yes, Tom, brilliant show. I'd love to do it again," Jamie said.

"Why thank you both. I am humbled. I try to--"

"You know, we could have invited Kitty," I interrupted.

Tom sighed.

"Sorry, it was amusing watching you squirm. 'Oh, em, ah, K..k..kitty, I'm flattered!" I aped in an uppity British accent. Jamie blurted out a loud laugh.

Tom looked at me sternly. "Testing the waters, m'dear? Best be careful."

My heart beat a little faster from his tone. I gave him an equally sinister grin.

We walked through St. John's Square and a small pedestrian alleyway called Jerusalem Passage. Well, we tried to walk through. People were drinking, crowding the alley. We managed to excuse our way into the pub and had the fortunate timing to find a table as another group was getting up. It was right in front of cute drawings of Tintin. Seamus continued complementing Tom, relaying parts back that he especially favored. I'm not sure if Tom was being nice and tolerating Seamus or if he actually liked him back.

After we ordered, Seamus asked, "So, who wants to play the favorites game?"

"Em... Favorites Game?" Tom asked.

"Yeah, it's to get to know someone a bit better. One person thinks of a topic and we go around saying our favorite," Seamus explained.

"Oh, Seamus, not again, we aren't 7 years old," chastised Jamie.

"Shut it, Jamie! Now, I'll go first, what's your favorite color?" He posed the question to Tom.

"Okay, I am fond of green and black," Tom answered.

Seamus looked to me, "Orange and black."

To Jamie, "I like purple."

"And I like red," Seamus remarked.

"Great, now we all really know each other!" Jamie sung, sarcastically.

I snorted. Tom flashed me another warning look.

"Okay, missy, your topic," pointed Seamus.

"Alright, um, favorite rock band, any style," I looked to Seamus.

"Butthole Surfers," Seamus proudly declared. I detected a spot of bother from Tom's face.

"Triumvirat, a progressive rock band," Tom professed.

"The Spice Girls!" crowed Jamie. Everyone at the table groaned.

"Um, there are so many! I'd say definitely The Damned and maybe Bauhaus as a close second."

Seamus looked up at me. "You like The Damned? Who else do you like?" And then Seamus and I got into a lengthy conversation about music. It turns out, Seamus and I liked a lot of the same bands. Jamie and Tom talked about more mundane things, at least from what I could tell.

We played more of the favorites game, getting onto topics like favorite hairdo and favorite movie. The game started to get a little louder and boisterous to match the late-night drinkers' sounds. In fact, most of us were drinking, pint after pint. Although I had a good buzz on, I didn't want to get drunk, so I held back. Seamus, Jamie, and to my surprise, Tom, were all sucking down the beers like water. This could get interesting.

"Eeriest occurrence?" Seamus asked. "But, I'll go first. So, when I was a teen, I used to play around with the Ouija Board. My mates and I got really into it and I was playing a lot, maybe a wee bit too much. So, anyway, one night we were playing and the planchette was racing around the board, spelling out the letters, "I L-I-E" and "D-O N-O-T P-L-A-Y" and freaky messages like that. I mean, the pull on the device was so intense," he mimicked moving the planchette, "so you can imagine we were pretty scared. Anyway, that night, in my room, it was dark, but the light from the street gave my room enough light for me to see wispy things on the walls and shadows moving in the corners. I was petrified. I reached over and turned on my clock radio, hoping some music would get me to sleep. I set the timer to count down about 30 minutes until the radio would turn off. So, I finally start to drift off to sleep after some time. But then, I hear "Imagine" come on. So, what's the first line?" He asked us, all captivated from his story.

"Imagine there's no heaven," Tom slurred.

"Exactly!" Seamus pounded the table; our drinks splashing angrily around in our glasses. "And you know what? The fucking radio shuts off right after that line!" I shivered, my mouth agape.

"I've not played with the Ouija Board ever since," Seamus declared.

We all sat in silence for a minute from the chilling story, goose bumps running up my arms.

"You never told me that," accused Jamie, breaking the silence at our table.

"You never asked," he grumbled.

"Why would I think to ask such a question?"

And then, the Karaoke was broken out. Like a dog hearing a siren, Seamus's head snapped in the direction of the stage, promptly stood up and barreled his way to the small stage.

"Oh, God, here we go again. I bet it's going to be Hootie and the Blowfish." Jamie said as she took another swig of her drink.

Sitting back in her chair, she nodded, knowingly, as he started singing a horrible rendition of "Hold My Hand." But his performance was so earnest that at least some of the crowd seemed to enjoy it.

I nudged Tom, "Why don't you get up there? You can sing."

"Ah, no Anna."

"You can sing, Tom?" Asked Jamie.

"He has an awesome voice," I interjected.

"Of course he does." Jamie and I looked at each other, stood up, and each grabbed one of his arms and tugged. "Come on!"

"Hey, watch my ribs, please," he said as he stood up.

We pushed him through the crowd and up to the stage, Tom protesting the whole way while Seamus finished his "song."

"Okay, okay," he said. He got up on stage, looked at the choices and picked one. Jamie, Seamus and I walked back to our table.

Tom tapped the microphone, making a loud thumping sound, "Em, okay. I haven't done this before, so hopefully, I won't make a bloody fool of myself. Also, I've had a few pints. But, this is for myyyy girlfriend, Anna, hi love," he waved, "em, who thinks I am pretentious and em what's the word you always use?"

"Uppity!" I yelled.

"Yes, yes, uppity. Perhaps this song will prove I am *cool*," Tom slurred. I thought he was going to fall down for a second. He squinted at the screen, reached into his inside jacket pocket and donned his glasses. They *were* actually a little nerdy, completely making him un-cool.

And then the music started. The Screaming Trees. He grabbed the mic, leaving it on the stand, with both hands, closed his eyes and started. His voice was low and raspy and right on key. I was, as Jamie would say, gobsmacked. I wouldn't have thought he'd even know the song, let alone any of the lyrics. But, oh my God was it good. Every once in a while, he opened his eyes to look at the prompt.

He was mostly stiff except for a couple of hand gestures, but wow. Jamie, Seamus and I exchanged glances during the performance, eyebrows raised. In fact, the rest of the pub started to actually listen and groove to the music.

As he finished "I Nearly Lost You," he bowed, and then practically fell off the stage. Seamus ran up and helped him off. Everyone was clapping and saying how good he was as he worked his way back to the table. He flopped down in the chair.

Quickly, I got up from my chair and sat on his lap. I took off his glasses, folded them up and placed them on the table. I wrapped my arms around his neck and kissed his forehead. "That was fantastic, Tom!" I exclaimed. "How do you even know that song?"

Tom breathed out, "Just because I like classical music and prog rock does not mean I live under a rock. I told you I liked some alternative," he retorted, somewhat incoherently. He nudged me off him, saying I was too heavy. He really was drunk.

"Pretty good, mate." Seamus nodded.

I noticed some women looking over at Tom as if they wanted to eat him up.

Tom slurred, "Well, it was fffun. I think I'll order another beer." But as he attempted to finish the one he had, he just about missed his mouth. Then some woman walked casually passed us, dropped a folded napkin on the table in front of Tom, but kept walking.

He looked up at her, then down at the napkin, opened it up and started to read it, "Hi, sexy. Great performance. Call me." He attempted to stand.

"Where are you going, Tom?" I asked.

"I was going to explain to the girl that I have a girlfriend, but thank her for the compliment. I seem to be attracting the opposite gender tonight. Why is it right *after* I get a girlfriend, this happens?" He braced his hands on the back of the chair.

"Okay, Tom, sit back down and drink some water, then let's get you home," I suggested and yanked at his sleeve. He sat back down on the chair.

Seamus was amused, but changed the subject. I think he was slightly tired of the Tom Hall fan club.

"Hey, Tom, can you get us into one of the houses? I think I'd be willing to break out the Ouija Board again... in a haunted house. Wouldn't that be mental?" Seamus asked excitedly.

"Yeah, yeah, let's do it," Tom faltered as he stood up again and then sat right back down, "but maybe not tonight. I'm a little knackered," yawning.

"We don't have a Ouija Board in our purses, either," Jamie said, stating the obvious.

"I think I really better get Tom home," I urged, and with that, Seamus helped me get Tom up from the chair and out the door. I looked back at the table and saw Tom's glasses, so I retrieved them and put them in my backpack.

"He's a lightweight, Anna," Seamus observed.

"I don't think he drinks a whole lot," I agreed.

Tom, staggering outside with Seamus helping him, put up a hand and tried to hail a cab.

"Tom, no cabs are here, we've got to walk through the Square, okay?" Seamus coaxed.

"Right-o," Tom said as he found his feet and moved toward Clerkenwell Road. There, we found a cab. Before we got in, Seamus and Tom embraced goodbye and Tom kissed Jamie's hand.

"Still the gentleman, even drunk," Jamie said to Seamus. Seamus just shrugged.

"I'm not drunk," Tom slurred as he tried to find the door handle to the cab. I nudged him away and opened the door for him.

Tom flopped in the seat and I crawled in next to him. I gave the cab driver Tom's address, waved to Jamie and Seamus and off we went. Tom slouched, head on my shoulder.

After about a 30-minute ride, because of an accident on the way, we arrived at Tom's place. I woke him up and he immediately tried to pull out his wallet. I beat him to it and paid the driver. I got out, went around to the other side, opened the door and helped him out. "Thank you, Anna. You're wonderful," he said, quietly.

I grabbed his keys from his coat pocket, got in the elevator, and we went up to his flat. Tom was able to stand on his own, but wobbled a little on his feet. Déjà vu from last week, but without the fights, thank God.

I walked him to the bedroom, pulled his coat off, and guided him down as he collapsed onto the bed. I took his shoes and socks off. Then, I started to unbutton his shirt.

On his back, he started talking, "Anna, sometimes I black out. Like I don't know where I've been or what I've done. As if I'm dreaming or sleepwalking. Just sometimes. What does it mean?" He asked, sleepily.

"I don't know Tom, but right now you're drunk, so let's talk about it tomorrow."

"Okay, Anna," he said in a low, quiet voice. His eyes starting to close, he mumbled, "I love you, Anna." I stopped unbuttoning his shirt.

And then his breathing became much deeper and his head drooped to the left. I froze for a second, my breath catching in my throat. I sat on the edge of the bed with my eyes wide, watching him sleep in somewhat disbelief. Only one other person has said that to me, beyond my family. Graham. And he only said it because he was in trouble, big trouble, and wanted me on his side, completely manipulating me with his affections. With Tom, it was a totally different scenario. But, did I love him? So soon? And what about these blackouts, I mean, what is that about? Or, was all this just the alcohol talking? With my thoughts running on overdrive, I decided to get comfortable and surf the net. I needed a distraction, not wanting to over analyze anything he just said. Unfortunately, I had forgotten to put a change of clothes in my travel bag, so once again, I found myself in Tom's flat with nothing to change into. I grabbed a tee shirt from his dresser and pulled it on, breathing in his scent. Upon flipping on the computer, an article popped up about the Wainwright case.

It was dated today. I read… "turns out that Mr. Wainwright did indeed harm his son. There was never a case, trial or charges pressed. Being a wealthy family, they did not want to harm the family name, so they kept the abuse under wraps. The son came forward on social media after seeing that his father sustained the same injuries the boy endured from his father's hands. Through instant messaging, the boy told one of his Facebook friends that his father had dislocated his shoulder, broken his foot and harmed his knee on separate occasions. He confided in his friend that he thinks his father was a victim of the Vigilante. The boy almost bragged to his friend, sources say, that now his father is locally famous. The friend went to his own parents who contacted police. Wainwright denied these allegations. Did the Vigilante somehow know about this abuse? Was the Vigilante a friend or relative to the Wainwrights? Or, is this just a case of a boy wanting attention and fabricating the abuse to put his father in the limelight. Time will tell."

So much for distractions! My eyes were wide and I started to shiver. Another possible connection to the Vigilante. Christ this was insane! I wanted to talk to Tom, but I didn't want to while he was drunk. So, I pulled out my journal and wrote this down, too. Along with Tom's statement about his blackouts.

**

— *Sunday, September 14, 11:00 AM*

"To-om, Tom, wake up," I coaxed, pushing the hair out of his eyes. "Tom, come on, it's getting late."

His eyes fluttered open a few times, and then closed tightly as he rolled to his side, away from me.

"Come on Tom, let's get you up."

"Anna," he whispered, "please leave me be," and then he curled into a fetal position and put his arms around his head.

I pulled on his arms a little, but he wasn't budging.

"Headache?"

"Pounding."

"You don't really drink much, do you?"

"Clearly, no—not to that extreme."

"Why did you drink so much, then?"

In a muffled voice, because of his arms, he said, "I was having *fun*."

"Yeah, you and Seamus really seemed to hit it off."

"An unlikely pairing, but yes, I liked him, we even exchanged phone numbers and I think planned an outing, but Anna, please leave me alone and let me wallow in my misery," voice still muffled.

"Okay." I left the room to get some coffee brewing and make some oatmeal. About 20 minutes later, Tom staggered into the kitchen with his hair all messed up and his eyes half open. Even when he looked like shit, he looked good. I did notice that his black eye from last week was showing just a trace of purple and the cuts on his lip and cheek were barely noticeable.

"Well, hello," I said, eagerly drinking my coffee at the table.

"Hi," he mumbled as he dropped onto the chair.

"You want some coffee or tea?"

"Coffee, please," he whispered. He put his elbows on the table and rubbed his face, "I feel my head is going to explode."

"Sorry, sweetheart. You've got a massive hangover."

"Regrettably, I am aware."

I gave him his coffee with cream and sugar. "Thank you, love," he uttered quietly and then continued, trying to open his eyes wider. "You didn't have any odd experiences last night? No pain, right?"

"Right. So maybe I'm clear." I said in a monotone voice.

We sat in silence for a minute until I started.

"Um, Tom, last night, do you remember anything?"

He sat back in his chair and drank his coffee, "I think… oh my God. Did I sing?"

"Yes! You were great." I said a little too loudly, causing him to flinch.

He sighed, put his mug down and then covered his face with his hands. Separating two of his fingers allowing just one eye to peak through, he said, "I am mortified."

"Tom, believe me, you were fantastic. I mean, you slurred your words a bit and almost fell off the stage, but other than that… and geez, you sang a Screaming Trees song!" He slid his hands down to his mouth.

"And then a woman gave you her number."

Removing his hands from his face, he picked up his mug with both hands, drank a bit more and then asked, "Really? Was she cute? I can't remember."

I gave him half eyes and said, "How 'bout I go put on some Dead Kennedys and play it real loud?"

"Oh… God, no," gesturing 'surrender' with his hands.

I raised one eyebrow. "Um, you also said a few other things last night."

"Like?"

"You mentioned something about blacking out sometimes, not being able to remember where you were."

"I said that? It was probably the alcohol talking." But, he didn't elaborate any further.

"And also, I was checking my email on your computer and a story about the Wainwright case popped up."

"Yes, I started to read it, but didn't finish it. I meant to tell you about it. What did it say?"

"That his son claims he was abused by Wainwright in the same way he was assaulted."

"Which means…?"

"Right, which means it was probably the Vigilante."

"Hmm. Another connection to her, and yet you had no incidents last night."

"Or him."

"Oh, so now it's a him? What's changed your mind?"

I sighed, "Tom, I know this sounds crazy, but I have to ask. Are you, I mean, is it even possible, um, are you the Vigilante?" I faltered, sounding like a complete ass.

Tom started to laugh, "Ouch, my head. Em, no, Anna, I am not the Vigilante. What on earth would give you such a preposterous idea?" With his elbows on the table, he rested his chin on his clasped hands, giving me a disapproving look.

"Well, you clearly know how to fight even though you say you don't have training. You had that Wainwright article up. My episodes didn't start until I met you. You've had a traumatic childhood, which would explain the attacks—maybe you are exhibiting positive growth."

Tom, quite a bit cranky in his state exclaimed, "What the fuck is positive growth?" He looked at me bleary eyed, while I sat in silence, a little taken aback since he really doesn't cuss.

"Sorry. But love, you are grasping at straws."

"Yes, but…"

Tom took a deep breath, "Anna, I really am not in the mood or shape, obviously, to be put on trial today. Either you believe me or you don't. I'm going back to bed. But please, continue to make yourself at home," he offered, slightly sarcastically.

He stood up from his chair and staggered down the hall to his bedroom. I started to feel guilty for even suggesting this. When I said it out loud, it really sounded silly.

About fifteen minutes later, I walked down the hall to his room. He had changed into a T-shirt and pajama pants and he was lying on his side, facing the doorway.

"I'm sorry, Tom," I whispered.

Without opening his eyes, he quietly said, "It's okay. I think you're just trying to make sense of a nonsensical situation. I'm sorry I snapped at you."

I walked over to the other side of the bed and curled up next to him, my right arm around his waist.

Softly, he mused, "This is much better."

"Tom, you said something else last night."

"Mmm?"

"Do you remember?"

Tom rolled over to face me, wearing a very serious expression as he stared and paused. I imagine he was trying to muster up the strength to say it again, sober. "I love you, Anna," he professed, running his fingers through my hair. "You don't have to respond. I know it's only been less than a couple of weeks, but I've never said this to a girl nor have I ever felt like this before. For anyone."

CHAPTER 9

The stalker followed the woman, just like he was taught, in the shadows. Become a shadow. He knew her, at least a little. She had come on to him, pretty heavily. He didn't want anything to do with the filth and politely declined her advances. It would have been easy to go to bed with her and then do the deed, but he wouldn't have been a shadow. He'd get caught. So, he patiently watched and waited and then seized his opportunity. She walked alone, stupid girl, down the darkened street. Upon turning to walk toward her flat, instant panic ensued as the killer wrapped his arm around her neck and held her mouth closed with a gloved hand. She tried to scream, but only a muffled sound escaped. He turned her around so he could watch her face—he liked to watch. Her eyes opened wide in recognition of her assailant. He removed his hand, but quickly pressed his mouth to hers. He pushed his tongue into her mouth and his chest into her breasts, walking her backwards until she hit the stone wall near her flat. Her arms flailed, trying to claw at him, but it was pointless. He had her shoulders pinned hard against the wall. Had she had her wits about her, reacted a second earlier, she may have been able to bite his tongue and then scream and push him away, but it was too late. The stalker pulled back for a split second, cocked his head slightly, as if hearing what she wanted to do, bared his teeth and then sunk them into her lower lip. The woman panted, tried to scream as her eyes pulsed out of her head. Blood filled her mouth. The attacker pulled away and spit the piece of the shell-shocked woman's lip on the ground. The killer then placed one hand on her head, the other on her chin, and snapped her neck. Holding on, he delicately eased her down to the ground. Casually, but efficiently, he cleaned the area. No trace of his blood could be found. Pulling out a plastic bag, he placed the woman's lip inside and sealed it, pushing it down into his pea coat. He then used a rag he carried and a small bottle of alcohol to mop up any blood on the pavement. And then, he stood over the woman's body and spilled the alcohol on her face, swabbing it in and around her mouth. Once he was satisfied with his work, he stepped back and became, once again, just another shadow in the night.

— *Saturday, October 4*

"Anna, we're going to miss our flight. Come along, now."

"I know! I can't find my keys."

"If you kept your flat neat, you wouldn't be misplacing items all the time," Tom criticized.

I frowned, hands on my hips, "You better get used to it, buddy."

"Stop being such a child; here, here are your keys." Tom had found them under a pile of unopened mail and held them out for me.

I snatched them from his hand. Tom grimaced and huffed, obviously perturbed, "Okay, Anna, truce? I think getting ready for our trip on such short notice has been a little stressful, and we are taking it out on each other."

"Yeah, well if you stopped lambasting me for how I organize my things and my life, we wouldn't be arguing and *I* wouldn't be stressed."

Tom decided to ignore my petulance and sighed, "Okay. We have everything? Bags, keys, identification, passport?"

"Oh, shit!"

Tom held up his hand and went into the bedroom. I heard a drawer open, some shuffling, and then he appeared with my passport in hand.

"Thanks," I mumbled.

"Okay, the cab is waiting," Tom urged, but trying to be patient.

We lumbered down the three long flights with my bags in tow. Even though I had packed lightly, the bags were still somehow unwieldy. We were going to visit my parents for just a week since I had to work and Tom had to get back. With Halloween approaching, October is the busiest time of year for the tours. In fact, he has to work a couple extra weekdays as well as more weekends.

We crawled into the cab after my bags were stowed in the trunk next to Tom's.

Tom looked over at me and smiled, trying to change the mood, squeezing my knee, "Are you excited?"

"Yeah, I mean, I haven't seen my parents since I moved here. And, I'm anxious about them meeting you."

"You prompted them, I assume?"

"Yes, of course. I told them I had a boyfriend, but they don't know I'm moving in with you. I mean it's only been one month, right?"

"There's no time restriction on when you fall in love with someone," he said, his eyes somewhat pleading.

I gave him a half smile, but said nothing. He nodded, as if agreeing with his own sentiment, and closed his eyes until we got to the airport, his hand remaining on my knee.

***

The flight was smooth and uneventful, giving me plenty of time to reflect on the last couple of weeks leading up to this point. Outside work, Tom and I were spending most of our time together. Except for Thursday nights after his tour, which, much to Jamie's and my bewilderment, Tom and his new pal Seamus would spend together. In fact, one evening at dinner together, we asked if we could tag along with them on a future Thursday night. Tom looked at Seamus, Seamus looked at Tom, then they looked at us. Tom shifted in his chair, not wanting to offend and waivered, "Em, well, even though we enjoy your company, Seamus and I are building a comradery, which would be hard with, em, you two lovely ladies present." And I remember Seamus rolling his eyes and saying, "In other words, Fuck no! A bloke's gotta spend time with his mate." And he patted Tom's back. Jamie and I, of course, found this rather amusing. They were such complete opposites. But then again, so were Tom and I.

I wanted Tom to meet my parents. I had been planning a trip back around this time before I met Tom, and knew the timing was bad with his work, Halloween coming up and all, but when I mentioned it, he became really excited about the prospect and said he could work it out. I tried not to let him pay for the tickets, but he insisted. I agreed only if we flew economy. So, coming home to my flat the other day, I found two round trip e-tickets to BWI sitting on the kitchen counter.

Although I was a little nervous about telling my parents about my plan to move into his flat, I wanted to prove to them that I had matured and met someone who wasn't a psychopath, liar, cheat, or asshole. Tom was so different from the rest. I thought my parents were really going to like him. How could they not? I heard a thump, startling me from my thoughts. Tom's hardback book had fallen on the floor. His head was tilted to the aisle side of the plane and he was fast asleep. I picked up the book and placed it in the pocket of the seat in front of me. I then gently shifted his head so it was leaning toward me. He awoke briefly, looked at me, and then slumped down so his head rested on my shoulder. Although I hadn't told him yet, I knew I was in love with him.

Listening to his even breathing, I starting thinking again. Nothing more had happened with my odd premonitions. We were still, however, a bit on edge about the recent death of a professional escort. Two days after our outing with Jamie and Seamus, Kitty Myers, the same woman who flirted with Tom at the tour, turned up dead in an alleyway, not too far from the visitor center. I hadn't had any premonitions about it at all, which I guess was good, but it didn't fit Tom's theory that when I come in contact with someone who's about to be harmed, I get a premonition.

Speculation on the news went rampant about the sixth murder of a prostitute in the last two months. Social media was abuzz saying that the Vigilante had changed course and started to kill, and not just the "bad guys," but anyone deemed immoral. Champions of the Vigilante would say that it was someone else, the anti-Vigilante or something stupid like that. There was even a comic in the paper showing two black masked people fighting it out in a super hero versus villain kind of thing. It was all overblown, tabloidal and ridiculous. I, however, started to chalk up my experience to be something maybe out of the ordinary, but every time I said my original theory out loud, it sounded more and more preposterous. The more distance you have from a situation, the easier it is to rationalize it, and that's what I was doing. But I didn't care. I wanted to enjoy my life.

When they found Kitty the morning after her death, her head was cocked at an odd angle. On the Internet, there was a picture of her... dead. The person who found her actually took the shot and posted it before the police could get to her. And Tom's reaction?

"Oh my God!" I heard from his home office.

"What's wrong, sweetie?" I said after I came in the room, placing my hand on Tom's back and looking over his shoulder. He looked up at me and the expression on his face was of shear horror. He pushed the seat back, almost running over my foot, stood up and started pacing; he couldn't contain himself. I sat down at the desk and read the article. The gist of it was that Kitty Myers, an "escort," was found by a passerby in the early hours of the morning. There was a picture showing her head twisted, indicating her neck had been snapped, as her dead eyes stared into the camera. Her lower lip looked like it had been torn off. I quickly looked away, trying not to gag.

"What sick FUCK would do such a thing?" Tom yelled. I wasn't sure if he was talking about the murderer, the person who took the picture, or both.

Tom was obviously shaken. I mean, I was too, but Tom's reaction was a lot more visceral.

"I've got to get some air," he announced, storming out of the room and out of the flat. After I heard the door slam shut, I scooted back, still in a bit of shock, and looked out the window. The rain was coming down rather hard.

I called Jamie and told her to look at the news report. She freaked out a bit, too, worried that the killer could have been right near us that night. She asked if Tom had seen it, and when I told her how he reacted, she didn't seem all that surprised, saying that everyone reacts differently to shit. Jamie and I talked for a while until I heard the door open.

Coming out of the guest room, I found Tom leaning his back against the inside of the front door. His face was flushed, his eyes were red-rimmed, he was wet and he was out of breath.

"Sweetheart, are you okay?" I asked as I approached him.

He shook his head and looked down at his feet; drips from his wet hair hitting the floor. "I don't know… I don't know what came over me." He looked back up at me with sadness in his eyes. "Guilt, I suspect, or the fact that I was in contact with the young woman and then I see her dead."

My ears pricked up a little as I went to get him a towel.

He thanked me and started to dry his hair. Stooping down, he sopped up the water on the floor with the towel and then draped it over his shoulder. He tried slicking back his hair, darkened from the rain, but much of it fell immediately back into his face. He finished undressing, sans his jeans, kicked off his shoes and, holding onto the doorframe, took off his socks.

"I get it, Tom. I feel the same way, seeing her like that, but guilt?"

"Yes, guilt. It's not rational, Anna. Maybe if I had been politer to her or less polite or, I don't know."

"Seriously, Tom? You think you had any control over what happened to her that evening? Maybe you should have taken her up on her offer. That would have prevented her murder, right?"

Tom's jaw twitched as it often did when I said something sarcastic or insensitive.

I quickly apologized and tried to soothe him saying that this had nothing to do with him and he shouldn't feel guilty about any of this. I knew this stemmed from what happened to his sister. After a bit, I was able to pull him away from the front door and to the sofa, where I wrapped the paisley throw around him and then held him, for a long time.

I fell asleep thinking about this and woke up when we were descending into New York in the evening. We hopped on a commuter plane destined for Maryland, landing at BWI around 8:30 PM. We were both tired, despite my long nap, as it was really 1:30 AM in London. The long wait through customs didn't help, either.

"I can barely keep my eyes open," Tom complained while leaning on a column outside the airport.

"I thought you slept on the plane. I sure did."

"Em, I did for maybe the first hour or so, but while you were sleeping, I had the oh so fortunate experience of having a bloody child behind me constantly poking the telly buttons. I never should have listened to you about flying economy. I am changing our tickets to first class for the flight back."

"It's like triple the price!"

"And?" he stated rather meanly, so I left it alone. It's his money, so I guess he can do what he wants with it.

We climbed into the shuttle to take us to my parent's house in Eastport. They had offered to pick us up, but I didn't want to trouble them. On the half hour car ride to the house, I warned Tom about my mother. She's nice, but incredibly nosey and will hold grudges long after you've forgotten what they were ever about. I explained how she will remember something you did when you were five and then throw it back in your face twenty years later. Although he was only half listening, Tom assured me he would be on his best behavior as his eyes fluttered closed.

"Oh, and one more thing; she will bombard you with questions, so be prepared."

I guess I startled him awake, but he patted my hand reassuringly and remained quiet the rest of the way.

We arrived at their house around 11:00 PM, 4:00 AM London time. My parents, Richard and Jenny, live in an older restored home in Eastport, which is right across a small drawbridge connecting to downtown Annapolis. They bought the house while I was in college.

When the shuttle pulled up, my mother, wearing a pink sweater and jeans, came running out of the house. She saw me and almost knocked me down with the hug she gave me, "Oh, Anna, I've missed you so much!" She planted a number of kisses on my face. Tom was busy paying the driver and handling the bags. She walked over to him and said, "And you must be Tom," her suspicious tone angering me.

"Yes, I am very pleased to meet you," Tom answered as he took my mother's hand and kissed it.

She raised one eyebrow and then shrugged.

As we all walked in the house, their dog Barley jumped on Tom and me. My dad was walking downstairs when he saw us. "Anna!" and he gave me a very fatherly hug.

"Um, Dad, this is Tom."

"Very pleased to make your acquaintance, sir," Tom said, shaking my father's hand and bowing his head.

"So formal," my mom said out loud.

"Em, yes, we Brits tend to be that way. I can give you a high five if you'd rather."

"I like it," my dad said. "Maybe some of your manners will rub off on Anna. Does she still cuss a lot?"

"Incessantly," Tom confirmed.

I breathed outward, heavily, and rolled my eyes. "Great."

"Well, you two must be tired, it's what, 2:00 in the morning for you?"

"4:00," both Tom and I said in unison.

"Well, let's get you settled. Um, I hope you two were not expecting to share a room." My mom stated, a little pointedly.

"Em, no Mrs. Pearson, separate is just fine. We are in your house and want you to feel comfortable." Tom reasoned. Geez, we didn't even discuss this.

I looked at my mom with an "are you serious," expression. She just turned away and ignored me, smiling at Tom.

We walked up the beautiful staircase featuring an ornate banister that Dad had rescued from its peeling beige paint to its original oak finish. Off to the left was one guest bedroom to which my mother showed Tom to.

"Thank you, Mrs. Pearson."

"Please call me Jenny. Do you need anything else? I have towels in the bathroom which is right across the hall from you."

"No, thank you, I am fine. Good night, Mrs... Jenny."

My mom smiled at Tom and closed the door to his room.

"What's the deal? I'm 28 years old and he's my boyfriend." I challenged as we traipsed two doors down the hallway to the office that also served as a guest room.

"Sorry. My house, my rules." Then as usual when she wants to close the subject, she changed tack.

"He's quite formal. I wouldn't have expected you to go for his type, based on your previous boyfriends. But, he is gorgeous. My God, those eyes! It's hard to look away they're so captivating. Are you sure he isn't a vampire? He does kind of have fangs and you know, vampires can glamour you. Maybe that's how he piqued your interest."

"Very funny, Mom. You've been watching too much True Blood."

"So, how serious are you two?"

"Very," I answered while pulling a nightshirt out of my suitcase.

"Care to elaborate?"

I sighed. "I'm moving in with him. I mean, we practically have been living together for the past three weeks anyway."

"Oh, Anna!" Her shoulders sagged so much it looked like her bones had vanished.

I predicted a long, drawn out reprimand, so I quickly said, "Look, can we please talk about this later? I am so tired I can hardly see straight and I might say something even more incriminating."

My mother's forehead creased, spreading four horizontal lines across it. She was about to say something further, but held her tongue. "Okay. Yes, we'll talk about this tomorrow. But, regardless, I am glad you are happy. Good night, sweetheart."

And after that, I pulled my Franz Ferdinand long T-shirt on and walked down the hall to Tom's room. I opened the door to find him fast asleep on the bed, on top of the quilt, jacket and shoes still on. I took off his shoes and tried to get his coat off. He sat up, still mostly asleep, let me take it off, and then he lay back down. I crawled into bed next to him, my overtired eyes shutting heavily.

***

— *Sunday, October 5*

I awoke to a large tongue licking my face.

"Barley, stop," I yelled, pushing him away. I looked over at Tom, who was still asleep, but not for long since Barley pounced on his chest, instantly waking him up with a distinct "oomph." Barley licked his face until Tom rolled over for cover.

"Get down, boy." Tom snapped. Barley obliged and left the room.

"What time is it?" Tom asked in a muffled voice, still hiding his face.

"Um, around 9:00 AM."

He turned his head toward me, "I thought we weren't sharing a room."

"I broke the rules."

"Look, if your mother is uncomfortable with us sharing a room, we should be respectful of that."

"We're adults, Tom, so shouldn't she be respectful of that? Besides, we are almost living together."

"I realize that, but I still think we should respect your mother's wishes. And aside from that, I would very much like to give your parents a good impression of me. Didn't you tell me your mother can hold a grudge forever?"

I pursed my lips and ignored his question, getting out of bed. I assumed he hadn't heard anything I said on the shuttle bus.

***

"So, Tom, we hear you are a ghost tour guide. Do you do that full time?" asked my mom over breakfast. She served tea, bagels, and was thoughtful enough to buy vegan cream cheese for me. At least she's respectful of my diet.

"No, I just work some weekends, not all. The schedule really varies, but around Halloween I work a bit more."

My mom eyed Tom.

I looked up at the ceiling, "I know what you're thinking, Mom. He has an inheritance, so he doesn't have to work full time, okay?"

Tom gave me a sideways glance, obviously a little irritated.

"I wasn't thinking anything, Anna, I was just making conversation," and then she changed the subject. Another tactic she uses when she knows she is in the wrong. "So, we have a nice ghost tour here. I thought you might like to be a spectator instead of the leader."

"That would be lovely, Jenny," Tom replied, sincerely.

"Great, I assumed it would be okay so I already set it up for tonight."

Barley went over to Tom and put his chin on his lap.

"Don't feed him at the table. We're trying to train him not to beg," warned my dad.

"He's 8, Richard. I don't think he's going to change," Mom said.

Barley kept his chin on Tom's lap, not moving, so Tom reached down and scratched behind his ears.

"So, Anna told me you two were moving in together. Don't you think that's a little premature? I mean, you hardly know each other," Mom blurted out.

"Mom!"

She ignored me. "Really, how long have you two known each other?"

"Em, about a month," Tom answered, shifting nervously in his chair.

"Hmmm... a month?" my mom pressed. Dad just sat there reading his newspaper, pretending not to pay attention.

Tom sat up a little straighter. "I assure you, Jenny, we have spent a lot of time getting to know each other. I can unequivocally say that I love your daughter and want to spend as much time with her as possible, and that would be made easier by sharing a residence," Tom reasoned as he took my hand. "And, of course, there would be a cost savings for Anna. London can be quite expensive."

I felt red heat creeping up my neck and onto my cheeks. I just wanted to bury my head.

My mom bounced her head back and forth, contemplating what she just heard, "Well, no offense, Tom, but I'm a little weary of Anna's choice in men. We've lived through a couple of truly awful boyfriends. Her track record isn't so hot. I will say that you seem, well, different from the others." I groaned. Did they forget I was sitting at the table with them?

Tom looked curiously over at me. I was so embarrassed; I started to regret bringing Tom home.

"So Tom, what are your parents like?" My mom began.

Oh no.

Tom, in mid-chew, grimaced a little, and then swallowed hard. "Em, my mother passed on when I was a young boy and my father lives outside of London proper."

"Are you and your father close?"

God, my mom and her 20 fucking questions.

"Em, no."

My mom started to ask why, and I tried to come to Tom's rescue, "Mom, just leave it alone. He's just not close with his dad, okay?"

My mom shrugged, innocently, mildly offended.

Finally, my dad put down his newspaper and started to ask me about work and the friends I've made—the normal stuff a parent should ask when a guest is in the house. My mother remained quiet, loudly sipping her tea.

***

Later that day, Tom and I bugged out of the house, walked over the Eastport bridge into Annapolis, and browsed around downtown. We spent most of our time in the Annapolis Bookstore on Maryland Avenue, a historic house-turned-shop. This was one of my favorite places and Tom seemed to thoroughly enjoy poking around in it. The bookstore mainly carried used books, often in piles on the ground, on top of trunks, or in makeshift bookshelves in between exposed brick columns. My favorite room was down a spiral staircase, through a main room and then down a couple of brick steps. It was strewn with books, of course, but also old bottles, labelled as "Petrified Unicorn Tears," "Dried Gillyweed," and "Wool of Bat." Exposed wooden beams lined the ceilings; rustic lamps, old suitcases, and a couple of skulls in niches completed the décor. I always got a chill in this particular room; but it never scared me, it only intrigued me. I've always imagined benevolent ghosts must live here.

As if echoing my very thoughts, Tom surmised, "This room has got to be haunted," as he pulled a few mystery books from the shelf.

When we were ready to leave, Tom bought an armful of paperbacks on the ghosts of Annapolis and some other historical books, and we headed out.

We continued around State Circle, past the State House, and down a very clean alley to Main Street. We looked around for some souvenirs for Jamie and Seamus at Re:Source, a store where all the merchandise was made from recycled materials. I snagged a pair of distressed bottle cap earrings with a Raven Beer label featuring Edgar Allan Poe for Jamie and a wallet made out of used tires for Seamus.

When we came out of the store, I heard my name being called. Like Pavlov's dog, my palms became sweaty and my heart rate increased, a conditioned response to a voice I hadn't heard in ten years. I whipped my head around and saw Graham. He looked older, more haggard, especially for 28. His Mohawk was gone, and in its place was non-descript brown hair clipped short. He wore jeans and a polo-style shirt, and was just slightly heavier than in high school, but other than that, he looked about the same. I felt a little self-conscious, as I was wearing a Damned shirt from a concert we saw together in high school.

"Um, Graham, hi."

"Hi, Anna. You look great." He put his hands in the pockets of his brown bomber jacket.

"Thanks… um, you look good… um, different."

"Yeah, well, jail will do that to you. I got out about four months ago."

I had forgotten about Tom for a minute, came out of my daze, and introduced them, "Oh, um, Tom, this is Graham."

Tom looked him straight in the eye, extended his hand and just said "Graham," as they shook hands, firmly.

There was an awkward pause and then Tom graciously excused himself and went back into the store we had just left.

"So, ah, are you still in Annapolis?" He asked.

"Um, no, I live in London, now. We're just visiting my parents."

"London. I thought I heard an accent. So, are you two, um."

"Yeah, we are."

"He seems a little clean cut for you."

I just shrugged.

Graham looked down at his feet for a bit. Breaking the awkward silence, he looked up at me and said, "Look, Anna, I wanted to contact you for so long. While I was locked up, I wrote and rewrote letters to you, but just couldn't send them, I don't know why. I know I hurt you, really hurt you and I just wanted to apologize. You didn't deserve any of it."

I saw Tom in the window, casually looking out.

"Yeah, well, it took me a long time to get over you," I said, making eye contact with him, but then I quickly looked away.

"Yeah, well, um, I'm sure you're busy, but, I don't know, would you want to get a drink or something. I mean, you could bring your boyfriend."

I sighed and said, "I don't think so Graham. I'm glad you're getting your life back together and all, but we went through too much shit, it was a long time ago, and really, I don't have much interest in reminiscing about our past."

"Yeah, sure, I totally get it. Well, your friend is coming back out, so, well, it was great seeing you." And he gave me a tentative hug, nodded at Tom, and walked on with his head down.

"Alright, love?" Tom put his hand on my back.

"Yeah, it's just weird seeing him after all this time. I just had a visceral reaction. Don't be jealous, okay."

"I'm not jealous, love, just cautious. So, he was in jail? What did he do?"

"Geez, I mean, what didn't he do. He was into drugs, he dealt drugs and then he was arrested for a hate crime. I look back at how I was when I was with him, seeing how insecure I was, how I would do anything for him, believe anything he said, even though I knew he was all wrong for me. I thought I was so in love with him."

We started walking down Main Street toward the city dock; Tom listening patiently as I continued.

"So, one night, Graham calls and asks me to meet him at the mall. I told my parents I was going shopping with a friend since they always gave me grief about seeing Graham. When I got there, he was obviously high, but as usual, I ignored it. Anyway, he had a pool cue in his hand, which I thought was odd, so I asked him about it. He said that it was for self-defense and I'll see why. Even though the hairs on my neck stood up when he said this, I still remained, hanging out in front of the mall, waiting with him for whatever. After about a half hour, a couple of Hispanic guys came out of the mall, and that's when Graham struck. He hit the one guy really hard in the head with the pool cue, knocking him cold, and then hit the other guy a few times until he fell. I remember screaming at him and asking what the hell he was doing, but he just said that these two guys "disrespected" him earlier and needed to be taught a lesson. Well, I guess someone witnessed the altercation because a few minutes later, we heard sirens. Graham was too high to run away, I guess, but did tell me to tell the cops that the guys attacked him first. I couldn't believe what I was hearing and finally, I came to my senses after a year of shit. So, I told him that I wouldn't do that, that I couldn't believe he just maimed two guys for no reason, and that I wasn't going to lie. Well, he got in my face calling me a fucking cunt, that I was useless, that he never loved me, and so on. Then he pushed me to the ground and kicked me."

"Pardon?" Tom looked like he was about to run back and kick the shit out of him.

I quickly went on, "Luckily, it wasn't that hard and didn't cause any real damage, but mentally, it killed me. By then, the police were there. They pulled Graham away from me and hauled him off in the police cruiser. Long story short, they asked me some questions, and I told them the truth. After a long while and a trial with me as a witness, he went to jail."

"And he got out four months ago."

"Yeah," I said in a weak voice as we approached the dock, finding a bench in front of two sleeping Mallard ducks.

"And didn't you move to London four months ago?"

I shot him a look. Crap.

"I didn't just move to London to get away from him. I mean, maybe that was the catalyst, but I really wanted to get out of this area. Just like you, get away and maybe reinvent part of myself. I wanted to explore new things, become an adult. And, yeah, escape from my ghosts."

"Yes, the ghosts. Well, I'm glad you didn't just move out of state," he said as he put his arm around my shoulders and looked at the ducks who had started mildly quacking and wandering around.

"Me too. And really, I'm kind of happy I saw him. I wasn't scared at all. I mean, I didn't think he was going to hurt me. He just looked so pathetic. Anyway, seeing him like that and hearing him apologize kind of just shut that door the rest of the way for me. And besides, I have you."

"Yes, you do."

***

I told Tom not to mention our encounter with Graham. My parents and I really had a tough year when I was with him and I didn't want to dredge anything up.

We arrived back at their house around dinner time. My mom made a rice and tofu dish, mainly for my benefit since my parents aren't vegans. My mother usually complains about my protein intake—she really has no clue about nutrition—but she didn't go there this time.

We were able to relax for a small amount of time before heading back out to the ghost tour. My dad and Tom were chatting a bit on the screened-in porch, sipping some port Tom had picked up in town. It was a beautiful October evening. The smell of freshly fallen leaves and burning wood reminded me of Halloween.

***

Tom, my parents, and I walked across the Eastport Bridge, up to the top of Main Street, in front of the Maryland Inn. The guide, dressed in some Colonial regalia, handed us all light sticks. He was about as opposite from Tom as you could get. Older, not all that fit, and a little odd. He began his tale:

"Okay, ladies and gents, we start our tour with the story about a woman who," the tour guide paused and then continued in an affected tone, "haunts this hotel, hahahaha."

And so, he went on, in his weird way, continually dropping his voice to sound 'scary.' I had heard this story a number of times. In fact, I had recounted it to Tom earlier that day. Without the theatrics, it's about a woman who jumped out the top story window because after years at sea with the Navy, her long lost love was run over by a carriage right in front of the Inn. Apparently, the ghost of the would-be-bride has been seen reenacting the jump. Every time I walked by here, I always looked up at the window, but I've never seen the ghost. During the tale, I looked up at Tom, who seemed a bit amused by the guide's antics. Tom tried to stifle a laugh when the guide pantomimed the jump. The poor man's knees buckled upon landing. He panted as he stood back up, huffing and puffing. Regardless, the guide spoke very clearly and was entertaining.

We walked down the old sidewalks, Tom tripping but catching himself more than once on the uneven bricks raised up by tree roots.

At the cemetery on Church circle, the tour guide told the tale of a grave digger nicknamed Joe Morgue, whose ghost is said to grab people's ankles as they walk by. No ankles were grabbed, but the eeriness of the light cast around the raised graves added to the atmosphere. I huddled closer to Tom who put his arm around me.

We toured a few more haunts, finally ending up at the Brice House, touted as the most haunted house in Annapolis. Looming above us, the eerie brick colonial gave me chills. Maybe it was the lighting, the dark windows, or just the knowledge that it was haunted, but the sense of foreboding couldn't be denied. The guide wove the story about the Brice family's history as I stared up at the house on the quiet street.

> "Okay folks. Here we are at Colonel James Brice's house. Not only a Colonel in the Revolutionary War, Brice also served as mayor of Annapolis and even Governor of the great state of Maryland. The Colonel was said to be murdered by one of his servants, but this is speculation. However, the ghost of both James and his servant have been seen walking the halls. Other ghosts have been spotted lurking these hallways as well. In 1998, hoodoo spiritual talismans and other offerings were found during renovations, but the most chilling event happened when, during further renovations, the skeleton of a girl was found in a closet that had been walled off with bricks. Get it, skeleton in the closet?! But seriously, they think the girl was probably mentally challenged and maybe had even been abused. As a possible member of the Brice family, they probably kept her in the house as to not damage the family name. After the girl died, we can speculate that she was walled up here to conceal her existence…

And the guide continued in that same goofy affected voice, "and many, have heard cries and wails coming from the house, hahahaha." He went on a bit more about other sightings, all with gestures and changes in voice.

While the story continued, Tom, who had been holding my hand, dropped it and put both palms to his eyes, "Excuse me, Anna." I watched while he extradited himself from the crowd.

He approached the low brick wall in front of the house and laid both hands on it. He looked aggrieved as I saw him clutching the top of the short wall. No one else, including my parents, seemed to notice the odd behavior; they were all rapt in the story.

I nonchalantly walked over and put my hand on his back.

"Tom? Honey, are you okay?"

Both hands still on the brick wall, he turned his head and stared at me. His eyes glistened from the streetlamp as he looked straight through me. He then slowly looked up to one of the darkened windows of the house, his eyes completely fixated, glued to that window. Following his gaze took me to a window left of center on the upper floor. I focused on the window and then froze when I thought I saw a black shape. Squinting, I realized it was probably just a lamp or a part of a curtain. I then looked back at Tom. His eyes widened and his mouth dropped open as he started to shiver. I dared myself to look back at the window, hoping Tom was just messing with me. But then, I saw it. It was no lamp. A foreboding silhouette of a human figure started to move, swaying back and forth until it raised its arms. My heart pounded, pounded so loudly it was deafening. I squeezed my eyes shut and upon reopening them, the shadow was gone. A wave of nausea rolled through my head and stomach as the fear crept through every pore of my body.

Shaking. "T..Tom, did you see that?"

Still staring at the window and clutching the brick, he whispered something inaudible.

"Tom?" I tugged on his arm, but it was stone stiff.

And after about ten more seconds, he stood erect, looking rather confused.

"Tom, are you okay?" I asked. My voice sounded like a scared mouse.

"I," he started then took a breath. He wiped his eyes with one hand and sniffed, "I don't know."

"Did you see that figure? In the window? Oh my God, Tom." Squeaking my words, I looped both of my arms through his left arm and hugged it close.

"Yes, I believe I… saw something, but don't know what. My mind, it's all foggy." He lightly touched his temple.

"Can we get out of here?" I stared back up at the window, but only saw darkness.

Tom gently pulled his arm free from my grip, put his face in both hands, and slid them down to his mouth, steepling his fingers, then dropping his hands back down. "I think I just had one of my uncanny feelings. This…" He hesitated, then continued, "It sometimes occurs at places where horrible violence has occurred."

Dammit. I thought we were in the clear. "Let's get back to the crowd and talk about this later. I think the tour is almost done." I really just wanted to leave. My legs were so wobbly that I had to hold onto Tom's shoulder to keep steady.

We blended back into the crowd and found my parents, who hadn't noticed us gone. I took a deep breath, dropping my hand from Tom's shoulder. I wanted to scream, but stifled it.

Tom took my hand and started to clutch it too tightly. I looked up at him and saw he had a vacant look, staring off into space.

"Tom, you're hurting my hand." I whispered loudly.

He snapped out of his daze and immediately loosened his grip, "Sorry, love." He smiled quickly and brought my hand to his mouth, kissed the back of it, and then hugged it into his chest before he let go.

The tour guide gave some final thoughts and asked for tips. Tom walked over and handed him a twenty. My dad handed him some cash as well before we started back to their house. Pausing on the Eastport Bridge to look at the boats, I focused on their small green, blue, and white lights all reflecting beautifully on the water while the sounds of halyards slapped against masts and echoed in the wind. Tom rested his forearms on the railing as he peered over the edge.

"Well, what did you think?" My father asked Tom.

Tom's voice, trying to remain steady, answered, "Very well done. I especially enjoyed walking around Annapolis in the evening. It's really a lovely town." Tom replied, still looking over the water.

Trying to keep my mind off what happened at the Brice House, I joined the conversation. "This guide was good, but goofy. Definitely entertaining, but Tom is tons better, and not hokey at all." I bragged, placing my hand on his arm.

Tom half smiled and thanked me, but remained humble in his lack of a response.

"Well, maybe you can tell us a ghost story later." My mom suggested.

Tom nodded and told her "of course," then turned away from the water to face the downward incline of the bridge.

After we arrived back at the house, Tom dismissed himself once he thanked my parents and went up to bed. I followed a minute later, explaining that the jet lag was really starting to get to us. This was honest, but my true purpose was to speak with Tom in private.

I changed in my room and then walked down the hall in my flannels to his door and knocked lightly, but he didn't answer. I listened for a second more and then decided to go to bed. He probably wanted to be alone.

***

— *Monday, October 6, 12:22 AM*

I awoke gasping and sucking in air as if I had broken the surface of the ocean after being under for way too long. A bass drum pounded in my head. I massaged my face as best I could and then curled back up, placing a pillow over my head as I tried to sleep.

— *4:45 AM*

I awoke again in a cold sweat, but at least this time I had no headache. I grabbed my journal and wrote down the approximate time of my headache, even though I didn't think it meant anything, and also about Tom's reaction at the tour. Cringing, I described the silhouette in the window. Even though I only caught a glimpse of whatever "it" was, I felt as though a foreboding and sinister, churning, blackened fog would engulf me, squeeze me, and then swallow me up. I started to tremble. Sitting on the bed, alone, in the wee hours of the morning, I started to freak out, so I quickly flung my legs over the bed and scampered down to Tom's room. His door was ajar, so I opened it further. I went over to the bed and sat next to him, his back to me. My nostrils flared as I thought I detected cigarette smoke. Strange. I opened the blinds to cast a little bit of light into the room from the outside streetlamp, revealing a fully dressed Tom. I went back over to him and brushed the hair away from his eyes, the strands sticking to his damp forehead. My parents kept the house so warm that he had to be really hot in his coat. I gently rolled him over to his back and then started to pull the lapels apart from his unbuttoned coat. Reaching inside one sleeve to try and ease it off his arm, I brushed his right side with my left hand and felt something wet and sticky. It was still too dark in the room for me to see what it was, so I sniffed my fingers. My nerves went on overdrive as I gasped. A sickly metallic odor curdled in my stomach. Recoiling from the horribly familiar smell, I clumsily felt for and clicked on the switch of the bedside light, illuminating Tom's body. He was bleeding through his ripped shirt on his right side. Oh God, Oh God.

"Tom? Tom, wake up!" I was panicking and I started to shake him.

He took his right hand and grabbed mine. Startled, he popped his eyes open. "Anna, what is it?" He tried to sit up. "Oh. Wow. Ouch." He reached over and touched his side where the blood had pooled. He winced a bit and looked at the blood on his fingers," How did this happen?"

I scrambled to the bathroom to get some supplies: wet washcloth, rubbing alcohol, Neosporin and different sorts of bandages. I didn't know how deep it was. When I came back in, Tom had taken his coat and shirt off and was gently touching his wound.

"Stop touching it and let me clean it up." He flinched as I started to dab the washcloth around the cut, cleaning it the best I could. I then put some pressure on it, making Tom suck air through his teeth.

"It doesn't look very deep. I don't think this warrants a trip to the hospital. Okay, get ready… again," I said with an edge. I put the alcohol on the other corner of the washcloth and dabbed it on him.

"Mother fuck!" He jerked back.

"Shut up, you'll wake my parents."

"Then stop torturing me with your bloody first aid," he said grumpily.

Ignoring him, I kept the pressure on until the bleeding stopped and then stuck the square bandage to his side, covering the four-inch gash. I grabbed his shirt and washed the blood out with cold water in the bathroom sink and then hung it in the tub to dry. It was a fruitless effort as it was irreparable. When I came back in the room, he was sitting up, staring off into space. I placed both my hands on his knees and got right in his face.

"Yes?" He sharply spoke.

In an angry whisper, I said, "Is that all you have to say is, 'yes'? Tom, I come in here, your clothes and coat are on. You reek of cigarettes, and you have a large slash on your side. So, what the hell? What are you keeping from me?" I stood back up, pushing off his knees.

"Anna, I am not keeping anything from you. I don't know where I got this. I… I remember getting changed and getting into bed. Next thing I know I am being shaken awake by Nurse Ratchet."

"Should I have let you bleed to death? Or stain my parent's sheets? How would I explain that? But, more importantly, how can you not know what happened? And… and I thought you didn't smoke."

"I… don't." He hissed through gritted teeth. He stood up abruptly and then looked down at me.

I put my hand on his chest, keeping him at bay. "Alright Tom. It's 5:00 AM and I'm going back to bed. You sleep on it and let me know later if you want to tell me what's going on or not." I started to leave but he grabbed my arm and pulled me back with a bit too much force. Realizing what he did, he let go immediately, putting his hands up.

"Sorry. Look, I am telling you the truth. I don't smoke, I do not remember leaving this house and I certainly don't know why I am clothed and have an injury." His voice started to tremble a little and I could tell he was fighting back tears.

I sighed, softening a bit, "Okay, okay. Let's figure this out." We both sat back down on the bed, "You came upstairs as soon as we got back, right?"

"Right, and I brushed my teeth, got changed into my night clothes and got into bed. I read for a little until I started to fall asleep, and that's all I remember."

"Did you dream?"

"If I did, I cannot recall; it's buried in the recesses of my mind."

"Maybe you were sleepwalking. Maybe you wandered outside and scratched yourself on a fence or something."

"I suppose, Anna." He said, dourly.

"When we get back to London, I think maybe you should see someone or at least talk to Holly. You told me there were times when you couldn't remember things, that you had blackouts. But you were drunk when you told me and then you denied it in the morning. And last night at the Brice House, we both saw that figure in the window, which was freaky enough, but then it looked like you weren't, um, weren't quite all there."

Tom remained silent, chewing on his lower lip.

I continued, "Was that one of the blackouts you were talking about? Like back in London, in Berkley Square that night?"

He slowly nodded his head, "I'm sorry. I haven't been completely honest with you, nor myself for that matter. I find it hard to describe. Something just fogs over in my head, and I feel like a force has taken grasp of my mind—squeezing it—and I don't have the strength to break free. It eventually lets go, but then I can't remember a thing."

"And it only happens at tours, right?"

"Well, that feeling. But then, sometimes I find myself in, ah, odd circumstances. Like, now, being in my clothes when I clearly have changed."

"Tom, something very strange is going on between you and me. I don't know if there is a connection with my odd pains and your blackouts or not, but something is going on and we need to fix it. Especially if you're sleepwalking, I mean, you could walk right in the middle of the street and get hit by a car!"

"Okay." He sniffed, furrowing his brow, still distant.

Bending over, he took off his shoes and socks. The eyes of the happy face were peering up at me along with the newly bandaged wound right next door. He lay back down after taking off his jeans. I turned off the light and crawled next to him, but he did not complain. I didn't want him to sleepwalk again, if that's what had happened.

***

— *10:30 AM*

Knock… knock knock knock.

I sat up with a start. Crap.

"Anna, you in there? It's 10:30."

I looked over at Tom, whose eyes were open, but he seemed to have no intention of getting up. I took the blanket and covered him, just in case my mom got nosy and walked over to the bed. No way did I want her to ask about his scars.

I rolled out of bed on the other side and went to the door, opening it enough so my face just peeked out, "I was just checking on him this morning. I had a bad migraine during the night and later—I just wanted to look in."

My mom made a mom face, "Look, I know you are an adult, but I am uncomfortable with you sleeping with your boyfriend in my house. I don't know why you can't honor my wishes."

I rolled my eyes and breathed out, "I told you, I was checking on him. I didn't wander in here until 5:00 AM and then I fell back asleep, okay? And I'm not going to fuck my boyfriend in your house. Give me some credit."

"Oh Anna!" she exclaimed, giving me an indignant look. Resigned, she stated curtly, "We need to start getting ready. We are going to Quiet Waters Park to show Tom the scenery."

"Okay, can you just let him rest for another half hour, please?"

"Fine," and she left in a huff.

I went over to the bed to check on his wound. I pulled the covers off his back, exposing the raised scars. I then started to reach around to untape the gauze.

"Nurse Ratchet strikes again," he taunted.

"Very funny. How are you feeling?"

He turned back over to face me, ignoring my question, "You really shouldn't be so crass with your mother."

"She's being stupid and ridiculous," I retorted.

He closed his eyes, shook his head and then announced he was getting in the shower.

"Hold on, let me look, okay?" The wound was not deep, but definitely raw. Mimicking the rip on his shirt, it was a pretty straight, thin line, as if he was cut with a knife. I pulled the rest of the bandage off. "Make sure you wash it really well in the shower and then I'll put another bandage on."

"Yes, darling," he said sarcastically as I watched him go into the bathroom. The scars on his back matched nicely with this new injury.

***

We had a nice time at Quiet Waters Park, despite my worries. My parents drove us through the entrance and down to a parking lot across from the dog park. Barley was with us, so I suggested we take him into the dog park while my parents did some geo caching, my father's new hobby. Tom and I found a vacant wooden bench within the confines of the fenced dog park and watched as Barley ignored the playful dogs. He then peed, jumped up on the bench next to Tom, and sat down.

"I guess he just likes to watch," I said.

One dog in particular seemed to really like Tom. Zoey, a cute black dog, kept bringing a ball up to him, "asking" him to throw it. He tried once with his right hand, flinched and then threw it errantly into the ground with his left hand. Eventually, she just lied down at his feet to be pet. Tom's mood seemed to gradually get better.

After about 20 minutes, we left through the gate to find my parents. All the while, Zoey watched us go.

"She's so cute!" I exclaimed.

"Yes, indeed. I've never had a pet, but certainly see the merits of taking one in."

We then walked with Barley in tow down the tree-lined path leading to the water. We met my parents along the way. Tom and my dad lagged behind as they had an animated conversation. When I looked back, I saw them shaking hands. I wondered what they were discussing.

Two white gazebos flanked the end of the path. Tom and I went into the right one while my parents went to the left. We stood silently, taking in the beautiful water vista below and in front of us. Although the Chesapeake Bay always reminded me of a Hefty bag because of its murky greenish-brown color, the water still looked beautiful. A few boats were milling around Harness Creek and the sun beamed down on the soft ripples in the water. Large, million-dollar houses loomed, spying on us from across the water.

"It's really quite stunning here," Tom pronounced while starting to put his right arm around my shoulder. He stopped himself and then walked around to my other side to use his left.

"Is your cut hurting you?"

"Yes, a bit, but never mind that. I'm having a wonderful time."

As he looked out over the water, he said in a low voice, "You really make me very happy. I love you so much." He then turned to me and gazed straight into my eyes and smiled. He really can give a girl goosebumps. But, why does it have to be so complicated? I guess everyone has some baggage, but Tom seems to have a trunk full and it's still affecting his here and now.

As frightened as I was to say it just yet, I knew I was in love with him. But I was only able to croak out, "And you make me happy, too."

***

We ate at home that night. My mother wanted to have some kind of barbeque, and invited a bunch of her friends. It was your typical barbeque fare, but she had veggie burgers for me and even made a vegan potato salad. Tom, of course, was as charming as ever as he engaged in polite conversation with the guests. He talked about London, ghost stories, and a bit about me. Every once in a while, he would look up from his chats to find me and either smile or wink. Eventually, I stole him away, taking his arm and pulling him from the food table.

"So, what were you and my dad talking about in the park today?"

"Em, you know, politics, sports, that kind of thing."

"Sports? I didn't know you like sports."

"I like to watch tennis or an occasional rugby match."

"Anything else?"

"Pardon?"

"Did you talk about anything else?" I clarified.

"Em, like what?" He looked puzzled.

"I saw you two shaking hands. What was that about?" I pressed.

"I don't recall, probably a gentleman's handshake about something or other. Mmm. I see your mother is beckoning me," he turned abruptly and walked toward her.

"And this is Tom, Anna's boyfriend from London," I heard my mom introduce him to her friend Geena, and Geena's daughter, Sheila, who actually went to high school with me. She was and still is a very attractive red head, but someone I never really cared for. In fact, she was a bitch to me in school. I scrunched my nose as I saw her eyeing Tom up and down.

"Pleased to meet you," Tom replied; hands in his jacket pockets.

"Oooh, London! I've always wanted to go. I just looove your accent," Sheila flirted as she touched Tom's arm; my eyes narrowed in their direction. My mom started a conversation with Geena, leaving Tom and Sheila together. Thanks, Mom.

"Em, thank you." Tom said, but shifted away a little, looking down at the ground.

"So, you're with Anna? You know, we went to high school together."

Tom picked his head up. "Really? And what was she like?"

"Oh, she was, ah… interesting." She sidled up a little closer to him. I couldn't tell if Sheila knew how close I was standing to them, that I could hear every word and see every flirtatious gesture. She probably knew. Bitch.

Tom, who hadn't really been making eye contact with her, cocked his head and looked straight into her eyes and challenged, questioning, "Innn..teresting?"

I saw Sheila take a small step back; I knew the feeling.

"I don't mean in a bad way, she was just, um, y' know, a little rough around the edges."

"Hmmm… okay. Rough around the edges."

She moved closer to him again, "She kind of hung out with, well, the weirdoes who colored their hair blue and wore their bras on the outsides of their clothing. But, I assume she's grown out of that, right?"

Tom squinted at her, "You realize she is 28 and an adult, had the courage to move herself to London—alone, for that matter, and developed a life for herself?"

"Yes, I guess I just don't think of her like that. I haven't seen her since high school."

There was an awkward pause and more arm touching until she started in.

"Are you two serious, because if you're not, I could show you around town, maybe go to dinner or something. Hang out with someone perhaps more your type?" She squeezed his arm.

He glanced down at the arm she was grasping and then stared into her eyes. She was smiling, oblivious to Tom's intentions, or lack thereof. "Well, I suppose if you define 'my type' as someone with beauty, grace, kindness," he rocked up onto his toes, looked at the sky and drawled out, "and someone who is *utterly* sexy, and the most gorgeous woman I have ever met… then I better stick with Anna," rocking back down to his heals and sheepishly grinning at Sheila. "Now, if you will excuse me, I need to find the loo." Tom went into the house, leaving an open-mouthed Sheila behind. I was tempted to stuff a potato chip in the gaping hole.

"Nice try, Sheila," I said as I walked by her, following Tom into the house.

"Hey, everything okay?" I asked as I caught up to him. "Hey, that was awesome! Sheila was always a bitch to me in school and it looks like things haven't changed."

"Yes, well, I picked up on her shallowness from across the yard. Did she think I came here with *you* to meet *your* parents only to look for someone else to bed?"

"Yes, probably. I'm surprised she didn't give you her number." I almost said, "like Kitty," but stopped myself.

Tom gave me a sideways glance as if he knew I was thinking, but left it at that. He did ask me to check his wound since his side was starting to itch.

We went upstairs to the bedroom and sat on the edge of the bed. He lifted up his shirt and I took off the bandage. "It looks pretty good, but let me put some Neosporin on it." I came back from the bathroom to find Tom's head in his hands.

"Tom?"

"Anna, I think I did something last night." He softly spoke.

"What do you mean? While you were sleepwalking?"

"I don't know that I was sleepwalking. I think I had a dream—or not a dream. Something or someone at the party triggered the memory of it. I was walking down the street—I am not sure where—when I stumbled upon a man. I had an object in my hand, but I'm not sure what it was. The dream... I... I swung at the man's head with the object. He had a knife or something sharp. He evaded the swing and tried to cut me on the side, but missed. I took another swipe which landed squarely on the front of his head. He was alive, but badly hurt. And then," his speech faltered, "then I grabbed the knife. But, that's all I remember."

"You don't think this was a dream?"

"I... I don't know. It was so vivid. It would explain better why my clothes were on and perhaps how I succumbed to this wound." He took one of my hands and stared at me, his voice cracking, "Anna, I am frightened."

I sat next to him and ran my fingers through his hair, "It's going to be okay. Like I said, when we get back to London, we'll see someone, okay?" He closed his eyes and nodded.

"Anna, I love you," he professed again.

I hesitated briefly. "I love you, too Tom," stroking his face.

Relieved, he breathed out and opened his eyes, "Oh, thank God. I didn't want to press you. I mean, I hoped, and thought you may, but it's fantastic to hear you say it." He enveloped me in his arms and held on... for dear life, it felt like.

CHAPTER 10

Tuesday and Wednesday were uneventful. We basically hung out around the house, my dad and Tom conversing quite a bit, mainly about classic rock; they seemed to like the same music. Tom also helped him with a few physical chores he couldn't really do himself. It was kind of cute, as Tom really wasn't much of a handyman, so although he helped, he took complete direction from my father on what to do. I was really happy that they seemed to genuinely like each other. I was, however, getting a bit bored. We were going to DC on Friday, but nothing happening on Thursday so I occupied my time searching the net. I secretly was trying to find something on the attack Tom described, but I found nothing. I thought he was probably sleepwalking, somehow hurt himself, and had some very vivid dream. At least, that's what I convinced myself of. I searched a little more until satisfied, and then looked for things to do in the area.

"Hey, Tom. Do you want to go to the R-rated haunted house tonight? I really want to get out and do something, and this looks like fun."

He peered over my shoulder, "Hmm… 'House of Tortures.' Really? Why am I not surprised you want to do this."

I rolled my eyes. "Come on, it'll be fun. And why wouldn't *you* want to do this? You love Halloween. And besides, I really need to get away from my mom for a few hours," I whispered.

Resigned, he said, "Alright. A night out with just you would be good."

I bought the tickets online and informed my mom what we were doing that evening. Tom and I decided to get some dinner alone. We ate downtown at Tsunami, a Japanese restaurant with a New York feel. We relaxed in a secluded booth surrounded by the deep blue color of the ocean painted on the walls; a candle flickering on the table enhancing the romantic atmosphere. We ordered one dish to share—the Yamoto Tofu with sushi rice. There is really no comparison here to London restaurants, especially vegan/vegetarian ones, but this was one of the few dishes I missed. In addition to the bowl of the tofu, we ordered some avocado rolls. During the meal, I told Tom that I didn't find anything on an attack in this area and that it would have shown up in the paper. He seemed relatively relieved by this and agreed it was probably all in his head—except for, of course, the cut.

We skipped dessert and found our way to the car. I figured I would drive since Tom was used to the wrong side of the road. While driving to the haunted house, I put Bauhaus in the CD deck of my mom's car to get us in the mood. Luckily, I still had a few CDs in their basement. Eventually, we came to a dark, unpaved road through a forest and then to a dimly lit parking lot. Since it was Thursday and early in October, there weren't too many cars, yet. We showed our tickets to the ghoul and got in line. After waiting about 15 minutes, we were ushered into the house; really not a house at all but a warehouse. We actually had to sign a waiver stating that we wouldn't sue them if we got hurt. This should be good! Tom, however, wasn't too impressed.

"To be grabbed or not to be grabbed," another ghoul asked. According to one of the signs, you could opt to be grabbed, abducted, or touched if you wanted, but had to wear a large glow in the dark wrist band signifying this.

"YES!" I exclaimed while Tom said 'no.'

"Come on, Tom, it will be cool," I begged, tugging on his arm.

He sighed, succumbing to my pleading face, and held out his wrist to be adorned with the neon yellow band.

I took hold of Tom's arm as we walked through the dark. Pushing open what seemed to be a makeshift door, we came upon a room where skulls lined the walls. Eerie music played in the background, sounding like a remix of the theme from *The Exorcist*. We cautiously walked through the room, which resembled catacombs, when a skull suddenly pitched forward in front of us. I screamed; Tom remained steady. Walking through, a swamp room lay ahead of us. The humidity and stench in the room accosted our senses. Something resembling seaweed hung from the ceiling and brushed our faces as we trudged along. Tendrils of "sea grass" slapped at our feet while many gnarled hands lightly brushed our bodies; whispers came from the walls. The room became foggy, making it very hard to see, but we pushed forward. Jumping back, yanking Tom with me, I screamed upon seeing a swampy face, skin peeling and smelling greatly of mud. A webbed hand yanked a piece of skin off and dangled it in front of me.

We kept walking, quickening our steps to the next room, "Isn't this fun, Tom!?"

"It's mildly amusing, although I am very much enjoying your reactions." I lightly punched his shoulder, then wrapped and squeezed both my arms around his left arm, making it a little hard for him to walk. Soon we came to a very dark maze. Blacker than black, we felt our way through, hitting a few dead ends, when I decided to place my hand on the wall and guide us out. This seemed to work until we bumped into a large something. I saw red eyes glowing at us and then heard a click.

"Ah, brilliant," Tom mumbled, sarcastically, under his breath.

"What's wrong?"

"I think I've been handcuffed." And as he said that, he was a little forcibly pulled away from me. Then I felt a slimy something grab my free hand and felt and heard the click around my wrist. I squealed, both with glee and trepidation. I was led into a diffusely lit room where there were two jail cells on each side of the walkway. In each cell was a grungy metal bed with an even grungier mildewy mattresses. Beside the beds sat various implements of torture… filthy knives, rusty saws, and other pieces of metal that could be used for punishments or tortures I didn't want to (but sort of did want to) think of. The creature pushed me into one of the cells and handcuffed me to the bed.

My abductor then turned on a dim flashlight and shined it in my face, laughing. The creature said in a demonic voice, the words echoing off the walls, "You volunteered for our experimental procedures. We want to thank you for risking your life for the betterment of the human race."

Sitting on the disgusting damp bed, the all-black creature with red eyes "performed" various forms of experiments. He sprinkled some kind powder on my hand and then took a fake hammer and hit my hand. It didn't hurt, but I felt something wet and looked down seeing "blood." It then took my leg and started to "saw" into it. Once again, it didn't hurt, but scraping, sawing and cracking sounds echoed from the walls as if my leg bone was being severed. The creature then cut the dim light and left me alone for a bit in pitch black. Nasty, wet, slimy pieces of something were thrown at my face. I felt one ooze down my cheek. Then, I felt something like spiders crawling all over my body. "Oh God!" I whimpered.

"THERE'S NO GOD HERE!" I heard something say loudly from the shadows.

My heart rate was up and I started to sweat a little. Although I was thoroughly enjoying this, I was also a little afraid. The spiders got to me. The physical sensation was gone, but I still *felt* it. I know I will think something is crawling all over me all night. As I slapped at my arm with my free hand to rid my body of the phantom bugs, a bright light shined again in my face. I was unchained from the bed and led into another room. "STAY HERE!" the creature commanded. I did what I was told. As far as I could tell, the room was small, but otherwise devoid of anything too frightening.

"HERE IS YOUR COMPANION, NOW GO FORWARD!"

Tom was ushered in and pushed, slightly hard, into me. A green arrow appeared in front of us showing us the way out. I couldn't see Tom's face in the darkness, but I took his hand. He felt extremely cold and he seemed to be shivering.

"Tom, are you okay?"

He let out a breath, "Em, I guess. No, not really. Can we get through this attraction, please? I need air."

And so, we weaved ourselves through a number of rooms with various monsters, vampires, headless bodies and the like popping out at us. Eventually we came to the end, where we were chased by the obligatory chainsaw wielding zombie out into the autumn night.

Tom limped toward the parking lot, ignoring my questions until we found the car. Leaning against the door, hands in his pea coat pockets, he took a deep breath and looked at the star-studded sky.

"Are you okay? You're limping." I asked again, "What'd they do to you? They fake tortured me and it was scary, but I didn't get hurt."

I could see Tom's face a bit better from the yellow glow of the parking lot lights. He looked paler than usual, and his teeth were chattering.

"Em, some kind of ghoulish woman with blood oozing from her face and a whip in her hand led me to a room and chained me to the wall. She feigned doing some, ah, sexual theatrics with me while I remained immobile. It was quite a bit uncomfortable to say the least. I could handle it though for she wasn't touching me. Em, I could handle it until the walls started to literally close in on me, creating a box around me. By the time they stopped, the walls were about an inch from my face. I felt the box tilt back all the way until I was lying on my back. Sounds of screams and laughter and something hitting the top echoed in the box." Tom paused, still shaking. "It sounded like dirt, like I was being buried alive. Anna, I was terrified and started to panic. I started to sweat and shake. I wanted to pound on the walls, but it was so tight in there that I could not move my arms. I tried to pound the top with my knee as hard as I could, and that's why I'm limping. You know I'm somewhat claustrophobic, and this really got to me. I took deep breaths to calm myself, reminding myself this was a mere Halloween attraction, but it didn't do too much good. Eventually, they let me out and unchained me. Indeed, it was a coffin and dirt was all over the ground."

"Oh, Tom, I'm so sorry. I didn't realize they would go that far with this. I saw some disclaimer about claustrophobia, but didn't think much of it. Are you feeling better now?"

"Yes, I suppose."

"Do you know why you're so claustrophobic?"

"No. My guess is some repressed memory. But, who knows," he shrugged. I pressed my body against his, trying to steady his shivering, and hugged him. He, in turn, responded with his arms around me and resting his chin on my head.

"I'll make it up to you later, okay?" I said, as I gently released from the embrace.

On the ride home, Tom remained pretty silent, resting his head against the door, while I played some Ray LaMontagne. Fortunately, my parents were asleep when we arrived, so we quietly walked upstairs. I joined Tom in his room despite the inevitable repercussions from my mother. I think at this point, Tom didn't care.

"Alright, sweetheart, take off your shirt and I'll give you a massage to drive the demons out." Tom obliged, but still didn't say anything.

He lay face down on the bed as I started to knead his tight back. He sighed softly and I felt him begin to relax.

"Something is at the tip of my brain," he breathed out in a sleepy voice.

I kneaded some more.

"In that coffin, I experienced some sort of déjà vu. That's when the panic set in. But, I can't say why."

"All the more reason you should see someone." As I deepened my pressure on his back, I heard his soft breathing and knew he had fallen asleep. His scars really, really run deep.

***

The next morning, Tom's color and mood were a little better. My mother asked us a barrage of questions about the event last night, but Tom was relatively short with her and only disclosed what he wanted her to hear. He became more edgy than frightened. I guess that was better.

We did go into DC that day, my mother monopolizing the conversation most of the way down US 50. Tom and I sat in the back seat together, my mother often turning to face us and talk, asking question after question. On more than one occasion, I would see Tom close his eyes and pinch the bridge of his nose. Mom caught him doing this, which set off a series of questions as to whether he had a headache or not. I had my iPod with me, so I rudely plugged in, but I didn't feel bad. I had had to deal with this my whole life.

Finally, we arrived and found parking in front of The Natural History Museum. I swear my dad has parking mojo; he always finds the best spots. Anyway, walking through the museum, my mom and I ogled the gemstones and other rocks. I showed Tom the colorful ones I liked best, like the sapphires and rubies, although he clearly wasn't too interested. He did, however, love the giant squid bathing in formaldehyde downstairs. After visiting with cavemen, saber-toothed tigers, and other prehistoric creatures, we decided to go to the Adams Morgan district to shop and eat an early dinner.

Similar to Camdentown in some ways, although much, much smaller, Adams Morgan has some shops more my speed; bars, used bookstores, used CD and record stores, and funky vintage boutiques lined the streets in colorful buildings. As we walked along the sidewalk, I heard "The Strand" by Roxy Music playing deliciously loud. The music drew me down a few steps into "Smash," a little punk rock store that sold vinyl, CDs, and some clothes. My parents opted to stay outside; Tom entering a minute later.

"Oh My God!!!! Tom, look!" I held up two used imports by The Damned, ones I didn't have yet.

"Oh, goody, goody," he drawled over the loud music. "You know you live in London, right? You can probably buy those there and they wouldn't be imports."

"That's no fun." I wrinkled my nose at him, but he went over to the "T" section and showed me a Triumvirat CD. Tom has played a bunch of their songs for me and I do like them.

After my arms were loaded with CDs, Tom gently explained that we would never fit them all in our suitcases.

"Um, right, because you bought so many books at the used book store," I said with my eyes wide. Tom shrugged and quietly said sorry. I put back many of the CDs, but kept five, the two imports a definite. Tom plucked them from my hands, added the Triumvirat CD to the stack, and paid the overly pierced clerk. When we came outside, my parents informed us they were going to walk down the street and check out some restaurant menus and that they would text us when they found something. Happy to be alone with Tom, I took his hand and brought him into "Crooked Beat Records." Here, they were playing "PIL," but at a much higher decibel than in the other store.

"Must we?" he said in the doorframe.

I just ignored him, listening to the music and thumbing through the posters and patches. Not seeing anything I wanted, we left and then went into a consignment store. He checked out some of the long coats while I fell in love with some 1960s boots that were, incredibly, in my size. They were canvas and probably leather. I had a little internal dilemma with the leather, but figured since they were used, very used, it was okay. They laced all the way up to right below my knee and had about a one-inch heel. "Tom, look at these!" I called over.

"Groovy." He jeered.

"Aw come on, they're really cool!"

"Yes, they are *cool*." While I was admiring myself in the mirror Tom went over to the clerk and paid once again.

Outside the store, I complained that he stop buying everything I touch.

"But, I like to. I've not been able to frivolously spend my money on a girl before, not in a long time. It's one of my indulgences." I guess I just needed to accept it.

We wound up eating at Casa Oaxaca, a really tasty Mexican restaurant with a few vegan options. Tom and my father argued over the bill, but, of course, Tom won and paid for the meal. Besides my mother's annoying questions and insinuations, we had a pretty good day.

***

The last full day in the States, we all went to Homestead Gardens to see the llamas. The large nursery cared for the llamas in a barn and field across the parking lot from where the flowers and plants are sold. I always enjoyed communing with the llamas, ever since I was a kid. Tom seemed to enjoy watching them, although, I don't think he loved the dusty and smelly environment. We then dropped my parents off at the house while Tom and I picked up Barley and headed back to the dog park. Unfortunately, Zoey wasn't there, but this time, Tom coaxed Barley into playing ball. Barley really perked up, in fact; he started running and darting around faster than I'd ever seen.

He's usually pretty lazy. After a bit, Barley came back to the bench and lied down at my feet, his tongue far longer than before.

"So, would you eat a dog?" I asked Tom; my arms spread wide on the back of the bench.

Tom squinted at me, "No, of course not."

"Then why would you eat a cow?"

Tom pursed his lips, "Anna, since I've been courting you, have you seen me ingest any animal products?"

I thought for a second, "No, I guess not—did you just say 'courting'?"

"I told you when we first met that food, as long as it's good, doesn't really matter to me. And you've convinced me. I've read your magazines and looked at a couple of your books, so there you have it."

"Okay, good. I was kind of concerned moving in with you."

"You're safe, love. And yes, what's wrong with the word 'courting?'" Before I could answer, he stood up and urged Barley to play for one last round.

***

The next morning, my parents drove us to BWI. It was the longest half hour ride I'd ever spent, since my mom started telling Tom about a couple of my past boyfriends. The woman has no filter.

"One was a sociopath and another was literally a psychopath, winding up in jail."

"Pardon? Really?" I was glad he played dumb.

"Yes, so I'm happy to see she's found someone so well adjusted and, well, nice and proper. She doesn't have to 'fix' you."

"Thank you, Jenny." But, I saw that eye twitch.

Upon arriving at the airport after my mom recounted my relationship with Graham, she gave Tom and me a teary goodbye and my dad crushed me into his chest. He even embraced Tom; I had rarely seen him show affection to anyone other than me or my mother.

And then we left. I was happy to be going home, although I was going to miss my parents and Barley.

After we boarded the plane, we settled in, knowing it was going to be a long flight. After a lot of arguing with the airline,

Tom was unable to change our tickets to first class since there was no room. So, economy it was. Tom craned his neck and casually looked behind him. He was smiling slightly when he turned back to me, "Elderly woman, thank God."

I started to put my iPod earphones in when Tom touched my knee. "After you move in, do you want to adopt a dog?" He seemed very excited about this.

"Maybe. Does your flat allow animals?"

"Yes, I've seen other dogs in there. I figure with your work schedule and mine, he or she won't be alone that often."

"The only pain is going to be taking the dog out. Having a fenced in yard is so much easier—especially when it's raining or cold." I reasoned.

"True, true. Well, let's get you moved in first and then we'll revisit the notion. However, I think it's a splendid idea!"

"Splendid." I smiled, shook my head, and plugged in.

***

We landed in London on Saturday at 5:00 PM London time. Even though we both slept most of the plane ride, we were still exhausted. After dragging ourselves through customs and hailing a cab, the clock rolled to 7:30 by the time we walked into Tom's—soon to be our flat. When Tom is tired, he's not the best company, and he was a bear going through customs.

"I'm going to need to see my father," Tom grumbled. "It's been a couple of weeks now, so I really need to check on him. I'm afraid I've been neglectful."

I nodded and shrugged at the same time.

"I thought tomorrow, we could go see him," Tom said as he gave me a pleading expression, "and then go to your flat to pick up some more of your belongings. We should probably go through your kitchenware to see if you want to keep anything or not."

"I'll go with you to your father's, but if he makes one condescending comment toward you or me, I'm out of there. As for the kitchen, most of that stuff belongs to the landlord—he stocked it pretty well. In fact, almost everything in the flat, except my clothes and my music, belongs to the landlord. I think we can probably get all my things over here in two trips."

"Fine. Well, let's get some dinner and go to bed early." With that, Tom phoned an Italian delivery restaurant and ordered us some pasta dishes; a little impatient with having to repeat the order twice.

We went into the bedroom to unpack. My mom did all our laundry the night before we left, so we had very few dirty clothes, thankfully.

"It was kind of your mother to do our laundry. But, em, she's an odd bird," Tom said. "Nice, but, her incessant questioning can get to you. I am not sure how your father lives with it. Sorry, I'm being rude and catty."

"No, not at all. You nailed it. I don't know how I lived with it."

"She took me aside and wanted to see if I could influence you to get rid of your T-shirts. She said you've had most of them since college. Some even from high school," he mentioned as I was unpacking them.

Hands on my hips, "And what did you say?"

Tom raised both hands, surrendering, "I told her it added to your character, that I thought it fit your personality and then I told a white lie and said that you didn't wear them out... much."

"Okay," dropping my hands from my hips. "And just so you know, my T-shirts define me, so if you even think about getting rid of them, even the ones with holes, we are getting a divorce."

Tom looked at me, intrigued.

"You know what I mean," I countered.

"I wouldn't dream of touching your shirts in a destructive way, nor would I want a... divorce."

The doorbell rang. Tom shot past me to pay for the delivery.

When I came out of the bedroom, the table was set and the delivered food was on plates, a candle lit in the center.

"Are you always going to be like this after I move in? I think we are past the trying-to-impress stage." I said as I took a seat. "Sorry, the 'courting' stage," I said as I smiled.

He knitted his eyebrows together. "I'm not trying to impress. I eat like this all the time." He said it as if it were the most obvious thing in the world. "And you really have a lot of nerve teasing me about the way I speak. I guess I should start using such descriptive words as 'things' and 'stuff' and start to curse. Or maybe I should have dinner in front of the telly every night."

"Oh lighten up, Tom. Look, if you have reservations about me moving in, you had better tell me now." I said, then stuffed a bunch of pasta in my mouth. I realized I was starving. I had barely touched the airplane vegan meal because it tasted like sewage.

He sighed and tempered the edge in his voice a little, "Em… no, of course not. Em, except one," he paused a little too long.

My eyes widened, flipping my palms up, waiting for a response.

"Okay… well, em… I cannot live in filth or clutter."

I rolled my eyes, "Is that all? I know that, Tom. I wouldn't dream of fouling your sink with a dirty dish."

"Please, Anna, I'm serious. We all have our preferences. I don't mind compromising on some things, but just like you won't with your graphic tees, I won't with this." He looked at me sternly.

"Geez, okay *Dad*. Look, I'll try my best, that's all I can offer, okay?"

Tom just stared at me, not too pleased, and then started on his food.

"What made you such a clean freak anyway?"

"What made you such a slob?" Tom retorted quickly, looking up from under his brows. Oh, I wish he would just go to bed.

I sat straighter in my chair, a little offended at his response, but I offered, "Laziness, I guess. My mom was always cleaning up after me and I rarely had any repercussions, so I guess I never really learned the habit of cleaning up myself," I stated reflectively, trying to quell his mood.

Tom slowly nodded, "My father was and still is messy. I kept my room tidy, wanting to be as far from my father's ways as possible."

"Mmmm, more daddy issues, I should have figured as much," I flippantly added.

Tom dropped his fork on the plate, making a loud clatter, "Fuck off, Anna." He wiped his mouth with his napkin, stood up and went to his room, slamming the door.

I chewed on my upper lip. Oops. That was a stupid thing for me to say. Especially when he's so tired and dickish.

I sat there, quite embarrassed. Then the guilt set in. Man, I can be such a bitch sometimes.

My conscious feeling rather heavy, I mustered the courage to stand up, put the leftovers in the fridge, and wash the dishes. I then blew the candle out, took another deep breath and crept down the hall to Tom's bedroom. I knocked softly.

"Tom? Tom, I'm sorry, I… I shouldn't have said that. It was really inconsiderate of me." I tried the knob, but it was locked. I knocked again. I could just picture him, stewing.

"Tom, please, open the door," I pleaded. The door suddenly swung open. Tom, still seething. Eyes ablaze looking rather sinister and scary. I took a step back.

He was looking at me pretty intently, obviously trying to work something out when finally he spoke, although tersely, "I accept your apology, Anna," and stepped to the side to allow me to enter.

He made a bee-line to the lounge chair by the window, flopped down in it, crossed his legs and looked out. He started chewing on his thumb nail.

I stayed by the door and apologized again. "I really am sorry, I can be, um, insensitive at times, if you haven't noticed."

"Hard to miss," he hissed with his thumb nail between his teeth.

He turned his head back to me and stopped biting his nail. "I'm sorry I cursed at you, although I am not sorry for the intent. I am afraid your mouth is rubbing off on me."

"Yeah, well, I'm fucking sorry for that, too, I guess," I remarked sarcastically, starting to feel a bit defensive.

"Okay. Well, I am extremely knackered and a bit on edge. I am going to sleep," he informed me as he rose up from the chair and went into the bathroom to brush his teeth.

"Um, do you want me to stay tonight?" I asked, a little put off by his actions. I really wasn't used to this side of Tom. It was a bit intimidating.

He spit out his toothpaste, rinsed and splashed his face with water, "Yes, Anna, I want you to stay. We are going to have arguments, love. You just have to give me time to calm down and let it go. And when I don't have enough sleep I can get cantankerous, I'm sure you've noticed."

I almost gave him another snarky remark, but stopped myself.

Still feeling self-conscious and guilty, I undressed out of Tom's site and turned in. A few minutes later, Tom came to bed but we slept with our backs to each other.

***

— *Very early morning, Sunday, October 12*

"No Elizabeth, no, no!"

Awaking with a start, I focused my eyes on Tom's silhouette, thrashing in the early morning dark.

"Tom, wake up," I said as I nudged him and then flipped on the light.

Then a little louder, "Tom?!"

Startled out of sleep, he sat up quickly, clutching the blanket. Pale and sweating, he breathed heavily as if he had just run a couple miles.

"It's okay. You were having a dream."

He took another deep breath, trying to calm himself down. He shook his head as his confusion started to quell.

"Hey, it's okay, just a dream." I reiterated.

"I can't remember, but I feel, I feel, oh God," he scrambled out of bed and ran to the bathroom; a barrage of retching sounds ensued.

Quickly, I followed and filled the cup on the sink with water. When he finished and his breathing subsided, he sat heavily on the floor and leaned up against the shower. A bead of sweat formed on his forehead.

I crouched down to his level and offered him the water. He held up his index finger, and then once again, leaned his face over the toilet. I stood back up and placed the glass back on the sink, waiting for the heaves and convulsions to end. I felt a bit helpless as there really was nothing I could do. After a few minutes, seemingly to have expelled all the evil from his dream, he slowly pushed himself up, flushed the toilet and took the water from the sink. He rinsed his mouth and then placed both hands on the sink, leaning into it. Softly he said, "Sorry, love. That was intense. I don't know what came over me. I can't remember anything." He then grabbed the toothpaste and squeezed out an enormous blob onto his toothbrush and rigorously brushed his teeth.

Rubbing his back, I explained, "You kept saying 'No, Elizabeth, no.'"

After rinsing once again, he said, "I know she was somehow in it, but I can't remember what happened."

He wiped the sweat off his face with a towel, stretched his arms and went back to bed, lying down on his back. Flopping down on the bed next to him, I asked him about his sister.

"What would you like to know?" he asked, a little calmer.

I sat up on my elbow. "What was she like? What was your relationship like? I mean, you rarely talk in specifics about her."

Tom ran his fingers through his hair.

"Em, we had an interesting relationship. On the one hand, she stuck up for me, whether we were in school and someone was picking on me or my father was abusing me. However, she could be quite mean. She used to berate me for not fighting back, not trying to stick up for myself. I think that's why I got so defensive with you earlier. The tone you took reminded me so much of her assaults on my character."

"I'm so sorry, Tom," I reemphasized, shaking my head.

He turned his head to me. "It's okay, love, I overreacted. I should never have uttered those words to you. I am ashamed and embarrassed."

I smiled a little in the dimly lit room.

"Anyway, even though Elizabeth felt it was her obligation to protect me, she resented this burden as well. For when she defended me against my father, she would catch the brunt of the abuse. And I was too young, too weak to help her. I really wasn't a very good brother to her."

"But, she was the older one."

"She was, true, but I should have tried. I remember an absolutely horrible night when…

> *Elizabeth and I were playing chess after dinner. I think I was around 10, putting Elizabeth at about 14. My father, drunk from his ale, started moving the pieces around, just to be an arse. Both my sister and I asked him to stop, that he was ruining our game. I guess that angered him further for he flipped the board over, took the pieces and started pelting me with them. It may sound funny, but these were not plastic pieces, rather they were marble. My sister had enough, stood up, grabbed a bishop and winged it at my father's head. I remember the skin on his forehead start to change color. Then his whole face matched the mark. His face became a red balloon, blown up too big and about to pop. He turned on Elizabeth. I recall her trying to fight back, kicking, punching, scratching, but to no avail. My father just kept slapping her and slapping her. It was humiliating for her and I know painful as well. She was pleading with me to help, but I didn't*

know what to do—I was scared to death, petrified. Finally, my father grabbed her by the hair, pulled her head back and spit right in her face. Then, he let go and left the house. Elizabeth ran to her room crying and stayed there most of the night, until she decided to come into my room, late.

Tom took a shuddered breath.

She woke me up by shaking me vigorously.

'What, what is it?' I remember saying, a little disoriented from being startled out of my slumber.

She hopped on top of me, straddling my stomach, looking directly into my face.

'Hey, "brother," putting the word in air quotes.

'Why didn't you defend me? Or stick up for yourself? You could have done something, Tom.'

I recall telling her I was afraid. She then held my arms down above my head and said something like, 'You listen here, brother, you'd better start fighting back or I'm going to start in on you more than usual. Then you'll have two people beating the crap out of you. You need to learn to be a man, you fucking coward." Then she got off me, balled up her hand and hammer fisted me right in the bollocks. I remember the excruciating pain coursing through my body as I cried myself to sleep.

"So, you could say my relationship with my sister, was, ah, a bit schizophrenic."

"Jesus Christ, Tom. So you got it from both your father *and* your sister?"

"Yes and no. Sometimes my sister would only get after me when I didn't stand my ground with my father; coward was her little nickname for me. The other times, she was okay with me. Nice, even."

"I think you need to see a therapist," I stated matter-of-factly.

Tom let out a short laugh, "Anna, please leave it alone. These events happened over 15 years ago."

"You can't say it isn't affecting you. Geez, you just had a violent physical reaction to a dream about her. I mean, look what happened in Maryland. Your possible sleepwalking and your reaction at the haunted house? What about the guy you beat up. This stuff isn't normal."

"I didn't harm that homophobe at the ghost tour, did I? He goaded me at the pub—in fact he grabbed my crotch—I think I was warranted. I have no regrets pummeling that man, only that you were there to witness it. And that has nothing to do with my upbringing."

"How do you know?"

"Because I know. And what about you? Do you think your mysterious pains can be explained by your upbringing? Hmmm, I know. The pain you felt was a delayed reaction from your mother's constant jabbing comments and questions," he said sarcastically.

I just sighed. He wasn't getting it.

His face softened. "Sorry, that was rather crass of me—but kind of funny." He smirked. It *was* funny.

Picking up my pillow, laughing, I swung it at his face, but he blocked it with his hands, grabbed the pillow and threw it to the side. Then he grasped my arms and held them above my head while swinging his legs around me, straddling my torso. He tried to kiss me, but I turned away.

"Puke breath, c'mon man." I scrunched my nose.

"I just scoured my teeth!" He exclaimed, releasing my arms and sitting back, careful not to put pressure on my stomach.

"Still there." I said, snatching the pillow again, and this time making contact with his face.

"Alright, alright, you got me. I'll go brush my teeth again."

So, he quickly got off of me and went back into the bathroom. "I'm worried about you, Tom. What about what happened in Maryland?" I said when he came back. Switching off the light, he sat gently on the bed, his disheveled hair outlined by the outside light.

"I really don't know. I think you are probably right, I was probably sleepwalking. And at the haunted house, I reacted to being locked in a coffin. I think a lot of people would have such a reaction."

"I don't know. And remember also, you thought you harmed someone."

"Didn't we decide it was just a vivid dream? You didn't find anything in the paper."

I ignored his excuses. "Then where did the cut come from? Look, you promised you'd see someone when we got back."

Resigned, Tom blew out, "Fine, to make you happy I will see a sleep therapist. Now please, let me get back to it."

CHAPTER 11

— A week before Halloween

"I bought pumpkins!" Tom sang as he came into the flat, over "Evil Eye" by Franz Ferdinand blasting from the speakers. I was fully moved in, although I was still paying rent until the end of the month for my flat. Tom offered to pay the rest, but I emphatically told him no. Besides, it was only one month. The landlord was kind and let me out of my lease early. He had a waiting list for the place, so he said it was fine.

"Aw, cute! Look at the small one! "

"I'm going to make dinner and then we can carve these after." Tom happily kissed me on the lips, holding the small pumpkin in his left hand by the base and the bigger one in his right hand by the stem.

"Can you make pasta? I've been craving spaghetti," I implored.

"Anything you wish," Tom replied with a huge grin. He sure was in a good mood, "Em, may I turn down the music?" Usually, he doesn't ask, he just does it, reminding me of my father.

I had the remote in hand and turned it down to a more reasonable level… for talking, that is.

"So, how was work today, love?" Tom inquired.

"It was fine. We finished up our book a couple of days prior to our deadline, so that was good. Hey, did you see your father today?"

Tom exhaled, "Yes."

I waited for him to elaborate.

"He was as ghastly as ever, but I tried my best to ignore his comments. I told him I was going to hire a male nurse, which he complained about. I told him I would not subject a female nurse to his crassness, so if he starts to get worse, the male nurse is going to happen."

"Christ, Tom. I just don't get it."

"Leave it alone, Anna, please. I am in a wonderful mood and don't want to spoil it."

"Well, did you at least call the sleep therapist, yet?" I questioned, the same question I'd been asking for days.

As Tom was filling a pot with water he admitted he had not. "Em, no. I've been sleeping fine since the jet lag wore off and you haven't seen me sleepwalk or anything, so let's just see if anything happens again, okay?" His back was to me, so he didn't see my expression. I figured I'd leave it alone for now. I didn't want to pick a fight.

Tom put the pot on the stove and began his homemade marinara sauce.

"I'm going to take a quick shower and get changed," I announced, but I don't think he heard me. He was humming some tune and focusing on slicing tomatoes.

I took a long hot shower. When I was done, I towel dried my hair and brushed it out. Fumbling through my night clothes in one of the drawers of the new bureau Tom had bought for me, I found and put on my *Coraline* T-shirt and some yoga pants and then went out to the dinner table. The CD had been switched to Paul McCartney's "Maybe I'm Amazed." Tom was singing along in his fantastic voice. He had the table set beautifully, as usual, with candles and the small pumpkin in the center. A basket of sliced sour dough and a green salad were perfectly arranged on the table. Still singing, he offered me a glass of Malbec. I took a sip while he poured a glass for himself. His hand was shaking for some reason and he spilled a little wine on the table.

"You okay, hon? Your hands are shaking."

"Em, yes, I think I had too much coffee. You've gotten me addicted to soy flat whites."

After cleaning up the spill, we sat down. The CD switched to Elbow's "One Day Like This."

"Cheers, to Halloween," he toasted as he raised his glass. I clinked mine to his.

"Do you like the little pumpkin?" Tom asked, nudging it toward me.

"Yes, it's adorable."

"I cleaned it out so you may carve it after dinner."

"It's pretty small to carve, but I can draw something on it."

"Em, well, look inside at how I cleaned it out, I think I did a pretty good job. I haven't done this in a while."

Okaaay... he was acting kind of weird.

Perplexed by his obtuse mood, I lifted up the lid. It was hollowed out, but by no means empty. In it sat a very small box. I reached my thumb and forefinger in to pull it out. Tilting my head to one side, I gave Tom a questioning look.

He stood up from his chair and gently took the box from me.

"Anna, you know I love you more than anything?"

The lead singer on the CD sang something about a beautiful day, mirroring the sentiment.

Then, Tom got down on one knee and opened the box. Inside was the most beautiful diamond ring surrounded by sapphires atop a silver band. My heart started to pick up speed, seemingly in time with the anthem-like outro of the song.

"Anna, would you do me the honor of being my wife? Will you marry me?"

I was frozen and at a loss for words.

"I, um… oh my God, Tom, um…" This was so unexpected. We'd never discussed marriage, and I sure have never been proposed to. My mind started to race. I was screaming "hell yes" in my head, the Elbow song coming to a crescendo. I swallowed hard, unable to speak. I imaged my life with this man in front of me. The most gorgeous man I'd ever known, both inside and out. And he would be all mine. My eyes started to tear up, knowing that this was what I wanted, what I've always wanted—to be with someone kind and caring and sensitive.

"You don't have to answer me right now. You take your time to think about it, but please wear the ring. See, I was listening to you in the museum. I assume I picked the correct stones?" Hands still shaking, he took my left hand and slid the ring on; fitting beautifully.

He stood up, smiled at me and went back to the kitchen to serve our salads. I was in a bit in a daze. He put the plates on the table, but I only half noticed. I was still in a bit of shock, staring at the ring on my finger.

Tom sat down and started to pour dressing on his salad.

I finally found my voice and looked up at him, tears rolling down my face, "Yes, Tom."

He put the dressing down, "Yes? Are you sure? You don't want to think about it?" He asked, sounding rather giddy.

"I'm sure. I'm just blown away. And in a pumpkin? How could I say no to that?" We both stood up at the same time; Tom practically knocked me over with his embrace.

"Oh, Anna," he said into my ear, "you've made me so happy. Thank you, thank you! I truly am the luckiest man," and he kissed me intensely. He then pulled away, hands on my shoulders.

"Now, we can eat," he said, overjoyed, and spun around, back to his chair. "By the way, I did my research on the ring, and made sure the diamonds are not blood diamonds."

He knows me so well.

"How long have you been planning this?" I couldn't stop smiling.

"Oh, I've been thinking about marrying you ever since the morning after our first date; when I found you curled up asleep on the chair, wearing my shirt. I think I fell in love with you right then and there. And then, during our trip to Maryland, I solidified it. The handshake with your father you asked me about, that was about this."

"You asked him?"

"Of course! I wouldn't dream of asking a girl to marry me without consulting her father."

I snorted, "You are so funny, Tom."

He looked mildly confused, "Why is that funny?"

"You're just so formal sometimes. I think you were meant to be born in a different era. But, don't get me wrong, it's cute, too."

"Cute? Okay," he said as he shrugged his shoulders.

"Maybe charming is a better word. So, did you have a time in mind?" I probed, my head still spinning. This was all so surreal.

"Well, I thought we could have it in the spring, this spring. And, I am not sure if we should have it here or in Maryland. I hate the thought of all your friends and family having to come to London. But, we could pay for everyone's travel."

"That could get really expensive. And besides, I don't have that many friends back home that I feel the need to be invited. I'm closer to my London friends. So, we could just have my parents come out. I'd rather it be in London being that we can plan it better here. "

"Okay, London it is. One check off the list."

"Oh! I've got to call Jamie!"

"Can it wait until after supper? She may already know, anyway."

"Huh? You told her?"

"Well, I didn't tell her, but Seamus already knows, since we went ring shopping together."

"You did what?! Oh my God! I would have loved to have witnessed that! "

Tom looked a little insulted. "He was actually very helpful, I'll have you know. I am really quite fond of the man."

"I know, but just the thought of you two ring shopping is, well, hilarious! If Jamie doesn't already know, she's going to die!"

Tom raised one eyebrow. "You know, I just gave you a very, very, *very* expensive ring, not to mention my heart, so you may want to try and exercise just a little restraint."

Squeezing my lips together, I tried not to laugh, but it didn't work too well. Tom sighed and resumed eating.

Elbow continued to play on the stereo on a continuous loop. The thought of getting married was starting to settle in. We talked a little further about possible places and dates, but I really wanted to call Jamie. I excused myself as soon as we were done.

"He what? And in a pumpkin?! You lucky, lucky girl!" Jamie exclaimed into the phone.

"I know! Hey, Seamus didn't tell you? You know they went ring shopping together?"

"What?! No, he didn't tell me! And that bastard went ring shopping for you?"

"He'll come around, someday. Maybe Tom will be a good influence on him. Hey, but, can you imagine the two of them ring shopping together? I mean, just picture it."

Tom's gaze bored a hole into my head, his arms crossed.

Jamie roared, "Oh my! You are right!"

"We can play act this later, I think I'm in trouble," I said, glancing back at Tom with a grin.

Giving me half eyes, Tom shook his head and then went back to the kitchen.

After Jamie's laughter died down a little, she became slightly more serious. "Well, I am completely gobsmacked about this. But, are you sure? You've only known him for a little over a month."

"Almost two months, and besides, I love him. I've never really had a healthy relationship before."

"Well, I'm very happy for you two. Maybe this *will* get Seamus to act."

"Would you marry him?

"Yes, God help me."

***

After a night of pumpkin mousse, a sappy romantic comedy and fantastic love making, I slept deeply and peacefully. I woke up purposely early so I could call my parents, even though I was dreading telling my mom. Four in the morning, Tom fast asleep, I gathered myself and dialed. Mom answered.

"Hi, Mom."

"Anna! How are you? Isn't it quite early there?"

"Yeah, it's around four, but I've got some news. Um, could you get Dad on the phone, too?"

"News? Oh God, Anna, please tell me you're not pregnant."

"Geez, Mom, no, I'm not pregnant. Could you just get Dad?" I rolled my eyes.

"Well, good. Richard?! Anna's on the phone." I heard some rustling in the background and then my dad's comforting voice.

"Hi, sweetheart, how are things in London? How's Tom?" My dad asked.

"Good, ah, great! Look, I have some news… um, well, Tom proposed to me last night and I accepted."

"Oh, that's great, honey, congratulations!" my dad exclaimed. My mother remained silent, but I could feel her steely glare over the phone line.

"He told me he asked you first," I reminded him.

"Yes, yes, he di…"

"What?" my mom said loudly into the phone, "You knew about this and didn't tell me?" Oops.

"I thought it would be a nice surprise," my dad countered.

And the bickering went on and on between the two of them while I waited patiently, adding up the cost of the call in my head. Finally, my mom said to me, "Anna, it's too soon. You don't know him well enough. Why don't you just take some time getting to know him while you live together, and then get married?"

"Mom, we aren't getting married tomorrow. We're thinking the spring, so that will give us a few more months anyway, not that anything is going to change."

"Anna, you can't know a person that well in two months. Remember Eric? You dated him for four months before you found out what a destructive person he was, even though you suspected something was awry. And then there was Graham, of course. You dated him for a year and…"

"Please, Mom, cut it out. I know all this and lived through it. I was also much younger then. Besides, you've met Tom, you know what he's like."

Tom came into the living room half asleep and tilted his head, seeing the exasperated look on my face. He stretched his arms above his head, took a breath and then held out his hand for me to give him the phone.

I interrupted my mom's complaints and informed her Tom wanted to talk to her and I gladly handed it over. I slumped down on the living room chair in a huff.

"Hi, Jenny, how are you?" Tom asked, his voice deeper from just waking up.

Tom's voice went up a notch and his eyes got wider, "What was I thinking? Clearly, I…" he then ran his free hand through his hair.

"Yes, yes, I know it's only been a couple of months, but I assure…"

"Yes, I understand, but…"

"I…"

And it went on and on like this, Tom trying to get a word in, unsuccessfully. He often pursed his lips, closed his eyes tightly, and even once, held the phone out and pretended to strangle it, which made me snort.

He was trying to keep his composure, but he's never had to deal with the wrath of my mother. He finally took a deep breath and I assume interrupted her diatribe, "Jenny, stop, just… stop. Please. And listen. I love your daughter very much. I've never met anyone like her and I know we are meant to be. I also would be very proud to be your and Richard's son-in-law. I did not have a close relationship with my parents, especially since I lost my mother at such a young age, so I am hopeful I can forge one with you two." He winked at me.

After a few more minutes of silence from Tom, listening with his eyes shut and nodding his head, he finally smiled and said, "Thank you, Jenny... Yes... Yes, and... okay, me too. Bye." And he hung up the phone.

I looked up at him.

He took a deep breath and slowly breathed out in disbelief.

"Wow. That was... well, anyway." He stared at me, almost haggard looking, as if he got into another bar fight.

"What did she say?"

"After her long, long litany of complaints, she started to come around—a bit. She at least stated that I'm the only boyfriend she's ever liked of yours, so I guess that's a start. And she said that even though she wishes we'd wait a bit, she expressed that she is happy for us."

"You are a miracle worker," I exclaimed.

"It just takes some patience, em, a lot of patience. I understand where she is coming from—I could see it being a bit soon from a parent's perspective. Especially, after your track record of men."

"That... was a long time ago." I eyed my ring, hoping that was true.

"I want you to meet my grandfather as soon as possible. I've told him all about you and he is over the moon that I found someone special."

"He's in Scotland, right?"

"Yes, and since you haven't been, I thought we could steal away for a few days. Maybe after all the Halloween madness is over. Would you be able to take off the Friday after so we could make it a three-day holiday?"

"Probably. We don't seem that busy, I'll see what I can do."

"Brilliant! Now, if you don't mind, I am going back to bed. Not only is it rather early, but talking to your mother is exhausting."

CHAPTER 12

— *October 28, Tuesday*

I called Tom from work to see if he wanted to meet Jamie and me around 5:30 for drinks. He didn't have to work tonight, but the next few nights were going to be pretty hectic for him.

"Will Seamus be along?" he asked with hope in his voice.

"I don't know. Does that matter?" I asked, slightly entertained.

"No, I guess not. Sure, I'll come. Just text me a little bit before you're about to leave."

Later, Tom met Jamie and me at the pub around the corner from our work. Seamus couldn't make it, and Tom seemed a little disappointed. We took our seats at a high top while Tom went to order three ales. Coming back to the table with three glasses in hand, he carefully set them down on the table and then took a seat opposite me and next to Jamie.

Leaning back in his chair, Tom took a long sip and closed his eyes.

"You tired?" asked Jamie.

Keeping his eyes closed, he responded, "Em, yes. I didn't get much sleep last night."

Jamie nudged me; I rolled my eyes and told her to grow up. Then, to my peripheral view on the left, I saw a petite, eloquently dressed woman start to approach our table. She wore a tailored velvet rose colored jacket over an ecru blouse with a charcoal pencil line skirt. Her blond hair was pulled back in a high ponytail and her rouge was perfectly applied, showing off her high cheekbones. She looked to be about my age, maybe a couple years older.

"Tom?" The woman asked as she stopped next to him. His left eye opened slowly and then, startled, his right popped open. He tried to compose himself, stood up, bumped the table and spilled a little of our drinks.

"Lily, h..hi." He kissed her right on her left chiseled cheekbone. Their baby would be beautiful, I thought, then admonished myself internally.

"It's been a long time, Tom. You look fantastic, as usual. How have you been?" she asked with an air of skepticism. Or was that just my imagination?

"Em, good, good, ah splendid, actually. Em, this is my fiancée Anna, and our dear friend, Jamie. Would you like to join us?" Jamie and I said our hellos and then exchanged glances.

"Mmm, no, thank you, I've got my boyfriend waiting for me. So, you're getting married?"

"Yes. We haven't set a date yet, but probably in the spring."

"Okay, well good luck. It was great to see you, Tom. Nice meeting you," she nodded to Jamie and me and then started to leave.

"Wait, Lily, how have you been?" Tom asked, sincerely, touching her shoulder. I noticed an almost imperceptible flinch.

"I'm good, Tom, really good. I'll see you sometime okay." She patted his hand that touched her shoulder and floated to the back of the pub, Tom following her gait.

With his head still turned in her direction, I asked, "Ex-girlfriend, Tom? She's quite pretty."

Slowly, turning his head back to me, his eyes lagging behind, he answered, "Yes, yes she is."

Realizing his preoccupation, he gathered himself and quickly said, "B..but, not as pretty as you, love… or Jamie." He took his seat back, but was obviously a bit discomposed.

"Hmm," Jamie said as she raised her eyebrow at Tom.

"I haven't seen her in four years, so it's a bit of a shock, that's all." Innocently, he opened up his hands and shrugged. "I recall you had a similar reaction to *Graham*."

"Yeah, well, your eyes just about fell out of your head." I said.

In a strangled voice, Tom denied this.

"How long did you two date?" I asked.

"Not long, maybe a month. And we were never committed to each other. We ended very anti-climatically. And I never saw her again until right now. Nothing more, nothing less."

I decided not to press, at least not right now, so we changed the subject. After about a half hour and two ales, my bladder felt like it was going to explode, so I excused myself, leaving Jamie and Tom alone.

After taking what seemed to be five minutes to pee, I came out of the stall to wash my hands when in walked Lily.

"Hi, again," I said, as she looked at her reflection in the mirror.

"Hello, Anne, is it?" She pulled out her mascara and started to reapply it, thickening and darkening her long blond lashes. "So, you and Tom? I gather it's going rather well if you are engaged."

"Anna. Yeah, we're pretty happy."

"How long have you two known each other?" she asked, pulling out her rouge.

"Um, around two months now."

"Huh. Okay." That air of skepticism again.

I paused, faced her high cheek bone and then asked, "Is there a problem or something? I'm just kinda getting a vibe from you, if you don't mind me being so blunt."

She was on her lipstick now. She blotted her lips, then snapped the lid to the base and placed the shiny silver tube back in her clutch. She turned toward me; her beautiful made up face loomed in front of me. "Well, people can change, so I'm not really sure if I should disclose anything. I am not in the business of potentially causing problems."

"Just say it." I said, tersely.

She obviously wanted to tell me since there was no hesitation. "Well, Tom is pretty charming, I'm sure you're aware. I mean, he's very smart, well-spoken, generous, a gentleman at all costs and physically very, *very* attractive, but...." She cut herself off, checked herself in the mirror again, and then continued as she made eye contact with herself. "He's got some issues. Or at least he did. Maybe he's fine now."

I just stared and she continued.

"Our courtship was wonderful at first. We met after work almost every other day. We would walk through the parks or rent a chair while sipping wine. And on the weekends, he took me to outrageously expensive restaurants. We had an all-around good time, but I found it strange he never wanted to do much of anything physical beyond holding hands and kissing. I wanted more, so I pushed a little one night, trying to unbutton his shirt, but he became very guarded and a bit belligerent. I guess I was a little too pushy so he asked me to go. Em, so I just chalked that up to him being nervous, maybe it was too soon for him. Maybe he liked to take things slowly."

I wanted to tell her I didn't have an issue with that, but decided not to act petty. Maybe he just wasn't all that attracted to her. I kept listening, folding my arms.

"So, I let that go. In fact, I thought it was kind of sweet—that maybe he was a virgin."

It took all my energy not to roll my eyes. She finally turned her head and looked straight at me.

"But, I didn't hear from him after that, mind you, this was about a month or so of dating. He called me on the days we didn't meet, so it truly was a full month of being with each other in some form or another. I started to worry because besides that evening, things were going quite famously and I really liked him, I mean, how could you not? He's attractive and rich. So, I decided to go to his flat. Someone let me in downstairs and when I came upon his flat door, it was ajar. I went in, called his name, and found him on his sofa lying down. He was asleep. I approached him and saw he was wearing a short sleeve shirt. I've never seen him in one and I could see why. He had cuts all up and down his arms. One looked really new, like it just happened. I was concerned, so I woke him up. When he saw me, he became mental! He was mad at me for entering his flat unbeknownst to him. And when I started asking him about his cuts, asking if he did this to himself, he completely denied it. He said something about his father but then clammed up, saying that he'd rather not talk about it.

"Anyway, we both calmed down after a bit and made up. So, again, I tried to, you know, get a little physical. I don't want to say what, but I did something he didn't care for, but instead of telling me to stop, he drew into himself and he cowered and cried like a little schoolboy."

"What did you do to him?" I narrowed my eyes at her.

"Nothing much. I guess I was a little too intense for him. But, that's beside the point. I apologized and tried to get him to calm down, but he wouldn't. When he stopped crying, he sat there, catatonic. Anyway, as much as I liked the gent, this was too much and too weird, so I left. Tonight was the first time I've seen him since that night. Have you had any similar experiences with him?"

I shook my head no. I wasn't really lying, at least. I don't think she believed me, however.

"Well, good. Maybe he's cured of whatever that was. I was quite shaken that night and it took me a while to get over it. But, I wish you all the luck in the world. He's quite a catch, ah, if he's okay mentally now. Bye, Anne." And then she abruptly flitted out of the bathroom.

Dammit! I mean, what the hell? I was angry. What a bitch! Was she telling the truth or was she just jealous and trying to make trouble for us? She sure seemed like the type. Did it matter if she was telling the truth—it's certainly not a secret that he's guarded about his scars, but I didn't like that she thought his wounds were self-inflicted. That gave me pause.

I came out of the bathroom a minute later and headed to our table, Tom eyeing me the whole way over.

"Everything alright, love? You were in there for some time."

"Yeah, everything's alright." I said without too much enthusiasm. Tom looked at me with suspicion, but then went back to his drink and conversation with Jamie.

— *October 29*

It was Wednesday evening and Tom had to work every night through Saturday, Halloween falling on a Friday. This is my favorite time of the year; I absolutely love Halloween. Tom invited Andrea and her boyfriend, Jack and his boyfriend, Seamus and Jamie, and Steven (who declined) to an after-tour get together on Halloween. Tom was planning to take us into a few of the haunted houses. Neither Tom nor I had had an incident since Maryland, so we were hoping all that was behind us. It's easier to push problems aside when there is so much to look forward to. I decided not to tell him about my conversation with Lily, at least not yet. Besides, that situation was a long time ago, if it was even true. And Lily seemed really shallow, so how could he open up to someone like that anyway. Any other doubts, I just let go.

While Tom was at work, I busied myself with going online and looking up wedding checklists and ideas. I surfed the net for an hour or so, listening to The Damned. The phone very rudely interrupted "Maid for Pleasure."

"Hello?"

"'ello Anna, it's Thomas,"

I paused and took a breath, making sure I wouldn't lose my cool. He had been a little more civil the second time I saw him, but not much.

"Hello, Thomas." I said, monotone.

He started to have a bit of a coughing fit before he could speak again.

"Is Tom there? He hasn't been by in a bit."

"He's at work. Being that it's close to Halloween, he has to work more hours."

"I don't," cough, cough, cough, "I don't understand why he works there. My father gave him a shit-load of money in a trust fund and bought him his flat."

"He enjoys the work," I said directly. "Not everything is about money."

"Well, could you see if he could come over tomorrow during the day? I need some help with some financial things."

I hesitated and then said, "What do you need?"

"Well, I just need some financial advice and maybe help to tidy up the place."

It was 6:00 PM, and Tom wouldn't be home for another four or five hours, so I offered to go that night. I figured I could save Tom the trouble and at least help clean the place. Thomas's standards were more on par with mine.

Tom's father sounded a little happier when I said I'd be over tonight and I even offered to bring him some carry-out Chinese.

So, off I went. I picked up the Chinese and took a cab to his house. I figured if he was going to be my father-in-law, I'd need to start acting civil, even though every time I saw Tom without his shirt, I hated Thomas more and more.

I had taken Tom's key, so I could let myself in when I got to the house.

"Who's there?" I heard Thomas call from the kitchen.

"It's me, Anna," I announced as I walked to the kitchen. I saw his father, looking in pretty bad shape, sitting at the table, sifting through some paperwork. A full glass of water sat in the center of the table.

"'ello," he said, not bothering to get up. It probably would have been hard for him anyway.

"So, what did you need sorted out?" I said as I sat down, placing the Chinese food on the table. He just nodded. I guess that was his "thanks."

He pushed the pile of bills toward me. There were a lot of them. I started to organize them in piles with the most urgent due dates on top. He had utility bills, four credit card bills, mortgage, and a few others.

"How do you amass so many credit card charges in one month?" I looked down the list of charges, seeing mostly Amazon and eBay purchases, "Do you spend this kind of money every month?"

"Dunno. I'm a lonely old man who gets his jollies buying things off the Internet. It's not like I can go out shopping often."

"Can you afford all this stuff? I mean, I couldn't and I work."

"What's it to you?"

"Well, it kind of pisses me off you somehow get Tom to pay for all this shit."

He looked away.

I narrowed my eyes at him "Are you doing this on purpose?"

"I don't know what you're talking about," he said quietly.

"You are doing this on purpose! My God, Thomas. Tom would still come over here without a reason, y' know. And you shouldn't be using his money to buy your crap."

He pondered for a second, sniffed and then asked, "How well do you really know my boy?"

"I hope pretty well since we're getting married."

"Married? He proposed?" He barked out a guffaw.

"He didn't tell you?"

"No, he didn't. I think he knows how I would react."

I bristled, "You have a problem with me or something?"

"You? Not at all. It's him." He smiled, wryly.

"What the hell is wrong with you? He's your son. He comes over here to help you, against his better judgment, and I don't understand why he does it! You beat him over and over again when he was just a kid! Do you know he has tons of scars all over his body? Even a fucking smiley face from cigarette burns?"

His father remained silent.

"Yeah, I thought so. Look, I'm going. I thought I could be civil, but every time I look at you, I want to punch you in your smug face." I got up to leave as Thomas grabbed my wrist.

"Let go of me!" His gross, clammy hand made my skin crawl.

"You know Tom is a very, very gifted storyteller?"

"What are you talking about?" I tried to pull my hand away, but he tightened his grip.

"He tells stories for a living and he tells stories for attention. If you sit down, I'll tell you some things you may want to know before you marry him." He finally released his meaty hand from mine.

I was torn between wanting and not wanting to hear him out, but I sat, hesitantly.

"Well, first of all. He's a faggot. I caught him a couple of times with another male."

"He told me that, Thomas. You misinterpreted what you saw with Robbie."

"It wasn't just Robbie. I saw him just a couple years ago—an adult. They were here in his sister's room. I think he thought I wasn't home or somethin', but I caught him fucking another man. He didn't even look surprised when I caught him, he just stared at me and smiled."

"Thomas, I really…"

"Shut it, and listen, girl. There's more." Unwavering, he looked straight into my eyes and leaned in. "He told you I beat him and I put those burns on him? He tell you I kilt his sister, right? He tell you his mum died in a car accident, right?"

I refused to drop my gaze first. I just sat there, arms crossed, fuming. To my surprise, Thomas lowered his eyes and sat back, lacing his fingers together and placing them on the table. His whole demeanor changed; became softer.

"Where should I begin? I guess with his mum. Eloise, my wife, was cursed with bouts of depression. We di'nt really know that's what she suffered from, but looking back, it's quite obvious now. She grew up with a very rich family, but married my poor arse. Even though my side of the family was wealthy, very wealthy, my father wouldn't give me one red cent, the fucker. But, that didn't seem to matter to Eloise. I think she loved me and I don't think it was the lack of money that drove her to depression, I just think something was wrong with her. So, one day, I was out… probably drinking, I'll admit. Eloise was home with Tom, who was nearing five at the time. Elizabeth was God knows where—even at nine she was independent and often away from the house. So, as far as I know, since I wasn't here, Tom found Eloise in the car parked in the garage, a knife in her hand and her wrists slit. When I got home, Tom was just sitting in the kitchen, cross-legged on the floor, eyes wide, but not moving. He was, em, what's the word? Catatonic. So, you see, Tom found his mother dead." A tear escaped his eye.

"My God!" I gasped.

"Well, sit tight, missy, that's not the end of it. I don't think Tom remembers what happened and I'm not going to remind him. But, after that, he started to hurt himself. I would find bruises on his leg or face, just thinking he fell or got into a skirmish at school. But, later, I'd find little cuts on his arms and the like. He got into a lot of fights at school; fights with his sister, too. He could be a pretty mean child, but then he'd show remorse. If he harmed someone at school, he'd go ahead and harm himself. "

"So you're telling me, all those scars and burns, he did to himself? You didn't ever lay a hand on him?" I asked, getting rather defensive, especially after what I had heard from his ex-girlfriend.

"I'm not going to say I never laid a hand on him. Course I did. I'd spank him if he was out of line—especially when he got into fights at school. And I did wail on him a few times, especially when I caught him with Robbie. But no, I never burned him or whipped him like he told you." Thomas then grabbed his drink and downed it in a series of loud gulps. He wiped his mouth and pointed to his drink, gesturing for me to get him more. I rolled my eyes, but did it anyway. After refilling the glass in the messy sink, I set it back down a little harder than I would have for anybody else.

"So, the night his sister died, Tom was in his room and Elizabeth and I were having a row. That wicked girl lashed out at me all the time." He took a long drink. "I told you I di'nt hit Tom much, and that's the truth, but Goddamn right I'd hit her; she needed to be knocked around. That night, I slapped her hard across her face for being so disrespectful to her father. Cursing up a storm, as I told you before, over not allowing her to use the car. Tom must have seen this, and he flies out of the room charging right at me. The boy couldn't even see where he was goin' with his head down, so I stepped to the side. Elizabeth was right behind me, but Tom was blind with rage and couldn't see a thing. He barreled into Elizabeth and knocked her right down the stairs. Down, down she went, arms and legs flailing, screamin' until she hit her head hard on the edge of one of the steps halfway down. Her screams stopped, but she continued her roll until she landed heavily on the last step. My God, the way her face was contorted, she barely looked human, more like a slain monster. I had caught Tom by the arm before he could go careening down with her. So, Tom kilt her, I saved Tom's life. Now go ahead and call me a liar."

It was like he read my thoughts. "You are! You're a liar!" The louder I yelled it, the more it would drown out my doubts, I thought.

He shrugged, "Not about this."

He wasn't done with his story. My heart was beating out of my chest. "I grabbed Tom and shoved him back in his room. I think he was in shock. I left him there while I called 999. She was pronounced dead right over there," he pointed to the bottom of the step and I shuddered.

"I went to hospital anyway, hoping the medics were wrong, but she was dead alright. Hours later, I came home and went up to check on Tom. He was passed out on the bed and that's when I saw them, the burns. His face was a bloody mess as well. I saw his third-place team rugby trophy all bloodied up on the floor next to the bed. He must have taken it and broke his nose with it. When he awoke I told him that Elizabeth had died. Tom didn't remember a thing about what he did—not to 'imself or to his sister, so I let it go. I di'nt want more of the self-mutilation, so I kept telling him that Elizabeth lost her footing. A lot a good it did though. He started cutting 'imself again after. Not sure if he's still doing it, he always wears long sleeves. I'm sure you've seen him undressed. Has he more cuts?"

I didn't want to answer. I thought about the deep cut on his hand when I first met him and then all the blood in Maryland… all the scars on his arms that looked like knife cuts. And then, of course, what Lily said. I didn't want to admit that any of this could be true.

I ignored his question, "Oh my God, Thomas. If this is true—and I'm not saying I believe a word of it—did you consider that maybe he needed some help, therapy? You've helped to create a time bomb!"

He nodded, then he spat, "He was in therapy. Cost me all my savings. From the time he was 14 until he left me high and dry, and alone, he saw that therapist. I had to put him in because he was flying off the handle at school. I remember once, Tom must have been about 14 or so. I was called into the school by the Headmistress. Tom had beat the piss out of some poor bloke, and I mean literally. Tom pummeled the boy so much, the kid pissed himself. And you wanna know why? The boy said something Tom didn't like, so Tom took it upon 'imself to teach 'im a lesson. Later, Tom claimed he didn't remember this at all. He sat there blubbering in the Headmistress's office that he didn't do it. She didn't believe him, of course, and so Tom was suspended. Then, later that night, Tom takes a knife to 'imself. Cuts his arms all up and good. So, I had no choice but to put him in therapy or they wouldn't let 'im back in school. They drugged him up pretty good, trying to figure out what was wrong with him. Antidepressants, lithium, you name it. They diagnosed him with Borderline Personality Disorder. It probably started after he found his mum, which would explain all the self-mutilatin' behavior and the trouble he got into as a child. He likes to hurt people."

"No… that can't be right. He's kind and gentle and caring!" My eyes started to water.

"Okay, missy, who's known my boy for all of what? Two months?! I've known him his whole bloody life and had to deal with his shit. Always gettin' into trouble at school, beating up someone, then cuttin' 'imself! Yeah, it happened more than once, a lot more. And killin' Lizzie? Then he has the nerve to blame me for all his crap. You've seen Tom's temper, yeah? And maybe I made him like that a little. I know I made some mistakes. But, I was a widower with two children to raise without help from my wife's family or from my father. So, don't you judge me, missy. I admit, I was hard on the boy growing up, especially when I saw him with his faggot friend. No son of mine was going to be buggering another mate."

I put my head in my hands, trying to control my shaking. "I don't believe you. If I believe you, then this would mean Tom's been lying to me this whole time."

"It doesn't matter if you believe me or not. It's still the truth. He's a storyteller. He can't help it, Anna; he's sick. He can't deal with who or what he is on the inside, so he lies his way out. In truth, I think he believes his lies. The boy acts like a pretentious prig, an upperclassman with impeccable clothes and taste in wines—it's all an act that he's convinced you of, but most of all, 'imself. I think he does this to protect 'imself… you know, what do they call it? A defense mechanism? But then, he's not completely apathetic; he cuts 'imself as punishment for what he's done or who he's lied to. Like an atonement. It makes him feel better and then life goes on."

I got up quickly to leave, but Thomas grabbed my hand kind of hard and squeezed, talking softly, but sternly, "Does he still claim to have blackouts? Oh, I hit a nerve, didn't I. Well, if you believe that, you're stupider than I thought. He's playing you, Anna. I don't know why, but he's playing you. So, I'd be careful… watch that boy's temper. If I were you, Anna, I'd pawn that very pretty, very expensive ring on your finger and go back to America."

I wrenched my hand from his grip and yelled, "You can go to hell."

"I'm already there," Cough, cough, cough.

I ran out the door, my world spinning. I pulled out my cell and hysterically called for a cab. Tom would be home soon and I didn't want him to worry. But oh, God, what was I going to do?

***

— *Later that night*

I arrived home a little before Tom. During the long ride, the driver kept looking back at me asking if I was alright. I just wanted him to shut up and drive, so I finally lied to him and told him my cousin died and I really wanted to sit in silent prayer. He said he was sorry and stayed quiet the rest of the way. When I got home, I went on autopilot and changed into my Peter Murphy over-sized T-shirt and threw on some sweat pants. My emotions were on high and I needed desperately to calm down and think. I did not know what I was going to do. I couldn't hide this from Tom, could I? Fuck. Fuck. Fuck!

I sat down in the living room chair, staring at the fireplace, staring at the paisley patterned tiles. I struggled to organize in my head the oceans of thoughts, the waves of emotions, until I could no longer contain any of it. I cried and cried and couldn't stop. I didn't even hear the door open, so when Tom was crouched in front of me, I jumped.

"Anna, love, what's wrong?!" he asked, lines deepening on his forehead. I was such an idiot. Seeing him, so concerned, made me cry harder.

"Anna, come on, is it your mum?" He asked as he wiped the tears from my eyes with a handkerchief, but the faucet was relentless.

I shook my head.

"Richard? Jamie? What is it?"

I sucked in air with staggered breaths, trying to regain control, but it didn't work. My emotions pulled at each other—anger at Tom, hatred toward Thomas and Lily, compassion for Tom. I didn't know who was right, who was lying. Or, was there some kind of truth in between. Looking at Tom, my thoughts pounding at my temples, I couldn't take it anymore, so, I screamed. I screamed a relentless barrage of profanity at Tom, who just looked bewildered. I pushed him away from me while I stood up from the chair and went into the kitchen. Walking over to the faucet, I turned it on and splashed water on my face, the water diluting the salty streaks on my cheeks. Finally, my breathing and emotions started to ebb. Feeling a soft hand on my shoulder, I turned from the sink and stared into Tom's concerned face. He put his arm around me, while I let him guide me back into the living room. Silently, we sat down on the sofa, Tom waiting patiently until I was ready to speak. I took a breath and then started, "At the pub, I had a conversation with Lily." I spoke into his chest, my head in the crook of his shoulder.

"Lily? Is that why you took so long in the loo?" Tom asked, as he stroked my hair.

I nodded and recounted what she told me, calming slightly more as I spoke.

"Well, she's got it partially right."

I sat up and looked at him, tears starting again, but slower, wetting my shirt, waiting for him to elaborate.

"Lily had some pretty salacious proclivities, which I was not into. I had called her less and less and thought she'd get the hint. I guess I should have just told her. But, she *did* walk into my flat one night while I was asleep and we *did* argue and we *did* calm down after our row. I didn't feel the need to bring up my abusive past, especially since I really wasn't interested in pursuing a relationship with her. But then, one thing led to another and we started to kiss. I remember her trying to take off my shirt, for which I told her to stop, but she was relentless. I was very self-conscious about my scars, as I still am, and didn't want to show them. She got pissed and slapped me across my face incredibly hard; as I said, she was into that sort of thing. I told her to get out, and that was that the end of it."

"So, you didn't react the way she said you did?"

"Of course not, love. She wanted to scare you off, get me back for breaking it off. But, that can't be what's gotten you this upset."

I sniffed some more and said, "Um, your father called and..."

"I am going to murder him." Tom took a deep breath to calm himself down. "What did he say to you?" He stood up, took off his coat, and threw it on the plush arm of the sofa.

My breath shuddered as I inhaled and exhaled, trying to calm down.

"He asked if you could come over tomorrow during the day, that you hadn't been over there in a bit. I asked him what he needed and he told me he needed help with some bills and to help clean up some. So, I offered to go over so you didn't have to and that's what I did. I even brought him some take-out."

"You did not have to do that. My father is my burden and I wouldn't wish that onus upon anyone… especially you." Tom said, sternly. He sat down on the sofa, facing me.

"I know. I was just trying to help. So, I got there and I helped him organize his bills, which he could have done himself. He just wants attention, so he makes up any excuse he can think of. Plus, he wants you to pay the bills. I even called him on it."

"Yes, Anna. I know he does it on purpose."

I sniffed a few times and wiped my eyes with the back of my hand. "Okay. So, anyway, I mentioned something about our engagement. He didn't know."

"No, I didn't tell him. I was going to wait. I just didn't want to hear all the guffaws and criticism."

"That's fine. I don't care. But, Tom, he told me," and then I hesitated, worried it could set him off—time bomb, time bomb echoed in my head. Tom looked at me with such unconditional concern it about killed me. He stood up from the sofa and crouched in front of me again.

"What is it, sweetheart, you can tell me." He caressed my face.

I covered my mouth with my hand, trying to hold back the tears. Tom gently took my hand away from my face.

"Will this cause you to leave me?" he asked, voice cracking.

I shook my head 'no.'

"Because I can handle anything— besides that."

I barely nodded and I decided to take my chances.

"Tom, before I start, you have to know that no matter what, I am committed to you, okay? No matter what."

Tom was quiet, but his breathing was getting a little faster, in fact I swear I could hear his heart beating.

"Well, first your father told me that he rarely laid a finger on you. That he spanked you a bit and was a bit rough with you when he found you with Robbie, but other than that, he denied all the abuse."

"So, how in the world did I acquire so much scarring on my body that I'm too self-conscious about to even go swimming? Or the cigarette burns? Did those come from merely being spanked?"

I sighed, here goes. "He said you did it."

"What do you mean, I did it?"

"Self-flagellation, self-mutilation, whatever. What Lily kind of insinuated."

"THAT'S what he told you?"

"He also said that the reason you did this was because when you were a young boy, you were the one who found your mother. Geez, this is hard to say." I teared up some more, then took a breath and continued. "He said she committed suicide in the car in the garage and you found her. Not a car accident. He said that after that, you started acting out and harming others, and then yourself, probably from the guilt." I looked up at him, my tears blurring his face.

Tom started to seethe. He stood up and started pacing.

Finally, he spoke, "That… piece of… I'm going to kill him." Then he turned to me and looked down into my face.

"Please tell me you don't believe him. I mean, two days and two different people tell you similar things… I'm astonished. It's as if they're plotting against me." He looked hurt and frightened.

"He just sounded so convincing. And he told me you were placed in therapy after Elizabeth died, that you were on all sorts of medication for Borderline Disorder, and…"

Tom interrupted, "Borderline Disorder? What the fuck?" He began pacing again, clenching his fists.

I continued, "It was after you beat some kid up in school really badly, and you started cutting yourself more. He said that you liked to hurt people, and that you still do. Tom, you've got to tell me the truth, right now. Just tell me and I'll believe whatever you say." I bowed my head, ashamed that I could even think ill of him, and then I started to cry harder.

Tom grabbed two fistfuls of his hair. "Anna, as I told you before, the therapy I was in did nothing. It was some two-bit counsellor who asked me inane questions and drugged me up, and that was it. I didn't harm others in school, I didn't cut myself, I didn't have sexual relations with Robbie. I was a good kid with a fucked up, abusive father and a dead mother and a sister who ran hot and cold with me. Again, I dealt with it, and I am who I say I am. The man whom you see in front of you is the real thing."

He crouched down again to be even with my face, lifting up my chin with his hand. He looked deep into my eyes as he dropped his hand to my knee. "Anna, do you really think I fabricated all the abuse? That I made up these memories? These scars? I'm going to be your husband for Christ's sake. You've accused me of being that ridiculous Vigilante and now you're taking the word of my father and a sadistic ex-girlfriend you've spoken to once?" His eyes started to glisten.

"Tom, please don't cry. I… I believe you… I do. I'm just trying to make sense of it all. I mean, why would your father tell me this? Why would your ex-girlfriend?"

"Because my father is a fucking arse!" He stood up and pounded his fist on the fireplace mantle. "You think he's going to admit what he did to me? What he did to Elizabeth? And I… I don't know what to say about my mother. I don't recall any of what he said—I remember the police coming by and telling us my mother had a car accident and died on the scene. I'm going to call him." He went for the phone.

I jumped up and grabbed his arm. "No, Tom, please don't call him. It's not going to do any good; it will only exacerbate the situation."

Tom set the receiver down and then sat on the sofa. He leaned his head back, bounced his leg up and down and stared at the ceiling, "As you wish, Anna." But his hands were shaking badly.

I did not tell him about Elizabeth or ask him about Thomas catching him with another guy. This was enough.

CHAPTER 13

*The stalker, murderer, attacker was out of sorts. He was frustrated and didn't
know what to do. He was reeling from the news. How was he going to handle this?
He needed a release. He took a cab to the Docklands. Dressed in all black, he
found a gay bar. He went in and watched, watched everyone until his eyes glazed
over, waited until ultimately his patience paid off. Sitting alone at a table, the man
was tall and attractive with medium-length black hair slicked back, out of his
eyes. He wore a fitted satin button-down shirt tucked into skinny jeans, ending in
a pair of black Italian loafers. The stalker strolled over to the man's table, tapped
him on his shoulder, and... offered him a cigarette.*

— *Thursday morning, October 30*

Drained from an emotional night, I passed out pretty quickly, sleeping deeply
until my alarm went off at 6:30 AM. I assumed Tom hadn't come into the
room last night since I found him lying on the sofa, all curled up and still in
his clothes. I kneeled on the floor next to him and brushed his hair away.

"Tom, honey?"

He opened his eyes; his mouth set in a deep frown. He sat up and asked the
time, his voice a little hoarse.

"It's about 6:30. I have to go to work soon. Are you okay? I missed you last
night."

He sat there crestfallen, looking sideways, chewing on his lower lip. "I'm just
glad you're still here."

"Oh, Tom. Of course I'm still here. We'll work this out, okay? I believe you,
not them." I decided at that moment that this would be my mantra; trust Tom,
nobody else.

I kissed his forehead and left him alone so I could get ready for work.

After showering and getting dressed, I went back into the living room. Tom
was no longer on the sofa. In fact, I started to wonder if he was even in the
flat, it was so quiet.

"Tom?" I went into the kitchen and found the coffee made and a note next to
it:

Gone to see my father. Please do not worry or follow me. I can handle this.

I love you,

Tom

Oh, great. I poured myself some coffee, drank it, turned off the pot and went on to work. I was torn, but I felt I needed to respect his wishes. I hoped he wasn't going to do anything rash.

***

Noon rolled around at work and I still hadn't heard from Tom. I made it a point to try him after lunch. I sat with my regular crew, who all peppered me with questions about tomorrow night. I tried my best to seem cheery.

At 1:00, I tried his cell. No answer. No answer when I tried the flat, either. Dammit! I then tried his father's house.

"'ello?"

"Thomas, it's Anna. Is Tom over there?" I asked with venom.

"He was and oh, was he in a state."

"What do you mean? What happened?"

"He accused me of lying and trying to sabotage his relationship with you. And then that temper flared up further and he punched me right in the chest," he started coughing.

"I really don't believe you, Thomas."

"I don't give a toss what you believe and don't believe, missy! But, when you do something to piss him off, watch out. He'll hurt himself, oh yes, but he'll hurt you first."

"Whatever Thomas. What time did he leave?"

"9:30."

I just sighed into the receiver.

"Awright?" he asked.

And I hung up the phone abruptly. Shit!

I did the best I could to concentrate on work, but I was really concerned. Jamie asked me a couple of times if everything was okay, despite my efforts to hide my worry. I assured her things were fine, that I was just tired. At least I was being half honest.

Around 2:00, my office phone rang.

"Hello, Anna Pearson." I answered curtly.

"Anna?"

"Oh God, Tom. Are you all right? I was so worried," I whispered into the phone as Steven walked by and glanced into my cube.

"I'm fine. I'm sorry I didn't call earlier. I just had to be alone after I saw my father. I went to Hyde Park and walked around a lot."

"Okay. How are you feeling?"

"How am I feeling? Em, I'm feeling my father is a bastard. I just wanted to yank that oxygen tank from him and throw it at his head and be done with him. His main concern was to get me to give him 5,000 pounds toward a new car. When I confronted him on the lies he told about the self-mutilation and everything else you told me he said, he just smiled at me. When I asked him about my mother, however, he told me what he told you. I don't know if that's true or not... I'm going to talk to my grandfather. Maybe he can shed some light on this."

I breathed out into the phone.

Maybe Thomas was lying, but why? He sounded so convincing. Then again, so did Tom. I was confused.

"On the phone, he claimed you punched him."

"Bloody hell! When? Today? By God, I wanted to badly, but no, I didn't lay a hand on him." Tom refuted.

"Um, do you want me to cancel with the group tomorrow night?"

"For this? Of course not. Besides, it will be a good distraction," he reasoned, calming ever so slightly.

"Okay, sweetheart. I'll see you in a few hours." Steven walked by again, this time with a grimace.

"I love you, Anna," and then he hung up.

Christ.

***

— *After work*

I took a cab home because I wanted to get there quickly. Upon opening the door to the flat, my nostrils flared from a commingling of aromatic spices. Tom must be cooking some kind of ethnic dish.

"You're home early," Tom said with a smile, giving me a kiss when I walked into the kitchen. It was good to see him smile, although his eyes were a bit red and puffy. I'm sure he had a very emotional day.

"I took a cab. I felt so bad today leaving you alone," I said as he went back to the stove.

"Why? You don't think I've been dealing with this crap my whole life? I had quite the cathartic experience. Yelling at him felt, well, wonderful. But, Anna, I did ask him about my mum. He told me she committed suicide and I found her," he said, looking down at the dish he was making. "I really can't remember, but something about it seems so familiar. He could be right; I just don't know. It was so long ago."

"I still think you should see a therapist, Tom. I really do."

"Well, dinner is ready. Are you hungry? I found a recipe for a Massaman curry tofu and I think you will like it. I also made some green beans." He ignored me, again.

"Okay," dropping it. "Let me just get changed." I hurried to the bedroom, relieved that Tom seemed okay, but trying to decide whether I should tell him about his sister or not. I put on my jeans and a plain green T-shirt. Barefoot, I went to the dining room table, already set.

"Are you still going to work tonight?" I asked as he joined me at the table.

He stared at me, head cocked, paused and said, "Yes, I have an obligation."

"Do you want me to go with you?"

"You can if you want to, but…. Is something else wrong?"

I thought for a minute, then decided to leave it alone. "No, it's just been a confusing and emotional couple of days."

Softly, "He really got to you, didn't he? He has a way with stories."

Startled, I looked up at him, "That's what he said about you."

Flicking his eyes at me and not completely getting it, he said, "Very different sort of stories. I tell lore, he tells lies."

I continued eating and tried to change the subject.

"I think I'm going to look into some wedding stuff tonight, while you're at work."

"Mmmm… on that, I thought it would be good to hire a wedding planner to help us with the festivities. We would still be able to make the decisions, but at least we would have someone keeping us straight. I don't want this to be stressful, I want it to be fun."

"Aren't they expensive?"

"We really don't have to concern ourselves with money, as I've told you before. I've got enough money for us to live a fulfilling life right into our old age. In fact, you don't have to work." I stiffened at this, but he held up his hand, "You don't *have* to work, but I certainly wouldn't stop you if you wanted to keep it up."

"I'll want to keep working, definitely."

"That's fine. So, then, there really is no issue at all with a wedding planner."

"No, you're right, I think it would be a good idea. I'll look at reviews online tonight."

We finished our meal. I told Tom I would clean up so he could get ready for work. He raised one eyebrow at me.

"What?"

He scratched his head, "Em, I know you've been trying, but I often find your clothes strewn about in the morning, dishes in the sink and the coffee grounds all over the counter or the pot not cleaned after you've finished. So, maybe you are not trying so much, like you promised to?"

I sighed, "Sorry, I'll try harder."

"That's my girl," Tom smiled, kissed me, and went into the bedroom to get his clothes for the night. After a few minutes, he flitted back out and said, "I'll be back in a few hours, love," as he closed the front door behind him.

— *Friday, October 31—Halloween*

There was absolutely no way my Halloween was going to be ruined. So, I did what I do well. I pushed all doubts and fears far back into my mind. And besides, Halloween is all about pretending, so that's what I chose to do. The office was a blast. Everyone was dressed up in something. Even Steven wore a costume. I came in as a punk rocker—tribute to my old high school days. I wore fish nets, black pleather Doc Martens, a holey Sex Pistols shirt, and my pleather jacket adorned with chains, safety pins and studs. I borrowed Tom's gel and used it to make my hair go in all sorts of directions. A studded dog collar choked my neck, and I was even able to reinsert a hoop nose ring through the hole I thought had closed up. Jamie, on the other hand came in as some kind of schizophrenic witch, I think.

"I'm so looking forward to tonight! Seamus bought a Ouija Board." Jamie said.

"That should be interesting."

"Let's go eat. There are all sorts of treats in the cafeteria." Jamie rubbed her hands together, quickly, with a smile.

We found Steven dressed as a vampire, picking through the array of tasty Halloween treats: Bloody finger cookies, a graveyard cake, candied eyeballs. It was fantastic.

"Hey Steven, are you sure you won't come tonight?" I asked.

"No, han yu," he tried to say with white, plastic fangs in his mouth.

"Come on, Steven, are you afraid?" Jamie teased.

He reached in his mouth and removed the fangs; a line of spit attached from his lip to the fake teeth.

As he sucked in, he said with irritation, "No Jamie, I am not afraid. I just don't want to."

"Oh, okay, Steven, but I…"

"Jamie, leave him alone, he doesn't want to come." I said. Steven had become really mopey, especially since he found out I was engaged. He grabbed a bloody finger and walked out of the room.

"He's got it bad," Jamie noted, watching him leave.

"You're so mean, Jamie. I feel really guilty whenever he's around. He's always staring at my ring or grimacing when I talk about Tom. He shouldn't have waited to ask me out."

"Would you have gone with him?"

"Ah, maybe as a friend, but no. I don't have chemistry with him. He's too, ah…"

"Safe and ordinary?"

I raised one eyebrow, but then nodded as I stuffed some graveyard cake into my mouth.

***

I went home in my punk rock outfit, not really getting any odd looks on the tube. I entered the flat and found Tom sitting on the sofa going over some note cards.

"Hi. Oh, hi! Look at you!" He beamed and stood up.

"Yeah, I got into costume at work, but decided to wear it home on the subway, um tube. You like it?"

"Em, yes… very sexy, that is if you're into punk rockers."

"And are you?"

He laughed, "No, not really, but it's you, so I'll make an exception."

I pressed my lips hard to his cheek, putting a black lipstick print on his face, "Nice," I said. He gave me a sideways glance and sat back down, resuming studying his cards.

"I'm preparing for tonight. It's going to be a large crowd."

"You know, Seamus bought a Ouija Board."

"That was the plan."

"Do you believe in that?"

Tom shrugged, "When I feel something at some of the haunted places, it makes me believe. I think the Ouija Board may just be another conduit to those feelings, so we'll see. I've never experimented with one."

"I'm going to get a quick bite to eat, then we can go, okay?"

"Yup," Tom vacantly answered, rapt in his note cards, holding them at arm's length. He wasn't wearing his reading glasses.

"Did you eat?" I hollered from the kitchen.

I didn't get an answer, so I walked back into the living room.

Then softer, "Tom, did you eat?"

"Uh huh."

"What's got you so engrossed, don't you know that stuff by heart yet?"

"Mmmm… some new *stuff*." He flicked his eyes up at me, then back down to his reading. He hates that word, once admonishing me about how lazy it was to say.

"Okay, well enjoy your new *stuff*." I saw him tighten his mouth. He can be so stodgy at times. Am I cruel to push his buttons? Nah, he deserves it. Then Thomas's voice rang in my head, 'wait 'til you say something that pisses him off.' I quickly thought of something else—food.

I went back to the kitchen and grabbed some leftovers from the fridge, ate them up and drank some water. After going into the bathroom to reapply my makeup and redo my hair, Tom came in right behind me and looked in the mirror above my head, seeing the black lips marked on his face.

"Cute." He crowded me out of the way and washed his face, smudging the black lip marks until they were gone.

"Are you ready?" Tom dried his face on the towel.

"Yup… lemme grab my *stuff*." I responded.

"You are really asking for it."

"Yeah, right." But then Thomas's warnings punched through my mind… again. I quickly squashed them down.

***

Tom wanted to get there a little early, so he could prepare more. In the cab, I asked him what we were going to do after his tour.

"We are going back to a couple of places in Clerkenwell and trying out one or two new spots."

"Okay, I'm planning on getting some drinks with the crew and then we'll meet you after your last tour?"

"Yes, around 2200 hours. Em, were you able to research a wedding planner?"

"Ah, no, not really time to."

"Yes, of course. Well, maybe tomorrow."

We got to the tourist center and my friends were already there.

I introduced Tom to Andrea's boyfriend, Lee, and Jack's boyfriend, Christopher. Seamus gave Tom a huge handshake and a big hug. Andrea was in a Playboy Bunny costume (she had enough sense not to wear this one to work, she just wore the bunny ears), and Jack and Christopher were Kirk and

Spock. I think Lee was going for Hugh Heffner, based on the robe, and Seamus was Beetlejuice. Jamie was still the odd-looking witch. She had a broom and a long black dress and the witch's hat, but also Barbie dolls attached to her dress. I think she was confused. I didn't feel like asking her about it. The mystery of it was more intriguing.

"Hey, mate, look at this," and Seamus grabbed the Ouija Board sitting on the step.

"Ah, yes, it's a Ouija Board," Tom acknowledged.

"This is dog's bollocks! We're going to get pissed first and then we're on it!"

"Seamus, calm down. Tom, this is all he's been talking about since the last tour we did with you," Jamie said taking Tom by the arm.

"Eh. Would you stop flirting with 'im?" Seamus said, obviously irritated.

"Well, I must be off to work, but I'll meet you right here after. I have a few places to take you." Tom pulled out of Jamie's grasp, kissed her on the cheek, came over to me, and did the same.

"Have fun, love." And off he went.

"Did you see his eyes?" Jack asked Christopher.

"What's the deal with his eyes? They're fucking eyes. That's all I hear from Jamie; you all are mental," Seamus huffed.

Christopher looked at Seamus, "Are you serious? Look at them, they're beautiful. I got shivers when he looked at me." And Jamie, Andrea, Jack and Christopher all nodded in agreement. Lee and Seamus put their hands in their pockets.

"All right guys, stop fawning over my fiancé, okay? Let's go to the pub." I ordered.

Lee and Seamus cheered, and off we went, costumes and all.

We hit a pub I hadn't been to yet, around the corner from the visitor center. It looked like a place a vampire would like to hang out, dimly lit and somewhat chilly. The walls all had a black background with a raised, red, velvety pattern. There were small chandeliers above the tables that looked as if the dangling glass pieces were drops of blood. The tables were wooden, old and scratched, as were the chairs. The cushions on the chairs were worn velvet, but comfortable. We all took our seats and ordered some appetizers and ales.

"Where is Tom taking us tonight?" Seamus probed.

"I'm not positive, but we are definitely going back to the Farrington tube station and Charterhouse Square, but he told me there may be a couple other places."

Seamus started bouncing in his seat.

"Calm down, you git. You look like you need to use the loo," Jamie scolded.

"Shut it, woman!"

The table erupted in laughter, especially Jamie. Seamus didn't find it too funny, though.

Christopher said, "So Anna, we were all talking at the visitor center."

Jack gave Christopher a sideways look.

"What?"

Jamie blurted out, "What's he like in bed?"

Seamus let out a big groan, "Why are you all so fascinated with Tom. He's just a regular bloke, like me."

Jamie barked a laugh.

"Well if you think so highly of 'im and not me, you, Anna and Jack can have a ménage a trois with him and I'll stay out of it."

"Em, that would be only three," said Jamie, stating the obvious.

"What would be only three?" Seamus asked innocently. Even though I was stifling a laugh, I felt bad for Seamus. Jamie can be pretty obnoxious, sometimes. I guess that's why we get along so well.

"Em, nothing. Relax, Seamus. You know I love you. We're just having fun and we're just a little curious." She looked at me pleadingly, "He's so proper... I mean..."

I rolled my eyes. "Oh, come on. I'm not going to give you details. I don't think Tom would appreciate it either."

"Just rank it, from a scale from one to ten," Andrea pushed, Lee giving her a "what the fuck" look.

"You guys really suck," I said. "I mean, what is with you? I know he's attractive, but geez," I complained, but honestly it felt pretty good inside.

"You are kidding, right Anna?" Christopher remarked.

"What?"

"He's gorgeous, I mean, he could be People's sexiest man if he were an actor. And he's so... mysterious." Jack proclaimed.

"Can we please drop this? You're obviously making Anna uncomfortable. Let alone me and Lee. The bloke is cool and I really like him as well, but I don't want to be going around with him, knowing my girlfriend wants to bed him." Seamus implored.

"What happened to the stereotypical British reserve? I'm changing the subject." I interjected, "So tonight, who is going to play the Ouija Board?" I said, curtly.

Most everyone raised their hands, Seamus's shooting up first, Lee's staying down.

"Not you, Lee?" I raised my eyebrows.

"No, I'll just watch. Those things get me all jittery."

We ordered a couple more rounds, the conversations breaking into groups, rather than the whole table. I had Jamie and Andrea's attention, asking me about the wedding plans.

"I've been wanting to ask you two, um, Jamie, I wanted to see if you'd be my maid of honor and Andrea, if you'd be one of my bridesmaids?"

Jamie jumped up and gave me a huge hug, "I was hoping you'd ask me. Of course!" The guys seemed to not notice.

"Yes, that would be fabulous," exclaimed Andrea. "What about Jack?" she whispered. "He's been talking about it since you got engaged."

Jack was engrossed in a conversation with the rest of the guys.

"Tom and I already talked about it. He doesn't have a lot of close friends or family, more acquaintances, so he's going to ask him to be a groomsman. He thought Seamus might be a good choice for best man, especially since Jamie's my maid of honor. Don't tell either of them, though." I said, quietly.

Jamie whisper-yelled, "Seamus is going to wet his pants! As jealous as he is of Tom, he talks about him all the time and loves their Thursday nights together. If he were a girl or gay, he'd swoon like the rest of us," Jamie divulged, quietly.

"Geez, you'd think I was marrying Benedict Cumberbatch," I said a little loudly, the alcohol taking effect.

"Better," Jack said.

***

Besides Lee, we were all a little drunk. Just a little. Enough to lower some inhibitions, like going to known haunted places and conjuring up spirits. I was nervous, though. I didn't want to have another episode, but I figured if I was going to have one, this may be the way to give me some answers.

We headed back to the visitor center to meet Tom. He was finishing up with the group, who were all enrapt in his final thoughts. Once he finished answering questions and thanking people for their tips, he came over to me and gave me a huge embrace, knocking me off balance, but holding me up.

"How did it go?" I asked as he let go.

"Brilliant, I think. It was a very good group tonight and I believe I was more 'on' than usual. How was the pub?" He tilted his head and looked at me, questioning, "Are you drunk?"

"Just a little," I slurred.

"Mmmm…" His expression was inscrutable. But, he put one arm around my shoulder and greeted everyone else with a nod. "Let me get changed and I'll be right back. Please see Claudia inside who will lend you a few lanterns."

Jamie and I went in and brought out three lanterns for the group, figuring Tom would have his own. After about ten minutes, Tom emerged from the glass doors in ripped black jeans with safety pins holding the holes closed, black Doc Martens, a worn Ministry T-shirt and an old, beaten up leather jacket. His hair was too long to be spikey, but it was messy in a Robert Smith sort of way. He even had an earring, a clip-on. A dog's choker chain adorned his neck and he wore black eyeliner, accenting his penetrating eyes; his lantern in hand. My jaw must have dropped open.

"Flies are going to enter your mouth, Anna," Tom taunted as he walked by me.

"I… just… I like your costume." I leered at him.

"I figured as much. Just remember, it's just a costume," he winked. The others came over to say how cool he looked.

"Well, shall we? Off to the Clerkenwell House of Detention."

"How are we getting in there?" Lee's voice was a bit shaky.

"I know people," Tom stated in a low, cryptic voice.

We walked through the streets, crowded with pub patrons and partiers. Black cabs, double decker buses, and cars whirled by us as we made our way to Clerkenwell Close and then onto a tiny road that led to a large building. Tom walked us around until we found what we came for. In front of us loomed an alleyway with a creepy set of steps descending to an old closed door. Tom began with a flourish of his hand: "I give you... The Catacombs!" Everyone oohed. A devilish expression quickly crossed Tom's face as he extracted his keys, walked down the steps, and unlocked the door.

We followed him down and cautiously entered a very dank, barely lit tomb-like room. The walls were all weathered brick, with holding cell doors trapped between the brick walls. The musty smell accosted us all as we went through the arched tunnels. The lanterns gave us no comfort; they only cast an eerie glow. Cautiously, we walked further into the bowels of the tunnel until Seamus suggested we stop. We set our four lanterns down onto the dusty floor while Seamus started unboxing the Ouija Board, but only with one hand because Jamie was clutching his other arm very tightly.

"Some of you may know the history of the Clerkenwell House of Detention," Tom began in a deep, menacing voice, "It was erected in 1847, built on two previous prisons, dating back to 1616. In 1890, the prison was destroyed, but these tunnels remain. The Hugh Myddleton Primary School was built on the site, on top of these catacombs. The school later moved, and the building was converted to trendy flats. I find the juxtaposition very unsettling, first when children played gleefully above the catacombs and second, currently how people are watching the telly, surfing the net, eating with their loved ones, all above this place that housed prisoners. In fact, thousands of men, women and children have been incarcerated here throughout its history. Historians say that this prison was not as bad as some others as people could don their own clothes, however, I can only imagine what it is was really like. No sun, horrible provisions, and possibly torture, all ensued where we stand now. There have been many accounts of ghostly activity here, but I don't want you to experience anything because of the power of suggestion, rather, I'll leave it to Seamus."

"Awright," Seamus said as he sat down cross legged on the cold, dark floor, pulling Jamie down with him, who had not released her death grip. "Who's up first with me?"

Jack sat right down. They placed their fingers on the planchette, a three-legged triangular piece of plastic with a clear round window toward the apex. It immediately started to move.

"You're not moving it, are you mate?" Asked Seamus, his voice a high whisper.

Jack, wide-eyed, slowly shook his head. We all stooped down to get a closer look. All the lanterns were huddled around the board, so the darkness stretched outwardly even further.

"Ask it a question," encouraged Jamie. We all closed in on the board and each other. I wrapped my arms tightly around Tom's right arm, leaving it immobile. I noticed Lee holding Andrea; Lee just looked like he wanted to leave. Christopher sat closely next to Jack, their shoulders touching.

"Em, okay, em, 'are there any spirits here who would like to chat with us?'" Seamus asked, warily.

The planchette, scraping the board, moved slowly, but directly to "yes." Seamus looked up at all of us, then down again. Jack's eyes were plastered to the board.

The planchette then spelled out "S-A-L-Y"

"Sally? Is that your name?" Jack questioned in a pinched voice. He cleared his throat.

The planchette moved to "yes."

"What do you want to tell us, Sally?" Jack probed further, his voice back to normal.

The planchette started to move in slow, but deliberate concentric circles, spiraling out and then spiraling back in, almost hypnotizing us. The scratching of the three legs was all that could be heard aside from our breathing. After three or four spiral round-trips, the planchette stopped in the center. After about 30 seconds, it started to move again, but only the front, wavering back and forth as if it were thinking of what to say. Then, it journeyed to a letter, deliberately pausing so the round window displayed "R." It continued this way until the rest of the word or words were formed: "A-P-E-H-E-L-P."

"Rapheal?" Seamus asked.

It moved quickly to "No."

Seamus figured it out. "Were you raped? Were you a prisoner here," asked Seamus.

"YES"

"How can we help you?" Interjected Tom, softly.

"H-E-L-P"

"Sally, how can we help you? What can we do?" Tom asked, a little louder.

"I-T-H-U-R-T-S"

"M-K-E-I-T-S-T-O-P"

I looked up at Tom who was getting upset. His breathing quickened and his body began to lightly tremble.

"Tom," I whispered in his ear, "are you okay?"

He didn't answer, but his breathing started to slow down. Jamie's eyes were shut tight, mumbling some sort of prayer.

"E-V-L"

"Evil?" Lee whispered.

Then the planchette started moving very, very fast and went in counter-clockwise circles. All of a sudden, it directly pulled Seamus's and Jack's hands very pointedly to the letters that spelled "L-E-A-V-E-N-O-W."

A cold breeze, colder than the air surrounding us, passed through me. It was like a thin sheet of ice hit me straight on and then burrowed into every pore on my skin. I stifled a scream, whimpering instead. "T... Tom, please can we go?" My arms squeezed his like a boa constrictor.

Tom, still shaking a bit, agreed. "I think it wise; that is probably not Sally anymore. We cannot help the dead." Tom said tersely.

Seamus and Jack quickly lifted their fingers off the planchette, which came to a complete halt. The room was silent, except for some dripping pipes and all of our quickened breathing.

Seamus quickly packed up the board while the rest of us gathered our lanterns, and we spilled out of the place, fast.

Once on the street, we all breathed a sigh of relief.

"Wow, that was scary," Lee said, a little tremble in his voice.

"That's the problem with the Ouija Board, you never know what kind of spirit you are going to get, if you believe it." Tom reasoned, "are you all game to go to Charterhouse Square?"

Seamus and Jack timidly nodded; the rest of us just didn't answer. I looked back at the menacing door we just escaped through and shuddered.

The walk was a few blocks away and we all were pretty quiet and reflective, holding on to our better halves maybe just a little less tightly than a minute ago. Tom had his arm around my waist.

Whispering in my ear, he asked, "Are you okay, love? Did you feel any pain in there?"

"I'm fine now, just a little freaked. I felt this bone-chilling coldness pass right through me, though. It didn't hurt, but oh my God was it horrifying. I'm trying to shake it off."

Tom pulled me closer, "This was not a good idea. Maybe we should stop."

"No, I don't want to. I'm fine, just a little scared. Isn't that the point? Anyway, *you* looked really upset and you were shaking. Did you feel something—the chill as well?"

"I felt a little prick, I guess. When she spelled out "rape" it brought a chill to my spine. If I let myself believe all this, I find it is depressing that these spirits have to relive their horror over and over again; their pain never relents," Tom said with a crack in his voice. He obviously felt a connection, at least to their stories, and rightfully so. I started thinking about which scenario would be better, finding out that Tom was telling the truth about the abuse he endured as a child, or his father's version, where Tom inflicted pain on himself. I thought neither, but still hoped Tom was being honest. I dismissed the thoughts, once again, and concentrated on the night.

We walked silently until we entered Charterhouse Square. With people spilling out of the noisy nearby pubs, it wasn't nearly as spooky as the catacombs.

"Do we want to do this here?" asked Tom. "I'm not sure it's going to work with so many people around. I should have anticipated this."

"Let's try, anyway," Seamus replied, opening the box again and laying it on the grass.

"Okay, who wants to try?" asked Seamus, echoing his question from the catacombs.

"Since it's not so scary here, I'll do it," Jamie volunteered.

"Me, too." Andrea stepped forward a half second before I could.

So, once again they sat down and tentatively placed their fingers on the planchette. It didn't budge.

"Em, anybody there?" Asked Andrea.

Didn't move.

"Concentrate," Tom urged in a soothing voice.

Both Jamie and Andrea closed their eyes.

The planchette stuttered and moved maybe a few millimeters and then stopped.

After about 30 seconds, Andrea took her fingers off the triangular shaped piece of plastic. "It's not working here, let's move on." I think she was secretly glad about it.

"Alright, let's go to the Farrington Station," Tom suggested. "However, that too may prove to be a bust."

"Is that the one with the girl who was abused?" Asked Jamie.

"Yes, Anne Naylor."

So, on we traversed to our next horror story. Tom was going to purchase tube fares for each of us, but Jamie convinced the guard that we were on a ghost tour and not actually riding the tube. The nice woman had been on one of Tom's tours, and was easily convinced when he smiled and bowed toward her. She let us pass, and gave Tom her direct line, in case he needed "anything at all."

We took the steps down into the tube station and edged down the platform a bit to escape the small crowd waiting to board the train. Seamus found a secluded bench and laid the Board out on it.

"Did you two want to try again?" Seamus offered to Jamie and Andrea. They violently shook their heads "no."

"Let Anna and Tom try," Christopher proposed.

"Alright, Tom, you okay with that?" I looked at him wide eyed.

He breathed out and sat on the bench, turning his body toward the board.

Before he placed his fingers down, Tom first recounted the story of Anne Naylor for the people who hadn't already heard it. Tom's story amplified the uneasiness that everyone in our group had been feeling this night, despite the brightly lit and modern tube station.

"Lightly, now," Seamus instructed.

I sat down, one leg bent fully on the bench, the other dangling off. We put our fingers on the planchette in unison. It immediately started moving, and fast. Startled, I let go and it stopped.

"Holy crap!" I panted.

"You must have some electricity between the two of you," Jack observed.

Frowning, Tom looked back up at me. I took a deep breath and put my fingers back on, this time, determined to not let go. The group crowded around as a train came to a screeching halt.

It started moving again quickly.

"You ask the questions," I suggested anxiously. He grimaced at me.

E-A-T

"Hello, what is your name?" Tom inquired.

H-N-G-R-Y

"You are hungry? Is this Anne?" Tom asked.

It went to YES then NO.

"Are you someone else?

Same thing, only NO then YES.

"What is your name?"

A-N-N-E

"Anne... Anne Naylor?" Tom pressed.

YES

A shriek came from the platform, making us all jump. The group all breathed a sigh of relief when we realized it was just an excited commuter from the crowd further down.

"Shite." Seamus mumbled.

We kept playing, but the planchette moved to the corner where the YES was written, and continued until one leg fell off the board. I looked up at Tom, shrugged and placed it back in the center of the board. We lightly re-placed our finger tips and then it went to the NO corner and did the same thing.

"I guess it doesn't want to play?" Jamie asked.

"Okay, one more time," and I placed the piece back in the middle. This time it moved directly to letters.

I-A-M-Y-O-U

"Iamyou?" Seamus questioned.

"I think it was 'I am you.'" I whispered.

Tom continued, "Em, what does that mean? Is this still Anne?"

The planchette went back and forth, thinking again.

K-I-L-L

We just looked up at each other.

W-H-E-R-E-I-S-S-I-S-T-E-R

"Are you looking for your sister? Is this Anne?"

This time it went to YES then YES again.

"I'm sorry, but we don't know where your sister is."

D-E-A-D

"Yes, I… I'm sorry."

W-H-Y?

"Em, there is a lot of evil in this world. Can you leave this platform and go someplace safe? Someplace happy? Perhaps you can find your sister."

It paused again, then went to "NO." The planchette pulled our hands in slow, but large perfect circles until it slowed to a stop. We kept our hands in place, waiting for it to move. Then, I felt a tingling in my fingertips. Violently, the planchette shot around the board.

L-I-Z-D-E-A-D

"Lizdead? What's that?" Asked Seamus.

E-L-I-Z-A-D-E-A-D

I looked up at Tom. His face contorted and I swear I saw all the blood drain out; his pale complexion became even paler, devoid of any color at all.

"Elizabeth?" He whispered.

T-O-M

"Oh, My, God," Jamie said.

"Elizabeth, is it really you?"

T-O-O-O-M-M-M-Y-B-R-T-H-R

I looked up at Tom who was staring at the board, tears starting to mix with his with black eyeliner, but he did not dare remove his hands.

"B-R-T-H-R-B-R-O-T-H-R-B-R-O-T-H-E-R-H-A-T-E-U"

The planchette pulled our hands around the board, spelling out the next message.

"D-O-I-T"

"Do it? Do what?" Tom asked, his voice quivering.

"H-A-T-E-U-H-A-T-E-U

My hands felt electrified, the pull of the spirit or whatever it could be, was unquestionable. It guided our hands, pointedly to the letters that made Tom lose it.

S-O-R-R-Y- F-U-C-K-I-N-G-C-O-W-A...

And with that, Tom lifted his hands abruptly, as if he were shocked by the planchette. He closed his eyes while covering his mouth and nose, black tears streaked down over his hands. Like a strong magnet, the draw of the electric current kept my hands stuck on the plastic piece as it continued to the letter "R."

Yanking my fingertips hard off the planchette, it finally came to a halt.

I stood up quickly while Tom stayed put, trembling, his eyes drowning in the black mixture of sorrow and guilt.

Seamus started, "What was that all about? Eh, Tom, mate? You okay?" Tom put his hands now over his eyes and looked away to hide his reaction from the group, who were all uncomfortably silent.

"S..sorry, I think I'm going to be sick." Tom swallowed hard.

Jamie gently urged the rest, "Come on, come on, let's give Tom some space... and get the hell out of here," and she ushered the group a little further down the platform, leaving Seamus and me.

"Seamus, thanks, I... I got this." Seamus nodded, gathered up the board and pat Tom on the shoulder, then left to join the rest of the group.

I moved closer to Tom and put my arm around his shoulder.

"Hey, you okay? Do we need to get you to the bathroom?"

He finally took his hands from his face.

"I think I'm okay. I just had a tidal wave of nausea."

He sniffed and continued, "What the hell was that, Anna? That's what she used to call me... fucking coward. And, now I see that she hates me. Why?" I squeezed him a little harder trying to quell his shivering.

"We can't be for sure it was her. I mean, it might have been your subconscious talking, right?"

"I don't think so, Anna. I felt something, too. I felt her. And I had this horrible sensation of evil washing through me. Uncontrollable thoughts went through my head of abuse and rape and torture." He cried, his voice starting to get a little hoarse.

"Yes, well, look at the circumstances surrounding us. You led a ghost tour tonight, then we had the experience in the catacombs; it's no wonder those thoughts were there. And then maybe we contacted Anne Naylor, who's looking for her sister. I'm sure if we asked everyone over there, they'd say the same thing." But even as I spoke the words, in my head, all I could hear was Thomas's version of how Elizabeth had died.

Tom ran his fingers through his hair, messing it up further.

Exasperated, Tom said, "But, Anna, it was her. I'm sure of it."

"Oh, Tom, you can't be sure, okay. It's a Ouija Board. Who knows what gets dredged up from those things? Look, I think we all want to get out of here; we can either call it a night or get a drink with the group. I'll tell them that you don't want to talk about it."

"It's okay. I'm quite embarrassed and should probably offer them some sort of explanation. I can handle it. I think your girlfriends won't be as enamored with me as before."

I laughed out loud, "You obviously don't know women. Here." I handed him a tissue, "Your makeup is running."

Tom let out a small laugh and wiped his face, "Okay?"

I pulled out my black eyeliner from my purse, moved my face in close, tilted his head up and started reapplying.

"You can't be serious."

"Gotta stay in costume," I proclaimed. He was shaking so much, I had to be careful not to stab his eye. When I completed both eyes to my liking, I kissed him hard on his trembling mouth, then offered him my hand.

"I think you are trying to keep your sexual fantasy going with this," Tom said in a shaky voice, trying to lighten up.

I shrugged, "Maybe." We walked over to our group.

"Are you okay, mate?" Seamus asked, his concern evident.

"Ah, yes, let's go get a pint and I'll explain, a little."

"Anna really laid it on thick with the eyeliner," Jack noted.

Tom rolled his eyes and sighed, "I'm sure she did."

We left the station, the guard smiling at Tom as she let us back through. We crossed the street and went into the nearest pub, The Castle. It was around eleven, so the pubs were still packed, but we were lucky enough to find a large table away from the ruckus.

Tom lowered his gaze to the table and started to speak as he tried to tuck an errant strand of hair behind his ear. "I apologize for my behavior tonight. I won't go into details, because they are very personal, but basically, I had an older sister named Elizabeth. She died at the age of 17, falling down the stairs after a fight with my father."

"Aw, mate, I'm sorry," Seamus said.

"Do you think that was her on the Ouija Board?" asked Christopher.

"It's certainly possible, or my subconscious coming out. Either way, it's quite unnerving." Tom's eyes skimmed around the table and the room.

"What did Fucking Cowa mean?" Seamus innocently inquired. Oh, Seamus.

Tom grimaced. "Em, coward, a little nickname for me, growing up. Em, if you will excuse me, I have to run to the loo," Tom announced as he rose from his chair.

"Don't you wipe any of that off," I yelled to his back as he held up his hands in surrender.

When he was out of earshot, the talk started.

"Oh, Anna, he's so sensitive" and "Anna, I just want to hold him." My God, they were ridiculous!

Seamus started, "So, if I start to cry, right now, would that make every woman in the world, em... and gay blokes swoon?"

Andrea just laughed while Jamie remained quiet. I guess she finally thought it might have been too much.

Tom came back from the bathroom and quietly took his seat. The eyeliner was untouched.

"I don't know what you got, mate, but I wish I had some of that." Seamus commented.

Tom looked a bit baffled. "Pardon?"

"Don't worry about it, Tom." Jamie stood up and announced she was going to get a round.

Seamus steered the conversation away from Tom and onto lighter things. The pub normally closes at midnight, but being Halloween, they were staying open later. 12:30 rolled around and I was getting really tired and Tom was practically falling asleep at the table.

"I think we should probably head out now," I suggested and everyone seemed to agree.

Seamus went to the bar and actually paid the tab. This was rare; even rarer was Tom allowing anyone else to pay.

As we left the pub, Tom took Jack and Seamus aside.

While talking to Jamie, I saw Seamus raise his arm over his head and pump it up and down while Jack smiled from ear to ear. I figured Tom just asked them to be in the wedding. Seamus then engulfed Tom in a full embrace, squeezing him hard enough that I heard a muffled "oomph" from Tom. Seamus then pulled back and kissed Tom square on his forehead. Jamie was watching with mild amusement. "I told you he was in love with him."

CHAPTER 14

Tom and I hit the bed pretty much immediately after arriving home. We were so tired we fell asleep in our costumes, Doc Martens and all. I awoke to the shower running and glanced over at the clock. 11:00 AM. Scrambling out of bed, not wanting to waste any more of the morning, I changed out of my costume and threw on one of Tom's T-shirts. I walked into the kitchen planning to make coffee, but Tom had already taken care of that.

I ambled back to the bathroom and opened the door. Tom then cleared a little of the condensation away from the shower enclosure with a wave of his hand.

"Good morning, love," he said, peeking his face into the spot he just cleared.

"Morning. You doing okay?"

"Yup."

I washed my face in the sink and brushed my teeth. Tom stopped the water and I saw the towel hanging over the top part of the enclosure get shorter and shorter as it disappeared into the stall. Tom then emerged from the shower, towel around his waist and his hair slicked back.

"You sure you're alright?" I asked as I stepped away from the sink.

"Yes, love, I feel fine." He gently touched my face.

"I really, really think you should see someone."

Tom dropped his hand and rolled his eyes and glowered, "Would you please stop with this?"

He turned to the mirror and started applying shave cream. After a few strokes with his razor, he stopped and looked back at me.

"Look, I am touched by your concern and I appreciate it. But, I can handle this! I've been left alone most of my life to deal with obstacles, so this is just one more. And besides, I have you." He turned back to the mirror and continued shaving. I watched him a little bit before bringing up my concerns.

"I'm not sure what you mean by handling it. You keep saying that, but what I see is someone deeply, deeply scarred both mentally and physically by his upbringing. I see someone who is literally haunted by his past. And I don't think I've seen a man cry even a tenth of what I've seen from you...."

He finished shaving, wiped his face and rinsed his razor. Placing both hands on the sink, he gazed at me in the mirror. He was not happy.

"Are you saying I am less of a man because I express my feelings?"

"No... NO! Not at all. I'm saying that most people don't cry this much, men or women. Most people don't have their dead sister talking to them through the Ouija Board, most people didn't endure the trauma you've suffered through and most people don't have a fucking psychopath for a father! And the fact is, we don't really know what's true, especially about your mother."

"I'm not most people, Anna," he said, turning to face me, arms across his bare chest.

I blew out some air. "Tom, I don't want you to change. I love you exactly the way you are, tortured soul and all, but you are hurting. And when you hurt, I hurt. I don't understand why you are so reluctant to see someone. I mean, last night you told everyone at the table a little about your past, so it can't be that you're embarrassed."

"Believe me, I wish I hadn't said anything, but I felt compelled to tell them something after what they had witnessed. They must think I'm a freak."

I laughed, "Tom, they were even more into you after the Ouija Board incident. You should have heard them when you went to the bathroom."

Tom mouthed "what the fuck" to himself while looking down and shaking his head. "Are your friends mental?"

"Um, our friends? You are a rock star to them. Your looks, your mannerisms, the way you treat me, your performance at the karaoke bar, and the ghost tour. And any flaw you show only draws them in more. Stop being so hard on yourself. You didn't grow up with a lot of friends, but now you've got quite a crew. Did you see how happy Seamus and Jack were when you asked them to be in the wedding?"

"I'll think about it," he said quietly after a brief pause.

"Think about what?"

"Seeing someone. I'm reluctant because of the treatment I received as a teen. It was utterly useless and even, perhaps, damaging."

Relieved, I encircled my arms around him, laying my head on his chest, the scent of soap and shave cream pleasantly filling my nose. "That's all I'm asking, sweetheart. I'll be there with you the whole way."

"I haven't made any promises Anna. I only said I'll think about it."

— *Friday, November 7*

Tom had bought us tickets earlier in the week for our trip to Scotland so I could meet Trevor, his paternal grandfather. His grandmother, Elizabeth, died a number of years ago, so Trevor lives alone, at least without family. Trevor, at 80 years old, was pretty with it from what Tom said. He was rather fond of his grandfather, unlike his father.

We boarded the plane and took the short trip to Scotland, presents and suitcases in hand. We rented a car and drove through the countryside to Trevor's place in Dumfries and Galloway. The journey took us through beautiful green hills and stunning landscapes until we arrived at a magnificent house, or small castle, overlooking vistas of uneven hillsides.

"I guess I can see why you have money." I surmised as I eyeballed the amazing house with turrets and castle-like doors.

"Ah, yes."

"And your father? Why doesn't he have any?"

"You really have to ask that question?" Tom stopped the car in front of the circular driveway and we both got out. Tom stretched his arms over his head and took a deep breath. "The air is much cleaner here." He took our bags out of the back seat and handed me the lightest one. We walked up to the wooden and iron clad door and Tom used the gargoyle knocker, which echoed with three thunks.

A minute later, the door opened with a spooky squeak and in the frame stood a man, a rather tall man with long grey hair pulled back in a ponytail, a trimmed goatee and striking blue eyes. He wore pressed tan pants, a black button-down shirt, and black dress shoes. When he saw Tom, his face lit up like a sunbeam, deepening the wrinkles on his distinguished face. So, this is where Tom inherited his looks. At 80, Trevor looked to be more around 65, and although his eyes were not quite as piercing as Tom's, he still had a gaze that penetrated through to your core.

Tom put his bags down and embraced his grandfather.

"Let me look at you! Eh, you could use a haircut, but so could I," he jested as he ruffled Tom's hair. "And who is this lovely vision? Anna, I presume?"

"Yes Granddad, this is my fiancée, Anna." Similar to Tom, he took my hand and kissed it, his goatee tickling my knuckle.

Things started to make a little more sense after meeting Trevor. In this two-minute encounter, I ascertained not only where Tom attained his money, but also his looks, manners, mannerisms and attire. It never made sense to me that Tom came from Thomas.

"Well, come in, please! I'll have Anthony take your bags to your room. Let's sit and have some tea."

We walked through to the living room and sat on the plush Victorian era red velvet sofa. Trevor asked about the plane ride and the drive over and inquired about my job and so forth. But, then he started telling stories about visits from Tom and Elizabeth when they were children. He was charming, engaging and just a wonderful man. It made me wonder why Trevor didn't get Tom out from under Thomas. Maybe he didn't know or have any control of the situation.

After about a half hour, Tom announced he was tired and wanted to take a quick nap before dinner. Not me! I wanted to explore the house and the grounds, so Trevor took me around. The grandiose entrance to the house boasted a white marble floor, white columns separating the two wings, and a staircase that tapered up to the second floor. The ornate, wood banister had gargoyles carved into it. The left wing of the house fanned out with dark wood floors and columns galore. This theme spread tastefully to the rest of the wing into the living room where we were just sitting, the library, and a den. The right wing of the house mirrored the left wing in décor, but housed a large kitchen with a farmhouse sink, white granite tops, dark wood cabinets, and stainless-steel appliances. Anthony's bedroom was down here along with a bathroom. Throughout the house, the walls were white, but colored with ornately framed photographs and artwork. Up the wooden staircase, to the left, sat Trevor's cavernous bedroom, a sitting room, and a few hall closets. The right of the steps boasted a rustic guest bathroom and three extra bedrooms, Tom sleeping soundly in the middle one.

We continued back down the steps to walk along the grounds.

"Your house is beautiful, Trevor."

"Thank you."

"I see where Tom gets, well, gets everything from."

Trevor gave me a sideways glance, just like Tom. "Yes, well, we are close. I only wish we were able to see each other more."

I nodded.

"You know, Anna, I think you are good for Tom. He's been alone for a long time. As far as I know, not many friends and certainly not any serious girlfriends have been a part of his life, recently. He thinks the world of you and I can see why. I believe it was right after he met you, he was, well giddy on the phone! I've never heard him so happy."

I smiled as we walked, then asked "Do you know why he never had a lot of friends or girls? He's so attractive and engaging, you'd think he would have been pretty popular."

We walked through a canopy of trees, which opened up to vast views of the hilly landscape. Trevor guided me to a bench underneath a low branched tree. It was chilly, so when we sat down, we huddled close together.

"Anna," Trevor started, looking off into the distance, "Tom may seem like he has self-confidence and a high opinion of himself, but, I assure you, inside he's constantly doubting and self-deprecating. He's worked very hard to hide this and he does a good job. He's a very good actor."

I stiffened a little, remembering my conversation with Thomas. "Um, it comes out sometimes. You can't get him to wear a short-sleeved shirt outside of the flat, and he's often very sensitive about things."

"Yes, of course, the scars. Well, let's not talk about that right now. But, what I'm trying to tell you is Tom is a wonderful boy. He's very intelligent, witty, and is genuine when it comes to others. If he likes you, he'll do anything for you. Even, sometimes, if he doesn't like you. But, inside, I think he's still battling his demons from the past, and he tries very, very hard to quash them and live life as he'd like. And, honestly, the past couple of months, thanks to you, I think he's succeeding. I'm so grateful that you're in his life."

I shivered and nodded. I wanted to ask him about Thomas, about his past, but I didn't feel right doing it. Not now, at least. In any event, Trevor seemed to be an amazing father figure. Seeing how much he truly loved Tom made me feel better. At least there was one sane person in Tom's family.

Making our way back to the house, Trevor pointed out the different trees on the property and animals he's seen. He asked me about veganism, and told me Anthony had bought some cookbooks to accommodate me. I was a little embarrassed that they went to all that trouble, but Trevor told me Anthony loves to delve into new types of food.

Tom was in the living room looking at a photo album when we came back. He had put on some cologne, which always does something to me.

"Did you two have a nice walk?" He asked, looking up from the pictures.

"Lovely! Your Anna is wonderful," Trevor complimented as he sat down next to Tom. I wasn't great at taking so many compliments, but, of course, it was nice to hear. I sat down on the other side of Tom and looked at the photos.

A boy of about ten with striking eyes, messy black hair, and a skinny frame filled the photo. Looking into the camera, his face wore a very familiar contemplative expression, head tilted to one side, brow furrowed, and that vertical crease between his eyebrows. "Is that you?" I asked, stating the obvious.

"Em, yes." Tom said, coyly.

"You were so cute! You still make that same expression." I pulled the album from his lap to get a better look.

"And who is that?" I pointed to a blond-haired girl of about 14. She wore glasses and an England National Rugby hat. Her arms were crossed and the look on her face pretty much said 'don't fuck with me.'

"That's Elizabeth. She was much prettier without the glasses and hat. There are a few more pictures of her in here." Tom said, a little sadly.

"She was a tough bird. Stubborn as they come," Trevor said.

Tom took the book back so Trevor could see better. As he turned the page, Tom looked intently at the next photograph.

"Not a great picture," said Trevor. He pointed out all the people in the shot. Tom wore jeans and a T-shirt, looking to be about four years old; his hair was long and unruly. His paisley bear dangled from one hand while his other hand pointed to something. Elizabeth's hair was down and she was not wearing glasses in this one, she was quite beautiful. Her hands were on her hips while she was peering down at Tom. A young, beefy Thomas was to the left of the kids, leaning against a doorframe, wryly, and shooting a sinister smile in their direction while Eloise sat in a plush chair, shoulders hunched and head in her hands.

"Mmmhmm. This picture is quite telling of my family. Look at mother. She was so unhappy."

"What happened here?" I asked.

"If I am remembering correctly, Elizabeth broke something and was blaming me for it. I seem to recall it was one of Granddad's priceless vases being smashed to bits. Why on earth did you take this picture?"

"Oh, your grandmother was always snapping that camera at everything, regardless of the appropriateness. But, you are remembering correctly, although the vase wasn't priceless, just expensive. Your father didn't seem to care, but your mother apologized profusely."

Tom stared at the picture some more and said, "I do remember. When we got home, that's when Thomas started to care. He used it as an excuse to bend me over and beat me with a ruler." He sighed. "I recall Elizabeth feeling guilty about it, I guess, and she comforted me afterward."

"I should get rid of that picture, but I have so few of you and Elizabeth. And even fewer of Eloise."

"Well, that was uplifting," Tom said sarcastically. "Shall we do something else?" He shut the book.

***

The rest of the visit was very relaxing. We talked a lot about wedding plans and went on long walks around the property. I can see why Trevor moved here permanently. He used to live in London and only came here during the summers, but he wanted to retire here.

Tom seemed to be quite a bit more at peace; I think Trevor has a calming effect on him. When it came time to leave, Tom's eyes welled up as he embraced his grandfather.

CHAPTER 15

"He still hasn't seen anyone?" asked Jamie at lunchtime. Everyone else was out on appointments or out to lunch, so it was just us at the table.

"No, and I don't want to mention it again. It will just cause another argument."

"Since when do you care if you argue or not?"

I shrugged, "I don't know. It's just a touchy subject. I mean, nothing really weird has happened since Halloween, except for a few nightmares waking him up. So, maybe things are alright." I closed my eyes. "I don't know."

"Are you two planning on having kids?"

"It's funny, we never really talked about it. I guess it's just not on my radar yet... we've discussed adopting a dog. He's brought that up a few times now."

"I just think if he wants to be a good father and husband, he needs to get his shit together. I love the guy, but he's obviously got some issues from the few details you've given me and what I saw in the tube station. You don't want them to really surface after you have kids."

"Yeah, well, you don't know the half of it, and no, I'm not going to give you more details. But, I will tell you that he had a pretty rough upbringing."

"Really, in what way?" Jamie asked.

"Look, I don't want to betray him at all, so as much as I want to confide in you, I... I can't. I'll just say that he was abused by his father... pretty heavily, from what I understand."

"Oh, Anna, that poor man."

"I told him that it's normal for him to have some problems and that's what therapy is for. He's just so stubborn and he wants to figure everything out himself. His favorite phrase is "I can handle it," I mocked, in a deep British accent.

Jamie nodded. "Well, keep on him anyway. Hey, how are the wedding plans coming?"

"Oh, well, we found a planner. His name is Theo and he's real cute and peppy."

"Is he gay?"

I rolled my eyes, "Just because he's a wedding planner does not make him gay... but yeah, he's gay."

"Talking about me?" Jack queried as he strolled to our table.

"No, my wedding planner, Theo."

"I've been trying to figure out what to do for Tom's bachelor party. Seamus, of course, wants to go to a strip club, but Tom doesn't strike me as the type," Jack surmised.

"THAT... would be funny to watch," I laughed, "could you image him in his formal oxford shirt, dress pants and jacket and a five pound note in his hand? He wouldn't know what to do with it. He'd probably hand the note to her while looking away, not wanting to offend her or touch her body."

We all started laughing about it, picturing it. "Oh, and God forbid if the stripper took off her shirt and threw it on him..."

"He'd probably fold it," Jamie said, boisterously laughing. We all started rolling, when my cell phone rang.

"Quiet, quiet it's Tom," I answered hello and when I heard his voice I started cracking up again, as did Jack and Jamie. It took me a minute to calm down.

"Hi, Tom, sorry," I said as I got up from the table, wiping the tears from my cheeks.

"What's so funny?"

"You."

"Hmmm... are you making fun of me behind my back? Nice."

"I'll tell you about it later, otherwise I'll start laughing again. Anyway, what's up?"

"Em, I wanted to know what time you'll be home tonight. I have a surprise."

"Probably earlier than later since we finished the book yesterday. I won't have to work overtime, so 5:30ish."

"Brilliant."

"What's the surprise?"

"If I told you, it wouldn't be a surprise, now would it?"

I looked over at Jamie and Jack, who were obviously acting out Tom at a strip club. I tried not to laugh, but a big guffaw escaped.

"Are you done?"

"Sorry. I'll be there at 5:30. Love you, bye!" I said quickly before I burst out again.

And then I snorted and had a hard time stopping. My stomach started to hurt, but it was really great to laugh so hard.

"Was he mad?" Jamie questioned through her own tears and subsequent chuckles.

"I don't know, probably. But, he did say he has a surprise for me at home."

***

I took the tube home, wanting to save money for the wedding even though Tom said not to worry about our finances. I'm just not one to spend unnecessarily.

I took the steps instead of the elevator, as I usually do now, to get some exercise. I unlocked the door, and as I opened it, I saw him. A cute orange dog wagging its tail at me. I let out the most uncool squeal as my eyes bulged out.

"Oh my God! You are so cute!" I crouched down to the dog's eye level and he started licking my face with his tiny tongue. Through the licks, I saw Tom leaning against the column, hands in his tailored black dress pants pockets.

"Surprise," he drawled.

The puppy was male, about 25 pounds, young, but not too young, maybe four or five months. When I scooped him up to hug him, he relaxed in my arms.

"Where did you get him?" I squealed again, burying my face in his soft fur.

"The RSPCA, of course."

"What is he?"

"I don't know. Some odd mix. I thought he was adorable, so I adopted him. I take it you don't mind."

"No, of course not. I am just a little worried about all the walks without having a yard, but he's great!" He began squirming in my arms.

"Mango."

"Is that his name? I love it!"

I put Mango down since I couldn't hold him anymore and he went running around the sofa three times, jumped on it, jumped off and then skidded out of sight into the kitchen. I heard the loud lapping of water.

"Are you going to be okay with all the fur?"

"I'll just have to vacuum more often. We can train him to stay off the furniture."

"I don't mind dogs on the furniture."

"Of course you don't. But, I do."

"We'll see what happens," and I went into the kitchen to check on Mango, who was licking the bowl even though there was nothing left. I took it and filled the bowl with more water.

"Is he house broken?" I called from the kitchen.

"Yes, at least that's what they told me at the shelter. I've made a vet appointment for tomorrow just to check him out. He's already neutered and fully up to date on his shots." Tom explained as he came into the kitchen, "He's supposedly five months and he was found in a dumpster by someone walking by who heard whimpering."

"OOOHHH, you poor boy," I cried, picking him up again and squeezing him.

"You know, you hardly acknowledged my presence when you came in."

"Sorry," I put Mango down and gave Tom a huge hug. "Thank you!"

"You're welcome, love. So, tell me about your day. What was so funny at work?"

I took Tom's hand and guided him to the sofa and we sat down. Mango followed us and jumped right into Tom's lap.

"Get down, boy," Tom commanded, Mango jumping right off.

"Oh, we were just imagining you at a strip club." I tried to hide my smile.

"Ah, the bachelor party discussion. No, not really my thing."

"I know, that's what was so funny, imagining it."

Tom just sighed.

"Jamie brought something up today that we've not spoken about and we probably should. Um," I was a little nervous bringing it up, but dove right in, "what's your take on having kids?"

Tom paused a few moments before answering. "I can tell you I'm not ready right now, but I think in the future, I might want one. What about you?"

"Pretty much the same feeling. I wasn't sure how you'd feel about it."

Mango put his chin on Tom's leg and looked up at him with the saddest eyes ever, really wanting to jump up, but Tom just stared at him and said 'no.'

"Why? Because of my experience? I think I could do better. The bar was set pretty low."

"Well, a dog is a good start."

Mango ran to the door and punched it with his paw.

"I think he has to go out," Tom observed, so the three of us went outside for a walk.

CHAPTER 16

I awoke to a low rumble. Realizing the sound was coming from Mango, nervously, I reached for Tom.

"Tom? Tom, wake up," but Tom wasn't in the bed. Rolling over, I turned on the light and looked around the flat. Mango followed me, but Tom was nowhere. The clock read 1:30 AM. I looked around for a note, but didn't find one.

"Oh crap. Ouch!" I said aloud as I felt this dull, but relentless pain in my wrist. I figured I slept on it funny and started to rub it, but the pain continued to intensify. Sweat started to bead on my forehead as I felt my wrist become immobilized. The room started warping, the walls undulating, mirroring my dizziness, until…

Blackness enveloped me. My head spun. My wrist, trapped in a vise, a torture devise. The crank turned, squeaking as the pressure increased on my trapped wrist. Tighter and tighter and tighter. Pounding heart, labored breathing, face contorted in agony. Snap, crunch, pop. Bones splintering, shattering, skin bruising. Blood.

I screamed out, clutched my wrist, and fell to my knees. I tried to focus as sweat dripped onto the floor, breathing in and out, slowly and deliberately. The blackness dissipated, but I still felt as though I was going to throw up right on the floor. I almost passed out as the nausea started to get worse. But then, as suddenly as the intense pain and dizziness came on, it stopped. I looked at my wrist, flipped it around, shook it. Nothing. No ache, no throbbing. It was good as new. Mango was staring at me, but as soon as I made eye contact with him, he wagged his tail and licked my wrist. He knew something was up.

I sat down on the floor and leaned up against the sofa when the realization hit me. Just when I got comfortable and complacent, convincing myself that we were in the clear, that Tom's blackouts were a thing of the past and my pain was all in my head, all the fretting and worrying and paranoia came stampeding back into my brain like a buffalo herd. I started to cry, not from the pain, but from such a feeling of helplessness. Where the hell was Tom? Where the hell was he? I need him! Why the fuck is he not here?

I tried his cell, but I heard it ringing in the bedroom. I knew calling the police would be fruitless and I didn't want to wake Seamus up, so I just climbed back into bed and curled up with Mango, hoping Tom couldn't sleep and went out for a walk. I put the pillow to my face and screamed into it as loudly as I could.

***

You've got to try harder, dear girl.

Creak.

Growl.

BarkBarkBark

"Mango!" I said, disoriented, my heart beating out of my chest for some reason. I looked at the clock and it was 3:45 AM. Tom still was not in the room. Mango stopped barking, jumped off the bed and bounded out the bedroom door. I quickly followed him into the living room. And there Tom stood, in the foyer, taking off his coat, scarf and gloves.

"Tom?" I said shakily as I approached.

He looked really out of it. His eyes were half open and bloodshot. His hair was all over the place as if he had been wearing a hat, and his shirt was untucked.

"Tom?"

"Anna… what time is it, why are you out of bed?" he asked as he walked by me. He ignored Mango and plopped down on the sofa, took off his shoes and socks, and laid down, closing his eyes.

"Why am I out of bed? What about you?"

"Leave me alone, please. I'm knackered."

"You need to tell me where you've been," I demanded.

"I don't have to tell you anythin', please shut it and let me sleep."

I just stared at him in amazement. I didn't know what to say so I sat in the chair and watched him for a long while. He had fallen asleep almost immediately. Was he on something? Drunk? I looked to see if there was any white powder near his nose or if he smelled of alcohol. No, but the cigarette odor made my stomach roll. I sat back down on the chair and Mango immediately jumped into my lap—a welcomed comfort. Bewildered more than scared, I eventually drifted back to sleep with Mango in my arms.

***

"Down, boy, you know you're not supposed to be up there," I faintly heard Tom's firm voice.

"Tom?"

"Yes, love, why did you sleep out here?" he asked innocently.

I looked at him like he was crazy, "Are you serious?"

He looked perplexed. "Yes, of course."

"Where the hell were you last night? I woke up to Mango growling around 1:30 and you were nowhere to be found. Then, around 3:45, you saunter in like nothing happened, smelling horribly of smoke, being an all-around prick to me and then falling back asleep on the sofa."

"What are you talking about? I awoke in our bed and you were gone."

I gaped at him, perplexed by the complete and total denial of what had happened earlier this morning.

"Do you really not remember?"

"I'm not sure there is something *to* remember. I was asleep in our room, all night, and I awoke in our bed this morning, only to find you curled up with Mango on the furniture that I'm trying to keep him off. Maybe you were dreaming all this or your active imagination has run amok," he said a little too caustically. Fuming, I got up, marched over to where his coat hung, yanked it off the hanger and threw it at him.

"You smell that? I didn't dream or imagine anything, asshole. Don't you dare turn this around on me."

Tom's jaw stiffened at my frankness, but then he started to look a little concerned as he smelled his coat.

"You break anybody's wrist in the wee hours of the morning?"

"Pardon?"

"You heard me. While you were "sleepwalking" or blacking out or whatever you call it, I actually felt my wrist break. I was in sheer agony, Tom, and you weren't here."

"Is… is it okay?" He took ahold of my wrist gently to examine it, but I slapped his hand away, startling him.

"You weren't here, Goddammit. Who did you attack?"

"Calm down, please… I didn't attack anyone. Are you sure I wasn't here? I mean, I had some vivid dreams, but I think that's all they were."

I didn't offer a response. Tom held up his hands.

"I'll call, I'll call a sleeping clinic today, I promise."

I've heard that before. I turned away from him and stomped down the hall to the bedroom to get ready for work.

About 45 minutes later, I came out to see Tom sitting at the table, drinking tea. He wore his light green "Life is Good" T-shirt and jeans.

"I made you some coffee, love," he said tentatively.

"Thanks," I mumbled and got myself a cup.

"I'll try to call someone today. I will, I promise. But, Anna, you had another episode, too. You are supposed to write this down and call Holly."

"I plan to," I stated matter-of-factly.

Tom stood up and came to where I was standing. "Please don't be angry with me," he pleaded as he touched my shoulder. But then, I noticed a gash on Tom's bicep. It wasn't bleeding, but it was definitely fresh.

"Where did you get this? And don't tell me it was another tree branch." I pointed to his cut.

He looked at me and in a hushed voice said, "I don't know."

"Did you do this to yourself, Tom? Think." I urged.

He rubbed his face with his hands and stammered, "I… I… no, of course not."

"Tom, I'm really scared—about both of us, okay?"

"Come here," and he took me in his arms, but I was stiff. I worried his father was right; I worried that my own freaky condition was somehow connected to this. I was at a loss and needed air, needed to be away from him.

Sensing my obvious reluctance to be with him right now, he let go and softly spoke, "I'll give you some time. I'm going to take Mango out for a walk. Go get your leash, boy!"

Mango plodded to the foyer and then came back with his leash in his mouth, dropping it into Tom's hands. After clasping the metal clip on Mango's collar, Tom threw on a sweater that was hanging in the foyer and then opened the door, giving me a shy wave as he left.

***

I was seething all the way to work. He wasn't there for me when I needed him. Worse, he never called a therapist to get the help he needed, and I found it hard to trust that he would make that call today. And worst of all, I was more confused than ever about what it all meant, how it was all connected, who was telling the truth!

"Argh!" I yelled on the way too quiet tube, getting plenty of stares from the reserved Brits, but I didn't really care.

Everyone pretty much left me alone at work; they could tell I was not in a good mood. Even Steven stayed away, which was a rarity. Jamie tried to broach the subject of Tom, but I just didn't feel like talking about it, so I did my work. I got a lot done, in fact, and the day was ending before I knew it.

I decided to call Holly.

"Anna, what a pleasant surprise! How are things?"

"They were fine for a little while, but it started again. Are you able to meet me for some tea around 6:15? I know it's short notice." I was terser than I meant to be.

"Yes, absolutely. My husband is on a business trip, so I have all night. How about we meet at Tibits again?"

"That would be great. I'll see you in about an hour," I hung up the phone.

I felt I did enough work for the day, so I pulled out my journal and looked over the notes I had taken and the time and dates.

"All right, Anna?" Jamie asked. "Is there anything I can do?"

"Not now, but thanks, Jamie."

For the next 45 minutes, I checked my notes against my memory and the Internet and started filling in the blanks as best I could:

> September 4: ghost tour: mouth hurt, face hurt, felt something being shoved up my ass (gross)—felt like I was in some kind of weird dream—that's the night I met Tom. That night Richard Brown was found with his teeth knocked out and a metal rod shoved up his ass (gross again!)—he was a bad dude—abused his girlfriend. Was I with Tom when the attack occurred? No time or date on the net. Said that the Vigilante did the deed.

September 5: another ghost tour: afterward, stomach really, really hurt, jaw really hurt—Tom escorted me home that night... I threw up after getting home. Homophobe at the tour—goaded Tom. During the tour, Tom was really weird in the room.

September 6: Went on date with Tom. At dinner, Tom and homophobe had a fight—Tom was beaten up badly by the bartender—did I feel Tom's pain or the homophobe's? Both had been hit in the stomach and repeatedly in the face.

September 10/11: woke up at my flat, by myself, with my shoulder, foot and knee in excruciating pain. I tried Tom, but he didn't answer (but, it was during the wee hours of the morning). Then, in the morning, I see the news—Wainwright had the same injuries I had. Speculation that it was the Vigilante.

September 13: Turns out, Wainwright did abuse his kid! (note: Tom told me he has blackouts... wtf?... but, he was also drunk at the time).

September 12: Julius Thompson found dead with a gunshot wound... but I felt nothing, but they didn't think it was the Vigilante, anyway.

October: Kitty (the prostitute) was murdered. Was at Tom's tour, but I didn't feel anything, nor did they think this was linked to the Vigilante.

October in Maryland-at ghost tour: Saw a figure in the Brice house – gave me the CREEPS! Tom was acting funny... was out of it for a few minutes. I had a migraine that night, but it could have just been a migraine. Tom may have been sleepwalking—had a gash on his side and was bleeding... couldn't explain how he got it. I wasn't in the same room with him during the night, so he could have been sleepwalking? Blacking out? Don't know.

Halloween: weirdness at the catacombs (felt chill go through me), Ouija Board with Tom's sister???

December 4: felt like my wrist was broken—very dizzy, disoriented, nauseous—Tom was not in the flat and didn't remember leaving—claimed he was home all night. New unexplained cut on his arm and coat smelling of smoke. Was the smell just residual? Was I going nuts? Did I imagine all this or is he in total denial??

I then looked on the net to see if there were any reports of someone's wrist being broken or any other attack while Tom was out of the flat. Nothing. And then, I looked again to see if anything happened in Annapolis the night he was gone. Still nothing. "You're grasping, Anna," I said to myself. I closed the diary, turned off my computer, said good night to Jamie, and then walked out into the cold December night. I quickened my pace, walking past the bright lights of Piccadilly Circus.

Holly was already sitting at a table when I walked into Tibits. She wore a red blouse tucked into her small waisted black pants and a stunning velvet scarf. Her hair was not up this time; it cascaded down her head and onto her shoulders. She was the epitome of classy. Waving, she gave me a big smile when I came to the table.

When she stood up and then kissed me on both cheeks, the sweet smell of lilacs wafted into my nose. "Hi, Anna. Please, please, have a seat!"

I took off my coat and sat down, relieved to be talking to someone who might be able to help.

"I took the liberty and ordered you a fresh mint tea," she said as she pushed the cup toward me. I inhaled the aroma and took a long sip, calming me down a little.

"Thank you, I needed that."

She smiled and said, "Well, tell me all about it."

So,

I gave her a brief synopsis of the last two months. I included the Wainwright case, and Tom's sleepwalking episode in Maryland. And I told her about the Ouija Board on Halloween night. And then, of course, what happened last night.

"Were there any attacks yesterday? I didn't hear anything even remotely related to the Vigilante."

"No, I didn't either. I scoured the Internet. But, maybe it'll come out later or maybe it won't get reported."

"Or maybe it has nothing to do with the Vigilante. All this means is that you may have some sort of psychic ability, as I've said before. You may just have a gift."

"Wait, wait. A gift? This 'gift' hurts like hell and is not helping anybody. And what's the connection? Is it Tom? I mean, his behavior has been pretty whack. Blacking out, sleepwalking, having unexplained injuries. Maybe he's the one harming these people!"

"Shhh. Keep your voice down. Do you really believe that?"

"You said yourself you don't believe in coincidences."

"True. And according to your story, you were not with him during most of the attacks, except for the night he got into that ridiculous bar fight?"

"Right, but he did attack the guy in the bar."

"Hmmm."

"Oh, and I forgot to mention, when we were at that ghost tour in Maryland, we saw something in the window of one of the houses. It was really creepy and Tom started to act weird again, a lot like he did before at the haunted houses here. He looked right through me and said something unintelligible. But regardless, Holly, there is something wrong with Tom. He was so out of it last night when he came home. He claimed he didn't remember any of it. Is it really possible he is sleepwalking? Drugs? And what about all the cutting? Do you know anything about his childhood? He had a really, really awful upbringing with lots of tragedy and lots of abuse; at least that's what he says. His father denies it…, says that Tom hurts himself."

"No, I was not aware of his history. Oh that poor, dear boy," she said, wistfully.

Holly took my hand. "I can say; however, I am not all that surprised. He's always been a bit guarded, always glossing over any questions I asked about his youth. And there is something rather deep and troubled in those gorgeous eyes he has. But, listen, you mustn't be angry with him for things he cannot remember; you can't blame him for things he can't control. If he had such an upbringing, that is bound to affect him, but I would be very surprised if it were drugs; he's just not that type, and I think you know that. The mind has a funny way to wrestle with its demons. Maybe that's why he blacks out or sleepwalks, to deal with these tragedies that he's probably never come to terms with on a conscious level."

"I'm not mad at that. It's just that he never called anyone for help. I begged him for weeks, but he either argued about it or ignored me."

"Well, he did call me today, earlier."

I breathed out a sigh of relief, "He did? What did he say?"

"Well, he was mainly concerned about you and your episodes, but he touched a little bit on the sleepwalking. I gave him the number to a clinic that can possibly help with that, but he may need a little more than that."

"But, what do I do?"

"We just need to figure out the connection, if there is one. We need to understand why you are only having psychic premonitions with victims of assault, if that is what it is. Maybe because you have such a strong connection with Tom, you feel for victims of assault since he was a victim himself. But, I reiterate, we don't know if all the feelings you had occurred from the Vigilante's hand and we certainly can't assume Tom is this person. I mean, come on. Tom? The idea is preposterous."

I put my face in my hands. This was all too surreal.

Holly interrupted my wallowing. "We could have you check into Hospital and run a brain scan."

"What would that tell us?" I asked, looking up, bleary-eyed. I took another sip of my drink.

"To see if your brain is normal… if any more or less activity displays abnormally in different parts of your brain. The only problem is, if there is something to see, it probably won't register unless you are having an episode, and I quite doubt we'd be able to hit that mark. But, I have a better idea, if you're open to it. I'd like for you and Tom to see a psychic"

"A psychic, really? Aren't most of them frauds?"

"Yes, a lot are, but there is one in particular I would recommend whole-heartedly. Her name is April Simms. She's a wonderful and kind person who has helped me with a number of things. In fact, she even consults for the police on investigations they have trouble solving."

"I guess it wouldn't hurt to talk to her. I'll have a hard time convincing Tom, though."

Holly nodded, "Well, let me try to get in touch with her. She is sometimes very hard to reach, but I'll do my best." Her whole face crinkled when she smiled at me. "If there's something supernatural going on here, April is the woman to sort it all out."

"Thank you so much, Holly. Sorry for being so terse on the phone earlier, and for being bad company, overall."

"Nonsense. You and Tom are going through something extraordinary and tough. This, however, is my specialty and I am happy to help. Besides, I would do anything for that boy. And you are a part of his life now, so that means I would do anything for you."

I thanked her again as we said our goodbyes and I headed for home. I checked my cell phone and saw five missed calls from Tom. I probably should have told him I'd be late, but I may have wanted him to worry a little. My mean streak coming out.

I took a circuitous way home, walking to an underground stop much further than the one I usually take. I didn't care that it was late, I just didn't want to see Tom yet; I had to think. What if he was the Vigilante? Holly did not see him attack that homophobe and I did, so I'm not so sure the idea is *preposterous*. And what if his father is telling me the truth? I had to do something and just asking him obviously wouldn't cut it.

***

I arrived home around 9:00, put my key in the door and opened it to see Mango sitting there wagging his tail at me. I heard Tom's footsteps hurrying toward the foyer. He was talking to someone.

"Thanks Jamie, she's here now… yes, she looks fine… oh, yes, please, thank you," and he hung up. He looked really worried.

"Anna, thank God! What happened? Are you alright?" He asked as he embraced me.

"I'm fine, Tom," I replied into his chest.

He pulled away, but still held my shoulders at arm's length, looking me over.

"Are you sure you're okay? Where were you? I tried your phone…"

"I know, I saw the missed calls."

Confusion set in. He removed his hands from my shoulders.

"Pardon?"

"I worked a little late, then I met with Holly to talk about what's been happening with the two of us, and then I took the long way home."

"And, you couldn't call to tell me? I expected you home four hours ago. I called Jamie, Jack, Andrea, I even called my father. I walked around the area for an hour and I was even about to call the police!" Tom's voice amplified with every word.

"I'm sorry. I just needed some time. Can't you respect that?" I asked as I tried to push passed him.

He blocked my way, letting out a breath, nostrils flaring and eyes aflame. "Respect? Really, Anna, you can be unbelievably thick at times. How much respect did you have for me tonight, allowing me to fret and worry? How is that respect? One *fucking* phone call, Anna, that's all! And yes, I would have *respected* your wishes," he spat as he stepped aside.

Mango came up to Tom, slowly, ears back and head down. He clearly did not like the yelling, and neither did I. Tom reached down, scratched Mango's head, and told him it was alright in a very soft voice.

"Well, what about you? You don't think I was worried sick last night?"

"If I was sleepwalking, that obviously couldn't be helped. I hardly see a comparison here."

"You really think you were sleepwalking? Maybe you blacked out instead, Tom, so who knows where you were and what you were doing. For all I know, you're fully aware of your actions. Maybe you were out fucking Lily! And then I see a cut on your arm? Again! If you had just called someone in October, when you *promised*, we wouldn't be having this issue, now would we?"

"Dammit, Anna! You really think I would cheat on you? And I didn't cut myself! My father fed you a line and you chose to believe him over me. And I did call someone today, I am sure Holly told you. If you can't trust me, can't support me, how is this all going to work? And tonight? You were getting revenge and that's not the way to solve anything, *now is it?* Especially when it's against the man you are supposed to marry?"

My face untwisted as I said, "Alright, I should have called. I'm sorry. And it's not that I believe your father over you. It's just that I don't think you know what really happened in your past, not fully. And I think it's time we got to the bottom of it, okay?"

Tom softened a bit and lightly touched my face. "Okay. I can't stand it when we fight." He dropped his hand and sniffed, "Well, there is dinner if you are hungry. Jamie said she would call Jack and Andrea, so they don't worry."

Embarrassed, I told him I was going to get changed and I went into the bedroom, the guilt setting in. He was right, I should have called him. Tom called it revenge, and he was right. Not a good way to start a marriage.

I decided to take a shower. The warm water felt wonderful on my skin, but I had so many thoughts spinning in my head, I just didn't know what to do. Maybe this psychic could help. I just kept going back to Tom being the Vigilante. Why else would I be feeling the pain that is inflicted on his victims? And did he really have Borderline Disorder as a kid? Does he still have it? Can you really ever be cured?

I turned off the shower, but I heard water rushing on the roof. Sounded like a heavy rain.

After getting into my night clothes, I went into the kitchen to heat up the homemade veggie burgers left out for me.

Tom was watching the news. Against my better judgement, I decided to try one more time, so I sat down on the sofa next to him and took his hands.

"Tom… Tom, please, just be honest with me," I pleaded.

"About what?"

"I asked you before and I'll ask you again, are you the Vigilante?"

He turned to me and pulled his hands out of my grip, standing up. "Goddammit Anna, again? No, it's not me. You really think I could beat people to a pulp or torture them? Regardless of the justification?"

"You beat that man in the bar *to a pulp*. And you weren't here last night and that night in Maryland and you were not with me when the other two attacks occurred."

"Christ, Anna! So I'm a criminal because I was out, *not with you*, when these crimes were committed? You're trying to wrap up my past, my blackouts and your premonitions into some neat little box. Things are never that simple. I am tired of this, and I'm not sure how much more of it I can take. Either you love me and trust me and trust that we will find a logical explanation to this, or… or we're done." His voice faltered. "You are sabotaging us, Anna. You're destroying the best thing that's ever happened to me." He quickly turned away and walked determinedly down the hallway to the bedroom and slammed the door.

Dammit. I knew mentioning this would do no good and yet I still said something. I can be so stupid! I went into the kitchen and tried to eat the veggie burger while I listened to the rain. When I finished, I placed my dish in the dishwasher and then listened at the closed bedroom door. The shower was running. I waited until I heard the water stop and walked into the bedroom. I took two deep breaths.

Tom emerged from the shower in his robe, his unruly wet hair going every which way.

"I'm sorry, Tom," I said as I started to approach him, but decided against it because of the look on his face.

"Are we done fighting for the evening? I'm spent," he said, tersely.

I nodded.

After a long pause, he stated, "I'm seeing the sleep specialist next week."

I gave him a weak smile, "You're dripping."

"So I am," and he got a towel.

CHAPTER 17

I did not sleep last night, or at least not much. My mind was on overdrive, analyzing and reanalyzing, until I came up with a plan. I was going to follow him. I reasoned if he is unaware of his actions, maybe whatever I end up seeing could help figure out the cure. Tom had to work tonight, so I figured I would leave the flat and arrive at the tour right before his shift ended. I would also tell him that I was going out with Jamie so, just in case he went straight home, he wouldn't have any questions or worry. I didn't know what to expect. Another woman? Drugs? Him beating someone up? Or nothing at all.

9:00 that night, I was ready. I wore dark clothes and a winter hat. I grabbed my purse with my fully charged smartphone, gave Mango a kiss on the head, and left for the tour.

When I got there, I saw Tom's lantern in the distance walking toward the center, then the group of tourists came more into view. I hid on the side of the building and waited.

I heard Tom give his final remarks as I peered through a bush near the corner of the building. I started to feel really stupid and really guilty, but this had to be done.

Tom went into the center, I assume, to change. A few minutes later, he emerged, took out his phone, and dialed a number. My phone vibrated, but I didn't pick it up. I felt too guilty to talk to him and I didn't want him to hear any wavering in my voice.

I waited and then sent him a text that I just missed his call and that I would be home soon. Seeing him read the text really started to make me feel horrible.

He held his hand up to hail a cab. Shit! As soon as he pulled away, I got lucky and flagged down another taxi, stole into it quickly, and nonchalantly asked the driver to follow the cab in front, that I was going to surprise my boyfriend. The cabbie obliged and off we went, straight to our flat.

"Stop here," I said when we were a block from the flat. I paid the cabbie and once again, the guilt set in.

I saw Tom get out and go into the building.

I waited on the corner for about fifteen minutes, berating myself for deceiving Tom. When I went up to the flat and saw him, I acted as natural as I could. I told him very few details about my made up evening with Jamie and quickly got him talking about the tour. And then we went to bed. I softly cried while he slept, trying to wipe my conscience. I'm not sure I could do this again.

***

Our fight mostly forgotten and my betrayal pushed to the side, we went around town to look at different places for the wedding. Since neither of us were religious, a church just seemed a little hypocritical. We thought maybe on the bridge overlooking the water in St. James Park. If you looked out one way, Buckingham Palace loomed. The other way, the London Eye came into view. The bridge is touted as the most romantic place in London. Logistically, however, it might be a pain to work out.

"How about my grandfather's house?"

"In Scotland?" I asked, critically.

"Yes! It's not that far from London and shouldn't cost too much to bring people out. We'd save on the venue and even have a free place for people, at least family, to stay. He actually suggested this the other day on the phone. I told him I didn't think it would be feasible, but I don't know; what do you think?"

"It's a pretty big place, so I guess it could accommodate everything, right?"

"Oh, yes."

"Well, let's think about that if we don't really find a great place here." I said.

The rest of the day was really nice on the surface. Underneath, I was plagued by this damned guilt.

To make matters worse, we had to stop by his father's house, which, as usual, sucked. He and Tom got into it about money again; always something about money. Tom went to the grocery store to get his father some things, leaving me to clean up the kitchen, and worse, listen to Thomas rant.

"So, how are things going at the love nest? My boy seems a little agitated. He cutting himself anymore?"

I didn't answer.

"Mmm, so somethin' did happen. You don't have to tell me. I lived with it, I know the signs. He buggering some chap?"

I dropped the dish I was washing in the sink, almost breaking it, and turned to face him.

"No, Thomas. Can you just leave it alone, please?"

"I'll warn you one more time. My boy is not who you think he is. I just don't want to see you get hurt."

I rolled my eyes. As if he gave a damn about me.

Then we heard the click of the door and Tom walked in with groceries in his arms.

***

I debated heavily with myself as to whether I was going to follow him again or not. I did not want to betray him anymore, and I knew he was seeing someone next week, so maybe that would shed some light on things. But, then it happened. Soon after Tom left for work, I was reaching for Mango's leash to take him for a quick walk when I started to feel a sharp burning sensation in my eyes. I began rubbing them, but the burning just got worse and worse. I couldn't take it anymore. I screamed out in agony, falling to my knees hard on the bare floor. My hands instinctively covered my eyes… they were on fire. My eyes began to tear up as my palms pressed harder into them, trying to dull the pain. It didn't work. My heart raced and the panic started to set it. My breathing quickened as I fell to my side, almost blacking out. Curling up into a ball, I lay helpless as the pain intensified.

Acid burning flesh. Hot pokers. Searing pain. Blacker than black. Blindness, blindness, blindness.

Body trembling, the pain started to dissipate, but I couldn't move. I was literally scared stiff. As I started to come out of my fog and excruciating pain, I heard a whimpering. Mango started to lick the back of my hands, which were still covering my face. The word "blindness" pounded in my ears over and over again. I cried out on the floor until finally, finally the pain subsided into a dull ache. I shakily stood up and ran to the bathroom to examine my watering eyes, but I didn't see anything awry. No red, no broken blood vessels, just normal eyes. And I could see just fine. Splashing water on my face, I started to shake, uncontrollably.

"Fuck!" I screamed, making Mango run away from me. He slowly slinked back in.

That's it! All my guilt and self-doubt vaporized. Tonight is the night. I decided to trust in my so-called psychic ability. Tom or someone was going to hurt someone tonight, and badly. I just knew it.

So, I performed the same ritual as the night before, only I texted Tom telling him that I was going to do some wedding planning with Jamie. I made sure to tell her that if he called, she had to act like I was with her. I promised her that I would explain it to her later. Although suspicious and reluctant, she agreed.

Earlier, I had nonchalantly asked him where the tour was going to be tonight, and he told me he was going to be around Covent Gardens, so I took a cab to the to the plaza. After finding him, I waited in a tea shop for him to finish up. He went into a store and came out a few minutes later with his travel bag in hand, making his way out of the plaza and onto the street. Walking down King Street, with me following far behind, I thought I saw him get into a cab, but there were so many people wearing black pea coats that I found it hard to keep Tom in sight. Somehow I managed while still staying far away. If I got too close and he saw me, it could be the end of our relationship. As this awful thought came into my mind, I questioned the sanity of what I was doing.

Then, something odd happened. I was pretty sure it was Tom in the distance, but I couldn't be positive. I noticed a distinct change in his gait. He usually has a long, very smooth stride, but now, he had a slight hitch in his step as if something was wrong with his leg. I edged a little closer to him when I saw him stop. He reached into his coat pocket and then put on what looked like his reading glasses. Then he reached in again and hunched his shoulders as if he were cupping something. Smoke rose up, swirling around his head. Oh God. He took a deep inhale and then lifted his face to the sky, letting the smoke out slowly. He continued walking down King Street as it turned into New Row, until he came to the Round House Pub. He threw his cigarette on the ground and walked in. My heart pumped noisily as the dread set in. But, I pushed on.

The pub was crowded, so it was hard to keep an eye on him through the windows. Knowing it was a bad idea, I ventured inside, ducking behind people as best I could. I spied him talking to some female, a bit too closely for me. My heart beat even more rapidly. But, then, he moved to the other side of the bar, put up his collar, and then pulled out a baseball cap from his bag. He put it on backwards, looking nothing like the Tom I knew. Even his mannerisms were different, making me question whether I was watching Tom or someone who looked a lot like him from a distance.

I tried hard to get a good look at his face, just to be sure, but his back was to me and I didn't want to risk him seeing me, so I stayed put.

"Hi, there. Buy you a drink?" An Indian man asked me, causing me to look away and lose contact with Tom.

"Um, no thank you. I'm here with someone." The man nodded politely and I heard him ask some other woman the same question. Tom had moved in that brief second, but I caught sight of the baseball cap way over to the left of the pub.

He was now speaking with a man. From what I could tell, it was a very grizzled man in his thirties, obviously a bit drunk. He and Tom were leaning into the bar, drinking, having a very animated conversation. Before long, they took their drinks to a nearby table. Although I couldn't hear what they were saying, they were obviously enjoying each other's company. The crowd kept shifting, making me bob and weave my head to keep an eye on them. I pulled out my smartphone and started to record them talking, but it was no use. It was just too crowded and too loud.

Both men were leaning back in their chairs, taking sip after sip of their ales. Tom's back was still turned to me. I then saw him sit up a bit straighter and then slowly lean into the man's space. The crowd parted enough for me to catch a glimpse of Tom's hand resting on the guy's knee. I froze, all the blood in my head draining to my toes. What the hell? What I saw almost caused me to faint. Tom leaned further in and kissed the man, passionately, on the lips. The man pulled away slowly from him, stood up, and walked right passed me and out of the bar. Very soon after, Tom followed. I ducked and turned away so he couldn't see me. After a minute, I left the pub as well, trying to keep as close an eye on them as possible without making a noise. Tom put his arm around the guy and guided him to a nearby alley, Goodwin's Court. I knew this alley, as we featured it in the book I was working on. Brown brick buildings with bowed front glass windows flanked each side of the alley, making an enchanting, but somewhat sinister backdrop for two men staggering down its path. I was able to hide in a doorway niche while keeping a watchful eye. I took out my phone again, hitting record, my hands shaking uncontrollably.

My heart continued to throb as I saw Tom push the man lightly in the chest, flattening him up against the brick wall. He kissed him again and said something I couldn't quite hear. The normal timbre of his voice was not there; rather, it seemed to be quite a bit higher. My God, am I really watching my fiancé? I started questioning myself when I distinctly heard the other man say, "I'll try not to bruise you too much."

The man started unbuckling his belt. And then he started on Tom's.

I couldn't hold my emotions in any longer and I let out a choked cry, causing both the man and Tom to look up in my direction; however, I turned away quickly before they got a good look at my face. I ran, pumping my legs and arms as fast as they would go until I was back at the pub. I pushed my way through the crowd and into the bathroom, threw open the stall door, and vomited into the toilet. Sitting heavily on the floor, I sobbed, waiting for the dry heaves to subside. I remained on that nasty stall floor for what seemed like an eternity as I replayed over and over again my whole world collapsing into nothingness.

***

— *Very early Sunday morning*

After I got the courage to leave the bathroom, I decided I was going to go back to the alley. I wanted to see if anyone was lying in a pool of blood or beaten badly. Helplessness and hopelessness weighed heavily on me as I walked out of the bathroom on autopilot. Glancing up, I saw the man who was with Tom before, speaking with someone else. I let out a sigh of relief, but then I thought about Tom, so I cautiously walked to the alley. Fortunately, I didn't see anyone. At least I was relieved a little, but now I had to deal with my fiancé. I took a cab home, thankful that the driver wasn't chatty and that I could sit quietly with my thoughts. As scared as I was, I had to go and confront Tom. I couldn't bear the lies or the betrayal, nor was I thinking too straight and I really didn't care about my self-preservation at this point.

When I walked in, Tom was sprawled out asleep on the sofa, Mango next to him on the floor.

Tom's coat was neatly hung up and he was already in his night clothes. He looked so fucking peaceful. I checked his coat pockets, but didn't find the glasses or the hat, or cigarettes for that matter. His coat smelled of smoke, however.

I turned on one of the reading lamps in the room.

Nudging him, I commanded, "Tom? Get up."

He stirred a little bit, opened his eyes slightly until they adjusted to the light, and then he sat up, rubbing his face and yawning.

"Oh, hi, love, what time is it?" He inquired with a rasp in his voice.

"Early."

"Did you have fun with Jamie?" He asked, innocently, as he sat forward, squinting and blinking from the light, both hands clasped between his knees.

I ignored his question, "Where were you tonight?"

"Em, Covent Gardens, remember?" he reiterated, sleepily.

"Anywhere else?"

"No, I came home directly. I was so knackered I fell asleep on the sofa waiting for you."

My rage had been building and building since my journey home from the pub and this lie was the last straw.

I reeled back my arm and slapped his face as hard as I could. So hard, it turned his head to the right and a red mark started to form against his white skin. Mango shrunk away, out of the room.

Fully awake now, he yelled, "What the hell was that for?" and he rubbed his chin and left cheek, his eyes brimming with tears from the sting.

Saying nothing, I slammed my open hand once again, on the other side of his face, and on the third attempt, he grabbed my wrist to stop me and stood up.

"What is wrong with you, Anna?" His eyes told me he was terrified.

"Let go of me!" And so he did, but he backed away from me, standing in shock.

"What's wrong with me? I'm an idiot for falling in love with you. For thinking that I finally found someone good and nice and genuine!"

"What are you talking about?!"

"I followed you, you fucking liar! I saw you. I saw you smoking and drinking and then kissing some guy from the pub, Tom! And then I… I saw you… you went into an alley and kissed him again and then… the man started to undo his belt. Were you going to blow him, Tom?!" Everything pouring out of me in anguish. My body shook from the culminating fact that my whole relationship with Tom was one big farce.

Tom looked scared out of his mind, "Anna, I..I..don't know what you are talking about. I was here. I was asleep on the sofa. What's gotten into you?" Then a realization. "Wait, you, you followed me?"

I took out my phone and pushed play, handing it over to him. He watched intently, but said, "I can hardly see anything here. This isn't me; this could be anybody!"

"But—I—followed—you," I seethed through gritted teeth as I grabbed back the phone. "You had a baseball cap on and your reading glasses!"

"Anna, I misplaced my glasses long ago and I don't wear baseball hats. *This isn't me.* Please believe me. I think you're confused. My father planted this idea in your head and you chose to believe it. Chose to see what you wanted to see. It is entirely in your head!" he pleaded.

I shoved him with both hands with all my might, causing him to stagger back against the fireplace mantel; the look of shock on his face was paramount as he regained his footing. I continued my rant. "You think I'm an idiot? You think I'm *thick?*" pointing at the side of my head, "well, now I've gotten smart."

Mango scurried next to his leg.

I yanked off my engagement ring and threw it at Tom's face. He tried to catch it, but missed, the ring making a small ping on the floor. Mango pounced to capture it, but it skidded under the sofa.

"Anna, please, I beg you, you've got to believe me, I am at an utter loss." He stammered as he attempted to reach for my arm. The long sleeve of his dark blue night shirt looked wet. I grabbed his hand and shoved the sleeve up to his elbow. He recoiled in pain as the fabric rubbed hard against a long, fresh cut on his arm.

"And this?! Let me guess, another tree branch?"

"I… I don't know."

I gripped tighter on his cut, making him cringe. "You don't know. You want to know what I think? I think your asshole father was telling the truth. I think you do things, Tom, and then you feel guilty about them and cut yourself. Well, you've sucked me in, and my friends in, and caused all kinds of havoc and pain. If this is some viciously sick game you're playing, then you've won, you FUCKING LIAR! Congratulations. You've won."

I violently dropped his arm, grabbed my purse, and went out the door, slamming it behind me. I heard the door reopen and heard Tom calling my name as I ran down the steps. He followed me out into the street, his bare feet slapping against the cold pavement.

"Anna! Please, I'll... I'll see someone, a therapist, I'll call Holly again, anything you want. If I blacked out and did this, I don't remember. God, what am I saying? This isn't me! Please, don't leave. I love you Anna; it's no game," he begged. Tears were pouring out of his eyes.

"Goodbye, Tom," I firmly stated as I walked down the street to hail a cab. I needed to get away from there, away from him. I spotted a cab and flagged it down. I started to open the car door, not really sure where I was going or what I wanted to do, when Tom ran up to me and pushed the door shut.

I stared into his tear-stained face. "What are you going to do, Tom? Blind me?"

The cabbie got out of the car and walked around to where we were standing.

"Awright, mate, let the girl get in the car or I'll call the police," he warned, approaching Tom.

Tom, shivering, ignored the cabbie, hand still on the door, "Anna, you know me. There has to be some mistake or explanation, please, come back up." He cried.

"Tom... you need to let go of the door now. I mean *now*." My voice quivered as tears started to stream down my face.

He stared at me with a combination of fright, disbelief, and confusion, but he acquiesced, allowing me to open the door and get inside.

I left him on the pavement, not once looking out the window, as we drove off.

CHAPTER 18

I instructed the cab driver to drop me off at Jamie's flat, the only place I could think of to go. I know I freaked her out a little since she had a baseball bat in her hand when she opened the door.

"Anna? What's wrong? You look like hell." She pulled me into the flat and into an embrace.

And then the sobs came. Uncontrollable sobs. I couldn't catch my breath.

Jamie guided me to the sofa and held me until finally, I stopped.

"Anna, what happened?" She asked. Seamus came out of the bedroom and quietly sat down on the chair opposite, obviously concerned, but remained silent.

So, I told them. I told them most everything about Tom, but not about my own visions. It sounded so ridiculous out loud. I recounted Tom's alleged upbringing and what his father told me about his supposed self-inflicted wounds and his sister's death, and I relayed what I had witnessed tonight. Seamus and Jamie listened, against Jamie's character, patiently. After about a half hour, I was done talking, starting to lose my voice.

"Oh, honey, oh, I am so sorry." She hugged me. My tears started once again.

"Anna, I want you to listen to me for a second, okay? Let's try to sort this out objectively. First, is it possible, any possibility at all, that it wasn't him or maybe that he didn't know what he was doing?"

I sniffed between tears as Jamie continued.

"Look, the man is probably damaged. No wonder! He's had a very, very hard life from what you've said. So let's say that his father is right and he did this to himself. Why? Because he found his mother dead. He's got issues no matter what story is correct and he's had to deal with this all on his own, until you came along. And then regarding earlier, you said yourself that his mannerisms were different, that his whole demeanor was different, that he wore a cap, and that he smoked—which is something the Tom we know cannot stand."

"And he kissed a bloke," Seamus stated. "Anna, I've spent loads of time with him. There is just no way he's cheating on you... or gay for that matter. I just don't buy it."

"So what's the explanation, Seamus?" My cynicism came out in my question.

"I wish I knew. I just… I just… I can't buy this. You think you know a person," Seamus considered, a crack in his voice. He straightened up and spoke assertively. "I cannot, and will not believe my mate, Tom, the most upstanding person I know, is a liar and a cheat. There has to be an explanation other than he's been conning us all. I want you to look deep down into your heart and really, really ask yourself. I mean, are you a hundred percent sure it was him? You said it was dark and your cell phone really doesn't show much of any proof."

"I mean, one hundred percent, no, but 95 percent, yeah. But, he's pretty fucked up—his dad said he had been in therapy and placed on a lot of drugs. He had or has Borderline Disorder, he's got these crazy cuts on him, he blacks out. I mean his dad says he likes to hurt people," I said, sniffing. "Now I really am thinking that he did self-mutilate himself, that he made the stories up about his father, I guess to avoid embarrassment… to pull me in… to..to.." I started to bawl, my face started to feel like raw meat.

"The way I see it," Jamie reasoned, "we have a couple of choices. We either believe he's been playing us all and be done with him or we give him the benefit of the doubt and confront him. You said he was in dire straits when you left him, right? That he genuinely looked as if he didn't know what happened?"

"No one can act that well—and why on earth would he? What would be his motive? It's not like he's after your money. If he knew what he was doing, why would he get involved with you in the first place?" Seamus added, but obviously upset.

"Why would he? Because he's sick!" I stated what I thought was the obvious. "Maybe he gets his kicks out of leading a double life?"

"Look, we're going 'round in circles and making too many assumptions. It's late, we're all knackered. Can we get some sleep and figure this out in the daylight?" Jamie bemoaned and then softened, "you may stay as long as you like, love. I'll make up the sofa."

"I think I'm going to go over there," Seamus stated as he stood up.

Jamie looked up at him, a little concerned.

"I'm his best friend. I'm going to make sure he's alright."

Even though my emotions were running at an all-time high as well as my confusion, I was worried about Tom, so I handed Seamus my key.

***

I lay awake on Jamie's small sofa, bouncing between worry and fear to anger and resentment.

The phone rang, interrupting my thoughts. Jamie was in her room, so I ran to get it.

"Hello?" I asked, anxiously.

"Hi, Anna, it's Seamus. Em, look, your boy is, well, he's been in a bit of a state. I knocked on the door to the flat, he didn't let me in, so I used the key you gave me. Em, Anna, I've already called 999."

"What? What do you mean?" My voice started to rise as Jamie walked in rubbing her eyes.

"Don't panic, but, when I let myself in, the place was dark and Mango wasn't even at the door. So, I went looking through the apartment and I found Tom on your bed. His shirt was off and Mango was lying next to him, licking him, trying to wake him up. A knife was next to the bed on the floor."

"Seamus, please, cut to the chase for God's sake!" I yelled.

Seamus's voice started to quiver. "He was all cut up, Anna. I mean all cut up, all over his chest and arms. I found the kitchen knife on the floor next to him. I mean he's breathing and all. Look, I'm going to clean him up a bit and try to rouse him while I'm waiting."

"Okay, yes, okay, we're leaving now."

Jamie and I rushed out of the flat and found a cab, but not quick enough for me. On the way, Seamus called saying that the ambulance had arrived and was taking him to University Hospital. I redirected the cabbie; Jamie took my hand and I started to cry. When we approached the Hospital, I took out my wallet, handed the cabbie a wad of pounds and opened the cab door prior to him coming to a full stop.

"Eh, lassie, you tryin' to kill yerself?"

I ignored the man and ran through the hospital doors. Seamus was waiting for me right inside. He started to report what happened as soon as I saw him. "I think he'll be okay. I tried to mop up all the blood, but, there was so much. Tom was completely out; he wouldn't awaken, but at least he was breathing. Em, the paramedics said something about a transfusion, but I was so upset, I wasn't really paying much attention. Em, Mango had been by his side, lying next to him on the bed." Seamus's eyes started to glisten, but he blinked and composed himself.

"Where is Tom now?" I asked.

Jamie silently walked up next to me, gently touching my back.

Seamus shrugged. "They took 'im somewhere to get fixed up, I presume."

"Anna, this may be a while and I'm sure Mango needs to go out. I bet he stayed with Tom the whole time. When the EMTs arrived, Mango growled at them and wasn't too happy with them touching his pop. Anyway, I'm going to run back to your place and take care of a few, em, things."

I figured he didn't want me coming back to a blood bath and for that, I was grateful. I gave Seamus a big hug. "See, you are a rock star, too." He looked at me bewildered, but smiled anyway. He squeezed Jamie's hand and left.

After getting nowhere with obtaining information, I sat with Jamie in the waiting room. We tried to pass the time doing crossword puzzles and reading magazines, but the hours crawled. I wrestled with so many thoughts and emotions. I should hate him after all the lies he's told me, but I couldn't. What if he died? What if he died thinking I hated him? I felt so hollow, so empty, at the thought of him being out of my life forever. And if he lived, did I want to deal with his issues? His sickness? I bowed my head as the tears started to come, Jamie hugging me in close. I knew I would deal with it, knew I would try to be his savior. It's who I am.

"Jamie, go home. I really appreciate this, but I'm okay for now."

"I'll stay until we get some information, okay love? Then I'll go when we know he's okay."

It took about another hour and a half until a nurse finally came out to talk to us. She explained that Tom had to have a blood transfusion. He was now stable, and I could see him. I let out a huge sigh of relief, but my feelings were staggering. Jamie and I embraced as she said "I told you so," and then she left. The nurse then led me to his room.

Tom was a mess. His hair was disheveled, his skin a sickly white. He was hooked up to machines and an IV. His arms and chest were cleaned and bandaged, but I could tell that he had been horribly cut up. It looked like a couple gashes had been stitched up. And then I saw them. Circling his wrists and ankles were taught, leather restraints.

I quietly bent over him, brushed the hair out of his eyes, and touched his face. The hospital room smell assaulted my nose.

His eyes started to flit open, then widened.

"Anna? Oh my God." He pulled on his arms to reach me, but couldn't move. He tried to move his legs, but to no avail.

"Anna, where... what's going on? Why am I restrained? Get these off of me." He started to panic.

A nurse came in and tried to calm Tom down.

"Are these necessary?" I exclaimed in a high voice.

"I'm afraid they are miss," she whispered. "Mr. Hall is on suicide watch." Tom heard.

"Suicide watch? Are you mental, take these bloody manacles off of me!"

"Mr. Hall, I'm going to give you a sedative."

"N..No, I don't want a sedative. I want to get out of here!"

"It's just to take the edge off; you'll still be able to talk. There you go," the nurse babied as she put something into his IV bag.

"Goddammit!" Tom yelled. The nurse left the room.

In a matter of minutes, Tom's fright and anger dissipated into a sleepy, but lucid, calmness.

"What happened," Tom whispered.

"You don't remember?"

"No. I only remember you leaving me on the cold sidewalk after accusing me of things I didn't do, after hitting me and throwing your engagement ring at me," he stated matter-of-factly.

"Tom, look at me, okay? We're going to figure this all out, okay? Just try and keep it together." I sensed a meltdown, despite the sedative, but instead, he nodded slightly.

"But, why am I here? I don't understand." His voice flattened.

"You cut yourself up really badly."

"What?"

Seeing him like this, so weak, so damaged, solidified my resolve to help him. He couldn't have known what he was doing, could he? Could he even lie like this while drugged? I wouldn't think so.

"Look, I'll be right back. I've got to call Seamus. He's really upset. He's the one who found you, you know."

Tom looked like he was going to have a nervous breakdown. "Seamus?" he said quietly.

"I went to Jamie's after our fight. They know most everything. I had to tell them. He and Jamie are really worried about you."

He didn't respond.

"Why did you do this to yourself? Was it punishment for cheating on me? For being bi..bisexual?" I stammered, afraid of the answer, but I had to know.

Dismayed, Tom explained in a slightly slurred tongue, "Anna, I want you to listen to me. I beg you. Number one, I am not bisexual. I have no inclinations regarding men. However, if I were, I'd like to think I wouldn't have issue with owning up to it. Number two, I would not cheat on you—not ever. I love you and only you. And thirdly, I do not remember anything but coming home after the tour. The last thing I remember is my feet freezing. I find this so hard to believe, but maybe, maybe I had a blackout, so…"

"Okay, well, you MUST see someone about this Tom, and not just a sleep therapist. This goes way beyond."

A nurse walked into the room and checked on Tom's vitals and IV fluids. Then the doctor came in.

"Good to see you're awake, Mr. Hall." The doctor shook my hand and introduced herself.

She started to speak much louder than necessary, "So, here's where we are, Mr. Hall. You had a number of lacerations on your body. You lost a bit of blood, requiring the need for a transfusion, and, we did have to stitch up some of the lacerations on your chest, stomach, and right arm. You are in no physical danger. I will be prescribing some antibiotics to prevent infection. Your movement is going to be a little painful for a number of days. Now, I understand you cut yourself with your kitchen knife, is that correct?"

The doctor was extremely blunt and had absolutely no bedside manner.

"Em, I don't recall."

"Mmm hmmm. Well, the gentleman who found you informed us that a bloody kitchen knife was found next to your bed on the floor and that the wounds were self-inflicted. The angles of the cuts indicate that as well."

Tom sat in silence.

"So, Mr. Hall, we are going to transfer you to the psychiatric ward at Havendash Hospital, which can help you better. They'll place you under suicide watch for your own benefit."

"Em, no. I'm not suicidal, I just can't remember. I'm prone to blackouts. I'm quite aware now and don't need these restraints. Please take them off. I... I get claustrophobic."

"I'm sorry, Mr. Hall, we have no choice in the matter under the Mental Health Act."

Tom looked pleadingly at me.

"Can't he just come home and I'll watch him." I didn't know if this was what I really wanted, but Tom looked so pathetic.

"Miss, I would think you would want your husband to get some help. The doctors will take good care of him there. If they deem he is mentally fit to go home, then they will allow that, but first, he needs to be evaluated."

Tom, despite the mild sedative, started to hyperventilate and strain his body against the restraints. The doctor snapped her fingers at the nurse in the room who quickly turned some nozzle on the IV bag. The dosage was probably more potent because Tom immediately calmed and closed his eyes.

The doctor turned to me, unamused, and said they would be taking him soon, and she left the room.

"Tom, it will be okay," I whispered, slicking his hair back in the way he liked.

CHAPTER 19

I took a taxi home to the flat after Tom was transferred since I couldn't stay with him. I was so worn out from everything that happened last night and today, I just wanted to cry myself to sleep. Or run away, I wasn't sure which was better.

I knocked on the door of our flat since Seamus had my key. He let me in, Mango waiting patiently at the door. I told Seamus that I wanted to take Mango out, that I really needed air and to be alone for a bit and then we could talk. He said he'd be happy to wait.

I fetched Mango's leash since he won't get it for me, only Tom. And Mango and I set out on a long walk through the London streets. Reflecting on all that had happened, I tried my best to be optimistic. My brain started to wander in twenty different directions as my resolve started to wane a bit. From leaving Tom, to staying and dealing with this, to moving back to the States, to marrying the man. My legs moved on autopilot. Mango would occasionally sniff the ground and pee and we ultimately wound up in Regent's Park. I sat on a bench near a pond with a number of birds swimming around, and I invited Mango up with me. He immediately accepted and jumped into my lap. I hugged him tightly for warmth and comfort. We had been sitting like that for quite some time, when my cell phone rang.

"Hi, Jamie."

She asked me for an update and told me she was at my flat with Seamus.

"They're transferring him to another hospital, a psych hospital, I guess. He's been placed on suicide watch, although, I don't think he's suicidal... at least not consciously."

"I'm sorry, Anna," she said into the phone. "But, maybe this is a good thing, after all."

"Well, he obviously needs help, he can't keep living like this. Neither can I. Jamie, he's got to have some kind of disorder, right? Maybe they can fix it with therapy or drugs or something. I just don't want to believe what he did was for real. I mean, what if he's had sex with other people? What if he has an STD or AIDS or something?"

"Don't jump to conclusions, okay? And I'm sure they'll test for all that at Hospital."

"Right. Look, Mango is getting restless, so we're going to keep walking, but we'll be back in about 20 minutes."

"Okay, love. We'll see you back. I'll cook something up; breakfast at this point."

"Thanks, Jamie," and I hung up and continued our walk.

***

— *Monday, December 8*

Jamie was kind enough to let me take the day off. She said she might also after the late night and early morning. I did not feel like moping around the house and second guessing and worrying about everything, so I decided to find some facts on my own. I obviously couldn't trust Thomas. So, I called Tom's old secondary school's office and set up an appointment with the Headmistress and luckily, she was able to see me today.

When I arrived at the school by cab, I walked straight to the office and waited on a not-so-comfortable chair, but not for very long. Our appointment was for 11:30 and at 11:32 an elderly woman with short white hair wearing a tailored blue business suit introduced herself.

"Hi, Ms. Pearson. I am Claudia Gates. Please come in." I thanked her and followed her into her office. The single window overlooked a green field, probably for rugby. The walls were decorated with many plaques for "best this" and "best that" along with her university diplomas. She had a mass of papers on her desk and four wooden filing cabinets.

"So, how may I help you? My secretary's message about the purpose of your visit wasn't too clear, just something about a former student."

"Yes, thank you. My fiancé is an alumnus to this school—he was here about 16 or 17 years ago—I understand you were here at that time?"

"Oh yes, I've been working here for, oh, I'd say about forty years now. I started as an English teacher, but eventually made it to Headmistress. Who is the lucky chap?" She gave me a very big, yellow-tinged toothy smile.

"Um, do you remember Tom Hall?"

The smile from Headmistress Gates evaporated rather quickly and a look of sorrow crossed her face. "Yes, of course, I remember Tom Hall. I often wondered about how he was doing."

"A lot of stuff from his past has been dredged up, and he doesn't remember a whole lot from his time here, at least after his sister died."

"Yes, Lizzie." But, she didn't elaborate. "So, how may I help you?"

"I was wondering if you could tell me a little about how Tom was when he was here. I mean, how he behaved, stuff like that." I felt myself tripping over my words. I felt so weird being here.

She sighed, "Tom was one of my favorites. He was a dear sweet boy, charming and quite handsome. But, he was quiet and got bullied quite a bit."

"Oh?"

"Please forgive me, as I'm sure your intentions are true, but I'm not sure if I should be disclosing any information about a former student."

I nodded, figuring something like this would happen, but I pushed anyway. "I understand, but he's really having trouble wrestling with his past right now. He's in the hospital because of his past and I'm just trying to gather some facts for him to help him get better."

Headmistress Gates bit her lip and nodded as she began.

"Well, you seem like an honest person. I guess no harm can be done by telling you," she said while nodding. That was easier than I thought.

"He was a bit of a loner, and after his sister died, he became more so. I don't think the other children knew how to act around someone like him—you know, someone who had such tragic losses in his family—so they would push him around and tease him."

"So, he never beat anyone up?"

"Tom Hall? Well, overall, he was gentle as a lamb, but one time and only once, a lad pushed his buttons pretty hard. This was after Lizzie had died. It seemed Tom had finally had enough, and he lashed out. He almost put the boy in hospital, but afterward Tom claimed he couldn't remember what had happened. It's like he was literally 'blind with rage.' I didn't want to do it, I truly believed him, but I had no choice but to suspend him so he could get the help he needed. That decision has weighed heavily on me for years. I always wondered if something was awry at home, but whenever I questioned him on it, he assured me everything was fine."

"What about the cutting? I've been told he was in therapy and diagnosed with Borderline Disorder."

The Headmistress sat back in her chair, looking rather concerned, "Yes, he did cut himself, or so we think. It happened quite a bit after his sister died. We only found out about it because his friend Robbie came forward and told us so. It seemed he would do it when he felt guilty about something. Like, if he did poorly on a test or in a rugby game. We recommended, well, insisted to his father that he needed therapy, but I don't know how much good it did. Tom became even more quiet and reserved. Probably the drugs they put him on, I gather. Unfortunately, the bullying didn't stop—we would intervene when we knew it was going on, but of course, we couldn't watch him all the time."

"So, the Borderline Disorder?"

"No, not that I know of. His therapist would have given us that information. If I recall, the medication they put him on was something akin to Ritalin. It really subdued him."

"So, you all didn't investigate his home situation ever?"

"Well, times were different then, and I suspect different here then where you come from. We just didn't pry. And when we thought he was probably doing all this to himself, that's when we took action and required him to get therapy. We figured the tragedy caused his, ah, mental problems." She pursed her lips together, the pink lipstick diminishing to a thin line. Then she asked, "But, how is he now?"

"I don't know. But, I think he's getting the help he needs. He really is a wonderful person—he's just got a lot of shit, oh, sorry, stuff to deal with."

"Well, I hope I was some help to you. Do you have a picture of him?"

I smiled and took out my phone and handed it to her, showing her some of the pictures I had taken on Millennium Bridge.

She breathed in and smiled, her eyes crinkling, "Oh, would you look at that. So handsome, and he looks so very happy," she said as she handed the phone back to me. "Do tell him I said hello and that he should come and visit. I'd love to see him. I hope he truly is going to get better. Bad things really do happen to good people." She nodded, as if reassuring herself.

I thanked her profusely and left. Thomas had told me partial truths, and I wondered how many other partial truths or lies he chose to tell me. One fight, not many. Gentle child, not mean. No Borderline Disorder. But, he did cut himself, at least after Lizzie died, and it seems he's had at least a couple blackouts since he was a kid. But what is Thomas's motive in twisting everything around? Or is he just the sadist Tom claims him to be?

***

— *Wednesday night, December 10*

I was getting restless. I hadn't been able to speak with Tom, and the nurses kept telling me he's in observation or therapy or whatever. I didn't expect it would be such a long time. I thought he'd just go in for maybe the evening. With him gone, the flat felt extremely lonely, despite Mango's presence.

The last couple days, I stayed as busy as possible at work and I went to bed early in the evening. Time passed, but at a crawl; tonight, seeming to drag out even more. After making myself a simple dinner, I decided to do some more research. I had been staying away from the news the whole week, not wanting to hear anything about the Vigilante, but tonight I poured through the net with searches on anything I could find, especially looking for any attacks on someone's eyes. I felt compelled to gather any clues to see what possible connection I had with him or her. And, I really wanted to rule out Tom as a possibility.

Search: London Vigilante

October, 2013:

> *…Gerard Nicholson found cowering in his basement by his wife. Nicholson's mouth was duct taped, and his wrists and ankles were cinched together with zip ties. Nicholson was rushed to Hospital, suffering from blood loss as his right pinky and ring finger were severed. Nicholson received a transfusion for blood loss and is currently in stable condition.*

I read later articles on the case:

> *…turns out Nicholson slammed his wife's hand in their car door after an argument. He did so repeatedly, breaking her hand in countless places… eventually lost two of her fingers… possible work of the Vigilante… described as a tall person, probably male, smoked cigarettes, wore a mask… motive seems obvious, but victim did not seem to know the person… Nicholson said his*

> *attacker knew about how he broke his wife's hand... assumes wife told*
> *someone... police have no leads.*

This was the only story I found on a harmed hand, and it was last year, anyway.

Another link:

> *...Alleged Vigilante severely burned Sebastian Pike... found in a loo in*
> *Barbican Station... cigarette burns all up and down his arms and on his face...*
> *found later that Pike had burned his own son in such a way... son told teachers*
> *at his school after the attack on his father occurred.*

I found many more links on the subject. All of them had to do with the abusers maimed in the same way they abused their own. The victims of the Vigilante's targets were mostly women and children, but some were homosexuals and a couple were animals. The Vigilante never once killed anyone, but definitely did some permanent damage in many cases. Some of the victims saw the Vigilante, but could only describe him or her much like the Nicholson's description.

I decided to have another look at the Annapolis papers to see if there was anything reported that night. I found nothing, but the local newspaper there was not all that great.

When I finally found the clue I was searching for, my hands starting to tremble:

> *"Father George Sunderland, a Priest at Our Lady of the Assumption and St.*
> *Gregory chapel, was found by an anonymous passerby with brutal injuries to his*
> *eyes on Saturday night, December 6th . Father Sunderland was taken to Hospital*
> *that evening. We will know more on his condition later when the police make a*
> *statement."*

Further down:

> *"...the Father has lost his sight in both eyes. We will get to the bottom of this*
> *vicious attack... no, we do not have any leads. No, we do not have reason to*
> *suspect this is the work of the Vigilante or even Jack the Ripper II... or someone*
> *else... when the Father feels up to talking to police, we will issue another*
> *statement..."*

Then, the report from yesterday:

"Father George Sunderland, known best for his focus on helping the mentally challenged and abused children, was blinded in a horrendous attack on Saturday, December 6. The Father made a statement to the police indicating that, although he did not get a great view of the assailant, he thinks the person was a woman, based on her mannerisms, but couldn't be sure. The Father, of course, wants justice, but also says he forgives this woman if she would turn herself in."

And then the report from today:

"...not only did he sexually abuse a number of boys, he accidently blinded one while he was disciplining the boy. Sources say that while the priest was beating him, the boy tripped forward and hit the corner of the priest's desk, blinding the boy in one eye. Nothing came out about this or the abuse until one of the assaulted children, now teenager, tweeted it to a few people. Word got out fast, causing more boys to come forward and claim their abuse by the priest. Following the Vigilante's modus operandi and the description given by the priest, Scotland Yard is quite certain this is the work of the Vigilante..."

I put my hand to my mouth and started to cry tears of relief. The article listed the time at the end, doing the math in my head, it turns out the attack would have taken place at 9:00 PM. Tom is not the Vigilante. He couldn't be... the attack happened while he was finishing up the tour—I saw him. Unless this was a copycat, but the police seem relatively certain it's a female. That means it's not Tom. That means I have some other connection to the Vigilante, but it's not Tom. I breathed a small sigh of relief. Still, he's either lying to me or he has... something else, but at least it's not criminal. I started to search a little more.

Disorder of Jekyll and Hyde:

... thought to have split personality disorder, known today as Dissociative Disorder or DID

Search DID

Dissociative Disorder thought to be caused by significant trauma... related to PTSD... coping mechanism to deal with trauma... rape or severe abuse, perhaps as a child... 2nd personality can have different physical aspects like a change in vision or hearing, different mannerisms, can be of a different gender... changing to different personalities a subtle eye roll occurs... change usually happens with a trigger... dominant personality does not know 2nd personality... complaints of blackouts... treatments include psychotherapy, dance therapy, art therapy, drug

therapy... new controversial EDMR therapy... patient re-experiences trauma...
track eye movement... gain control.

I read this a couple of times. So many of the symptoms here fit. From wearing
his reading eyeglasses when he didn't need them, smoking, to a different gait
and of course, different behavior. Did his eyes ever roll back? And, of course,
the blackouts and cutting. As I rubbed my temples, the phone rang.

"Hello?"

"'ello Anna, where is my boy... haven't seen him in a bit."

"He's out."

"Mmm... well tell him he should stop by and take care of his father."

I hung up the phone. I wanted nothing to do with Thomas Hall at the
moment and I sure wasn't going to tell him where his son was. I should have,
however, called Trevor. I was reluctant, feeling that Tom should tell him what
happened, not me. So, I went to bed early and unfortunately dreamed.

> *In the catacombs the dank air clogged my nostrils causing me to gasp for air. The*
> *putrid odor became worse as I walked through corridor after corridor, hearing*
> *screams and moans. I plodded along, wearily, looking for something or someone*
> *and then I tripped, barely catching myself. Looking down, worried it was a body,*
> *relief swept over me when I saw a thin box. I hesitated, but the box beckoned, so I*
> *stooped down and opened it, revealing a pair of glasses and baseball cap. The smell*
> *of smoke mixed unpleasantly with the mustiness... my gag reflex kicking in. I*
> *squinted and scanned the darkness around me for the source. I could faintly make*
> *out a dark figure against the catacomb wall to the left of me and another one to the*
> *right. Holding my lantern up, I saw a face, vaguely familiar... it was Tom, but*
> *then again it wasn't. The figure to my right was certainly Tom. He was intently*
> *looking at the figure across from him, over my head. Surprise crossed his face, he*
> *tilted back his head, opened his mouth wide; his fangs extremely sharp and long,*
> *and then he screamed in anguish, causing the ceiling to rain dirt upon my head.*
> *The earth pounded me from above, filling my nostrils, my eyes, my mouth. The*
> *pounding kept getting louder and louder.*

I awoke with a start. The rain outside pelted the roof. Tilting my head back, I
sighed. Mango, on all fours on the bed, stared down at me and cocked his
head. I must have been doing something odd in my sleep for he looked at me
quizzically and then started licking my face.

"Stop, boy," I half-heartedly ordered. I looked over at the clock…5:30 AM. I figured Mango had to go out, so I put on some jeans and a sweater, found my raincoat and took him out the door. The rain and gloom outside mirrored my feelings inside. In a way it was a comfort to bask in my despondency. Mango stepped gingerly on the pavement, not really liking to get his paws wet, but eventually did his business.

Back upstairs, I stripped off my raincoat and dried Mango off with the towel that was neatly folded in the foyer closet. When I went to feed him, I noticed the answering machine was blinking. Upon pressing play, I heard Tom's hoarse voice, telling me he could probably be released today as long as I came in and had a chat with the therapist. He went on to say that he really wanted to come home, his voice faltering on the words "come home." He sounded incredibly upset and distraught. He also said not to bother coming in until around 9:00 since the doctor wouldn't be in until then and that he hoped he wasn't impacting my work schedule, apologizing for it. He whispered he loved me and hung up. Missing his call sent me over the edge. My eyes welled up and I let out an anguished cry, but then, I became almost giddy with the prospect of him coming home today. Mango ran up to me with his ears back and gave me a wrinkly, worried face, which I cupped with both hands and kissed reassuringly.

"It's okay, boy. Daddy's coming home today." Mango started wagging his tail in big circles, making his whole butt move.

I looked around the flat and grimaced a little. The place wasn't horrible, but it certainly wasn't up to Tom's standards either. So, I got to work, vacuuming the dog hair, making the bed, folding the clothes I had all over the floor. I then took care of the dirty dishes in the sink I somehow amassed. During a quick break, I emailed Jamie, explaining I wouldn't be in and why. I figured she'd be okay with this since I put in a bit of overtime this past week. Plus, she knows the situation.

I went into the bedroom and gathered some clothes for Tom, assuming the ones he went to the hospital in were ruined. On the dresser, my ring sat, beckoning me. Jamie had found it under the sofa and placed it in my room, saying I should wear it when and if I felt comfortable. I was confused about so many things, but during these days apart, I knew, even more so, that I loved Tom. I also knew he was quite mentally sick and needed help and I wasn't about to abandon him.

After showering, eating breakfast, and finishing tidying up the place, I gave Mango a treat and then locked up the flat. I went back in, forgetting the bag I had put together for Tom, so I ran back to the bedroom and as I grabbed the bag, the engagement ring caught my eye again, but this time I did not hesitate to seize it from the dresser and slide it back on my finger. It felt good and right to have it back on. I pulled Tom's coat from the hanger in the foyer and sped out of the flat.

The streets were a bit crowded, as usual this time of morning, but my driver seemed to realize I was in a hurry, so he maneuvered the cab as best he could through the traffic, avoiding the double-deckers that stopped to pick up the awaiting passengers. Arriving right before 9:00, I told the receptionist who I was there for. She nodded and directed me to the seats in the waiting room. I plopped down on a stiff vinyl blue chair with a wood frame and picked up a random magazine, aimlessly flipping through it when a nurse came out and called my name. I quickly rose out of the uncomfortable chair, which squeaked as I stood. Following the nurse down the beige hall with the beige floor and the beige doors, I was led into a sterile office with a window overlooking the street—the only thing of any interest in this place.

A middle-aged doctor with a sandy blond, receding hair line shook my hand and motioned for me to have a seat, introducing himself as Dr. Mason.

"Ms. Pearson, I've completed Mr. Hall's discharge papers and he is free to go. However, I wanted to speak with you in private before you pick him up. Mr. Hall gave us permission to disclose information so I am not violating any patient confidentiality here. The good news is that we don't think he is suicidal. After keeping him on watch and then asking him a number of questions, we believe he was unaware of his self-mutilation."

The doctor cleared his throat.

"I've dealt with many good 'actors' so there is always that chance that he's covering, but after studying him, he seems to be telling the truth. But, Ms. Pearson, I wanted to hear your side, to know what you've seen from him. Any other odd behaviors? Anything?"

Pushing my hair behind my ears, I began. "Well, yes. I've confronted him about various wounds. He claims he doesn't know where they came from, or sometimes he makes some assumption or maybe even makes something up. In fact, when I first met him, he had a huge gash on his hand and claimed it was from a tree branch. And then there have been a couple of other times when I've found mysterious wounds on him. Um, I've seen him smoking twice. He vehemently abhors smoking and swears up and down he does not do it. And, I've seen him wearing glasses on the street, but he only needs them to read. One night, I observed him from a distance. I..I did this because I was spying on him. I started to get suspicious because of some of the odd behaviors he was exhibiting, so I followed him. Not only did I see him smoke and wear the glasses and a baseball hat, but his gait was different, his mannerisms were different, even his speech, as far as I could tell. And," I shook my head to try and get the image out, "and I saw him kiss someone... a man."

"Mmm Hmmm."

"What does that mean?" I asked, scared of the answer.

"Well, Ms. Pearson, I hate to be blunt and alarm you, but is it possible Tom hasn't come to terms with being a homosexual? Or bisexual?"

"I..I don't know, but I don't think so. He really does seem to have blackouts where he can't remember where he was or what he did. I've witnessed this two times now... at least, the aftermath."

The doctor nodded and told me that Tom had mentioned he's had blackouts here and there over the years. The doctor then suggested we carry on this conversation with Tom. He motioned me to follow him to the room where Tom had been admitted. I was a bit nervous to see him, but also excited.

Another sterile and depressing hallway led us to yet another beige colored door with a small piece of glass at eye level, surrounded by bars. The doctor knocked softly and pulled out a key. When we entered the room, Tom was in a chair by the barred, but larger window, looking out. The room was small and devoid of any warmth or creature comforts. Two pieces of furniture, a bed and the chair Tom sat upon, were bolted to the ground. A single florescent light above cast a yellowing gloom to the room, matching the colorless walls. Tom's malaise mirrored the room's dourness.

Tom looked, well for him, like crap. His hair was unkempt, like he had just woken up, and his facial hair was longer than I've seen before. Not yet a beard and mustache, but stubble well on its way. His eyes were red and puffy and his hands were shaking as if he had seven cups of coffee. He looked like he was beaten down emotionally. He seemed not to notice our presence, so I approached him tentatively, not wanting to startle him.

And then as if someone flicked on a light switch, Tom snapped out of whatever "trance" he was in and gave me the biggest look of relief I've ever seen. He stood up and took me in his arms, burying his face into my shoulder.

He squeezed me like a boa constrictor while kneading my back like a cat. He whispered how he missed me and loved me and that he was sorry. It felt good to be in his arms again.

"Please, Mr. Hall, Ms. Pearson, let's sit down and chat so you may carry on with your day." We unfurled ourselves from each other, but kept holding hands as we sat on the rock-solid mattress. "Well, Mr. Hall, Ms. Pearson and I were going over what behaviors she's seen from you, confirming some of what you've disclosed to me." Tom gave me a slightly worried sideways glance. "About your different mannerisms and habits. She told me you kissed a man? Are you a bisexual, Mr. Hall?"

"No, I've already gone over this with you. I am devoted to my fiancée and seemingly have never been happier, sans this bit of a setback. Like the self-inflicted wounds, I don't remember any of this."

I interjected, "Is it possible he has Dissociative Disorder?"

"Well, Ms. Pearson, I see you've done your homework. We are considering that possibility, but without further therapy… well, I like to take my time before diagnosing someone."

"Em, what is Dissociative Disorder?" Tom wore a bewildered expression.

"It's like multiple personality disorder," I muttered.

"That's right, Ms. Pearson, although we don't call it that anymore."

"Pardon?" Tom let go of my hand and crossed his arms across his chest.

"Mr. Hall, some people who have had a traumatic childhood like rape or severe abuse, like you've allegedly experienced, create an alter ego. The brain works in funny ways. Sometimes in order to cope with these abuses, your brain can suppress memories and even create a new identity, one that can deal with these traumas better. Something usually triggers the change; it could be a smell, a word, a taste. Whatever the cause of the transition, your alter ego protects you from dealing with your past trauma. Your other personality might be male or female… you may have different values or habits, your tastes may be different. Even your eyesight can change. And yes, you may even have different sexual tendencies or even accents. It truly is like someone else inhabiting your body. But, please keep in mind, this disorder is highly controversial and very hard to diagnose. It may look like you check a lot of these boxes based on what you and Ms. Pearson have said, but we cannot be sure at this point, not at all. I would suggest you having an ECG and an EEG just to see if anything medical is going on because I am concerned about your blackouts. Now, if you truly kissed a man that evening, if Ms. Pearson is sure what she saw, then you are either lying to us or yourself about your tendencies, Ms. Pearson was gravely mistaken, or maybe, you have Dissociative Disorder. I will say, however, to you Ms. Pearson, you can take almost any abnormal psychological disorder and be able to attribute 75 percent of the symptoms to yourself or someone else. That is the danger of trying to self-diagnose."

I looked over at Tom; his face was tense and his jaw muscle was pulsing.

"What about all the scars on his back?" I asked.

Tom stared at me.

"What about them?" The doctor probed.

Tom interjected, "My dubious fiancée would like to know if the scars were self-inflicted."

"Well, I suppose some could have been, but based on the angle or position and the severity of the scars, it would seem that it would be very difficult to inflict that much damage by oneself. However, the cigarette burns and the older scars on the arms could have been. Were they Mr. Hall?"

"I clearly remember my father burning me, so no, they were not." He said, defensively.

"So, where do we go from here?" I asked.

"As I said, I am going to recommend some tests. I also would recommend therapy. It seems, Mr. Hall, you had a pretty traumatic childhood, your mother's death, your sister's death, and obviously at least some abuse from your father. Since you have never truly learned to deal with it, it would behoove you to take such a course of action. Especially if you are mutilating yourself unwittingly."

"We'll think about it," Tom interjected a bit brusquely.

Imploringly, I placed my hand on his shoulder. He looked over at me as if to say, leave it alone.

The doctor agreed, but emphasized we should not wait—to at least get the EEG and EKG done. He gave Tom his discharge papers and a prescription for antibiotics. He also mentioned that Tom was tested for AIDS among other STDs and the results all came back negative. After that, we thanked the doctor and he left. I handed Tom the bag of clothes and stepped out of the room to breathe, hugging his coat. About five minutes later, Tom came out, looking a bit better. His hair was wetted and combed back, plus, he looked much more like "him" in his own clothing. Handing him his coat, he smiled faintly as he shrugged it on.

As soon as we stepped out the main door to the outside, Tom took my face in his hands and kissed my mouth, desperately. He ran his hands through my hair, dislodging my orange and black scrunchie as he continued to plant numerous kisses on my face, his stubble scratching me. And then he abruptly stopped, piercing me with his eyes. They looked so lost and sad.

I grasped his hands and pulled them down, squeezed them and let go. "Sweetheart, it's going to be okay. We're at least getting some possible answers."

"Anna, you have no idea what happened in there. When I was admitted, they put me on suicide watch which entailed stripping me down and searching various parts of me to make sure I didn't have any objects on or in me to harm myself, put me in some other hospital garb and… and strapped me to the bed." He looked away, trying to suppress his feelings. "Not only was it demoralizing, but you can imagine how I felt being immobilized. I couldn't deal with it, and I tried to explain it, but I must have sounded mental. They gave me some kind of drug that put me in a fog and I didn't know where I was and I experienced so many horrid dreams while in that state. I… it… it was horrible," Tom faltered.

"Oh God, Tom. I'm so sorry. I tried to call and visit, but every time, they said you were under observation or something. Had I known, I would have tried to get you out of there." We started walking down the street, Tom inhaling London and his freedom.

"And not being able to talk to you, to know where we stood, was agony." Tom started to walk faster as a shadow crossed his face, making his already distraught expression more gloomy. But then, he picked up his pace even more. I tried to grab onto his arm to slow him down, but instead, he took my hand and started to jog. We weaved in and out of the crowd and then turned down a deserted street where Tom shifted gears into an all-out run, his Chuck Taylor's slapping the ground. I stumbled a bit, but kept up the best I could as he dragged me down the street. The chilly air burned my throat and I pleaded with him to stop, or at least release his death grip on my hand. Finally, he decelerated when we came upon the entrance to a greenspace. He let go of my hand and breathed in through his nose and out his mouth to catch his breath.

I put my hands on my thighs, gasping for air and trying to alleviate the stitch in my side.

Tom put his hand on my back and apologized. "Sorry, love, I just had to run. I shouldn't have done that, my sutures." He placed his hand on his stomach and sucked in through his teeth.

I righted myself and smiled as did he, and we broke out laughing, aggravating my cramp. We found a bench and sat down, Tom with his arm around me, pulling me close.

"I missed you, love. I missed my dog, my flat. I will not go back to that place. We'll find something more suitable… I will call Holly later today for a recommendation."

"I'm sorry I brought up the stuff your dad told me. It wasn't because I didn't believe you, but in light of everything, I had to know… I thought it best if we had an opinion on that."

"I understand." He delicately touched the ring on my finger. "Are you sure? My baggage is piling up and I don't know how long it will take me to get over it. I didn't want this for you."

"I'm in love with you. I can't just turn that off. And everyone has baggage."

Tom blinked and one tear made its way down his face. He wiped it away and whispered, "I don't know what I did to deserve you."

I smiled up at him and we sat quietly, watching squirrels run around the park, until I broke the silence.

"Well, what do you think about this Dissociative Disorder? "

"I think… it's bullshit."

"Why? I read about plenty of people having this, and your behavior and your history fit. The doctor didn't rule it out."

"Come on, Anna. A split personality? Really? You think I'm Dr. Jekyll and Mr. Hyde?" He asked as he removed his arm from my shoulder and turned on the bench to face me. Another couple came into the park and sat on a bench within earshot, so I dropped my voice.

"I just think it's important to explore all avenues. Let's look at the facts, okay? You have had many blackouts and didn't know where you were for a time… and mind you these weren't drug induced. I've witnessed your changes, your self-inflicted wounds. Geez, Tom, you made out with a man and did God knows what else."

Tom looked at me straight in the eyes. "You do believe me I had no idea about that night? I really think you saw someone else. Someone who perhaps looked like me." He looked so sincere.

"I… I guess it's possible it wasn't you, I mean I thought that was possible myself after the change in your whole demeanor, but I think I'd know if it was you, don't you?"

Tom started to perform his next diatribe with an affected voice and gestures. "How about looking at it this way, Ms. Sherlock Holmes… what if, we have a girl with an imagination that has run amok. The girl thinks her dashing fiancé is the *evil* Vigilante. He was abused," Tom looked wistfully to the sky and then back down into my eyes, "he blacks out every once in a while, which must mean, he goes on a rampage harming those demons who inflicted harm on the innocents. Not only that," his expressive eyebrows rose as his finger came up, "but he secretly has sex with men, smokes cigarettes and then, because he's a masochist, he cuts himself all *up*." He caressed my face and gave me a wry smile, raising one eyebrow.

I raised one eyebrow at him and then shook my head. "Y' know, some of that sounds ridiculous, especially the way you phrase it in your 'story telling mode.' But, you did cut yourself up. You could have died. And you have no recollection of this. I'd say there is something very wrong with you, to be blunt. And I'm here for you, okay? But, dammit, you cannot take this lightly, after what both you and I, let alone Seamus and Jamie went through!" My voice got a little louder. The people on the next bench didn't seem to notice.

Tom looked down and remained silent. He knew I was right.

I continued, "And whether you like it or not, I am pretty sure I am connected to this Vigilante. But! I now know it's not you."

He looked back up at me, his eyebrows raised, "Really? You've finally let that go? What changed your mind?"

"The night I followed you and saw you with the other guy, a priest was found blinded. The attack happened at 9:00 PM, while you were still at work, so, even if, and a big if, I mistook another guy for you, you couldn't have blinded the priest. The timing wouldn't work out."

"Is that what you meant the night you left me, when you asked if I was going to blind you? What happened?"

I recounted my experience in the flat and then the research I found.

Tom scratched his head, causing his usual strand of hair to fall forward. "Maybe you are right. If these so-called feelings you are having are actually happening."

"What, you don't believe me? You've witnessed this, you know what I've been through. Even Holly thinks I have some kind of psychic phenomenon happening!" This time, the well-dressed man on the bench skirted his eyes over to us.

"See, here's the thing, Anna. Yes, I believe you, whole-heartedly. I know you are telling me the truth, not because of what I witnessed, but because I trust you and have faith in you." His eyes glowered. "Do you understand what I'm saying to you?"

I breathed out, "Yes, I do."

"Okay, so please give me the benefit of the doubt that I did not bugger another man, blackout or not. Just as I told you I am not the Vigilante. We'll just dig deeper and figure out the rest. Obviously, I did cut myself, em, a lot, even though I don't remember any of it. All the other unexplained cuts, I don't remember, but I absolutely remember what my father did to me. And I'm not stupid, I realize I've been in complete and utter denial. But, I now know more than ever that I need help, and I promise, tomorrow, I will set up the tests and talk to Holly. Good?"

I smiled, somewhat relieved. I really wanted this to be true. "Good. And by the way, I think you have to allow Mango on the bed now."

"Oh, and why is that?"

"Because he took care of you after you, you know. When Seamus found you, he said Mango was with you, licking you. He even said he snarled at the EMTs when they tried to touch you."

"He's a good dog. You win." His mouth twitched up ever so slightly.

"Um, I should probably mention something else to you. I went to your secondary school."

Tom squinted at me, "Whatever for?"

"Well, remember how your dad told me that you used to cut yourself and you used to get into a lot of fights at school? So, I went to talk to Headmistress Gates, who was still there. She totally remembered you."

"So you went on a fishing expedition?" Tom sighed.

"Don't be mad at me, Tom. Your dad gave me half-truths, okay? Some of what he said was true. But, I now know more how he operates. This is what I think. He doesn't want to admit any wrongdoing, so it was convenient for you to hurt yourself, so he could disguise what he did to you. But look, Headmistress Gates said that you were super gentle and kind and never hurt anyone, except once and except yourself—much like you are today. She said you were bullied, too."

"As I've told you before, school, after Elizabeth died, is a big fog to me. I don't even recall ever hurting myself, but I am sure, now, that I did during the blackouts. So, did you learn anything else, Ms. Holmes?"

"Not really. Only that she really liked you. She said you were one of her favorites and she beamed when I showed her a current picture, saying how handsome you are."

"Yes, well, she was always kind to me and understanding. Did my father say anything else to you?"

There was no way I was going to tell him about Elizabeth. "Well, he said he caught you with another guy."

"Yes, we've been over this, time and time again."

"No, not Robbie. He said he saw you with another guy a couple years ago—in your sister's room. That he saw you in the act."

Tom took a deep breath, lowered his head, and shook it in disbelief, "Oh, Thomas. No, Anna, that did not happen. The only person I've ever brought to the house was you. His audacity is beyond comprehension."

"Okay, I figured as much. Look, let's stop talking about him. I've got an idea." I stood up, took both of his hands and pulled him off the bench. We walked to the street and Tom asked what was on my mind, but I just smiled at him as we waited a bit for a cab to slow for us.

"71 St. James Street, please," I directed. I looked over at Tom, who narrowed his eyes at me, but at least looked curious after his ordeal. He relaxed into the cab seat.

"This was going to be one of your Christmas presents, but I think it's much needed now. And you really smell of hospital," I explained as we drove up. I paid the driver and we hurried out of the cab. In front of us, a blue awning reading "Truefitt & Hill" covered the sidewalk.

A huge grin overtook his face, "You know me well," he said as he entered the store.

The formal clerk, clothed in a black suit and ecru shirt, greeted Tom and then took him back. I waited patiently in the foyer, looking at every shaving need one could want. Very expensive shaving "necessities," for that matter. I paid for Tom's treatment and then passed the time browsing through all the brushes, razors, creams, and after shaves, making mental notes for Christmas. Eventually, Tom came out looking like his normal self. Close shaven, hair slicked back with gel and as GQ as ever, walking a bit more upright—more confident. I touched his face… soft and smooth.

"I needed this, love. They, of course, wouldn't let me touch a razor in that institution. Thank you again for this, I feel somewhat whole again. But, let's get some food, I'm a bit peckish. I've actually missed veganism. The meals in that place where horrid. And then, after we eat, I would like to hug my dog."

CHAPTER 20

Tom slept soundly and deeply. With no restraints, no cement-hard mattress, and wrapped up in blankets like a caterpillar in a cocoon, he seemed at peace. I, however, struggled to fall asleep. I sat vigil with Mango, stroking his head, waiting for Tom to rise up, and change into, well, something. Would it be a beautiful butterfly, emerging triumphantly, flying away from his past, or would he go the opposite way and become a wasp, something sinister. I felt he was at a turning point and would, hopefully, persevere.

I must have drifted off eventually because I awoke to beautiful eyes staring at me. Tom was crouched by the side of the bed talking softly to me.

"Sweetheart, come on now, you've got to get to work." Tom stroked my hair.

"What time is it?" I groggily asked.

"It's around 6:30. Did you not get much sleep?"

"No, not really." I sat up on my elbow while Tom crossed his arms on the bed and rested his chin on his forearms, still staring at me.

"I never apologized for that night. I'm sorry I hit you."

"I would have hit me too if I thought I saw what you thought you saw. No harm done, although I'll know not to piss you off. You're pretty strong… your handprint lasted for hours." He stood up and smiled, and then he announced he was going to get breakfast going.

"Let me see them."

"See what?" Tom paused and then, quietly, embarrassed, "Oh. Didn't you see in Hospital?"

"Just the bandages," I said as I crawled out of bed.

Tom stood up, paused, and then took off his shirt. Raw, but healing pinkish red lines crossed over one another like railroad tracks. There were maybe four long gashes on his chest and a few on each arm. The top of his right bicep looked like a rag doll's arm, two four-inch slices stitched up into place, creating an X. His stomach also sported a deeper wound, stitched up as well. There were a number of smaller marks in various places, too. Tom stood there, expressionless, looking out the window as I examined him further, my eyes dropping to his raw wrists.

"What happened here?" I gently turned his hand over, softly running my fingers over the welts.

"The restraints. I became a bit belligerent when they shackled me to the bed. They, ah, made the restraints tighter than necessary and I constantly tried to break free, but to no avail of course. Eventually, they drugged me to get me to stop, but I guess the constant trauma to my wrists already created these welts and the redness."

"Are you in pain?"

"A little. When I move the wrong way, the sutures get stretched, like when I foolishly ran off yesterday." Wistfully, Tom continued, "But, being home, looking in the mirror, I cannot believe I did this to myself. I am so embarrassed and ashamed. What's wrong with me?"

"We're going to get through this, I know it, okay?" But, I couldn't hide the look of doubt in my face. Tom nodded, looked away and told me he was going to make some breakfast for me, leaving me in the room by myself. So, I finished getting ready, mad at myself for not being more reassuring. He needs that now.

I found two pancakes, strawberries, and vegan sweet cream sitting on a lonely white plate on the table. Tom must have taken Mango out.

***

"Anna Pearson," I answered when my work phone rang.

"Hi, love."

"Oh, hi, how are you? You left without saying goodbye. I'm sorry if I didn't seem more comforting. It's just hard," I said.

"I completely understand, I feel pretty okay now. Mango and I had a favorable walk. In fact, he's getting much better on the leash and a number of women approached me because of him. I should have gotten a dog long ago!"

"Haha. Well, I'm glad to see you haven't lost your obnoxiousness."

"It would take a lot for that to happen. Anyway, enough of that, em, I called the clinic. I have an ECG and EEG set. In fact, they were able to work me in Monday. And, I talked to Holly as well. She said she would set me up with a good therapist once we get the medical results back. Em, she also mentioned something about a friend of hers she wants us to meet; April Simms, her psychic friend? But, she hasn't reached her yet."

"Oh, great. I'm really happy you are taking some action on this. I think this all could have been avoided if you just had…"

"Anna," he sternly warned.

"Sorry, I'm trying, okay?"

"Okay, love. Well, I'll see you at home tonight. Em, I do have to be at work at 1900."

"You're going to work? Are you kidding me?"

"Em, yes, I'm going to work. Look, life goes on. I cannot and will not shirk my responsibilities or hide under the blankets. I've missed too much as it stands."

"What if you have another blackout and hurt yourself again?"

"If it will make you feel better, then join me."

"Okay, I will." I confirmed, petulantly.

"Suit yourself, love. I'll see you home." And he hung up.

***

The tour had rather a small group tonight. I stayed in the back, watching Tom to see if there was any kind of shift in his behavior. Nothing happened, and neither of us had any strange feelings. As I watched Tom, I began to scrutinize everything about him. I noticed the small flare in his nostrils when he got excited over a part of the story; the graceful wave of his hands when he gestured, and the deep cadence in his voice, slowing down to create dramatic tension. His hair often slipped down over his eyes regardless of the pint of gel he used to slick it back.

After the crowd dispersed, I followed Tom to his office, closed the door behind me, and locked it. Tom's back was turned to me, so he didn't notice. He started to gather his bag from the desk when I moved closer to him, tapping him on the shoulder. As he turned around, I pushed him gently against the desk.

"Yyess?" He drawled.

I started to unbuckle his belt. Puzzlement crossed his face, "What... are you doing?"

"What's it look like?" I stated the obvious as I unbuttoned and unzipped his pants.

"Here? There are people outside and, em..."

"Tom, shut it." And I moved in and kissed him. So many feelings were pulsing through me, brought on by the last few days. Excitement, fear, confusion, love. I got maybe too aggressive, bashing my teeth into his, but I didn't let up. I leaned more into him so he was further against the desk. I was about to lift up my skirt when there was a knock on the door and a turning of the lock.

"Mr. Tom? I have your paycheck here. May I come in?"

"Em, no, I'm getting changed, em, I'll be right out," he said in a high voice.

Tom grimaced at me, patted my rear and side stepped to the left.

"Later," he promised, buttoning back up his pants and buckling his belt.

After arriving at home, Tom quickly found Mango's leash and took him straight out into the cold night. I love having a dog, but taking him out in the cold and rain isn't all that fun. Tom, however, has never once complained about it.

Alone in the flat, I decided to make the place a little more romantic. I lit some candles, put on some Ray Lamontagne, and dimmed the lights.

While pouring some red wine, I heard the familiar jingling of Mango's collar. Tom walked into the kitchen, his coat already off, and grinned.

"What's gotten into you, Anna? No Cramps or PIL this evening?"

I leaned against the sink, facing him. "It's been a while, hasn't it? We've had a really emotional week and I need to bask in you, if I have to be blunt about it." I handed him a glass of wine. He took a small sip and set the glass down. After taking my glass from my hand, he started to unbutton my blouse while he kissed my mouth. He was slow, methodical.

Gently, he pulled away and rested his forehead against mine.

"I love you so much," he whispered.

I gave him one quick kiss, took his hand, and led him into the bedroom.

— *Monday, December 15*

I tapped my fingers on the desk, waiting for Tom to call. He wanted to go by himself, so I had to acquiesce. His appointment was at 9:00 AM and my watch read noon. But, eventually, I felt the familiar buzz in my pocket and fumbled around to pick up my phone.

"Tom. How did it go? I've been so nervous."

"Well, we got started late, but they ran a number of tests. Em, they took some blood tests to rule out drugs. But, I am not concerned with those results, obviously. They also performed an EEG to see if I have Epilepsy, believe it or not—because of the blackouts. The test was negative, of course."

"Well, that's good."

"Yes. And then they did an ECG to see if I had any kind of heart condition, which I don't. They had me run on a treadmill, really more of a light jog. They called it a 'stress test,' but it was the least stressful part of the whole ordeal, and it turns out my heart is in tip top shape."

"All this is good news, Tom, but I think you know where this is leading us."

"I've already phoned Holly, and she has set me up with her recommendation for a psychiatrist. And yes, I've already called him and he's making it a point to see me tomorrow, as a favor to Holly. She's also been trying to reach Ms. Simms, but that is still proving to be difficult."

"Should I take off and go with you?"

"It is an afternoon appointment, so you may want to ask Jamie… I'd like you there the first day, at least. Get your impressions and such."

"I'm sure it will be alright."

"And, I'd love to take Seamus and Jamie out to dinner for all their help. Could you please set that up for me?"

I agreed and hung up.

— *Tuesday, December 16, 3:00 PM*

My chair shook. Tom's incessant nervous habit of leg shaking was trying my patience. I darted him a look and placed my hand on his knee. He gave me a very small closed-mouth grin and stopped the shaking. Instead, he switched to biting his thumb nail.

"Mr. Hall? Dr. Jackson will see you now." The pretty receptionist led the way down the taupe colored hall to a plain oak door. We entered, finding a jovial looking man with short grey hair, round wire-rimmed glasses and dark skin, standing behind his ornate oak desk. Coming out from behind the desk, he immediately extended his hand to me and then Tom and gestured for us to take a seat in the upholstered light pink velvet guest chairs. The walls showcased the doctor's many degrees and certificates, along with a few pictures of his family, I assumed.

"Hello, hello. Welcome Mr. Hall and Ms. Pearson. I hear you two are engaged?" The doctor asked as he sat behind his desk. A manila folder sat opened.

Tom and I looked at each other and smiled, nodding our heads.

"Good, good. Well, Dr. Gaines speaks very highly of you, Mr. Hall. May I call you Tom?"

"Yes, of course."

"Good, good. Well, let's get started then. I've looked thoroughly over your files from your wounds at Hospital to the mental institution, as well as your visit yesterday. From the tests you have taken, there doesn't seem to be anything physically wrong. We certainly could delve deeper, but we were able to rule out a couple of big possibilities, ah, physically that is. Mentally, it gets a little trickier. Well, let's not waste any time. Tell me why you think you cut yourself?"

Tom leaned in a little, made his fingers into a pyramid and rested his chin on the tips. "Honestly, I don't remember ever cutting myself. I would often wake up from a slumber and find superficial marks on my arms, ever since I was a teen, but never anything too deep except for this last episode."

"And did you have a blackout... this last time?"

"I believe so. "

"Can you tell me about them?"

"Well, as best as I know, I just feel like I've woken up from a sleep. Sometimes I'll have vivid dreams... usually about hurting someone or myself, but they seem to be just dreams. The funny thing is, I've never found myself in odd places after a blackout. I always wake up at home, but sometimes my day clothes are still on, even though I thought I had changed into night clothes."

I interjected, "We thought he may have been sleepwalking, but the cutting and his odd behavior last week just didn't seem like something you could do while sleepwalking."

"The cutting, maybe, but Ms. Pearson, I read here you followed him and saw him in a compromising situation with another man?"

"Well, yes, and he smoked and wore glasses, but they looked like his reading glasses. His mannerisms were different as well."

This time, Tom interjected, "Yes, but we discussed this and think maybe Anna was witnessing someone else who looked like me. And besides, Anna, as I told you, I misplaced my reading glasses a while ago." Tom looked at me and I stared back at him, and shook my head. I had never come to that conclusion. I only thought it was a possibility—a small one.

"Mmmm… is that possible, Ms. Pearson? That it wasn't Tom?"

"Please call me Anna. Um, yeah, I guess. I lost him for a bit and then it was really crowded and dark in the pub. But I don't know, it sure looked like Tom. Um… is it possible he has Dissociative Disorder?"

"Well, Anna, reading his chart, a number of things certainly fit. The blackouts and lapses in memory, the cutting, the possible changes in behavior, are all consistent with dissociative symptoms. But, that is very hard to diagnose and would certainly take more than one therapy session. But, Anna, could you please step out of the room briefly? I'd like to talk to Tom alone, now."

Tom looked at me and said, "I'm quite comfortable with Anna being in here."

"I'm sure, but I'd really like to talk to you by myself, just for a bit."

"It's okay, Tom." I pushed myself out of my chair, patted Tom's shoulder and walked into the waiting room. The blond at the desk smiled as I took a seat and grabbed a magazine. After about a half hour, Tom came out of the office, made an appointment with the receptionist, and then held out his hand to me. I took it and stood up.

"Well?"

"He just asked me a lot of questions about my sexual preferences, whether I have had suicidal feelings ever and the like. He also asked me about my childhood and a few other things." A very slight twitch of his jaw made me think he wasn't telling me everything.

"And did you learn anything?"

"No, not yet, but I do like the man. He's easy to talk to. And I didn't disclose to him anything I haven't told you already... I think he believed me."

"Okay, when is your next appointment?"

"In two days' time." We held hands walking out the door. Tom gave a friendly wave to the receptionist.

***

— *Thursday, December 18*

I decided I would make dinner tonight as Tom was in a therapy session. When he arrived home, he told me it went well. I hoped that talking about his childhood with a therapist would finally allow Tom to deal with it. I still didn't know how much his father abused him and how much Tom did to himself, but regardless, at least we knew that both happened. And so, life went on. I hoped upon hope he didn't have DID. I wasn't sure how I would deal if he had it. I hadn't been so great dealing with things so far, I didn't think.

I finished dishing up and found him in the guest room clearing space in the closet.

"What are you doing?"

Tom looked over his shoulder, raised his eyebrow and smiled.

"What have you got up your sleeve?"

"I was going to let this be a surprise, but, well here." Tom took two strides to the desk and dug into the drawer, pulling out an itinerary: two round trip tickets to London from BWI, in my parent's name for this Sunday.

"You bought tickets for my parents?"

"Yup," he smiled, but upon seeing my reaction, his mouth turned downward a little. "You aren't happy."

"I mean, yeah, yes, it will be great to see them, but, Tom, you've got to stop spending so much money. Eventually, it's going to run out."

"Anna, please, I'm pretty savvy with money. I don't own a car, our flat is nice but not extraordinary, plus it's all paid for."

"And, you buy expensive clothes, you don't have a full-time job, you always treat when we go out to dinner with friends, this ring you bought must have cost a fortune, plane tickets, um..."

"Anna, stop. I think I've failed to tell you about my financial situation in detail. Not only was my trust over two million pounds, I've been fortunate with my investments. In fact, I loathe the day it will happen, but I am the sole benefactor of my grandfather's wealth. *We* are fine. If you wanted to leave your job, I could support both of us with no problem a'tall. But once again, I know you enjoy your job… and that's just extra spending money for you, okay?"

"Oh. I didn't realize you had that much. Nothing goes to your father?"

He laughed, "Ah… no. My grandfather has not spoken to, nor wishes to speak with my father. He basically disowned him once I was on my own and they didn't have to associate with one another. And, once again, *we* have a lot—now can you be a little excited about your parent's visit?"

I smiled and nodded, scratching my head.

"Anything else the matter?" he asked, tilting his head to the left.

"I guess I'm a little concerned about getting around explaining your therapy or worse, my mom wanting to meet your father."

"First, they will not meet my father, and second, if it comes up, I will tell them I am in therapy and *when* your mother asks why, I'll tell her I had a difficult childhood and I'm getting help dealing with it. Will that work?"

"I suppose, but she's going to bombard you with questions."

"I know. I'm preparing myself."

"Well, dinner is ready. I made that lentil loaf you like."

We sat at the table, talking about the wedding and thinking we should set a date soon, depending on how his therapy sessions were going. And, I still really wanted to talk to April Simms.

The buzzer rang while we were finishing up.

"Ohhh, that must be your boyfriend," I teased.

"Very funny, Anna," Tom said as he went to the intercom.

"Hello?"

"S'me."

"Alright."

And Tom buzzed Seamus up.

After about a minute, Tom opened the door to let him in. He must have taken the steps.

" 'allo, Anna," Seamus greeted as he patted my shoulder, a little too hard. He really doesn't know his own strength.

"Tom."

Tom nodded.

"What, no hug and kiss for Tom?"

"Shut it, Anna, what is it with you and Jamie?" asked Seamus. "What's so wrong with two blokes enjoying their time together away from you nagging lasses?" Seamus said, clearly agitated.

"Jamie still gives you grief?" asked Tom.

"All the fucking time. 'is that your boyfriend on the phone?' 'where is your boyfriend taking you tonight?' 'are you sleeping at your boyfriend's flat tonight?' She's relentless!" Seamus exclaimed. A smile escaped from me despite my ill attempts at remaining neutral.

"Just ignore it. Are you ready, Seamus?" Tom asked, shooting me an 'I'm disappointed in you' kind of look.

"Yeah, where are you taking me?"

"Ah, well, I found this lovely pub by the Thames," Tom explained.

This time I did laugh out loud.

Tom just sighed while he donned his pea coat, "Goodbye, Anna," and he kissed me quickly.

"Have fun on your date!" I yelled as they walked out the door.

"Fuck off," I faintly heard Tom say from the steps.

I decided to watch something on television until Tom got home. There were a lot of reruns on, so I watched the first *Sherlock* episode for the millionth time. During the show, I tried to figure out Christmas presents. I thought I would get Tom some clothes and actually make him that mixture CD. I wanted to get him something special, too, but I was at a loss. He is so particular with the things he likes, plus he's got everything he wants. I invited Mango to come up on the sofa with me, who gladly accepted, and I started writing out a couple ideas, scratching most of them out. Then, I thought of something great…
until I couldn't keep my eyes open.

A worn looking lady in the basement of my high school building, wearing all black, unveils her hood, revealing brilliant eyes with heavy eyeliner all around, "you must help him, Anna." Another entity in the room, a bad presence. It envelopes the lady, squeezing, squeezing… "Anna, Anna…"

"Anna, Anna, wake up… you're talking in your sleep." I felt Tom stroking my arm.

"Oh, Tom… geez. I just had a weird dream. What time is it?" I yawned.

"Half past one. *Sherlock* marathon again?"

"Yeah."

"Why is Mango on the sofa?"

"Because I invited him," I stated, completely ignoring his fatherly tone. "You guys were out late. What'd you do?" I said, sitting up rubbing my eyes and yawning some more. I reached over to scratch Mango's head, who was fast asleep, oblivious to Tom's irritation.

"I can't win with you, can I?" He said, flopping on the chair across from me.

"Nope. So where did you go?"

"We got a couple of pints from a pub on the Thames and chatted."

"What do you guys talk about?"

"I don't know, life, philosophy, sometimes paranormal subjects. I clarified some things from my past… I figured I owed him that much."

"Mmmm, Seamus philosophizes?"

"Actually, yes. He's a much smarter man than either you or Jamie give him credit for. He's developed some pretty profound ideas. Also, he was pretty affected by finding me in the state I was in, so we talked that out a bit." Tom stretched and said, "Well, I'm off to bed. Come along then," he got up and nudged Mango off the sofa. Mango did a downward dog stretch, then put his two front paws on the ground while leaving his two back legs on the sofa. He walked forward allowing his back legs to stretch out in full, behind him, and then dropped them to the floor, one at a time.

Tom stared, bewildered by this behavior.

"That was soooo cute!" I screeched, "did you see that?"

"Yes. He's an odd dog, isn't he," Tom said as he turned off Sherlock jumping from St. Bart's.

In the bedroom, Tom got in his night clothes as I set the alarm, Mango jumping on the bed.

Tom, resigned, shook his head and went to the lounge chair by the window to do some meditation exercises his therapist suggested.

"Good night, sweetheart," I said, leaning into him with my hands on each arm of the chair. I gave him a long kiss, and pulled away slowly.

"Sorry about Mango," I said as I turned to the bed.

"No, you're not," he said, in a dreamlike voice.

***

— *Sunday evening, December 21*

"Anna! Tom!" yelled my mom as she waved to us from the curb at Heathrow. I could actually hear her through the car window. Tom pulled the sporty, red Audi he rented up to the curb and popped the trunk. I jumped out and hugged and kissed my parents hello.

Tom loaded all the luggage in the trunk, greeted my parents with a hug, and then sat in the driver's seat.

"Oh, what a nice car you have," my mom said.

"It's a rental," I stated.

"You didn't rent this just to pick us up, did you?" my father asked, concerned.

"Partially. We'll mainly take cabs in town because parking is quite a challenge, however, I thought we might do some sightseeing out of London," Tom explained.

"Well, let me give you some money toward the rental," my dad offered.

"That won't be necessary, but thank you," Tom said as he pulled into traffic.

My father started to protest some more, stating that Tom bought them first class tickets which must have cost a fortune. I hadn't realized they were first class, but I was not surprised. I leaned forward from the back seat and interjected, "It's not worth it, Dad. He won't let you pay for anything, so give it up."

"Let me see your ring in person, Anna," Mom said, both of us in the back. I held out my hand to her and she investigated.

She let out a big breath, "Wow... wow... wow! How much did this cost? How can you afford such a ring on a tour guide salary?"

"MOM! We're in the car not twenty seconds and you are already starting."

"It's alright, Anna. Jenny, I believe Anna mentioned before I have a rather hefty trust fund. Please don't worry about my financial situation. I've got it under control. Besides, your daughter is worth it."

"Hokay," my mom said shaking her head slowly. This was going to be a long visit.

"Are you two hungry? Tired?" Tom politely asked.

"I'd say both," my dad answered.

"Let's get you situated at the flat so you may eat and relax." Tom suggested.

***

Tom dropped us and the suitcases at the curb in front of our flat and drove off to look for a parking space. Mom, Dad, and I went up the elevator and into the flat, finding Mango in his usual spot, sitting, but wagging his tail in the foyer.

"Aw, what a cutie," my mom said as she pet Mango's head.

We made another trip and brought the suitcases in as Tom followed. Mango went crazy! He's been doing this recently when Tom comes in. He tears around the flat three times and then sits at Tom's feet. I think he's so excited he needs to get his energy out so he doesn't jump on Tom as he knows the verbal lashing he'll get if he does.

"Hi, boy!" Tom said as he stooped down to rub Mango's face and head. Mango, very slowly, stuck out his tongue and curled it around Tom's cheek.

"He sure likes him," Dad said, pointing his chin in Tom's direction.

"Oh, yeah. Tom is his favorite, even though I let him do things Tom doesn't."

After situating my parents in the guest bedroom, I gave them a tour of the flat, my mom oohing and ahhing over the furnishings and interior elements. She noted the cute paisley bear on the bed, but I felt funny with him there, so I took him into our room.

After fixing them a dinner of pasta with pesto and a salad, they announced they wanted to sleep and try to adjust to London time.

***

— *Monday morning*

I walked into the kitchen bleary eyed, and was met by a bright-eyed Tom, happily making his special, now vegan, crepes, listening to some classical station on the radio.

"Good morning, my love," Tom said. "Did you sleep well?"

"Yeah, until you woke me by getting up so early."

"Sorry, love, but I wanted to get breakfast on. Your parents are already up and they've taken Mango for a walk."

"Oh, okay. Where are you going to take them today? Sorry I couldn't get off, but I really need to finish this chapter."

"I've got it all covered. We'll stroll along the Thames and then perhaps go to Trafalgar Square and the British Museum, whatever they like. Jamie and Seamus will meet us for dinner around 1830. Okay, love, here are your crepes so you can get to work on time."

"Thanks. 1830… that's 5:30, right?" I asked as Tom gave me a snarky look and shook his head.

I sat down at the table as he placed the savory dish in front of me.

"6:30. Can you not do mathematics in your head?"

"Look, I've had a lifetime of AM and PM, not military time. And besides, you seem to be the only Londoner who uses it, besides the trains and the news, sometimes. I may never get used to it, so you'll just have to deal."

"It's really not that hard to figure out."

I stuffed a huge bite into my mouth and ignored him. A few minutes later, my parents joined us after bringing Mango in.

"Good morning, Anna," my dad said as he kissed my head.

"Please, sit," Tom suggested.

My parents took off their coats and sat with me at the table.

"Oh, I wish you didn't have to work today," my mom said.

"I know, but I'll be off the rest of the week. I just have to finish this one chapter for my deadline. I should be able to get through it quickly since there won't be many people in the office to distract me. Tom's going to take you around today, so you'll have fun and stay really busy," I said in between bites.

I wolfed down the rest of my food, got ready for work, and left my parents in Tom's hands.

***

— *4:00, off from work early. Yay!*

I arrived home around 4:30. They weren't back quite yet, so I took Mango out for his walk and then fed him.

About twenty minutes later, everyone paraded in. My mom had a few bags of items and seemed to be quite the happy camper. My dad followed my mom with one bag and then Tom with about five. Mango did his laps. But then, I saw Tom's face. He looked tired and haggard, as if he had stayed up all night. His eyes were a quarter closed, shoulders hunched, and his mouth was set in a thin line. The vertical crease formed between his eyebrows, right above the bridge of his nose.

"Geez, you guys certainly bought a lot of stuff!" I remarked, darting my eyes over to Tom.

"Mainly souvenirs. How was your day, honey? We had a *wonderful* day! Tom was so *gracious*, taking us all around town!" She had a little sarcastic edge to her sentence. Her passive aggressiveness, I knew so well, oozed out of her pores.

"Thank you, Jenny," Tom answered softly while— smiling? No, more of a grimace. "Em, if you don't mind, I'm going to lie down for a few minutes before we head on to dinner." Tom dropped the bags in the foyer and made a bee line for the bedroom. His outstretched arm banged the door open. Uh oh. After a quick minute, I told my parents I would be right back and casually walked into our room. I closed the door behind me; Tom lay supine on the bed, palming both of his eyes and whispering over and over again, "shoot me now, shoot me now."

"What's wrong?" I asked, curious and a little amused.

"I have a huge migraine… And I've named it Jenny."

"Ah, Jenny strikes again." I climbed on top of him, straddling his stomach and moved his hands away from his eyes, pinning them on the pillow. I kissed his forehead, then his mouth. "Bad day?" I asked, staring into his drooping eyes.

I let go of his hands and like a magnet, they immediately stuck to his temples. "My God, Anna. She was… exhausting. The questions, the wanting to go into every bloody shop. I had it all planned that we would go to the Museum, the Thames, the attractions most tourists want to see, but she wasn't interested. I don't know how your father lives with her. Oh God, please kill me now. I even had to miss my appointment with Dr. Jackson."

"I told you, Tom."

"I know, I know! Don't get me wrong, I think she is a nice woman, but… my God. I tried to keep my temperament in check today and I succeeded for the most part, barring one time; I think she's angry with me."

"Why, what made you crack?" I asked, trying to suppress a smile.

He sat up on his elbows, causing me to fall back slightly. He chewed on his lower lip, looking much like a schoolboy who did something really bad and was about to fess up. "It was getting late and I really, really wanted to come home. I was so knackered from all the souvenir shopping we did today and all the questions I answered. We went into souvenir shop after souvenir shop after souvenir shop. At about the fifteenth one I said something like, 'Again? They are the same fucking store.' I said it kind of under my breath, but clearly she heard me."

"You didn't!" I laughed.

"I'm afraid I did. I apologized profusely as soon as I said it, but I think she is still angry with me. And it's not funny."

"What did my father say?" I asked, trying not to laugh again.

Tom sighed and said, "Nothing at first, but when your mum went into the store in a huff he turned to me and said, 'I'm glad someone had the nerve to say it.' But, I was mortified. I cannot believe I said that. The rest of the time was exceedingly uncomfortable, as I am sure you can imagine."

"Well, bud, you've dug this hole, good luck getting out of it. Remember, she is the master of grudge holding. You'll think everything is okay, then out of nowhere, she strikes like a big, nagging cobra." I started unbuttoning his shirt.

"Not now, Anna," he said, without too much behind it.

"Do you really have a migraine?" I asked, untucking his shirt from his pants and pushing it off his shoulders. His stitches had already dissolved, but the marks were very noticeable.

"No, not quite, just a headache," he said in a sleepy voice. "I think I can sleep it off."

"Alright, I'll leave you alone," I kissed his forehead once more and let him rest.

I pushed myself up and over his stomach and proceeded to the living room, finding my mother going through their souvenirs as Dad feigned interest.

"Everything alright?" My mom asked, still with a slight edge.

"Tom has a bad headache, so hopefully he'll sleep a little. I'll wake him up in a half hour. I'm sure he'll want to shower before dinner."

"Your boyfriend was very rude to me today."

"Oh, cut it out, Jenny. You were the rude one. He had a whole day planned for us to see London, not souvenir shops. He said exactly what I was thinking. Did you even consider I might want to see some of the sites?" My dad complained, "He even had an appointment he had to miss."

"Well, he wouldn't even tell us what the appointment was for and besides, why did he schedule an appointment while we were here anyway! Couldn't he do his hair another time?"

"It wasn't a hair appointment, Mom!"

"Well, what was so important, then? He was very insulting to me, Anna. Reminded me a little of boyfriends past."

I sat down, knowing this would come up, "He's in therapy, okay?"

"Therapy? For what?" She asked with venom.

"He had some, um, problems with his father growing up, but, it's private. But, please, for God's sake, don't ask him any questions about it."

"Anna, you're marrying someone who has mental issues? This is Graham all over again. Or maybe Eric? Or Theo?" She spat.

"Jenny! Just because the boy is in therapy doesn't mean he's crazy or a bad person. He seems pretty well adjusted to me and I am quite fond of him. He is in no way Graham!" my dad championed.

"Thanks, Dad. Mom, look, he told you he was sorry, so instead of harping on the one ungentlemanly thing he did, look at the hundred nice things he did for you. Buying you first class tickets, renting a car to take you around, feeding you, housing you, taking ti…"

"Alright, Anna, I don't need a lecture."

"And you really need to bring up Graham? First, that was high school and second, he was an abusive asshole who got his jollies from pissing off everyone around him. He was a cruel person and I moved on. Why do you have to bring something up that happened 12 years ago?"

My mother ignored me and announced, "I am going to get ready for dinner, okay?" And she practically stomped down the hall into the guest bedroom.

"Sorry, Anna. You know how she is. And *I* think Tom is great. You've got a winner there."

"Yeah, thanks." I sighed a long sigh and walked back to the bedroom to shower and change. Tom was shirtless and fast asleep on the bed.

"Marrying someone with mental issues." Those words ricocheted in my head. If only she knew the half of it—and she won't.

***

— *Dinner with Jamie and Seamus in Soho*

Tom was a little reserved at dinner. When I woke him up earlier, he said his head was still throbbing, so I brought him two Advil, but it apparently didn't do the trick. He was constantly rubbing his forehead and eyes.

"Is everything okay, Tom?" my mom asked with a little bit too much cheer.

"Em, just a bad headache I can't seem to shake. I'll be alright, thank you," he calmly said, taking the high road.

The conversation broke out into my mom talking to Jamie and my dad conversing with Seamus. Seamus kept glancing at Tom, obviously concerned about his best friend. I think he thought what I thought, that something else was going on.

"If you all would excuse me, I've got to go to the loo, Tom, you need to, too?" Seamus offered.

"Em, yes, that might be good."

Jamie and I looked at each other and smirked.

"Couple of girls," Jamie said under her breath. I caught what she said and so did Seamus, evidently, because I saw him discreetly give the American peace sign backwards in Jamie's direction; my parents oblivious to this all.

Tom got up, still rubbing his head.

"He doesn't look too good," my dad observed as Tom slowly followed Seamus. A minute later, my cell phone buzzed while my mom was recounting her shopping excursion with Jamie. "Sorry," I said, glancing at the text. Seamus was summoning me to the bathroom.

"I'll be right back," I said.

I maneuvered my way through the crowd around the bar to the back of the restaurant. Tom was leaning up against the exposed brick wall next to the bathroom, Seamus with his hand on Tom's shoulder.

"Hey, what's up? Getting worse?" I asked.

Tom nodded his head slightly, "I had a dream right before dinner and this headache is pounding."

"What was the dream about?" I asked.

Seamus told me instead, "He said he saw his mum being raped and killed, but couldn't see the face of the man who did it."

"And I was in a tiny cell or a box and… I couldn't help, couldn't get out or move. It was reminiscent of that blasted Halloween attraction. When I awoke, I thought my head was going to explode. I did some deep breathing, which only marginally helped, but it's gotten worse. And your mother's attitude doesn't help much." Tom complained.

"Yeah, she's… ah… an interesting sort," Seamus said.

"Do you want me to take you home?" I suggested.

"No… that would just make matters worse. I'm going to put some cold water on my face again and then come back. Perhaps eating something might help."

As Tom went back into the bathroom, I said to Seamus, "You know, despite Jamie and me teasing you and Tom, we really do love how you two are together."

"Come on, Anna," hands in his pocket, looking away from me.

"No… I'm being absolutely serious. Tom didn't have many friends growing up, so, believe me, I am grateful that you are a big part of his life." I kissed Seamus on the cheek as Tom came out of the bathroom and Seamus blushed.

Tom raised an eyebrow, "Should I be concerned?"

I smiled and raised my eyebrow back at him. Seamus looked at the ground in embarrassment.

As we approached the table, Jamie looked up at me with a pleading look on her face. My mom seemed to still be talking about souvenir shops."

Taking our seat, my mom started. "It takes two people to help Tom go to the bathroom?"

"I've had it, Jenny!" my dad abruptly bellowed as he pounded his fist on the table, making the water in the glasses swish. The next table looked over.

"It's alright, Richard," Tom said.

"No, it's not. All I've heard is your soon-to-be mother-in-law harping on you and I'm tired of it," my dad exclaimed.

My mom sat in stunned silence at his outburst.

"The boy has apologized to you enough and for something that he was justified with anyway. Now cut it out or we are going to have some real problems going forward."

My eyes widened a bit. I'd never heard my father speak to my mother this way. It was a bit unsettling, but also gratifying as well. I loved my mom, but she was hard to like, sometimes. Seamus and Jamie sat in quiet embarrassment while Tom chewed his thumbnail.

"You know, Richard, I don't know why you are pegging me as the bad guy here," my mom started to state in a lower voice, turning her head toward me. "Tom was incredibly disrespectful to me today. You don't know him, Anna. You haven't had enough time. I don't want you making a mistake. I have a right to be concerned," she said, tapping her index finger on the table with every point she was stressing. "Now I find out he's in therapy, and then I see a million scars all over his body. Am I really supposed to champion this marriage?"

My whole body tensed. "Were you spying, Mom? How did you see his scars?" I was horrified. This was such an invasion of privacy. I worried about something like this happening, but didn't think it would be this bad. Tom leaned his head back and stared at the ceiling while Jamie and Seamus shifted uncomfortably.

"Your door was ajar. I went to ask you something, but you were in the shower and Tom was sleeping. That's when I saw them."

Tom breathed out, trying to keep his composure. He tilted his head back down and addressed my mom. "Jenny, this really isn't the place to have a conversation like this."

"Don't you condescend me," she responded sternly, pointing a finger in Tom's direction. I felt the whole restaurant close in on us, as eyes skittered past us and soft murmurs could be heard. We were giving credence to the American stereotype.

"Fine. Would you like to know about the scars?" Tom asked in a quiet, but somewhat menacing voice; his agitation coming to a hilt. He winced a little, I assume from his headache.

"Tom," I soothed, placing my hand on his shoulder, "you don't need to do this. Especially not now." I looked over at Jamie, whose eyes were as big as Frisbees. Seamus was making fists with his hands.

"It's fine, Anna." He turned toward my mother, sat more upright and stared intently, his eyes burning a hole into her.

He began in a low voice, "My father used to hit me. Virtually every day of my childhood, he would beat me with a belt, a riding crop, his hands, his fists. He broke my nose by slamming me face first into the floor, he cracked my ribs with his feet, burned my skin over and over again with his cigarettes. The abuse was endless." He leaned in further, speaking a little quieter, but more sinisterly, "And the fresher cuts… I did to myself, so, yes, Jenny, I am in therapy. Something I should have done long ago. And, yes, I obviously have some issues to work out from all this coming to fruition. Are you satisfied now or are you going to ask me more inane questions or condemn and judge me further than you already have?" Tom's eyes were aflame as he sat back.

"Tom, that's enough, hon," I warned, touching his hand.

He held up his hand and shook his head, "I'm sorry. I've really lost my appetite, so please forgive my rudeness," and he got up, pulled out his wallet, yanked out about 200 pounds, threw the notes on the table and left restaurant.

The whole table was silent. I broke it, "Great, Mom, just great."

"I'm sorry, Anna, I didn't know. I didn't mean to cause such a reaction, but I worry about you—especially with your track record. And this proves my point, doesn't it? Maybe when you are a mother you'll understand."

I just shook my head, "Look, you cannot imagine how much stress he's been under recently. Although I think it's incredibly good for him, a lot of painful memories are being dredged up, so please, cut him some slack. And really, it's none of your business."

My father just sat there. I think he was trying to figure out what to say, but was at a loss for words.

"Anna, you want me to go check on him?" offered Seamus.

"No, please let's finish our meals. You all can get dessert and I'll run home, okay?"

We finished our meal with some pretty surface conversation. My father insisted on paying, pushing all the money toward me. I gave in, knowing Tom never would. Seamus said he would take my parents to get some coffee to give me a little time at home.

I said my goodbyes to everyone, trying not to make any eye contact with my mother, and took a cab back.

When I got there, there were flowers on the dining room table with a note for my mom… just saying "I'm sorry. Tom."

I went into the bedroom where Tom was sitting in the lounge chair by the window, looking out at the night, Mango at his feet.

"Hi."

"Hi," he said. A sad smile crossed his lips. "I blew it, didn't I?"

"Well, maybe, but the flowers should help. And besides, this is on her, not you."

"I've really got a short fuse these days. I'm really not liking myself."

"Hey, I like you," I said, walking over to him. I sat on his lap and put my arms around his neck. He continued to look out the window, but gently stroked his hand up and down my back.

***

My parents came home about an hour later. Tom's headache abated a little, probably from taking a prescription pain medication. He was at his computer doing some research for his tours while I was in our bedroom with the door open. I heard my mother tap lightly on the guest room door.

"Uh, hi, Tom. Am I interrupting you?" I heard my mom say.

"No, not at all. I'm just finishing up here."

"Thank you for the flowers, but you really didn't have to do that. I should not have been so nosey, and I shouldn't have jumped to so many conclusions." I don't think I've really ever heard my mother apologize. I have a feeling my father had something to do with it.

"That's alright. I sometimes have a temper. I'm trying to quell it, but have my moments. I am truly sorry for the way I behaved today."

"Okay, well, let's just forget about it all. Despite what I said earlier, I think you are pretty great and I'm very happy Anna found you. And your pal Seamus, boy, he gave me an earful! He really thinks the world of you."

I heard the scooting back of a chair. I walked out the door and peaked in, seeing Tom embracing my mom.

— *Christmas Eve*

"Mom and Dad are going to mass, um, not really my thing. I assume you don't want to go?"

"Em, no, not particularly." Tom answered, putting the Tofurky into the oven. He then sat down, grabbed a spare pair of wire-rimmed reading glasses, and started perusing the newspaper.

I glanced over, seeing the back of the paper, headlined as "Two more prostitutes found dead. Jack the Ripper Reincarnated?"

"Creepy." I mumbled. "Hey, are you going to see your father?"

Tom sighed, as he always does at the mention of Thomas, "Yes, I suppose I'll visit him tomorrow. Perhaps we should all have a lovely Christmas party with your parents and Thomas," the sarcasm dripping out of his mouth.

"Well, we're off," my mother said, all dressed up. "Are you sure you won't join us?"

"Quite sure, thank you. Do you need help finding the church?" Tom asked, lowering the paper.

"No, we know where we are going. I'm not sure the point of Christmas if you don't celebrate it," my mom said. We go through this every year.

I rolled my eyes. "Mom, you know the answer to that. Religion just isn't our thing. Christmas is just an excuse to give and get presents."

Mom just pursed her lips and shook her head as she and my dad walked out the door.

As soon as I heard the click, I pounced on Tom, ripping his newspaper. I grabbed a hold of his face and began kissing his lips.

"Aren't we the bold one." Tom breathed.

"Quiet, I figure we only have about an hour."

***

Exhausted, I put my shirt back on and flipped on the TV. Tom had gone into the bathroom. Just in time, because I heard the key in the door, Mango sitting patiently, wagging his tail.

"How was mass?"

"It was nice, the usual. The church was beautiful, though," my mother said as she took off her coat.

"...been a while since the Vigilante has attacked. It seems that the Jack the Ripper reincarnate has taken over the news and social media. Perhaps there should be a battle of the baddies...."

I rolled my eyes and flipped to another channel.

"What was that all about?" my mom asked as she sat down. My father touched the top of my head and went to the guest room to lie down for a bit.

"Oh, the tabloid type news here is worse than it is at home, at least some of the stations. Anyway, there has been a rash of violence against prostitutes and gay people, so they're thinking Jack the Ripper has resurfaced. And then, there's this, um, other. A vigilante who seems to attack people who have harmed others."

"Really? We had one of those stories in Annapolis."

I gave my mom a sideways glance, "Oh, really?"

"Yes, in fact we heard about it right before we left for London. Some poor man got assaulted with a baseball bat, right around the corner from us. Well, I shouldn't say 'poor' man."

"Why's that?" I asked with a tremble in my voice.

"Well, the man had been tried for beating his son with a baseball bat after the son had struck out at a Little League game. Apparently, the man got off on some technicality and did not serve time; however, his wife and child moved out of state to an undisclosed area."

"Oh, that's pretty... pretty scary," I was a little taken aback, but the timing was way off.

"Yes, it is. Sometimes I wonder about our court system. How a man like that can still be walking the streets."

I nodded slightly, then jumped when I felt a hand on my shoulder.

"Dinner's ready, love."

— *Christmas Day*

"Well, that's lovely," my mother spoke as she held up the cream-colored sweater Tom and I splurged on for her.

We bought my father a number of first edition books, ones that are harder to find in the States, and we all received a bunch of small items.

Tom opened his gift from me and laughed. "Finally! My mixture tape, em, CD. Let's see, Franz Ferdinand, Ministry, The Sex Pistols, Bauhaus, The Damned, of course. All my favorites," he chided. But, he kissed me and said he loved it. I also bought him a couple of new colorful, but not too bright, button down shirts and some new faux leather gloves. And, of course, some expensive aftershave from Truefitt and Hill. I then brought out my main gift, wrapped in a blanket.

"And what's this?" he asked as he "unwrapped" the covering. "Oh! A guitar! How creative of you!"

"Yeah, I got you some lessons, too, but you'll have to schedule them. I figured with your singing voice, you could also play—for me." I smiled and raised my eyebrows.

"Ah, your rock star fantasy. I don't see any punk rock outfit among your gifts for me."

"Well, not punk, at least." And I pulled out one last gift. Tom took the small present and carefully unwrapped the snowman adorned paper.

"A Triumvirat graphic T-shirt? Where ever did you find this?" he exclaimed, holding it up.

"I have my sources," I smiled, "I wasn't sure if you'd wear it, though."

"Don't you worry, I can make it look stylish with a fitted blazer and grey jeans. And, of course, Chuck Taylors."

My parents just sat quietly, observing, but oblivious to our little private jokes.

Mango received a few gourmet treats and a new green collar with mangoes embroidered all around. After we put it on, he pranced around as if he knew he was well dressed.

Tom bought me a gift certificate to the shoe store I bought my awful shoes from, reminiscent of our first date. He had a shit eating grin on when he handed it to me. He also bought me a number of new T-shirts: Screaming Trees, The Damned, and he even found a The The shirt. My mom rolled her eyes when she saw this. And then, Tom handed me one small gift. I unwrapped it and opened it. In it was the most exquisite piece of jewelry I have ever seen. It was a pendant necklace that matched my sapphire and diamond ring, only it was from *Nightmare Before Christmas*. It was pretty much a broach with the scene at the end where Sally and Jack stood on the black wave. The wave was made out of perhaps onyx, the background out of sapphires, and the moon from amber. It sounds gaudy, but it wasn't. It was tastefully done and not too big.

"Do you like it?" Tom implored, smiling.

"I..I love it. Thank you!"

"That's an interesting piece of jewelry. I mean, it's beautiful, but isn't Anna a little old for cartoons?" My mom asked.

"It's not a cartoon," I answered, wistfully as Tom helped me put it on. More than ever, I knew Tom was the one. The way he completely accepted me, and even enhanced the essence of who I am. I felt so lucky, despite his sordid past. I am trying to learn not to jump to so many conclusions. There were so many things I was wrong about or just not 100 percent sure and I let my imagination get to me. Even more so, I knew I had to accept this wonderful person, scars and all, and help him through his trials.

***

After presents and breakfast, Tom and I told my parents we were going over to see his father. They really wanted to come, but Tom sternly told them, "In no way will you be coming with us to meet my father." And from the tone of his voice, my parents backed down. Perhaps my mother learned her lesson from the other night. And so, Tom and I headed off, a couple of presents in hand.

We took the rental car to Thomas's; the journey taking less time than usual since there was little traffic. We ascended the steps to the tattered house. Tom used his key and upon entering, I noticed the place was clean and smelled fresh. That was odd.

"In here!" Tom's father yelled from the kitchen. He wasn't attached to his oxygen tank and he was pulling something out of the oven when we entered.

"Ah, my boy! Anna! So, nice to see you. It's been a while." He placed the sheet of cookies on a trivet, came over to us, and to our surprise, gave us big hugs. Tom looked confused.

"You're off your tank, Dad?"

"Yes… it seems more and more I am able to get along without it. I've been trying to take care of myself a bit more. Can't you see I've lost some weight?"

"Yeah, uh, you do look a little slimmer," I lied.

"Well, would you two like any cookies? They are vegan! And I have some gifts."

"Okay, Dad, what's up?"

"What do you mean, 'what's up'?"

"Well, to be frank, you're not acting like your usual brutish self."

"Oh yeah? Well, maybe I'm turning over a new leaf. I feel healthier than I have in a while, my son and his lovely fiancée are here, and it's Christmas day."

Tom shrugged his shoulders and shook his head while I took a cookie. They were actually quite good. Tom declined and then excused himself and went to the bathroom.

"Is this for real?" I asked.

"Look missy, I'm trying. I'm trying to get along with my son, okay? After you told him the things I told you, he hasn't been coming by as much, and I'm concerned he's going to hurt himself again. And, I want him to come over sometimes. I miss him." I squinted my eyes at him, not sure what to believe.

When Tom came out of the bathroom we sat around the kitchen table and had some Earl Grey that Thomas had prepared. All in all, the visit was actually, well, nice. Tom promised to come back soon and off we went.

CHAPTER 21

— *January 3*

The man finished up his work and started to walk home. He turned up the collar of his black pea coat, blocking the whistling wind in the chilly January night. He turned down an alley to further shield himself from the cold, pulled his right faux leather glove off with his teeth and reached for his phone. He texted his fiancée he was on the way home, glove dangling out of his mouth. He wasn't paying attention to his surroundings, only the lighted screen and the small letters he tapped were his focus. He didn't see or hear it until it was too late. An unsettling and ugly crack reached his ears right before the pain to the side of his knee set in. He buckled to the ground, the glove and phone falling to the cold pavement. He let out a small yell as he caught himself, preventing a face plant. Down on all fours, he looked over his shoulder and saw a masked figure looming above him. He couldn't see any features of the hulking form, but caught the gleam of a bat which squarely landed hard into his ribs... the ribs that had only been healed about a month. He cried out, falling to his side and instinctively curled up into a ball. He threw his arms over his head for protection. The assailant came around to the man's back and grabbed a fistful of hair, yanking his head back. The victim couldn't see his attacker, but heard a whispered, soft blow into his ear. "Take your punishment like a man... there will be more where that came from." Violently, the attacker pushed the man's head forward into the pavement, causing a nasty contusion above the victim's eyebrow. The attacker then let go, stood up, and stomped on the fallen body's already bruised knee. And then the attacker ran off, his laugh fading in the wind.

The phone rang and I jumped to get it. Tom should have been home a half hour ago, so I was starting to worry.

"Hello?"

"Hi, Anna, I'm at the police station. Could you please come?"

"What do you mean you're at the police station? What happened?" I squeaked.

"I'm alright, *I'm* not in trouble. I was attacked right after I texted you and after I got my wits about me, I used a passerby's cell phone to call the police who picked me up and took me to the station for a statement." Tom breathed out, sounding a little labored.

"Attacked? Oh my God, Tom, are you okay? Do you need to go to the hospital?"

"No, Anna. Please, just come get me. I'll just need your help getting in and out of the cab," Tom rebuked.

"But, if you're hurt…"

"I knew I should have called Seamus," Tom said quietly, then louder, "Anna, please?!"

"Alright, Tom, tell me where you are and I'll come right away." I sniffed. He gave me the address and I ran out the door. I called Seamus on the way, figuring I may need his help. He agreed, in fact he was close to Clerkenwell anyway.

When I arrived at the station, I asked at the front desk for Tom. The nice woman officer escorted me to another desk where Tom sat with one leg stretched completely straight and the other bent, bouncing up and down. If impatience were an emotion, it was clearly displayed in his facial expression. I noticed a pretty significant cut on his forehead. Taking a deep breath, I braced myself, walking over to him.

"Hi, sweetheart, are you okay?"

Tom glanced up at me and frowned, "It took you long enough."

I ignored his remark and said, "Let me look at you…"

"No, not here, just please get me home." Just then Seamus walked in, saw us, and scampered over.

"Hey, mate, what happened?"

Tom softened a bit when he saw his pal, but just a bit.

"Some mother*fucker* decided it would be fun to jump me after I texted Anna. He took a bat to my knee and ribs and before slamming my head into the ground and fucking up my knee, *again*, he said something like 'take your punishment like a man.'" Tom crossed his arms, his good leg still bouncing.

"What did the police say?" I asked.

"They had nothing to say. They took my statement and that was it. Nothing was taken from me, although my phone broke when I dropped it from the first strike to my leg. So, there you have it. Now, may we please go."

"Alright, mate, can you stand?"

"Em, I can't bend my leg."

Seamus and I looked at each other. "Tom, we need to get you to the hospital."

"Goddammit, Anna, no. I am not going back there. If I'm not better in the morning, I'll see a doctor… at an office. I am not waiting in an emergency room."

"Easy, mate, I know you're upset, but don't take it out on your girl."

"I know, I'm sorry. I just want to go home. I am so tired of being injured." He blinked away tears.

Seamus straddled Tom's legs, put his hands under his armpits and lifted. The sound of thunder echoed around the police station. All heads turned towards Tom's direction.

"Alright, he's alright," Seamus assured the puzzled faces.

Gasping, Tom placed his arm around Seamus's waist and leaned into him. I came around to Tom's other side and we hobbled out the door. I had told my cab driver to wait, so we were able to step right in. Well, I stepped in, Tom sort of oozed onto the seat; Seamus getting into the front.

We somehow made it up the steps and into the elevator. Some building occupants, the same ones who gave Tom condescending glances from the first time he was hurt, rode up the elevator with us. I could tell by their stiffness and slight shake of their heads, they were judging once again. I wanted to smack them. "I hate those people!" I exclaimed, loud enough so they could hear as they left the elevator.

When we stepped into the flat, Mango jumped on Tom, who in turn yelled, which in turn sent Mango cowering behind the sofa. This was going to be a long night.

We guided Tom to the sofa after removing his coat and then he melted into the cushions, stretching out his long legs.

"Ah, much better. Mango, come here boy." Tom patted the sofa. Mango slinked over, his ears back. Tom pet his head, reassuring him with kind words in a soft voice. Mango, ever resilient, wagged his tail.

"Seamus, could you please get some ice from the freezer, or whatever is in there that's cold? Alright, Tom, I'm going to look at you now." I rolled up his pant leg above his knee. A large, bulbous mass covered the area where his knee should have been. Angry red on the sides surrounded a small, purple balloon.

"Are you kidding me?" I said aloud.

Tom peered over and grimaced. "That doesn't look too good."

"No, it doesn't, idiot."

Tom sighed as Seamus walked in. "Holy shit, Tom. That looks really bad."

"I know, I know. Would both of you shut it! Remember, I was attacked tonight? Would you please give me a break?"

I took the ice pack from Seamus and laid it on Tom's knee. Cringing, Tom grabbed ahold of my hand and squeezed.

"Okay, honey, let me see your side."

Tom looked up at Seamus and pursed his lips. I'm sure he was embarrassed by his scars.

I helped him off with his shirt. The area where the bat must have hit him rippled with blacks and blues. I gently laid the other ice pack on him. "Here we go again," I muttered sadly. "I'll go get you some pain medicine, okay?"

I plodded down to the bathroom to fetch the Ibuprofen and a bandage for his head. Fortunately, that didn't look too bad. Still in earshot of Tom and Seamus, I heard them talking softly.

"Mate, you okay?"

"I don't want to scare Anna, but what I didn't tell you, my attacker whispered something to the effect of 'there will be more coming.' I mean, what the hell? Who did I piss off?"

"Did you tell the police this? Yeah? And what did they say?"

"Nothing really, just to keep my wits about me, don't walk alone, et cetera. They even asked if I harmed anyone. I think they were trying to link this to the Vigilante. Then they asked me other questions to determine if this was a hate crime."

I walked in on their conversation and handed Tom the pills with a glass of water from the bathroom. He gazed up at me, trying to gauge how much I had heard.

"Seamus, thanks for helping, but you can go now, if you like. I'm sure Jamie is worried."

"Yeah, well, if you go to the doctor tomorrow, phone me and I'll help you there, right mate?"

"Thank you, Seamus. You're a great friend," Tom said, sincerely.

After Seamus left, I sat across from Tom in the chair.

"I guess you heard my conversation."

"I did."

"Sorry. I just didn't want to frighten you."

"Frighten me? I've been scared since the day I met you, Tom! I mean, Christ, when is all this shit going to stop? I didn't sign up for this." I instinctively rubbed my pendant, trying to gain some reassurance.

Tom remained silent.

"Look, I'm sorry. I know I should be supporting you now, but it's enough! And then you, with your stubbornness about going to the hospital? You want to be able to walk again? I'm going to take Mango out, okay? I need some air."

I snatched Mango's collar and snapped it on.

"Please, walk where there are people," he implored as I left.

Damn him! I know I shouldn't blame him for what happened tonight, but this was the third time something awful has happened, plus his stay at the mental institution, his blackouts, his cuts. And then his fucking pigheadedness about not going to the hospital. Why couldn't we just have a normal life together? Why was I always attracted to the damaged, or deranged? I quickened my pace. Mango started to trot but then stopped abruptly, pulling me back, to pee on a lamppost. The cold, fresh air hitting my skin helped my mood somewhat. Then, of course, I felt guilty. He was the one attacked tonight. It's not his fault. So, we turned around and made our way back upstairs. I took off Mango's leash and he excitedly bounded over to Tom. I followed, kneeling next to the sofa. Tom had obviously been crying. His lashes were fat, but now his face was set, deep in thought.

"Anna, if this is too much for you, I'll understand."

"It's okay, Tom. I just needed to clear my head a little. I'm being selfish... I know. It's just... it's just so much."

"I know," he said, quietly.

"I'm not going anywhere, okay? We're getting married in a few months… I'm here. Just make sure you don't break your ribs again right before the wedding, okay?" I detected a miniscule upward twitch from the corner of his mouth. I leaned over and kissed his small smile.

"But, Tom, we're seeing a doctor tomorrow about your knee and side."

"Agreed. Em, bad news, though. I have to use the loo."

***

After talking to my parents about their trip home, I decided to call Trevor, despite how late it was. I needed someone to talk to, and I definitely didn't want it to be my mother. Besides, I felt Trevor should know what had happened. He was quite upset, as expected, and insisted on coming. He had been planning a trip here anyway, especially since he was away in Rome during Christmas, so he thought this would be as good a time as any, that he could help. While on the phone with me, he booked his train ticket and said he'd be here tomorrow afternoon.

After a lot of gasping and grunting, I was able to help Tom to bed. The swelling on his knee subsided somewhat with the ice, but he still couldn't bend it. The night was rough. The heaviness of the evening finally set in; the complete and utter violation Tom felt from the attack came to a hilt once he was settled and all was quiet. He did not cry, rather he just lay there, staring up at the ceiling, absentmindedly stroking Mango's back. Quietly, as if to himself, he said, "I don't know how much more I can take." His mental anguish apparent in the way his jaw was set, his forehead creased and his nostrils flared.

I had been mugged once, in New York. The person came out of nowhere, covered my mouth from behind, and then ripped my purse out of my hands. I never walked around with more than a few dollars and I kept my credit card and other identification in my jacket pocket. It wasn't what was stolen, though, it was what it did to my psyche. Afraid to walk around, always looking over my shoulder—the sense of violation was always there. It took me a long while to relax again. But, Tom's violation goes deeper. Not only from the attack and how it will impact the days to come, but also by the constant pummeling he is being subjected to. From my mother, from himself, from his father, from me. I stared at him. Like Tom himself, I also wondered how much more he could take. I just had to be stronger for him, and my actions earlier were far from it.

In the morning, I called the doctor, who said she could fit him in early, around 10:00 AM. Thankfully, Seamus made good on his promise and came out to help since I sure couldn't have managed alone. Helping him around the flat was hard enough.

Tom hobbled and complained the whole way, until we arrived with a few minutes to spare. We wound up being at the doctor's office for a couple of hours. The diagnosis? One of Tom's ribs was fractured, unfortunately, and a few were badly bruised. Fortunately, Tom did not have a fractured leg. The doctor said his knee was badly contused, but wasn't too concerned about any permanent damage, as long as Tom took care of the knee. She suggested to keep it elevated, ice it, then heat it, and take some Ibuprofen or something stronger. She told Tom that using crutches was going to be exceedingly uncomfortable because of his ribs, but he vehemently opposed a wheelchair.

Back home, Trevor arrived around 3:00 and greeted me with a huge hug and kiss. Tom, up on his crutches in the foyer, gave a slight wave to his grandfather. Trevor walked over to Tom and caressed his face like a mother would to her small child. He stayed like that, hand on Tom's cheek, a furrowed brow and a deep penetrating stare for slightly longer than normal. His concern moved me; there was something far deeper in that gesture that I couldn't read.

Mango licked Trevor's pants, breaking the stare. His whole face crinkled into a smile as he reached down and pet the fluffy orange fur.

"Trevor, would you like some tea?" I offered.

"Yes, I would love some." Trevor and Tom made their way to the living room while I started a pot of water and found some Earl Grey.

"I haven't been here in a while. The place looks nice," Trevor remarked as I placed the tea set on the coffee table.

Not patient for small talk, Tom admitted, "I am chagrined that you are here under these circumstances."

"Please, Tom," soothed Trevor, "I wanted to visit and discuss the wedding with you and Anna anyway, and it just so corresponds with you being injured. What did the doctor say?"

Tom recounted his diagnosis and then talked about the attack.

"And you have no idea who this may have been?"

Tom shook his head. Mango ran over to the front door and yelped.

"He has to go out," I announced, standing up and fetching his leash.

"Em, Anna, may I join you? Tom? You don't mind, do you?"

"Of course, not. I want you two to get to know each other more."

So Trevor and I set out, leaving Tom lying on the sofa with a book and some pillows under his leg.

"Do you have any idea who may have done this to him," Trevor asked as we stepped outside onto Harley Street and headed toward Reagent's Park. Some of the neighbors were already starting to take down their Christmas lights.

"No, I really don't know."

We walked in silence until we came to the entrance of the park. It was quite cold today and I wasn't dressed properly for the temperature. Shivering, I decided to tell Trevor all of it. I had to trust someone other than Tom.

"Trevor, there are some things you probably don't know, and I don't know if I'm violating Tom's trust, but I am worried about him and have been for quite some time." I paused, not sure if I was doing the right thing. I mean, a lot of this was Tom's business to tell.

Trevor put his free arm around me and guided me to a bench. "Please, love, you are not betraying Tom at all if you are concerned about his health. Please tell me." And so we sat down, huddled together, and I recounted my life with Tom, thus far. From my odd premonitions to Tom's blackouts to the cutting and the suicide watch. Trevor listened intently, not saying anything until I was done, but his face told me everything he was thinking.

Trevor rubbed his eyes and then laced his fingers together, putting his hands under his chin, his eyes glistening.

"I had no idea you two were going through all this. And Tom in Hospital and an institution? I am so sorry—this should be a happy time for you. I didn't know he was cutting himself again." He wiped his eyes, took out a handkerchief from his coat pocket, and blew his nose.

"So, you knew about that?"

"Yes and no. After Lizzie's death, Tom had a number of episodes. From the time he was around 14 through 18 or so, he had some unexplained injuries. When I saw him through the years, I would ask him what happened, thinking he was just accident prone, but he always claimed he didn't know how the injuries got there. I asked him if anyone at school did this to him or his father, but he said no. And so, we paid for some therapy sessions where the psychiatrist prescribed him some sort of anti-panic medication and lithium and the like, which made him, in my opinion, worse. He didn't respond well to the drugs, so we stopped the medication and the therapy."

"Thomas said he paid for the therapy, that it cost him much of his money." Trevor just shook his head and sighed, saying "bastard" under his breath.

I continued with my questions. "Then what's wrong with him? His therapist is kicking around Dissociative Disorder… you know, split personality," I trembled. Mango jumped into my lap, warming my legs.

Trevor raised an eyebrow, "I highly doubt that. I didn't even think that was a real thing. But, I wish I knew what was wrong with him. Tom is a very, very sensitive lad. He has so much guilt pent up in him from his sister's death, his mother's death, even about his relationship with his father. He carries all these burdens with him, and I think his body just takes over to, to give him a break. Maybe the cutting releases some sort of mental pain through physical pain? Maybe the blackouts he says he has are part of the break as well?"

I shrugged.

"But, I have no idea about your pain, or how any of it ties to the Vigilante. That is odd."

"I wish there was a simple explanation."

"Nothing is ever simple, Anna. Certainly not when it comes to my family. Let's keep walking to stay warm, but, I'll give you some history. It's not very pretty, but I think you have the right to know." And Trevor started his tale of his family's sordid past:

'I was born in 1935 in London. Piss poor and living with my kind mother, but wretched father. My father was not abusive towards me, but he was a drunk and, em, did things, things that were quite unsavory. Luckily, I took after my mum, who taught me manners, how to treat women, and how to be a gentleman. I never knew why she chose my father, but sometimes, love makes us foolish. I met Elizabeth in secondary school. We were sweethearts throughout school and as soon as we graduated, I asked her to marry me. I landed a job in the building industry and made my fortune when I started my own development company. I always pushed for sound practices; I didn't want to destroy nature like so many other companies did. I also treated my employees very well, so I had very little turnover.

We had one son. Thomas. Ah, Thomas. You try to love, unconditionally, but with Thomas, it was hard. You see, my father took a strong liking to Thomas. The two were inseparable. As my mother taught me respect and love, my father taught Thomas how to hate. How to hate women, blacks, Asians, Indians, anyone different from himself. As much as Elizabeth and I tried, my father injected Thomas with his venom, and unfortunately, it stayed in his veins."

A chilly wind blew and we walked a little faster. Mango stopped many times to stare at the ravens that hopped by. "Couldn't you have kept Thomas away from your father?"

"We tried Anna, but he would do things like pick him up from school or come over unannounced and offer to take him out for ice cream. It was hard to keep him away, especially when my father lived a block from our house at the time. And when Thomas was a teenager, it became even harder to keep him away from my father. Besides," Trevor said, giving me a steely look, "evil attracts evil." I shivered again, but not from the wind.

"You think your son and father were evil?"

"Yes, unequivocally, yes. Take my son. He beat Tom and Lizzie, especially Tom. You've seen the lashes on his back, I am sure."

"Yes, I know all this… and the burns."

"Yes, the burns." Trevor stared off.

"According to Thomas, Tom did that to himself. I think Tom cutting himself made it very convenient and very easy for Thomas to hide his abuse."

"Yes, no doubt. We know Tom did start to cut himself up after Elizabeth died, but most of the scars you see on his back were by my son's hand."

Mango started pulling Trevor toward his favorite fountain to have a drink. While Mango was lapping away, I got up the courage to ask the obvious. "Okay, pardon my bluntness, but why in the hell didn't you take Tom and Lizzie away from their father? Especially after their mother died?"

Trevor stared off, looking at the trees, his eyes starting to shimmer. "I regret that every day of my life, Anna. I didn't know back then and didn't question it, although I should have read the signs. I mean, the boy had a horrible stutter when he was around his father—that alone should have tipped me off. But I believed his therapist, and I believed my son, that Tom was doing it all to himself. I wish I had listened to my instincts. I knew something was awry, even when he was a young child; the way Tom would shy away from his father, the way he feared him. I knew my son and what he was like, but I never saw him lay a hand on Tom, not really, anyway. I was always so busy at work to really notice our grandchildren's living situation. And then after we moved to Scotland, we didn't see them as much." Trevor closed his eyes and shook his head, but continued.

"We would invite them out in the summer. We maintained weekly, sometimes daily contact with the kids. And we set up trusts for them. But, I wasn't really, really there for them, now was I? Tom finally told me what had really happened just a couple of years ago. Christmas, in fact. I don't know why he waited so long—shame, embarrassment, I don't know. But, when I found out, I tell you Anna, it took all the self-restraint I had to not strangle my son to death. I cut him completely out of my will, and basically disowned him. But, long ago, I should have paid more attention. Maybe all of this could have been prevented," he stated again, regret dripping from his words. I patted his back as we left the fountain and started to walk back home.

"Why do you think Thomas was so abusive to Tom?"

"I've thought long and hard about this. After Tom told me about the life I didn't know he had endured, I really thought back to when Tom was a child and teen. I came to the conclusion that Tom was a disappointment to Thomas, thinking him to be feeble. Tom was always very emotional and very sensitive, and Thomas viewed this as weakness. Thomas also resented having to raise two children. We tried to help, many, many times, but when we gave Thomas money, he drank and smoked it away. I finally refused to give him any more unless he straightened himself out. He didn't, so we set up trusts for the kids. We bought them clothing, bicycles, you name it, but I never gave their father any more. Thomas resented us tremendously after I cut him off, and I am afraid he took it out on the kids. Bad combination, right? A drunk, a person influenced by a wretched soul, and the son of a rich father who wouldn't give him money to sit on his bum and drink all day."

I nodded, understanding. "What about Eloise? Thomas told me she committed suicide in the garage and Tom found her. Is that true?"

Trevor looked rather confused. "No, she was in a car accident. At least, that is what Thomas led us to believe. Eloise was a kind woman, but weak and depressed, and Thomas treated her like chattel. After all, she was a woman. So it wouldn't surprise me if her accident was actually a suicide. But, I tell you, dear girl, you cannot trust anything my son says. I was told she drove off the road and crashed her car into a tree. Why on earth would he tell you something different? Or if that is true, why did he lie to us about it for all these years?"

I blew out, "Well, I guess he wouldn't want to tell you back then because you would probably have blamed him for it, and rightfully so. But, more so, I think Thomas is trying to instigate things between Tom and me. Thomas and I have talked privately a couple of times and the conversations are usually laced with warnings about Tom and his mental state. He actually told me Tom accidently killed Elizabeth."

This time Trevor laughed out loud. "Oh really? What a lying bastard. Now, I guess we can't be absolutely certain since we weren't there, but I can't see how Tom would have had the strength to do much of anything after his father got ahold of him. Tom told me everything that happened that night. That boy was beaten and burned the night of Lizzie's death. I don't and won't believe it, accident or not. Does Tom know about any of these accusations?"

"Not about Elizabeth, but yeah, I told him about his mom."

"And his reaction?"

"He wasn't sure. But, maybe therapy will bring something out."

"I worry about him, Anna. My family has a line of evil in it. From my father, to Thomas, to even Lizzie. I loved that girl, but she was mean. Not to us, mind, but she played Tom. She toyed with his affections. She would be all sugar and rainbows one minute to him and the next, she would be pushing him face first into the mud. He loved her dearly and she would give him just enough love back to keep his affections. She manipulated him, tremendously."

We came upon the street exit and walked on, contemplative.

"I hesitate to tell you this, Anna, but do you want to know what my father did?"

"Um… I guess."

Trevor grimaced a little and spoke. "Well, we didn't find out about this until he was caught, but my father was my family's own Jack the Ripper. He beat, maimed, and killed prostitutes and homosexuals. He thought them the scourge of the earth. He went to jail, but it was after he had his mitts into Thomas… long after. He was pure evil and I'm afraid that seeded Thomas and then even Lizzie. I am only glad that the gene missed dear Tom and me."

I looked over at Trevor. My lips parted as I tried to speak. Everything felt like it was in slow motion—the birds walking around, Mango's tail wagging, my steamy breath billowing in front of me. Trevor said something else, but I didn't hear him. He stared at me, his blue eyes wide—concern on his face.

I finally was able to croak out a whisper, "My God, Trevor. Your father was Phineas Hall."

CHAPTER 22

Back at the flat, Trevor decided to lie down. It had been a long day, plus, I think I overwhelmed him with what Tom had been through. Tom was up and about on his crutches, trying to get dinner started. I tried to process what Trevor told me. Phineas Hall was Tom's great-grandfather. He was the man who killed the prostitute in that first house where I met Tom. The first ghost tour. God, what does it mean?

"Love, did you have a nice chat with Trevor? You were gone for quite some time, and you were not really dressed for it." Tom tried to grab some rice from the top shelf, but gasped and recoiled his arm. I pushed up with my hands on the counter, swung my right knee on the cold granite, then my left and then pulled the bag from the cabinet for him.

"I'll make dinner, okay? Why don't you sit down?" Tom nodded and made his way to the table. He rested his leg on the adjacent chair while I busied myself with dinner, trying to focus on the recipe for a vegetable biryani Tom had picked out. Loud and abrupt with my preparation, Tom suspected a hint of anger in my actions.

"Em, everything alright, love?"

After starting the rice, I turned to face him. My heart sped up a little and my hands felt a little clammy.

"Why did you lie to me about Phineas Hall? He's your great-grandfather? I remember clearly, you told me that there are a *plethora* of Halls in the phonebook."

Tom grimaced and then quickly raised his eyebrow.

"Clearly, I wasn't about to disclose to a woman I wanted to—ah… that I was attracted to—that my great-grandfather was a murderer and the killer featured on my ghost tour. But, knowing you now, you probably would have thought that to be cool."

"Haha. You could have told me later."

"Honestly, I didn't think of it. I try to keep that little tidbit about my ancestry at bay, even from myself."

I turned back to the recipe, finding the spices and vegetables listed. "Well, it's pretty disconcerting and creepy. And with all the shit that's been happening, this just takes the cake. And just so you know, I told Trevor everything."

Tom sighed, "It's alright. I was planning on telling him anyway. He looked pretty distraught when he walked in the door, so I figured you said something."

The phone rang. Tom started to stand to get it, but in two steps, I beat him before his bad leg hit the floor.

"Anna, it's Holly."

"Oh, Holly, hi!"

"How are things? "

"That's a loaded question, but what can I do for you?"

Holly let me know that she finally reached April Simms. Apparently, she had been on a retreat in Africa where correspondence was not possible. But, April had returned and wanted to see us tonight, if possible. Apparently, my story intrigued her, and she wanted to help. Okay with the short notice, Holly texted April while we were on the phone and arranged for April to come to our flat in about two hours.

When I hung up the phone, I told Tom what was happening. I think he was slightly bothered by the late hour, but I really didn't care what he thought at this point. This needed to be dealt with.

***

Buzz...

Mango went to the door and sat patiently, wagging his tail. I opened the door to find a very attractive and glamourous elderly woman standing before me. She had long grey hair, twisted back in a French braid. Her beautiful figure was outlined by probably rather expensive designer clothes, and she wore just enough makeup to accentuate her facial features. She had greyish blue eyes, a slightly upturned nose, and high cheekbones. I couldn't get a gauge on her age... 65, maybe?

"Hello, you must be Anna." She extended a hand, and I took it. "And who is this cute little ball of fur?" She stooped down and let Mango lick her face... okay, first good sign.

"Dr. Simms, thank you so much for coming. Would you like anything to drink?"

"No thank you, I am eager to get started. I am sure you are too, given the late hour."

Tom emerged from the bedroom in black suit pants and a dark blue button-down shirt, no tie, as usual, and the first two buttons undone. He limped over, using the furniture as leverage.

"Dr. Simms, the pleasure is all mine." He took her hand and kissed it. I laughed a little inwardly.

"And I thought manners were dead. You have a nice-looking chap here, Anna." April said, in a very proper British accent. I pictured Tom and April sipping tea with their pinkies out.

I nodded in agreement. Trevor stood up from the sofa and copied Tom's chivalrous gesture. I introduced Trevor and we all had a seat, April on the chair opposite the sofa, Tom and Trevor flanking my sides on the sofa.

"And I see where young Tom gets his looks from," April said, smiling at Trevor. I think Trevor blushed a little.

"You are too kind, Ms. Simms," Trevor said, as he bowed his head.

"Well, let's get down to business." Dr. Simms took charge immediately. She sure commanded the room.

"I'll go put some tea on," Tom said as he attempted to stand.

April reached over the coffee table, put a hand on Tom's knee, but retracted it rather quickly as if she touched something hot. Quickly, she recomposed herself, "No, thank you, please let's get started. Besides, it doesn't look like you should be moving about so much."

Tom, obviously uncomfortable not being able to be a gracious host or perhaps because of her odd reaction, eased back into the sofa.

"So, before we start, I wanted to put a few things on the table. First, please let's drop the formalities and call me April. Second, everything you say is confidential. I have a strong reputation for not letting any information out, no matter the legality. I also charge an extraordinary rate after our first consultation. But, we can go over that later. If you choose not to hire me, I'll still keep our meeting tonight classified. Does that suit your needs?"

"Yes, of course, Ms. April," Tom agreed.

"Just April. So, tell me all about it. Don't leave anything out."

We sat for about an hour, me recounting what I remembered and Tom agreeing or telling his own part, especially his early years. Trevor chimed in a couple of times about Phineas and Thomas. We went over the different theories and when we were finished, we felt drained.

"Mmm hmm. So, let's see. You've been diagnosed as possibly having Dissociative Disorder because you have blackouts, you have cut yourself, and you have been possibly seen by Anna exhibiting behaviors opposite of your character. Well, that's one way to look at it."

Tom and I glanced at each other. "And, what is your explanation?" Tom inquired.

"I hardly know yet. I may be psychic, but I'm not omniscient. I'll need to investigate. But, there are other forces possibly working here, such as Anna's visions and your own feelings at the tours. It's all too coincidental. Anna, please give me your hands."

I leaned forward and offered her my hands, slightly embarrassed by my black fingernail polish.

April gripped tightly, but not painfully. She closed her eyes and rocked back and forth, taking deep breaths, in and out, in and out. I glanced over at Trevor, who stared at April intently.

She let go and popped her eyes open.

"You definitely have some nascent ability in you, Anna. You've probably always had it, but just never realized. It has only been obvious, recently."

"Okay. Why now?"

"It seems something happened at that ghost tour that probably jarred it. Ah, like when you have static on your telly, but you whack it and the picture is clear. I do think there is more to this story than just that."

She turned to Tom and asked for his hands.

Tom hesitated a moment, but leaned forward and reached his hands over the table. Upon, touching him, her eyes rolled back and her eyelids fluttered. She squeezed tighter and tighter until Tom gasped at the strength of this elderly woman; her blue veins puffing out. Tom's eyes darted to me, obviously at a loss for knowing what to do. I placed my hand on his shoulder for reassurance. Whispering nonsensical words, April spidered her hands up to Tom's wrists, applying more and more pressure. This went on for at least five minutes, Tom enduring the pain. And then, abruptly, April blinked, which righted her eyeballs and released Tom's wrists. He rubbed them to bring the circulation back.

April sat back, sweating, dabbing her forehead with her handkerchief. "I think we need to discuss further sessions."

"What did you see?" Tom asked, a bit startled. "That was a bit, em, intense."

Trevor stood up, walked around to Tom's side, and placed his hand lightly on Tom's shoulder.

"Tom, dear, I don't believe for a second you have Dissociative Disorder, Bipolar Disorder, or any other mental issues. I think something else is at work here, causing your blackouts and unexplained occurrences. Something powerful. This is more about you, much more about you, than Anna. Much of what I saw and felt were a jumbled mess, conflicting information between what you think you know and what is the truth. I suggest doing a life regression to really bring out these memories, the true ones. A regression will also bring out what happens during your blackouts so we can get to the bottom of this. And I would do it sooner than later. Because of the extreme nature of this, I will clear out some spots for you. If you agree to my terms." April seemed quite agitated.

"What is entailed in a life regression?" Trevor asked.

"Basically, hypnosis. I am not going to sugar coat it, however; it can be quite painful. Whatever is in your head, dear Tom, you have pushed it far, far down to be able to live a semblance of a normal life. Some of the things I saw…" April paused and shook her head. "But, I don't want to jump to conclusions. I want to be sure. And, I would like Anna there as well. She may be a key to this puzzle."

Tom and I looked at each other. "You can tell all this from one touch?" Tom was trying to not sound too skeptical.

April looked at him, not unkindly, and just said, "Paisley bear?"

Oh wow. No one had mentioned this. Tom swallowed hard and then said, "Yes, let's do this, ah, regression."

"You haven't heard my fee."

"Money is no object," Trevor offered.

"Granddad, you are not paying for this. You've given me plenty."

"I insist, lad. It will allow me, at least a little, to take away some of the guilt I feel for not abducting you and hiding you away from your sorry excuse for a father." Tom started to speak, but Trevor held up his hand and gave Tom a "case closed" look.

Tom nodded.

"Okay then, it's settled. I'll have my assistant draw up the paper–mainly confidentiality statements and the like–and we'll start. Is tomorrow too soon?"

CHAPTER 23

Trevor stayed home with Mango while I went to work, but I took the afternoon off to meet Tom for lunch before our appointment with April. We pretty much sat in silence in Sagar, our favorite Indian restaurant in the theater district. Tom pushed around his lentil dish, hardly taking a bite. The dark circles and exaggerated lines around his eyes marked the evidence of a sleepless night. Aside from the pain in his knee and side acting up, I knew he fretted about the memories that may resurface. Let alone, the surrealism and absurdity of all this.

"Hey. I love you," I said, reaching across the small table, lightly touching his hand. "You should eat; it's your favorite."

I was sidetracked by a waiter who carried a very large Dosai up the spiral staircase. "Look at that!"

Tom slowly turned his head, stared for a few seconds, then turned back. He gave me a small smile and squeezed my hand. "We'd better get going, love."

April's office was a few blocks away toward St. James Park. Tom had to use his crutches, but he didn't seem to have too much trouble with them. We entered the office building and rode the elevator to the tenth floor. Upon entering April's suite, we were taken in by the view over London. The sky was very blue with puffy clouds, the evergreens contrasting nicely in the park.

A pleasant, very young and golden-haired receptionist greeted us and showed us to the waiting area. Floor to ceiling windows surrounded the plush, modern furniture. Tom remained quiet and stared out the window, distant. I felt so bad for him.

After about ten minutes, the receptionist announced April was ready to see us, and walked us back to a gorgeous office. The calming leafy green colored walls accented the acanthus-leafed birch white crown molding with a lush burgundy rug in the middle of the room, covering part of the dark stained hardwood. The furniture juxtaposed a modern feel with rustic accents. The whole décor brought the outside in, creating a peaceful oasis on the top floor above a very busy city. An oversized, aubergine modern chaise sat to the right, with a matching guest chair next to it, back facing the large, tinted glass windows. A reclaimed wood desk sat to the left.

"Welcome, welcome," April said as she shook my hand. Tom kissed her hand, despite his mood.

"Ah, Tom, you are an old soul, but look I'm going to be noodling around in your mind, so I think we can forgo the formalities?"

"Alright. Em, where do you want me?" Tom asked, cutting to the chase. I think he wanted to get this over with, quickly.

"Aren't we eager to get started? Well, take your shoes, socks and coat off and have a seat on the chaise—please get as comfortable as you can. Anna, you can sit at the desk. I'm going to record this, if that's alright?" Tom said okay as he did what he was told. I took my seat at the desk.

April got up and pressed a button that lowered the blinds on the window, making the office dark, but still soothing as a small bit of light still came through. We exchanged a few more pleasantries, and then April began the process.

Tom laid down and rested his head on the pillow. "Okay, Tom, are you comfortable? Good. Would you prefer rain or ocean sounds? I've had very good success with hypnosis using the sounds of nature."

"Em, the rain, please," Tom said. April pushed a button and on came the sounds of a soft thunderstorm.

"Now, all cell phones need to be off and Anna, you cannot speak, no matter what you hear. Otherwise, I'll have to ask you to leave the room."

I made a zipper sign across my mouth and April nodded.

"Alright, let's begin. Tom, I am going to put you into a very deep sleep, but you will be aware and able to answer my questions. You will remember everything when you wake. I am going to try to delve deeper into your past and especially into memories of your sister. Understand?"

"Yes," Tom said in a deeper than usual voice. I could tell he was relaxing already.

Then, April, in her soothing voice, talked Tom through hypnosis, mainly by instructing him to really concentrate on the rain and her voice. After about five or so minutes, Tom was in a trance.

"Tom, I'm going to ask you to go back in time, back to when you were a child. What is your earliest memory?"

A short time passed and then Tom spoke, reminiscent of someone talking in their sleep. "Playing with some of my sister's toys on the floor of her room. I must have been about three years old."

"And what sort of feelings do you have with this?"

"Happy. My sister came into the room and started playing with me. She was being kind. She held me in her lap while we played. That's about all I remember."

"Okay, Tom, let's move on. What is the first memory you have of being severely abused by your father?"

Tom shifted uncomfortably and contorted his face a little, eyes still closed.

"It's okay, Tom. This is just a memory. Take your time, but I want you to relax, take deep breaths and allow your mind find it. You are safe here and surrounded by love. I reiterate, this is just a memory."

Tom took a number of deep breaths. I thought he drifted off, but then he started to speak. "I must have been near five. I remember my father asking me to fetch him a beer. I didn't know what beer was at the time, so I brought him a soda instead. He got up, forcibly grabbed me by my arm and took me to the refrigerator to show me what beer looked like, pointing at a green bottle. He took that bottle from the refrigerator, sat me down at the table and slammed it down in front of me. Pointing at it again, he ordered me to drink it. I did as he said, but after taking one sip I gagged and spit it out. I recall he smiled after that, but it wasn't a happy smile, it was more, well scary. He then told me to drink it all, but I refused, the taste was so vile. He, ah, he yanked me out of the chair, took me over his knee and spanked me… hard. I pleaded with him to stop, but to no avail. It felt like he hit me 20 times, yelling at me about how I should obey him. I recall my sister coming in the room telling him to stop, but he just ignored her pleas as well. When he was finally done with me, he sat me down hard on the wooden chair, which was excruciating, and told me to sit there until I finished the bottle with a warning that I better not even think about spilling it into the sink. He left leaving me squirming in the chair, the pain rippling through my body. I tried to drink it, but it tasted like piss."

Tom paused, "And then, yes, I remember, my sister sneaked back into the kitchen and drank it for me, put her finger to her lips for me to be quiet and left the room. I thought I heard her vomiting in the bathroom."

I fought back tears, not wanting to make a sound. I wanted more than ever to kill that asshole father of Tom's.

"So, your sister helped you sometimes?"

"Many."

"And many times, she hurt you, too?"

Tom didn't say anything.

"Okay Tom, let's go to another time when your sister helped you."

Tom took some time to think, but then started to speak again after the long silence.

"I think I was about six years old and in primary school. My sister was in her last year at the same school. She was tasked with walking me home every day. I was a small and quiet boy and got picked on quite a bit. After school, one day, I remember waiting for her at our meeting spot. She was sometimes late. This particular day, she was very late, late enough for two older boys to start harassing me. I remember they pushed me, knocked me to the ground, kicked dirt on me. Not long after while on the ground, I recall one of the boys being yanked off of me. My sister had come. She tackled the boy and started punching him in the face. I remember the blood running down his cheeks, mixing with the dirt on the ground, making it look like some vile cake batter. The other boy was so frightened, he ran away, but Elizabeth, like my father, was relentless. Blow after blow after blow. The color, brick red. I started to beg her to stop, not wanting to see this kind of violence, but she wouldn't until she was exhausted. Finally, she got up, but the boy didn't. In fact, he didn't come back to school for a couple of days after. Elizabeth got away with it, as the boy told people another boy from secondary school did this, I assume he didn't want to admit he was pummeled by a girl. I do remember the way home, Elizabeth telling me I had to learn to stand up to people like that and that she would show me how to punch, but I never wanted to learn after seeing what it did."

"Very, very good Tom, you are doing excellently. Now, I am going to ask you to search your mind for a memory of why your sister may have turned on you. What made her go from your savior to your foe? Take your time, but I need you to listen to the rain and really, really think."

After a number of minutes, Tom finally began, his voice at a lower and more solemn register.

"I was about eight years old, I think, in bed? No, I'm in another room, I think. Mum had been gone about three years now. I remember holding my paisley bear, but I kept hearing muffled sounds in the dark. The room was so dark, I remember, but... I... I can't see it... the memory is there, but I can't seem to grasp it."

"Tom, remember, this is just a memory from long ago, nothing is going to harm you now. You are safe."

"I c..c..can't." Tom stammered, scrunching his eyes tighter.

"Alright, Tom, you're doing great, we'll come back to that later. How about one last memory before we are done for the day? I want you to think back, maybe after that incident, and tell me something your sister did that was mean to you, where you felt she wasn't your protector anymore."

Another long pause ensued while I watched Tom's stomach rise and fall with his deep breaths. He began again.

"Em, eight or nine years old. Elizabeth was now in secondary school, but was still responsible for walking me home. She would meet me at the school and we would take the long journey home, usually not speaking much anymore. One day, she showed up with a group of her friends. I remember not really liking what they looked like. They were an intimidating lot. One lad, in particular, was rather sinister looking. Elizabeth informed me that we weren't going straight home, that we would be taking a small detour. So, I followed behind her and her friends. We walked a good while until we came to some woods where, deeper in, there was a run-down shack. It was creepy and looked haunted. We walked up to it. We went in. The floor boards were all worn, broken, creaky; the roof the same. I think I heard bugs and maybe rats scattering as we went inside. In the center sat a rickety chair. The sinister boy, named Alan, told me to take a seat. I didn't want to, but I did anyway and sat in that horrid chair. Elizabeth lit up a fag and Alan and the other boy and girl took drags off of it. Elizabeth then handed me the fag and told me to take it— that she was going to make a man out of me instead of a fucking coward. I told her no, but she told me that I better or she'll make me. I kept trying to talk to her, reason with her, but my words came out as a stutter. She instructed me to inhale, hold it, then blow out, so I tried and of course started coughing and coughing, my sister and her friends laughing at me and mimicking my stutter. Do it again, she commanded, but I told her no. And then... and then she tackled me, the chair falling backward as I whacked my head on the floor... I... I saw patterns of black and gray dots all the while as she held me down, forcing the fag into my mouth, but I wouldn't take it, so Alan held my arms above my head and then sat on my forearms while the other boy held my legs tight to the upturned chair legs. Elizabeth held the fag in front of my face, telling me they wouldn't let me up until I smoked it. So we sat there, a good long time until the pain in my arms and legs became unbearable. She put the fag to my lips and I tried again and again and again, through fits of coughing. They finally let me up and I remember throwing up in the corner. When we got home, Elizabeth told my dad that she caught me smoking, that I stole the cigarettes from him. I denied it, but of course he didn't believe me, after all he smelled the smoke on my clothes and I was still coughing. My father beat the tar out of me that night. This time with his belt. I vaguely remember hearing Elizabeth's laughter in the background."

I covered my mouth with my hand and started to cry, but quietly. My body ratcheted as I tried to hold in my emotions. I raised my head up and saw April looking over at me with kind eyes and she nodded.

"Tom, you did wonderfully. You are going to wake up when I count down to one. You are going to remember everything, but you are also going to wake up in a room where there is love and safety, okay? Five, four, three, two, one."

As Tom flitted his eyes open, he looked over at me, scared to death. I stood up, wheeling the desk chair back and went over to him, hugging him fiercely.

"Tom, oh my God. You didn't know about this?" I asked in between sobbing breaths.

"I, no, I didn't remember these little gems, until now."

"Tom," April interjected, "you've had a number of traumatic experiences in your past. No doubt there are more episodes you are suppressing, but the ones we discovered today were very, very big. We will get more answers, I promise you. These are just a few pieces of a very large puzzle. We can meet again if you are up to it, tomorrow evening if you like."

Tom looked very frightened and confused. He buried his face in his hands and then sat upright, placing his bare feet on the floor. April put her hand on Tom's back.

"Look, love, this is going to be a painful process, but you are strong now and certainly not a coward. Like it or not, your upbringing made you who you are today. You are proper, polite, clean, engaging, and well-liked. Instead of you succumbing to your experiences as a child and becoming that abuser, becoming that slovenly, fag smoking wicked man you could have easily become, you became the opposite. I get strong feelings about your character; I know you are a good, good man who's just battling some ghosts, that's all."

Tom nodded. He slowly started to put back on his shoes and socks. Standing up with his crutches and donning his coat, he gave April a friendly hug. She urged us to talk things through after each session, so we decided to go for a walk. He, however, was pretty silent. We walked along the embankment, Tom moving more easily with the crutches, until we came to a small greenspace with a bench. Leaning his crutches on the bench, he shuddered in some air and then took a seat. I plopped down right next to him.

"Tom, I cannot believe what you've been through."

Tom was staring forward into space, hands in his coat pockets with his injured leg straight out. He closed his eyes when I moved a strand of hair out of his eyes.

I quietly said, "Do you want me to leave you alone for a little?"

He shook his head, almost imperceptibly, and took ahold of my hand. We sat there, in quiet, for a good long time, watching the attractive Londoners walk by. Tom finally broke the silence. Quietly, he asked, "Why do you stay with me?"

I laughed a little. "Did you hear anything April said at the end about who you are? She is absolutely right. And besides, I love you more than anything." He didn't look at me. His eyes seemed fixated on a lamp post.

"Anna, I want you to have a life that isn't fraught with anguish all the time. We're trying to plan our wedding, for God sakes, but instead, we're dealing with all my issues."

"Your father did this to you, babe; none of this is your doing. Let him go to hell."

Breaking eye contact with the lamp post, he looked me squarely in the eyes. "He's in his own hell with his illness."

"Don't care."

"But, I do."

"Even after today?! What you remembered him doing to you—to a five-year-old?"

"He's still my father."

I let go of his hand and crossed my arms. Not thinking at all, I blurted, "Whatever, Tom. I can sort of see why your sister was so frustrated with you!"

Tom closed his eyes, jaw twitching. He leaned his head back on the bench, stared at the sky, and said nothing.

"Tom, I'm sorry, I didn't mean it." I quickly recovered, but it was too late.

"You did. And you better shut it before I say or do something we'll both regret."

I started to speak, but Tom interrupted me. "Anna, I don't want to hear your voice right now," he warned.

So, I sat, quiet as a mouse, on the bench, reprimanding myself once again.

CHAPTER 24

— *Tuesday, January 6*

The ever-resilient Tom started to get around just fine without the crutches. Albeit on pain killers, he was now able to bend his knee, and the swelling had gone way down. A good thing, because Trevor was leaving after breakfast. He had some business to attend to in Scotland—a woman, I presume—but vowed to come back soon. The night before, we had told him about the memories that were dredged up by the regression. Trevor was brought to tears, not realizing it had been that bad when Tom was young. Guilt plagues the Halls, at least the good Halls.

After work, Tom and I spent the evening looking over plans for the wedding. Theo had sent us some information on flowers, décor, invitations, and food he wanted us to approve. I think he was getting a bit frustrated with us since we'd been kind of neglectful.

Sitting cross legged on the floor in front of a blazing fire, wearing sweats and one of Tom's T-shirts, I read out loud the possible dishes we could serve. Tom sat on the floor with his back against the sofa, barefoot, with his legs straight out while stroking Mango, who seemed to enjoy basking in the heat. *Spartacus* by Triumvirat played softly in the background.

"We should probably discuss the guest list and get a rough estimate," Tom suggested. I'd like to invite my colleagues at work. And although we don't know April well right now, I have a feeling we will by then. Em, also, a few friends from University, of course your, em, our friends from your work, and…" he sighed.

"Your father?"

"Mmmm."

I started to shake my head. Tom mindlessly rubbed Mango's side.

"Why don't you invite him and ask him to make a toast? Can you imagine the insults he would spew at you? At any woman there," I said, trying to lighten back up the mood.

He smiled a little and nodded, "Yes, that would be amusing. Em, let's table this for a while. Maybe he'll be dead by then," he said under his breath.

I pretended I didn't hear his comment, although I had been thinking the same thing, "Okay, let's keep going. My mom said my grandparents actually might want to come."

"Both sides?"

"Probably just my mom's parents, although Grandmom Georgia said she would like to come, but couldn't afford it. I told her we would pay for it, but she wouldn't hear of it."

"So, we just buy and send her a non-refundable ticket when the time comes. Get Richard in on it to make sure she doesn't make plans."

I smiled, "Awesome! Okay, so how many people are we talking? Looks like only about twenty-five. But that's probably good since it's in Scotland."

"I've asked Trevor to investigate nice hotels in the area. He will put up the two of us, your parents and grandparents if they come, and Jamie and Seamus, of course. The rest, we'll pay for the hotel and transportation. Are you still sold on the black and orange theme?"

"Yes!"

"The wedding song might be an issue. I don't want to dance my first dance as your husband to The Damned."

"Give me a little credit. I've been thinking about this and thought that 'Maybe I'm Amazed' would be good."

"Ah, brilliant. Come over here, love." So, I crawled over and sidled up next to my fiancé. He put his arm around me, gingerly, as his ribs were healing much more slowly than his knee.

"If I could just stay like this for the rest of my life, I would be a happy man." A hint of sadness was in his tone. The fire crackled and popped, embers rose and fell. Tom inhaled deeply.

About fifteen minutes later, Mango stood up, stretched like a cat, and sauntered over to the front door.

"I'll take him; I think I can handle him." Tom offered. Releasing me from his arm, he pushed himself up with a bit of effort and said in a higher voice, "Go get your leash, boy! Good boy!"

When Mango brought it back, Tom stooped down and clasped the clip to Mango's collar. Mango licked him right in the eye. "Ick," he said, wiping his eye with his sleeve.

He stood up abruptly, kissed me, grabbed a poop bag and said he'd be back in a few minutes.

While he was gone, I sat on the sofa, put my feet up, and stared at the fire. I really hadn't had much of a chance to be by myself over the last couple of days and I welcomed the solitude. I absent mindedly turned my engagement ring around and around.

I must have dozed off because I was awoken by a dog breathing in my face.

"Mango! Off the sofa!" Tom shouted. Mango jumped right down.

"Do you still let him up there behind my back?"

I just shrugged and smiled, sheepishly.

"Mmmm… that sends him mixed messages you know. He won't be an obedient dog if you let him do the things I am trying to get him not to do."

"No, he just knows it's okay when I'm here, but not when you are… because I'm nice."

Tom narrowed his eyes. "That's hardly the point, love. I don't want him on the furniture. I've already acquiesced to the bed. Judging from the way you lived in your last flat, I realize you may actually prefer to live with hair all over the place, but not me. And since I'm the one who tidies up the most, you could at least respect that."

I tried to ignore his little snit, but he kept going. "You do realize he respects me more," Tom said. "Watch."

And then he said again, in a higher pitched voice, "Who do you love most, boy?" And Mango bounded right over to Tom.

I rolled my eyes, "It was because of your inflection, he thought you were calling him."

"Okay, you try."

"Who do you love most, boy?" Mango just sat next to Tom wagging his tail.

Tom winked at me and limped down the hall to the bedroom, Mango following him.

"Asshole," I said loud enough so they both could hear.

***

— *That night*

> *A boy… dark hair, black eyes, black eyeliner, whiter than white face, bouncing a black ball, a black lead ball. I stared at him quizzically, wondering how a lead, black ball could bounce on a hardwood floor. The boy just stared forward, his head cocked to one side, his movements jerky, like a stop motion movie. He just kept bouncing the lead ball, thunk, thunk, thunk….*

I awoke in the dark, a bit unnerved by my weird vivid dream. *Thunk, thunk, thunk.* Stiffening, I realized the noise was not from my dream. I reached over to wake Tom, but he wasn't in the bed. Out of the darkness, by the window, near the chair, the thunking continued in a steady, slow beat. The side of my face hurt, like it had been deeply scraped by something. I felt it, but nothing seemed awry. I wondered if Mango had scratched me, trying to wake me up, but then, just like that, the pain went away.

"Tom?" I called, petrified.

No answer. I counted to three, willing myself out of my stupefied panic, and then I turned on the bedside lamp nearest to the window. The light cast a glow around the room, revealing Tom, sitting on the floor, his back against the chair and feet flat on the ground; his knees drawn up. I bolted upright upon seeing the long kitchen knife he held in his left hand. Up, down, up, down, hitting the point of the knife hard into the wood floor between his feet.

His face was darkened, despite the light, and not by shadows, but by a sinister haze. He stared straight ahead, much like the boy in my lucid dream, jamming the knife into the floor, continuing the slow chop.

I felt the blood drain from my face, but swung my legs over the bed and shooed a curious Mango out of the room, closing him out. My legs feeling like jelly, I tentatively walked over to Tom and stood slightly in front of him, but out of his reach.

I tried to swallow, but my mouth was parched. "Tom? What are you doing?" I croaked.

Without lifting his head, he rolled his eyes up and looked at, no, through me. A very slow, maniacal upturning of his mouth crept in until a very wide "smile" overtook his face, his fangs looking as sharp as the knife. Then, the thunking noise abruptly stopped; the room a deafening silence. Still staring, still "smiling," and before I could react in time, he took the tip of the knife, placed it against his cheek bone and slid it down in an arch along his jawline to his chin; an angry crimson line followed the blade.

"TOM!" I screamed. His grip was somewhat loose, so I was able to grab the knife from his hand.

"Oh my God, Tom, WAKE UP!" I cried, crouching down, shaking his good knee vigorously. Blood started to ooze down his face from the curved line, like a red curtain cascading down.

I kept pleading with him to wake up as Mango started to whine, scratch, and bark from the other side of the door. Finally, Tom's mouth relaxed and his eyes refocused, and then widened. "Anna, what's happening, what…" he delicately touched his bleeding cheek and looked at his red painted fingertips. Startled, he looked at me in shock, seeing the knife in my hand. He scrambled to his feet and backed up against the window.

"What did you do to me, Anna?"

"N..nothing, Tom, you did this to yourself!" I dropped the knife on the floor.

"My God, Anna, is this some kind of sick joke? Did you cut me as well the evening you followed me? Blamed me for it? Like my father!? My psychologist suggested this and I thought it was preposterous, but, now?"

I stood up and looked directly at him, unwavering and said, "In no fucking way did I cut you tonight or that other night. I just watched you take a knife to your own face. You were not here Tom, you were somewhere… else." Blood started to seep onto his collar.

He side stepped me and went quickly into the bathroom. I slumped back onto the floor, my head swimming with his accusation and what he just did to himself. Water ran, the medicine cabinet opened and closed, a lot of profanity was uttered.

Not trusting my ability to stand, I inched my way over to the chair and leaned my body into the side of it and hugged myself, making myself as small as possible, the soft fabric comforting my head. The room started to spin… fear, grief, worry and helplessness jumbled together in an angry mess. I cried. I cried and cried, unable to stop, unable to control my breathing, my shuddering, my coughing.

I felt arms wrap around me, enveloping me in a cocoon of safety. I heard soothing words, "It's okay, shhh, it's okay. I'm sorry, I didn't mean it. I was just startled out of a stupor and I saw the knife. I'm so sorry, love, I'm so sorry." I tasted the relentless salty tears that kept coming and coming, overflowing, filling up the room.

Slowly, slowly, the waterworks tapered off to a few drips; however, while my body tried to break apart with convulsions, it stayed intact by the strong, scarred arms that held me tight. Unable to speak or just not wanting to, I closed my eyes and finally, relaxed into his arms. Emotionally exhausted, I fell into a deep sleep.

CHAPTER 25

With my hair plastered to my face and the covers drawn up to my chin, I awoke in bed, drained. I looked at the clock, my head throbbing. Work was not an option.

Leaving the bed, I stepped over to the chair against the window and cast my eyes down at the splintered hole in the scraped wood plank. It wasn't a dream.

In the bathroom, I washed my face and brushed my teeth, then hair, took a deep, deep breath and walked out of the bedroom.

Tom's back to me, leaning his elbows on the kitchen counter, he held his cell phone to his ear.

"Yes, April. Thank you. Of course, whatever is convenient for you. Thank you so much for seeing me earlier." And he hung up. Sensing I was behind him, he turned around to face me. He cupped his hands over his mouth and nose and closed his eyes.

I wanted to go to him, touch him, hold him, like he held me last night. I felt so safe in his arms, but his arms were protecting me from *him*. He was holding a gun to my head with one hand, but flicking on the safety with the other.

He removed his hands and opened his eyes. The red line on the left side of his face was raw, but fortunately not deep.

"I'm sorry, Anna." He quivered. "I shouldn't have accused you like that. I don't know what happened, don't remember anything. I scared you last night and I think it best if I stay somewhere else, until I get better. I'll… I'll stay in a hotel close by."

I sighed and crept closer to him until I circled my arms around his waist and rested my head on his chest. Tom wrapped his arms around my head while whispering how sorry he was and vowing he'll get better.

"I don't want you to leave your own place," I said as I pulled away, "and I don't want to go anywhere, either. This is something we need to deal with together."

"But you shouldn't have to deal with anything."

"Life is full of having to deal with things. At least you are making the effort to get better."

"But, I don't want to ever put you through something like that again. Can you tell me what happened?"

We sat down at the table, drinking coffee Tom had made earlier, and I recounted the fearful night. He sat with his face set with a concerned and frightened expression, a vertical line creased in between his eyebrows.

"How can this be? How do I not recall anything? Taking the knife, cutting myself, ruining the wood floor? I only remember seeing the horrified look on your face and the knife in your hand. You were so scared, Anna, so scared of me!" A single tear escaped from his left eye.

"I'll go with you to your appointment with April. There is no fucking way I'm going into work. And, Tom, why did I feel a cut on my face right before you cut yourself?"

Dejected, he looked at me and slowly shook his head. "I don't know. Look, April will be here in a couple of hours. She has an appointment nearby this morning and figured she would come over after. Hopefully, she can help us."

***

— *11:45 AM*

A knock at the door. Mango sitting patiently waiting.

April, as glamourous as ever, wore a blousy green silken top tucked into the slim waistband of her straight black skirt. A string of silver pearls decorated her neck which matched her earrings. This time, her blond hair was down, but pulled back from her face by two large silver and gold clamshell barrettes.

"Hello Tom, hello Anna." She took in Tom's long cut and then quickly looked away.

Tom led her to the lounge chair. The tea he had already prepared was elegantly arranged on the coffee table: three black-rimmed white tea cups, a matching teapot, small pitcher for cream, sugar bowl, three expertly folded napkins, and three small teaspoons sat on the tray.

"Thank you again for seeing us on such short notice. I know you are a busy woman and I am not your only client," Tom said, sitting on the sofa, pouring April a cup of tea.

"Well, true, but you are one of my most interesting cases; and you are the most handsome of my clients, even with that nasty cut on your face, so I'm making an exception for you," she winked at him and he looked away, slightly embarrassed, handing her the cup.

"Tom told me briefly what happened. Anna, could I please hear what you observed?"

"Yeah. I was having a weird dream, brought on by Tom chopping a knife into the floor only I didn't know that just yet. I felt some pain on my face, like I got cut or scratched. I thought it was Mango's claws, but it was a more severe pain, plus it went away almost immediately. Anyway, when I turned on the light, there was Tom, with the knife, only he was so... so out of it. And then, then he smiled, took the knife, and sliced his face. I felt it right before he did it."

April nodded, contemplatively. "Okay, let's figure this thing out. If we could darken the room as much as possible, that would help." I drew the dark shades down, blocking out the sun-filled room. April took it upon herself to dim the side table lamp. She then handed me her iPod set to the rain and had me plug it in.

"Is Mango prone to bark?" She asked.

"No, not usually, unless something alerts him." I said, taking a seat in the other chair.

April nodded and asked Tom to lie down and listen to the rain as she turned up the volume. The soft rain poured out of Tom's Bang & Olufsen speakers, lulling all of us into a welcome, relaxed state.

"Okay, Tom. We are going to continue with your life regression, but later, I am going to ask you about last night. For now, I want you to relax, listen to the rain, let it take you back, take you back to the day before your sister died. Breathe in, breathe out... keep doing that until you remember... until you are ready to let it come forward."

We sat in silence, thunder in the distance and the rain enveloping the room.

Before long, Tom began.

"Elizabeth came home in the afternoon with her boyfriend to find my father and me watching something on the telly. It was a Saturday, I remember. I wanted to go hang out with Robbie, but my father wouldn't allow it, so he made me watch inane American situation comedies with him. I... I remember Elizabeth calling me from

the kitchen, so I left my father to drink his beer and smoke his smoldering cigarettes to see what she wanted.

"Upon entering the kitchen, her boyfriend, an odorous sot, gripped the back of my neck tightly and escorted me out the back door into our small yard. It was a bit chilly out and I didn't have my jacket. 'Tom, we are going to show you something and you are going to help us, okay?' Her boyfriend shifted his grip to my hair and nodded my head for me, making me agree to whatever Elizabeth had concocted.

Elizabeth reached into her jacket and pulled something out… I can't see it.

"It's okay Tom," April assured. "Just take some breaths and listen to the rain. The rain is helping to wash away the dust that's blocking your memory. Slowly, but surely, it's washing the dust away… do you see it, Tom?" April's voice soothed Tom into a deeper meditative state, it seemed. Minutes ticked by until….

"A switch blade. Yes, she pulled out a switch blade. I remember now hearing the click and the spring of the blade. She held it right at my cheekbone. 'See Tom, what you are going to do is take this little knife and you are going to off our dearly beloved father. You are going to do it, Tom, because I've done enough for you through the years. It's your turn to grow some bollocks and do something for me. You are going to slit his throat, Tom. And if you don't do it, Peter here is going to hurt you, hurt you real bad.' And then… and then she quickly drew the knife down my face. God, did it hurt."

Involuntarily, I gasped. April shot me a warning glance.

"After that, they left me alone to cry and bleed. But, she told me she would give me the knife when the time was right. I… I can't remember any more."

"Alright, Tom, let's jump ahead to the night your sister died, the very next night."

Tom retold the events of his father's abuse, not wavering at all from what he had told me the morning after our first date. That his father slammed Tom's face to the ground and broke his nose, that his father burned that awful smiley face into him with his cigarettes.

"…I lay there, on the floor, my skin smoldering, my whole face throbbing from my obviously broken nose. I vaguely remember getting up and falling back into bed. I remember my paisley bear in bed with me. The only comfort I could glean from that house of horrors."

Tom took a series of deep breaths and then scrunched up his face, like he was trying to squeeze something out.

"Okay. Okay. I… I think I see it. I hear my sister yelling at my father right outside the door in the hallway. I hear her calling my name. 'Tom, it's time, get the fuck out here!' Somehow, I pushed myself out of that bed, the paisley bear pleading with me to stay put. I opened the door to see Elizabeth with one arm behind her back, holding the switch blade. My father was yelling at her, calling her a fucking cunt. He took a swing at her, but she side stepped him and he missed. She tossed me the knife, but I didn't catch it, I just let it fall to the floor in front of me. I was so confused and so panicked, I didn't know what to do, what I was supposed to do. I don't think my father noticed the knife; his back was to me and I couldn't see Elizabeth because his large frame was blocking her, but I remember her calling to me, 'Do it now, Tom!' I… I neglected to pick up the knife, but instead, I rushed at my father with whatever ounce of strength I had. Right at that moment, he turned his head, saw me coming and stepped out of the w..w..way."

His shallow breathing quickened as he became agitated.

"I..I..I kn..knocked into Elizabeth and she bounced down the st..st..steps like a bowling ball… like the dream I thought I had. I fffelt my arm being jolted back before I ca..careened down after her. Oh my God… oh my God."

April, wide eyed, but in control, leaned forward, taking hold of Tom's shaking hands. His entire body shivered.

April started with a very authoritative voice, "Okay, Tom, listen to me now. You are safe. You are safe at home with Anna and Mango, safe on your sofa. You are 31 years old, not 14. And you are going to wake when I snap my fingers." She pulled one hand away from Tom's and counted down from five, snapping her fingers at the end, snapping Tom out of his trance. His body stopped quaking, but his hands still violently shook.

He opened his eyes and sat up, ramrod straight. He blinked a few times, kneaded his long fingers into his thighs, and tried to speak. Nothing came out. Seemingly, the shock of the revelation, that defining moment in his life, was too much to process, too much to bear. I gingerly lifted myself from the chair and sat next to him. I rested my hand on his right hand that dug into his leg.

April leaned in further, placing her hands on each of his knees, staring at him in the face.

"Tom, love. Please, deep breaths. Anna, get him some water." Obeying, I hurried to the kitchen and back, glass in hand.

"What have I done?" Tom whispered. "I... I killed Elizabeth. I was the cause, Anna." The pain in Tom's eyes electrified my skin; the fine hairs on my arms stood up straight.

"Tom, no, it was an accident. Your father caused it, not you. You were trying to protect her," I urged.

"Anna, I was supposed to use the knife. I was supposed to kill him, not her!" Tom's agitation started to rise again.

April started, "Tom, in no way should you think you should have killed your father. Elizabeth was wrong to put that on you. No matter the circumstances. You did the best you could with what you had that night. Your father stepped out of the way when he saw you coming. Either he was just getting away from you or he knew it would cause you to crash into your sister. He is at fault for all of this, Tom, dear; he caused this, NOT you. Do you understand me?" April grasped Tom's chin, making him look her straight in the eyes, attempting to allay an oncoming panic attack.

Not thinking, I said, "Yes and your sick father actually credits himself for saving your life when he caught you."

Tom stopped kneading his legs, pulled out of April's boney grip, cocked his head and looked in my direction.

"Pardon?" He asked, accusingly. Oh, shit. I chewed on my lower lip.

"God, Tom, I didn't want to tell you this, I mean, I thought it was a lie."

"You thought, what was a lie, Anna?" He asked slowly as he squinted at me.

Despite my chewing, my lower lip started to tremble and my whole face flushed, "Um, do you remember the night you found me here, crying after the visit with your father, the things he told me about you?"

"Of course."

"He told me that... he told me pretty much the same thing you just relayed. Of course, he denied laying a hand on you to cause what happened, but you've confirmed what he told me about how your sister died. I didn't want to tell you... I didn't think it was true to begin with and I didn't want you to hurt any more than you already did."

Tom brusquely stood up and paced, then stopped in front of me, the hurt in his face raining down upon me.

He placed his fingertips on his temples and seethed. "How could you have kept something like this from me? What gave you the right to keep secrets from me about MY life? About my childhood? Who in the hell do you think you are?" His jaw was set tight, his nostrils flared, and his eyes were full of fire. I didn't know how many seconds I had until the bomb went off.

"I'm sorry, Tom, I was just trying to protect you," I cried.

"I DON'T NEED YOUR FUCKING PROTECTION!" he bellowed.

I sat there, paralyzed. Mango backed up but emitted a low growl. Tom shot him a warning glance.

"Tom, love, let's sit down and work this out. Anna was just trying to help. Remember, she loves and cares for you deeply. You've just been witness to some very troubling news and you want to lash out. We can all understand that, but let's not take it out on your fiancée or your dog."

Tom looked at April and spat, "I wouldn't hurt my dog." Then he turned toward me.

"Anna, I don't want you here right now. I don't want to see your face, I don't want to hear your voice. Just, please, please get out."

I stood up, crying, "Tom, please, don't do this."

The icy blue in his eyes became more pronounced as he stared at me, "Get… the… fuck… out of my flat."

April started to speak, but Tom interrupted, "April, with all due respect, I really need to be alone now. I am about to burst wide open and I need to be by myself. Please respect my wishes."

I ran and grabbed Mango's leash, hastily put it on him, sobbing all the while, snatched my small travel backpack, coat and purse, and then ran out the door.

***

I walked aimlessly around the city with Mango at my side. I had to sit a number of times to control my shaking and sobbing. Mango didn't know what to make of my reactions. He kept nudging me with his nose and licking me. Brits stared at me with their very reserved judgments.

I reached into my purse and took out my phone, hoping upon hope Tom tried to reach me. Nope.

I was about to dial his number, but thought better of it. I thought of calling Trevor. I picked up the phone and put it down a number of times. Then, I bit the bullet and called.

Upon hearing his voice, I started to cry on the park bench in the middle of the city.

"Anna, what's wrong? Please calm down. I can't hear what you are saying."

I took some shuddered breaths and recounted what happened, the best I could.

"Oh, Anna. Oh, I'm so sorry. I wish I were there with you. I shouldn't have left. I can try to call him."

"No, not yet. He's so angry, so hurt."

"Do you want to take a train and come here? I'd be happy to have you."

"Thank you, Trevor, but I think I need to stay around here, you know, just in case, in case Tom needs me. Besides, I need to work."

"Then, go and check into to a nice hotel. I'll take care of the bill. And don't fight me on this, I insist. I've told you my grandson can be rather sensitive, and he has a temper, as you've witnessed. Hang on. I've got the Internet up and I'll find you something right now that allows dogs. Sit tight, okay?"

I heard a bunch of clicking and after a few minutes, he explained, "Okay, I've got you checked in at the Langham on Reagent Street. It's less than half a mile from your flat and they allow dogs. I put in the reservation for tonight. I have an account there, so it's all settled."

"I don't have a change of clothes or dog food." I sniffed.

"Go buy a small bag of dog food, and you'll just have to live in the clothes you have on for the night. I'm going to speak with my grandson; this will all get worked out. He just needs a bit of time to calm down. This is, well, this is earth shattering news."

"I'm worried about his state of mind. What he's dealing with is immense!"

"I agree. Well, go and get yourself together for the night and we'll chat later. Listen, Anna, you are the best thing that's happened to Tom in all his life. He's not going to give you up; he's just upset for the moment."

I stifled another onset of sobs and thanked Trevor profusely.

I walked around to the shop that sold Mango's food and purchased a small bag and a bowl. I then went to the drug store and bought an oversized shirt to sleep in. It said "I Love London," but I was starting to wonder if I really did. I made my way over to Reagent's Street and looked up at the Langham. Oh, Trevor. It was a huge, beautiful hotel. Luxury was oozing out of its windows and onto the London pavement.

I approached the door with my bag and Mango in tow. The grand entrance revealed an even grander lobby, chock with grey and white marble columns and an extraordinary chandelier. I wondered how they changed the lightbulbs as I approached the main desk. Mango's nails clicked on the marble floor.

"Reservation for Anna Pearson? Um, Trevor Hall made the reservation?"

"Yes, Ms. Pearson. "Click, click, click. "Okay, here is your key card. Take the elevator to the fifth floor. I hope you enjoy your stay." The woman at the desk looked at me sympathetically. I guess my face told her enough.

I thanked the clerk and walked Mango to the elevator.

The room Trevor sprung for us was luxurious. The bed looked so inviting with its plush mattress and cozy comforter. Two purple lounge chairs sat under tall windows flanked by long cascading grey curtains. A vanity was positioned across from the bed, with a wooden desk that sat adjacent to the vanity. The room smelled like freshly cut flowers. I didn't deserve or want this luxury, I just wanted Tom.

I filled Mango's new stainless-steel water dish and placed it on the elegant bathroom floor. More marble, more luxury. I wondered how much this room cost.

As Mango lapped up his water, I took my travel bag and poured it out onto the taught white comforter. Toothbrush, toothpaste, contact lens solution, and... glasses. I picked up Tom's black framed, hipster reading glasses, turning them around in my hand. I was confused, until it dawned on me that I'd had them all along. I remembered now, the karaoke night, he left them on the table. A wave of dizziness overcame me and I thought I was going to pass out. I dropped the glasses on the bed and clutched the blanket in my fists. Oh my God. Maybe I did follow the wrong person. Maybe I caused Tom to cut himself.

***

Whimpering. Scratching.

"Mango, cut it out." It was dark outside and I was a little disoriented. I then heard a knock on the door.

I quickly bounced out of the bed and swung the door open. Tom.

He stood in the doorway, but didn't come in yet. So much pain was painted on his face. His eyes were red and swollen and the cut on his face looked angrier than before. His mouth settled in a slight frown and the crease between his eyebrows was cavernous. He looked like he'd been through hell and I supposed he had. I stepped back, allowing him to enter if he chose to. I wanted this to be his decision, not Trevor's.

Tom stepped through the door frame and quietly shut the door behind him. He leaned his back on the door, like a child in school might before facing the principal.

"Hi," he said.

"Hi," I returned.

Then it all poured out as he took one long stride and enveloped me.

"I'm so sorry, Anna. I cannot believe the way I spoke to you, the words that came out of my mouth. I should have been slapped. I just couldn't stop after the news. I needed to lash out and you were there."

We held each other for a while then sat on the bed. Mango cautiously approached Tom with his ears back, then wagged his tail once Tom pet him.

"What did you do while I was gone? Is the flat trashed?" I was also worried that he hurt himself, but I didn't ask.

"No, it's not. Em, April left soon after you, but upon parting told me that we need to delve further, that sometimes you have to get all the nastiness out before you can heal. And then? I screamed and cried and threw up, barely making it to the loo. And then Trevor called."

I nodded. "What did he say?"

"At first, he was sympathetic and told me it wasn't my fault, and then he gave me a rather stern tongue lashing about how I treated you. I needed to hear that; it helped me to finally come to my senses. He told me where you were. He certainly does know how to treat a woman and her dog." He smiled quickly, looking down at the ornately patterned rug.

"But, he also told me you had told him about Elizabeth during the visit. So, he knew too and didn't disclose the information. I don't agree with what either of you did, but I understand," he said, reflectively.

Turning toward me, he admitted, "Anna, there is something wrong with me. And I don't mean the blackouts. There is no excuse for the way I spoke to you."

"I forgive you, Tom. You remembered some pretty horrible times and it's going to take a while to come to terms with them." I touched his face. "I know you didn't mean what you said, and I probably should have told you what your father had told me right away, even if I did think it was all lies."

"God, Anna, how am I going to come to terms with what I did?"

"We will work through it, okay? I'm here, Trevor is here for you, and Jamie and Seamus, too."

He rubbed his eyes a bit and ran his fingers through his hair. "Well, what do you want to do? Trevor probably spent 450 pounds on the room, so you should use it. Do you want me to go? I'll understand."

"No, no, stay. Maybe we'll get a good night's sleep. And by the way, I found your reading glasses. They were in my travel bag the whole time."

Tom looked at me and said very quietly, "So, maybe it wasn't me that night."

CHAPTER 26

Life resumed, although often, when he thought I wasn't looking, Tom wore his pain in his expressions and mannerisms. Sometimes his eyelids would be clinched tight, sometimes he would stare at nothing in particular, and more often than not, I would see his face in his hands. He looked tired and haggard even after a seemingly good night's sleep. I was worried he was depressed. I wanted to help him, but didn't really know how. He stopped seeing his therapist altogether and avoided April's calls—which I felt was a mistake—probably because he was scared of what else might come out of the sessions. He had even put off Seamus a number of times.

It was Friday evening and Tom set off to work. I turned on the television about two hours after he left.

> *"This just in! The rash of brutal attacks on homosexuals continues. Yesterday, protesters lined the streets of Soho, snarling traffic to send their message to those who commit such heinous acts. However, their message was answered just now with another body. A man of about thirty was found allegedly murdered outside a bar frequented by homosexuals. His body was mangled from blunt force trauma on his arms and legs, and his throat was slit. If children are in the room, you may want to guide them out, for the next series of pictures are graphic."*

On screen flashed a picture of the victim's body. His entrails had been ripped out of him. How on earth could they show that on the news? Then, they flashed an older picture of the man. I almost fell of the sofa—it looked exactly like Tom! My head started to throb as I paused the remote. I ran to get my glasses and looked again. Okay, no, the man was thin with dark hair that fell in front of his face, but thank God! It wasn't Tom. But seeing such a brutal attack on someone that looked a lot like your significant other was rather disconcerting. The victim on the screen was not quite as attractive, but very similar, especially with blurry vision. I scrambled to the foyer, dug the cell phone out of my purse, and replayed the video from that awful night when I had followed Tom. The gait, the mannerisms, the behavior, wasn't Tom's. The glasses the victim wore looked very similar to Tom's reading glasses, the ones that I had had all along in my travel bag. I was much less positive it was Tom I had spied on. My mind started rationalizing and scrutinizing every detail of what I had seen that night—that I had convinced myself that something was up with Tom—that I was so determined to find something, to catch Tom in the act. My past relationships had caused this mistrust. I had thought so much about this until I thoroughly convinced myself that the murdered man was who I saw that night, not Tom. I felt so much relief, but then revulsion at what had happened to the poor man. And then the guilt set in. Had I trusted Tom and not followed him, he wouldn't have cut himself, wouldn't have ended up in the mental hospital, wouldn't have been strapped to a bed for four days. But, even so, I couldn't wait to tell him! My fault, all my fault, but at least this answers some questions. I decided to meet him at work. I kissed Mango and headed out, hailing a cab.

I arrived just when Tom was finishing up. I overheard his closing remarks. Still well-spoken with impeccable inflections, but not quite delivered like his usual self. Maybe this would cheer him up a bit.

He caught my eye and winked while answering an elderly man's question. When he said his goodbyes, he limped over to me and kissed my forehead.

"Anna, what a surprise. Is everything alright?"

"Yes, well, in a way." He gestured me to go with him to his shared office. As we walked in, I waved to Ms. Evans, who worked behind the visitor center desk, and then stepped into Tom's office.

"So," Tom asked, shutting the door, "what's up?"

"First, how's your knee? You weren't limping earlier."

"Em, probably too much walking. I think I aggravated it, but it's alright."

"Okay. Well, the reason I came is you know the night that we don't like to bring up, when I thought I saw you with another guy? Well, I'm not so sure it was you anymore."

Tom cocked his head, "Because of the glasses?"

"Well, that, but also, unfortunately, there was another attack on a homosexual last night, in the Docklands area. They showed a picture of him on the news. He looked a lot like you and even wore the same glasses. I mean, as far as I could tell from a distance and at night. I'm just so, so sorry for not trusting you."

Tom nodded his head. "Ah, well good. I really never believed it was me anyway, so I am not all that surprised."

"Aren't you a bit relieved?"

"Relieved?" He questioned the ceiling, then shook his head. "I still have no answers regarding my blackouts, and I am reminded of this every time I look in the mirror." He motioned to the line on his face from his eye down to his jaw. "And it seems I killed my sister. So, no, I wouldn't say I am relieved. But, thank you for trying," he said, not unkindly.

"But, Tom, I'm so sorry for doubting you so much and concocting these ridiculous stories. If I hadn't accused you that night—you wouldn't have wound up in the hospital."

He didn't respond. I slumped my shoulders, "I'm just trying to help. I thought at least this would be, although sideways, a good thing, an answer to one thing. I don't know what to do for you, Tom. I'm at a loss. You've been withdrawn and depressed; don't think I don't notice."

He nodded again. "I'm sorry, love. You're just going to have to give me some time."

"You need to call April back."

"No."

"No? That's it? She warned you that this was going to be painful, but you have to deal with your past!"

"Why? I was much happier without knowing all this..this *stuff!*" His hand flourished. "I cannot have another setback with you. I still haven't forgiven myself for the way I spoke to you. I threw you out of the flat—*our* flat. I didn't tell you this, but, but I almost struck you."

My eyes widened a bit. "But, you didn't. And I've forgiven you and I'll forgive you again if something else happens. But, by not calling April, by avoiding your past, you are just perpetuating the problem by not doing anything about it."

Tom chewed on his lower lip with a sideways glance.

"Em, Trevor called and talked to me earlier. He wants us to come up for a few days to go over wedding arrangements, but also talk to me. Would you grant me the time to do that first? After that, I promise I'll see April."

I agreed. I figured it was better than nothing at all. Besides, Trevor might be able to help. He seems to be able to relax Tom and get him to do what should be done.

CHAPTER 27

Tom fulfilled his promise and called April in the morning. He told her we were going away for a bit, but when we came back, he would see her. I think he was very embarrassed talking to her after what had happened. During the whole conversation, his head was down and his eyes were closed. She, however, was very excited to hear from Tom and told him she had a few ideas she would discuss with us when we returned.

Tom and I decided to do a little shopping this morning for some much needed fun and also to buy something for Trevor. We planned to rent a car and leave in the later afternoon for Scotland. I had already scheduled for time off this week to get on track with the wedding, so I was good to go. We were going to stay through Wednesday, come back Thursday and use Friday to meet with Theo.

So, after breakfast, we took a cab to Camden Town. That area is more my speed, not Tom or Trevor's, so I wondered why Tom had suggested it. Turns out, he found a store there that sells ethically sourced high-end clothes. He was actually kind of excited about taking me there and I was happy to see him smile.

Jamie had gone shopping with me here once, and I loved it. The street was filled with your typical souvenir vendors, but many of the stores had a very punk rock edge. Colorful buildings with three-dimensional artwork adorned many of the store fronts—large shoes, skulls, dragons, and even a huge glass window with tons of old sewing machines were featured. We weaved through the market, looking at used CDs, punk and rock band T-shirts, jewelry, and the food vendors. After stopping at Cookies and Scream to get a vegan chocolate chip cookie, Tom took me to the store he was really excited about. Turns out, it was a mecca for vegans, cool vegans. Lots of punk-type clothing and shoes decked the walls. The Dead Kennedys blasted over the sound system and used CDs lined bookshelves in the back of the store. This store proved to rival the punk stores in St. Marks in New York City I used to frequent during college; however, the prices here were a lot more outrageous. I didn't know what punk could afford this stuff. I picked up a T-shirt, putting it back right away as if it were on fire… it cost 50 pounds! I caught Tom walking toward me with a fake black leather jacket draped over his arm.

He presented the arm that held the jacket, bowed his head and said, "Madame."

I took the jacket and held it up. Emblazoned on the back was the cover of *Grave Disorder* by The Damned, one of my very favorite albums. A skeleton, a girl, a coffin all drawn in a cartoonish style, purple in color—that was the cover all right!

"OH MY GOD!" I squealed.

"I thought you might like this," he said with his arms crossed, leaning against a column in the middle of the store. "Try it on."

I took off my pea coat, handed it to Tom, and then slipped on the jacket. It was soft and sleek and uber-cool. I walked over to a full-length mirror and looked at my image from all sides. The cut accentuated my figure when closed up with the fasteners that were reminiscent of safety pins, but much thicker and less pointy. The "leather" was worn as if it had been used and abused, but there were no tears. Some metal studs rimmed the pockets and a small metal skull and crossbones was affixed to the left side, near the lapel. I was in love with this jacket. I caught Tom nodding his head in my direction. He looked so out of place in this store, wearing a light green button-down shirt, fitted charcoal blazer, dress pants, and expensive dress shoes.

"That was made for you. Why don't we purchase it?" he said.

"Oh, no. This jacket is 500 pounds! And besides, won't you be damaging your image, being seen walking around town with me in this jacket?"

"Mmmm… I've come to find your style of dress endearing." Ignoring my comment about the money, he pushed himself forward off the column and walked up to the clerk, while taking out his credit card.

"Tom, it's too expensive, and a bit overpriced," I whispered. But I wasn't very emphatic; I really wanted the jacket.

"At what other time are you going to find something like this? Besides, I know how disappointed you would be if we didn't buy it." He signed the credit card slip. "I'm sure you'll make it up to me, somehow." He winked.

After leaving the store, we took a cab back to Marylebone, the polar opposite of Camden Town. We made our way to a high-end liquor store where we bought Trevor some fine wine. I don't know my wines, but apparently, Tom chose a "magnificent" red. I couldn't stop rolling my eyes, listening to the conversation between Tom and the wine clerk. Oh, I mean the sommelier. The pretentiousness oozed onto the dark, hardwood floor. I felt really out of place, especially with my new jacket. Sometimes I feel like Tom is slumming it with me.

When we arrived home in the late afternoon, we packed, gathered Mango's items, and waited for the rental company to drop off our car in front of the flat. I felt we were spending money like water pouring through an open tap.

The three of us piled into the car and set out for Scotland. Tom seemed even more cheery at first. But when we were delayed trying to get out of London and onto the M6, Tom was far from patient. Plus, he had insisted on renting a stick shift, so he was constantly having to put pressure on his knee.

"Do you want me to drive?" I asked after about the fifth time I heard him gasp from the clutch.

"Really? Have you driven on this side of the road and with manual transmission?"

"No, but your knee…"

"Don't worry about my knee. It's fine," he said as he winced again when he had to push in the clutch. God, can he be stubborn. We eventually were able to pick up speed and Tom was able to get a bit more comfortable. As we drove, I happily blasted *Grave Disorder* as an homage to my new jacket. Tom listened patiently, even singing along to a couple of verses. By the time we hit A75, it was too dark to really take in a lot of the scenery, so I figured I would see more on the way back.

We arrived at Trevor's around 9:00 PM. Once again, he greeted us at the door with his charming smile. He held Tom tightly and then gave me a big hug as well. He had Anthony take our coats and lead us to the dining room where dinner was being served. Exquisite white china with a deep green rim featuring a Greek key pattern held even greener spinach leaves. Red tomatoes, purple onions, and avocados lay on top with some kind of vinaigrette that was swirled onto the salad. My mouth watered, as we hadn't stopped for food. Excusing myself, I went to the bathroom, splashed water on my face, and regarded myself in the mirror. I looked a little tired and older, the effects of the long drive and the last month wearing on me. I was glad to be here, however; glad Trevor could help me with Tom.

We had a delicious dinner, a polenta cake with a bean sauce and then a vegan cheesecake for dessert. Trevor informed us he was really liking the vegan food and started to eat a bit more like this recently. He said he felt sprier.

After dinner, Trevor took Tom into his study while I got ready for bed. Anthony took Mango for a walk, for which I was grateful. Brushing my teeth and hair, I heard a soft knock at the door. Anthony bid me good night and showed Mango into the room. I crawled into bed, waiting for Tom and Mango slinked up next to me. Trevor had whispered to me earlier that dogs on the furniture are a-okay with him.

***

"Bloody hell!" I heard, startled awake. I looked over and saw the back of Tom's head. Under the soft glow of the amber desk lamp, pages of some kind of book slammed closed with a 'thunk.'

"Everything alright over there? Way over there?" I asked, under the covers in the plushest bed I'd ever had the pleasure to sleep in.

Tom looked back at me over his shoulder and said with a slight edge, "Sorry, love, I didn't mean to wake you." He stood up, picked up the book and reopened it. He started to pace back and forth. He had a slight hitch in his stride, probably from using his bad knee too much on the clutch. He read a passage to me.

> *"I stalked, painstakingly, in the shadows, waiting for my time to pounce. Turning down an alleyway, I knew my opportunity had arrived. The wind uplifted her blond hair above her ear and as the strand fell back into place I swiftly grabbed her by the neck from behind her and slammed her against the wall. She tried to scream, but I stifled it by reaching around to her mouth and stuffing a rancid piece of garbage inside. I took pleasure in the gasps and cries as her head started to bleed from the impact of the brick wall. I had the urge to penetrate her, deep inside, but knew this was filth, so instead, I snapped her neck. The crack of her spine was more satisfying than any sexual climax. I let her fall to the pavement. I proceeded to…"*

"Why are you reading me this? Is this some sort of weird bedtime story?"

"I thought you'd be interested in my great-grandfather's journal."

I clutched the covers and sat upright, "Are you kidding? Trevor has his journal? Look, I don't want that book anywhere near me. It's echoing too much of what's going on back in London, and it's scary."

"Yes, echoing indeed. That's why I find it important to read."

"Well, you go ahead Tom, but don't get too obsessed with it, okay?"

"Obsessed?"

"Yes, obsessed. You tend to be like that about certain things."

He shrugged and sat back down at the desk.

***

Morning came. Tom was asleep, head down, cheek pressed to the desk. I turned off the lamp, noticing Tom's fingers stained with the brownish red color from the crumbling leather cover of the journal.

"Tom. Wake up."

He sat up, squinty-eyed, and looked around. He rubbed the back of his neck, trying to rid himself of the stiffness from the odd sleeping position.

"I guess I fell asleep reading."

"Mmm..hmmm. Learn anything about yourself?"

He looked back at me and grimaced a little. "I hope to God not. The man was a monster. It seems he wanted to carry on the work of Jack the Ripper. According to this journal he attacked over 30 prostitutes and five homosexuals. I knew he was brutal, even using old torture devices, but reading it firsthand is quite disconcerting, to say the least."

I took over rubbing his neck.

"Ah, that feels splendid," he whispered as he relaxed. "I'll tell you, however, being a descendant of that man—well, it's hard to wrestle with. I guess great-grandchildren of slave owners must feel much the same way."

"Yeah, but you can't feel guilty about it. It wasn't you and you are a completely different person." I worked my way to his shoulders.

"Yes, of course, logically that makes sense; however, feelings aren't always so logical." I stopped the massage and kissed his cheek.

"I'm hungry," I stated and headed out the bedroom door. Tom told me he'd be down soon and to eat without him.

I found Trevor at the table reading a newspaper. When he noticed me, he stood up, walked over and hugged me good morning, and offered me coffee. I sat down, warming my hands on the green mug.

"Sooo, Tom fell asleep at the desk, reading."

"Mmm, my father's journal, no doubt."

I nodded and made a disapproving expression.

"I thought it important he know his family's history a little more in depth. I want him to understand, so he can watch out… just to be cautious."

"Watch out for what?"

"I don't know. But, the more information he has, the better. And after what's transpired, well," his voice dropped, "Tom has a lot of rage pent up inside him and it comes out sometimes, as you've been witness to. He's got to come to terms with his past and if that means understanding our bloodline more, then so be it."

Trevor detected my uneasiness and rested a hand on mine, reassuring me that Tom is a good soul and just needs to sort out some issues. Just then, Tom walked in, looking quizzically at both Trevor and me, but didn't proceed to pry into our conversation. Tom held the journal in his left hand. After asking Tom for the book, he handed it to me and went to get some tea.

The very old leather-bound book had a faded cover that flaked onto the table. I opened it up and flipped through frail pages filled with beautiful cursive strokes in India black ink. If I hadn't known the contents, I would have thought it was an amazing piece of literature or poetry. But it was far, far from that. I scanned through the book seeing words pop out like "blood" and "disembowel" and "strangled." And then I saw an attack that caught my attention. I silently read the passage, eyes wide the whole time:

> *She was beautiful. She approached me while I sat at the pub, brushing her lovely fingers across my neck, taking a seat next to me. I offered to buy her a drink, of course she accepted. As I watched her sip her wine, I stared at her cleavage. Her breasts were practically falling out of her provocative dress. She purred her name to me… Candy. It's a shame so many pretty ones are whores. After drinks, I followed her outside. She walked in front of me, glancing back to be sure I was following. We went into the alleyway, where she whispered her modest fee. I placed my hands on each side of her young face, leaning in to kiss her lips. Then, I clamped down on her lower lip. I sunk my teeth hard into her flesh and tore, the blood pleasantly matching her red lipstick. She screamed out in pain and shock, but I was relentless. I snapped her neck and watched her ooze to the ground. After wiping the blood from my face with the back of my hand, I disappeared into the shadows.*

Tom walked back in and sat down with some tea in hand. Speechless, I shoved the book over to him and pecked my index finger at the passage I had just read.

"My God," he breathed after he read the paragraph.

"What's wrong," Trevor asked, concerned.

"Em, a couple months ago, there was a woman at my tour, an escort. She was murdered soon after and found in the same way as this woman in the journal was found; lower lip ripped off and her head snapped," Tom recounted warily.

"I guess it could be a coincidence?" Trevor reasoned.

"Perhaps," I said, doubtfully. "Is there another copy of this journal?"

"Not that I know of. I believe I am the only one who knows about it, except for now you two. I am sure this is a coincidence—a very uncanny coincidence, but what else could it be?"

I hugged myself, trying to keep my shuddering at bay. "Were any of the other murders in that book the same as the murders happening now?"

"I only read about half of the journal and didn't really think much about making a connection. When I read more, maybe I'll cross reference with the news reports and see. Unless we just want to leave this alone, but if it helps in a police investigation and could potentially save someone's life, perhaps I should read on."

"You know, Tom, I think maybe it was a mistake to give you the journal right now. You are supposed to be going over your wedding details, not solving murders." Trevor took the book from Tom's hands. A small argument ensued, but Trevor had the upper hand. Tom's expression reminded me of a child whose television privileges were taken away from him. Trevor noticed this and shot Tom a glance that clearly said to leave it alone. Tom's shoulders slumped a bit, but he didn't have a retort. I found the family dynamic rather comical.

So, the wedding plans went on. We decided to have the ceremony outside, in the back, overlooking the hills. If it rained, the covered veranda, also on the back of the house, could suffice for the ceremony and everyone could watch from inside. There were glass doors that opened all the way out, so the guests would still be very much a part of the wedding. We talked about the flowers, at least the color, which would be orange with black bows. The bridesmaid dresses were to be plain black with an orange sash. And the tuxedos would be black with a white shirt and have an orange flower for the lapel.

I really didn't want any meat. That would be so hypocritical of me, plus it would make me feel incredibly uncomfortable. Fortunately, neither Tom nor Trevor protested. In fact, Trevor said he had already looked into a caterer who specialized in vegan fare. Then, we got on the topic of the guest list. We were going to have to send some kind of save the date for those traveling from far away. So, we decided on Saturday, May 23rd. Then, Tom's father—Trevor's son—came up.

"Why do we have to invite him?"

"Because he's my father, Anna."

"No, Tom, *Trevor* is your true father."

Tom closed his eyes and sighed. "As much as a terrible father he was, I was wrong about Elizabeth, about how she died. He didn't do it… and… and I've blamed him for it after all these years."

"Christ, Tom! Listen to yourself! He caused the scene for it to happen. He stepped out of the way. He severely abused you that night. He's lied to me to get us to break up. He's…"

"Anna," Trevor broke in, resting his hand on my knee. "As much as I agree with you and really don't want him here either, it truly is Tom's decision, okay?" His steely blue eyes glamoured me into compliance. Damn these Halls.

"Alright, so we've gotten a lot accomplished. I'll email these notes to Theo so he can start finding florists, getting the save the date items, et cetera. Okay?" Tom stood up and asked his grandfather for the book back.

Trevor hesitated, but directed Tom to where he could find it. Tom saluted us both, turned and strode into another room to read. I'm not sure I liked his fascination.

"What good can come of him reading that?"

"I thought it might help him cope with what he's going through. To see why his father became what he became. And to show him how he's not like them. He's been beating himself up; I want him to realize the person he really is. I don't know if it will work, but even if it doesn't, I think he needs the truth."

I pursed my mouth and stared out the window.

***

A few hours later, Tom came out of the study, rubbing his eyes. After taking a seat next to me on the sofa, he slouched, then gently laid his head on my shoulder.

"Did you finish it?"

I felt a nod.

"And?"

"My great-grandfather was a sadist and a murderer. What more is there to tell?"

"Do you want me to read it?"

"No, I do not."

"Okay. Well, are you going to be able to get past this?"

"I suppose I'll have to." He slinked down the sofa more until he was lying down with his head on my lap. I stroked his hair, remaining quiet. Despite his determination to be pretentious and uber-mature, this frightened little boy sometimes emerges.

***

"…and I don't know what to do. I love her more than anything. But, I'm afraid I'm going to hurt her. I already have, with words at least. What if that night, that night I blacked out and cut myself, what if I had cut her instead? I don't have control, I don't know what I'm doing. And after reading this journal, why did some of it seem so familiar, so Goddamn familiar?"

"It only seems familiar because he was your blood relative and you've heard some of the stories before. Hell, you tell them at your ghost tours. I'm sure that good for nothing son of mine fed you some of these tales."

"Maybe. But, she doesn't deserve to live with all my baggage. She deserves someone who's not mental. Coming here was a mistake—to plan a wedding that shouldn't happen. I've been pretending, telling myself that all will get better, but it's only gotten worse. I swore to myself long ago that I would never get involved with someone, and I broke that rule—and worse, I fell in love."

"You have every right to love and have someone love you back. Anna is a strong person and knows what she's up against. She can handle this. Prior to her, you had what, one or two dates, one or two acquaintances? That's not a life. You were living like a bloody hermit."

"You're not listening, Trevor. I am terrified I'm going to harm her. I could not live with myself if I was the cause."

"So, what, you're going to call it off, break up with her?"

I could hear Tom's quiet sobs barely over mine. I sat down on the steps right outside the living room, shielded by the stairwell wall, and covered my face with my hands, holding on, trying not to cry out. My whole world started to dry out and crumble. Keep it together, Anna, keep it together. And then, a footstep.

I slowly raised my head, locking my eyes on Tom's. He knew I had heard it. The same look of shear panic and horror I've seen before overtook his face. He couldn't speak, couldn't form the words he was desperately trying to say. His eloquent speech, his baritone voice, his vernacular, were all gone. I needed to hear something, anything from him, but he just stared at me.

So, I took the reins. I could have let this happen, just left. It would have been easy to just walk out. But instead, I stood up on the steps, even in height now, and wrapped my arms around him. Nothing was said and nothing was going to be said; everything had already been said, over and over again, ad nauseum. But, he knew. He knew I wasn't going anywhere, that breaking up was not an option. He knew I could and would be his rock, that I was up to it. I've had plenty of practice. And I knew he wasn't like the others. He was good—I knew he was—that I could feel. I trusted my instincts, my psychic ability that I supposedly had, which all led me to know this. No more second guessing and theorizing. He needed help and he was going to get that help no matter how dangerous or how sad.

CHAPTER 28

"You ready, babe?"

"I am. I just need my coat."

I took a burgundy knit winter hat and pulled it down over Tom's head, covering his ears. I grabbed the lapels of his coat and kissed him. "Okay, let's go."

After taking the fifteen-minute cab ride to April's office, we bought some tea at the Pret a Manger right outside her building and then took the elevator up. April's receptionist asked us to have a seat at the window. I looked over at Tom, who was mindlessly leafing through some fan magazine.

Since Scotland, our relationship had shifted slightly. Tom had been a little less uptight, a little less on me about cleaning, a little less pretentious. He didn't complain when I cussed anymore or said "stuff" or even played my music too loudly. I think he was so freaked out by the conversation I overheard, that he became more delicate around me. It's as if he doesn't want anything to break, or that's the only way I can think to describe it. He knows I'm with him, no matter what we discover, but I think that's what scares him; I'm willing to stay with him, even if I get hurt.

April came out of the room, beaming at us, clapping her hands once. She took me in her arms and then Tom.

"I'm so sorry I couldn't see you sooner. I was working on a case in the US and couldn't get back here."

"Please, April. It's my fault for not calling you, em, avoiding you, I'll admit. I'm just… I'm terrified."

April nodded sympathetically and laced her arm through Tom's, guiding him into her office. I followed.

"Do you have the journal?" April asked. We had told her about it when we made the appointment.

"No, it's back at the flat," I said.

"Well, no matter, I will look at it later. We certainly have a lot of material to work through. Why don't we start with the night your mother died. I want to delve right in." Tom nodded, taking his place on the chaise lounge while I sat quietly at the desk, letting April work her magic.

Again, the windows were darkened by a shade of black, the rain started lightly gracing the room with a soft persistence, and Tom relaxed into the plush velvet. It was as if no time had passed at all.

April guided him to that night.

"Okay Tom, we're back, way back. You are about four years old. You are in your house, the house you grew up in. It's the same night your mother passed on. Tell me what happened. Reach back, far into that closet of truth and pull out the memory."

> *"I'm in my room, playing with Legos. There are racecars on my walls... red racecars... em, the wallpaper. The hardwood floor is partially covered with a brightly colored rug with many smiley faces. I seem to be creating some kind of robot out of the Legos scattered all over the rug. I want Elizabeth to play with me, but she says she is too old for Legos, but that she will inspect what I built when I am done.*
>
> *"Red, blue, yellow pieces I carefully snap together, revealing more smiley faces on the rug."*

Tom paused, sniffed and then continued.

> *"Then the shouting began. I was used to this by now, so I concentrated on the pieces, meticulously stacking them one at a time, drowning out the voices."*

Tom's hands started to pantomime the actions of snapping and building Legos.

> *"Em, the shouting grew louder until I heard a scream. I abandoned my creation and ran down the steps, stopping on the last. My father and mother. Thomas was on top of her... her skirt was lifted and his hands were around her neck. My feet were cemented into concrete and my throat closed up on me. Thomas noticed me, looked up and smiled—that sinister sneer.*
>
> *"Elizabeth came running down the stairs, almost knocking me over. She lunged at my father, clawed at his face. Thomas, struck with a back hand that sent her flying across the room. But, he at least got off Mum. Elizabeth ran out the door and my father followed while my mum lay crying on the ground, her skirt still up. Her blouse was ripped and I caught a glimpse of her breast. I didn't know it at the time, what it was, but I knew I wasn't supposed to see it. I finally found my*

legs and walked into the kitchen, opened the cabinet door and hid under the sink. It was dark in there, closed in, I don't like it at all. I feel, I feel claustrophobic."

He squeezed his eyes tighter.

"I heard my mother calling my name in a raspy voice. She was sobbing and gasping, but calling me. 'Tommy, where are you?' she kept croaking out. I was terrified. I didn't want to see her tattered clothes, or what was beneath them. Her voice frightened me. And I knew, I knew a husband wasn't supposed to do that to a wife, even though I couldn't understand it, I knew, but I stayed put.

"Eventually, I heard the door to the garage open and close. The exact same squeak, every time that door opened and closed, like a high C note. I stayed in the darkness until I couldn't bear it anymore. I must have been in there for a while because my eyes hurt when I stepped into the light of the kitchen. The house was silent. No Elizabeth, no Thomas, no Mum. I looked for her, opening the door to the garage, I saw her sitting in the car. I got a little excited, glad to not be alone. She looked to be asleep. I walked over to the car door and opened it."

Tom breathed out, sharply, pushing further into the pillow his head laid upon. His face contorted and he started to tremble. "Oh God," he breathed.

April placed her hand on Tom's that was covering his chest and grasped tightly, reminding him that he is safe and that this is just a memory. She prodded him, but gently, until he continued. His voice was a little hoarser when he started to speak again, as if the sharpness of the memory scratched at his throat.

"Her eyes were open, but they didn't blink. Her lips were parted ever so slightly, her expression was… peaceful, like a heavy load had been lifted from her. But then, I saw… I thought I saw red paint. Yes, em, she spilled a whole can of it on her stomach. I asked her about it, taking her hand. Her wrists were mottled with different hues of red… bright, dark and almost black. I shook her hand, making her whole arm shake as I called to her, asking her why she spilled red paint all over herself. I couldn't understand why she would do that. But then, her head lolled to the side and she slumped to the right and oozed down and halfway out of the car. I stepped back, away, and sat on the garage floor against the wall."

Tom's voice cracked as he started to gasp for air. I started to get up, but April forcibly gestured for me to stay put.

"Tom, dear, at the count of one, you are going to wake up, calm and safe; five, four, three, two, one.

Tom's eyes popped open. Slowly, he turned his head toward me, took one look, closed his eyes and as if in slow motion, drew his knees up, and draped his arms over his face.

I stood up from my chair and gingerly approached. Placing my hand on his arm, I tried to be as soothing and reassuring as possible, but he waved me away. April beckoned me to follow her out the door, telling Tom we were going to give him some privacy. We walked past the receptionist and into the pantry.

"My God April! What the hell!?"

"That poor young man in there. He has so many demons we need to expel, and all in the form of memory. He has repressed so much."

I stood there with my arms crossed, asking April, "Well, is this doing him good? Will this help with all the aberrant behavior? The blackouts?"

"I think it's all connected, but there is more. I'm certain there's more, and I think it has to do with his sister."

"What do you mean?"

"I don't know yet. And I know I'm letting you down, but, he's been so hard to get a read on. His memories are so jumbled, it's hard for me to tell what's going on. But these exercises, these memories are the truth."

April put the automatic kettle on and started making tea. "We'll get this sorted out, okay? Let's bring him some tea and we'll talk about this."

"How much more can he take?"

"That's why you're here."

I held a saucer and cup in each hand and walked toward the room. April opened the door but Tom was not on the sofa, nor in the room. I put the teacups down and quickly went to the receptionist, asking if she saw him leave.

"Em, yes, Ms. Pearson. He said he had to take care of something and said for you not to worry."

"Fuck!"

April asked me where I thought he would go. I got my coat and explained he would probably be going to see his father.

"I'll call you, April, okay? This is going to throw him over the edge." I ran out the door with my purse and cell phone in hand. I dialed Tom's number as I got in the elevator, but my cell lost the signal. Once I hit the lobby, I dialed the number again. No answer, of course. While in the cab and fretting, I braced myself, but called Thomas.

"ello?"

"Thomas."

"Oh, 'ello, Anna."

"Tom might be on the way over there, right now. Do not let him in the door. In fact, he has a key, so put a chair or something in front of the front door."

"Why the 'ell would I do that?"

"Because I am afraid he's going to hurt you really badly. And, I don't want him living with the guilt."

Pause.

"He knows, Thomas, he knows how Eloise died, how he found her, how you fucking raped her. I'm following him to your house."

"Tom's old room, on the dresser." Another pause, then a click. What the hell did that mean?

The cab ride seemed to be the longest I'd ever taken. We made good time, but it felt like forever. When I got there, I paid the driver, then ran up the steps and in through the open door. I looked to my right, into the living room. No one, just Thomas's oxygen tank. I looked into the kitchen and then opened the door to the garage. Tom was there, sitting on the garage floor, staring into the empty space where the car should have been. Sensing my presence, but not looking at me, he spoke.

"He's not here."

"I'm sorry, hon, but I called him. I told him not to let you in. I guess he took off instead."

Tom rubbed his face forcibly, "And why would you tell him that?"

"Because I was afraid of what you might do to him. I mean, you took off without telling us."

"I was only going to confront him with this little tidbit of my past."

"Really, Tom?" I asked as I slumped down right next to him.

No response.

"You know, I want to hurt him all the time, so it only makes sense if you wanted to. But you, I am afraid, would inflict some serious damage. I don't want my fiancé in jail. Let's go, okay? You can confront him when you're calmer."

He closed and opened his eyes slowly, stood up, and offered his hand to me.

"Can you call another cab? I have to run to the bathroom," I said as I went back through the kitchen and into the downstairs bathroom. After peeing, I washed my hands and face, assessing myself in the mirror. I started to see worry lines around my mouth. Crap. When I came out of the bathroom and back into the kitchen, I decided to go into Tom's old room, Thomas's comment needling at me. So, I ran up the steps, the steps where Elizabeth fell to her death. I reached the top, the top where Tom accidently pushed her, causing a mess for the rest of his life.

I walked into a room and took in Tom's childhood. The walls had peeling, faded racecar wallpaper. A twin bed sat near the window, stripped of linens. A small, wooden dresser sat to the left with one framed picture. I assumed it was Eloise and Elizabeth. Their arms were around each other, looking happy. Eloise looked very familiar. She wore heavy eye liner which contrasted with her beautiful eyes. Elizabeth wore a baseball cap that said "England Rugby" and glasses. Next to the picture, a manuscript of some sort perched on the dresser. Pages were stitch bound together… pages and pages of eloquent handwriting.

I swallowed hard as I leafed through the pages.

"Anna, are you upstairs? Is everything all right?" I heard footsteps getting closer and closer, echoing in the stairwell until they stopped at the doorway.

"Anna, what's the matter? You look like you've seen a ghost?"

I tentatively handed the manuscript over to him. He opened up to the first page and started to read; his eyes widened. He looked up at me and then down at the book. "What the hell?!"

"I thought Trevor said he had the only copy," I whispered.

"Obviously, he was mistaken. What do you think this means?"

I grabbed the book back from Tom's hands. Red pen marks with dates and Tom's name flashed by as I quickly flipped through more of the pages. I looked up at Tom and backed up.

"What is it?"

I found my voice, albeit shaky, "Is this your book? Is that why things look familiar?!" Crying now, "Tom, please tell me this can't be right. Please!"

Tom just looked at me.

I forcibly turned the pages until I found the passage that echoed Kitty's death. Tom's name was underlined in red followed by three exclamations points. The date, printed in big bold numbers, seemed to be the same date as her death. My head whirling, I started to sweat. Jack the Ripper II? Phineas Hall's great-grandson repeating history? Blackouts? Unexplained wounds? With a trembling hand, I tentatively handed the book back to Tom, open to the passage.

"No," he whispered.

I continued backing up, out of the room, not wanting to take my eyes off him. I didn't know what to do. I was in hell and didn't know how to climb out. Do I call the police? Do I call Trevor? Do I just leave?

Instead, I took a deep breath.

Tom melted down to the floor with the book in his hand. The look on his face pulled on my heart. It wrenched it out and squeezed until it popped. So, I took another deep breath. Instead of continuing to jump to conclusions, I paused and began to think. I thought about what happened on those steps in Trevor's house and my resolve.

I took a step towards Tom as we heard the cab beep its horn.

"Alright Tom, let's get out of this house. Take the book, okay? We'll make sense of it. We'll figure this out, okay?"

He didn't budge. The cab blared its horn once more.

"Tom, Mango has been alone for a long time, we've got to let him out, okay? Look, I'm not going anywhere, but we've got to figure this out. Now, please, get up off the floor. I don't want Thomas coming back while we're here. I'm scared, Tom, please."

He took a breath and stood up. I took his hand, walking down the steps and out the door and into the cab.

On the way back, I called April and asked her to meet us at our flat, that I had some important news, not wanting to disclose anything to the cab driver. The ride was uncomfortable to say the least. Both Tom and I withdrew into ourselves, imaginations—at least mine—running amok.

When we got back to the flat, April was waiting for us outside. Her face was like a darkened cloud. We all rode up the elevator in silence and walked into the flat. I told them I would take Mango out and that Tom could tell her what had happened. I really didn't want to hear it again. Mango nearly pulled me out the door and ran down the steps, me tripping behind. Upon leaving the building he made a bee line for a tree and peed a good long time. He wagged his tail when he was done and pulled me a little more down the street to go to his favorite grassy patch to finish his bathroom ritual. My head was spinning. What does all this mean? Am I cohabitating with a serial killer? A liar? A schizophrenic? Jekyll and Hyde? The thing is, I don't think he knows what he does. I don't think he is lying, but the rest of it? What's the explanation? My heart started to beat faster. I realized all my hopes lay in April, so I was anxious to get back. But first, I had to confront Thomas, so I found a bench, pulled out my cell phone, and called. He picked up on the first ring.

"You're lucky you were gone."

"I just went around the block and waited. Now tell me what the 'ell is going on. You accused me of raping my wife? Where on earth did you dream that up?"

"He remembered, Thomas. A lot of memories are coming back to him now. Things that you did to him and Elizabeth and your wife."

"He's remembering wrong."

"And I went to his room, following your cryptic message and found the journal, Phineas's journal."

Pause.

"Why do you have it, Thomas?"

"I came across it when I was going through some of Tom's books that he left here. It's his. I gave it to him when he started being a ghost tour guide. He used it at first to do some research for his presentations and left it here when he was done with it."

"And why are there notes and dates with his name on it?"

"Anna, do you really want to know? You aren't usually so amenable to my truths."

"Please, indulge me." I spat.

"Okay, girl, you asked for it. I want you, when you are away from Tom, to look at the dates on the pages I've marked and look at the crime committed and look on the Internet and compare. There is a person out there who is committing the same crimes, murdering the same type of people in the same way as in that journal. Now, you do the math. There are only three people, besides you now, who know about this book; me, Tom and Trevor. So, of the three, who would be able to carry out these crimes? My father lives in Scotland and is and old man. I am completely out of shape and am dying of emphysema."

I tried to retort. "But, Trevor gave Tom the book in Scotland. He gave him the original and Tom had never seen it or read it. He read it while he was there and was really upset about it! He... hadn't seen it before, I could tell."

Thomas barked out a laugh. "If I've told you once, missy, your fiancé is a professional storyteller. He's an actor. I'd give him a BAFTA for his performance with you." I hung up on him, screaming out in anguish. Mango looked at me quizzically and a passerby asked if I was okay.

I just sat on the bench, letting thoughts ebb and flow through my brain. I wanted to run. Take my dog and get the hell out of London. Go back home and get out of this mess. But, of course, I couldn't. My resolve was too strong, so I eventually went back to the flat.

Upon entering, I saw Tom sitting on the sofa next to April. The book was in her lap and she had a tight grasp on Tom's hands. Tom, like the first time, was bracing himself from April's claws gouging into his wrists. She was rocking back and forth, mumbling something. Unintelligible. Sinister. Whispered. Tom looked up at me, pleading with his eyes for help, but I really didn't know what to do.

Finally, April let go and pulled back. She had fear in her eyes and was looking intently at Tom with distrust, but then in a flash, it went away.

"What did you see?" Tom asked.

April shook her head and held up one finger. "Water, please," she croaked as I went to get her some.

"Anna, please sit down." I sat across from them on the chair as April started.

"Tom, there is something inside of you. Something, em, something sinister to be blunt. But, something is just not quite right. I'm having a difficult time sorting it out and I don't want to give you wrong information. The best I can put it is there is a presence. A presence somehow in you. It's not quite possession. But, my guess is, when you cut yourself, when you have those blackouts, that's when this, em, presence, takes over."

"I don't even know how to process this. What is it?"

"I don't know what it is, Tom, but I'll certainly try to help. It's no wonder the psychiatric hospital thought you could have a split personality. I believe sometimes, they misdiagnose the psychosis with true possessions."

"Possession? Like a demon?" I asked in a really high voice, unbelieving.

"No, not like a demon, I don't think so."

"Could it be Phineas?"

Tom shot me a look, a terrified look.

"Look, I just had a conversation with your father." I recounted what Thomas had told me.

Tom looked taken aback, but gathered himself and tried to reason with me.

"Yes, although some of the stories seem familiar, I guarantee I've never seen that book in my life, until Trevor gave it to me. Why would I lie about that? If I had seen it before to do research for my tour, why wouldn't I tell you that? My God, Anna, again, are you going to believe my father over me? He gives you half-truths to manipulate you. He wants you out of the picture!"

"Tom, I'm trying! I just don't know what to fucking believe anymore!"

"I don't blame you, Anna. You don't deserve this." And then I started to cry. I felt this foreboding pull that this was the beginning of the end. What Tom said in Scotland, 'planning a wedding that should never happen,' replayed in my head. I tried to shut it out; cover my ears tightly with my hands, but I couldn't drown out the sound.

"Anna, dear, we're going to work this out. Tom is a good person," April assured me, "no matter what is being insinuated in that book."

"Oh yeah, April? How can you be so sure? How can you be one hundred percent positive that this isn't all just one big hoax? Or that maybe he is psycho?" Tom looked away from me and closed his eyes tightly. I regretted what I said, instantly, but my resolve was shattering.

And then her calming tone shifted dramatically, putting me in my place. "Because, girl, I've been doing this for forty years and I am always right. There are times when I have to sort things out, but when I do, *I am always right*. I am one hundred percent sure there is another explanation here. Something, some entity, is in Tom. I can feel it. And I'm going to get to it."

Tom and I both stared at April in bewilderment. She continued.

"I'm going to channel whatever is in him."

"Channel?" Tom asked.

"Yes, I am going to try and pull whatever is in you, into me. Then we will know for sure who it is and you'll be able to talk directly to the person. Em, if we could move the chair closer, across from me, Tom can sit there."

"Pardon?" asked Tom in disbelief.

"The chair. I want to be in closer proximity to you, but across from you."

"No, not that," Tom said as he watched me vacate the chair, lift it, and place it closer to April.

"Yes, of course… I am going to channel that presence. I will be in a highly meditative state which will allow the spirit to enter my body, much as it does to you, I presume. The difference here is I will be fully aware and will be able to kick it out, if you will, if it gets too intense or I don't want it in there. You see, my terms, not the entity. That's what you will learn to do, Tom. Now, you will see my mannerisms change, my voice may slightly change, if this presence had any kind of dialect, that may come out, too. Understood?"

Tom was chewing on his nails.

April noticed and gently touched his hand, pulling it away from his mouth.

"It's okay, love. I promise, this will be safe. Now, let's go over what you need to say and ask. Okay, really, I want you to ask it what you want to ask. Why is it doing this? Then, I want you to be firm with this spirit. Tell it this isn't fair to you, that this is your body, not this spirit's to possess and handle. And, finally, you tell it you aren't going to allow it anymore."

"But, how?"

"Knowledge is power, love. We'll get you through it. But, let's get all the information first, then we'll have a plan. It needs to know that you will not stand for this anymore and you are aware. That's the first step, understand?"

"No, not really. This sounds so, em.."

"Absurd?" April finished.

"Well, yes, to put it bluntly," Tom said.

April leaned in again. "More absurd than having a spirit creating chaos for your life? This is your life, Tom. This spirit has already had one."

Tom stared at her for a second, then dropped his gaze to his lap and nodded. He looked up at me. I nodded, remaining silent.

"Alright, let's get on with it, shall we? Anna, please dim the lights. If you could turn on the rain, but please don't talk, I'm going to need some quiet to allow me to focus."

We sat and basically watched April for a while. She took long, deep breaths and rocked back and forth occasionally. Time passed, Tom closing his eyes, listening to the rain sounds. Finally, April opened her eyes. Her demeanor seemed somehow different, yet familiar. Her face contorted a bit and she slouched a little in her seat. A much more casual, less proper attitude seemed to take over.

"Anyone have a smoke," she said in a slightly different drawl, her accent not quite as formal as moments ago.

Startled, Tom opened his eyes wide. He looked at me, then back to her. Mango, lying down next to the chair, popped his head up, ears on full alert and emitted a low, guttural growl.

"April?" Tom asked, his voice quivering.

"No..ooo… guess again, Tom."

"Phineas?" Tom whispered.

"No, Tom, not even close. This is kind of fun. First, the Ouija Board and now this. Oh, God, are you going to cry again? You always were such a fucking crybaby." April rolled her eyes. The words, the accent, the crassness that came out of April's mouth were just uncanny. Just so wrong.

Tom's eyes had been welling up, but he quickly wiped any tears away.

"Elizabeth," he quivered.

"No shit, Sherlock."

"Elizabeth, oh my God. I've missed you so much."

"Oh, that's so sweet," she said, sarcastically.

"Have you been using me?"

"Oh yes! You are my puppet, and have been for a long time. And you want to know why? Because, dear brother, you deserve it. You deserve every fucking tragedy that comes to you and will come to you. I look at what you have little brother. You have Trevor's money, you have happiness, and you have a LIFE!" She bellowed, through gritted teeth, her eyes wild. Tom winced from her words.

"I..I..I'm sorry father did what he did to us, but I never harbored any hatred t-toward you. What I did to you, I was trying to save you. I just, I… he… he stepped aside." Tom stammered, visibly scared out of his mind. I just stared in morbid awe.

"Yeah, well, I-I-I g-g-guess." she mimicked. "But, what about before, Tom? All those years before? I used to always protect you. But, what ABOUT ME? I loved you, Tom. I loved you so much until you showed your true colors. I protected you from our dear father and what did you do in return, you fucking coward? You stood there and WATCHED!"

"I'm sorry, Elizabeth, I wanted to help you. I always wanted to, but I was so scared of him, I-I." He shook his head to try to compose himself. "I want you to stop using me. I want you to stop cutting me."

April's eyes darkened and a small sinister smirk crept up her cheeks. She stared directly into Tom's eyes.

"I never cut you, dear Tom. That's all you. All your guilt. You may not remember doing it, but you do. It's all you, well except for once." She reached out with her index finger and in an angry caress, traced the red line starting from the corner of Tom's eye down to his jaw line. She paused, firmly slapped his cheek twice, and whispered, "I hope this hurt like hell."

And then, April's body flung backwards as if the wind punched her. Her neck whiplashed violently, the back of her head hitting the back of the chair. She looked up at Tom, her eyes changing from their hardness back to the kind, all-knowing eyes of April. I knew Elizabeth had left, or April had kicked her out.

April took a huge breath in, and sweat started to bead on her forehead. She reached for the water and drank it down, her hands trembling.

Tom sat, shocked at what he had just experienced, digging his long fingers into his thighs.

"Tom, dear Tom," April said as she took ahold of his hands, which were shaking heavily. He didn't speak. What could he say? He pulled his hands from April's, stood up and walked down the hall, closing the bedroom door softly behind him.

I looked at April, blurred by my own tears. I couldn't process what had just transpired.

"What's it mean, April?"

"Elizabeth is a powerful force. Her feelings of hatred and revenge burn through her, and I am afraid she's gotten ahold of Tom."

"But how? Can't he stop her?"

"I believe with more work, he'll be able to stop her, but I don't know how, yet. She's not there all the time, but for some reason, Tom allows her in."

"So what do we do? And to what extent has she been using him?"

"I don't know yet. I'll come back here tomorrow. I can't come until the evening, but we'll work more and we will fix this. I promise." She stood up, a little wobbly, and walked to the door. As she was putting on her coat she said, "Keep him from falling apart, okay? You're the only one who can."

"But, what if she gets to him tonight?"

"I don't think she will. Now that Tom knows, I think she's going to be a lot more careful. Through all her bravado, I felt some panic as well."

I didn't feel all that reassured, but what could I do. Not wanting her to go, I asked, "Are you okay? Why don't you stay for a little while and regain your strength?"

"Oh, dear child, I'm fine. The best thing for me is a long walk and fresh air." She hugged me goodbye and left.

I sat back on the sofa to catch my breath before checking on Tom. Mango rested his chin on my lap. Tom was in the bedroom. The hall light flickered. The CD player stopped. All that was true, all that was real. I wanted to wake up from this surreal, tragic nightmare.

I walked sluggishly down the hall with Mango in tow and opened the door. Tom sat on top of the duvet with his back to the headboard and his arms hugging his drawn up knees. His head was down, hair falling forward.

I crawled onto the bed and touched his hands. He looked up at me, trying to keep it all together.

"That was…" I started.

"Insane?"

I bobbed my head up and down, fiercely. "Do you know what Elizabeth was talking about?"

He nodded his head, barely.

"You can tell me."

He sucked in a ragged breath, letting it out slowly.

"This… this memory. I locked this memory away for so long, I almost believed it didn't happen. Some memories are like that, right? The further you get from them, the easier it is to convince yourself it didn't happen. But, she yanked it out of me."

"What happened? It's okay."

He looked into my eyes and shook his head, "It's far from okay." And then he started to tell me.

"I was young, maybe seven, maybe younger. I was lying in bed hugging my paisley bear, trying to drown out the noises. There were always noises in my head. Screaming, shrill screams when the room was quiet and night had fallen. The noises were just my imagination or so I thought. But not this night; I knew these were real. I heard muffled sounds, and then a loud scream, and then muffled sounds again. I got up, holding the bear by its hand, letting it dangle to the floor. Slowly, I walked down the hall to Elizabeth's room. Through the door, I heard the low guttural voice of my father mixed in with sobs from my sister. I cautiously opened the door. My father turned his head toward me, stared and smiled. He… he was on top of Elizabeth. Her shirt was off, torn off. My mind flashed back to my mother, the night of her death. I knew, just like I knew then, what my father was doing was wrong. One hand was covering her mouth, holding back her screams. But then, she must have bitten it because he abruptly took it away long enough for her to turn her head toward me and beg me to help. But, I just stood there, turned to stone, unable to move. I just… watched."

"Oh, Tom. I am so sorry, for you, for Elizabeth. Your father should be in jail. But, Tom, honey, you were a child. A little kid! What the hell were you supposed to do?"

"Call the police? Throw something hard at him? More than just stand there. But, Anna, there is more. She's made me question so much."

"What is it?" My voice caught in my throat.

He stood up and unbuttoned his shirt, revealing old and new scars. He removed his arms from his sleeves and laid his shirt gently on the bed.

"These scars, not the ones on my back, not the burns or the whip marks, but these thin straight ones. I think I did it to myself."

"I know. You went to the hospital for that, remember?"

He rolled his eyes, "Of course I remember. But, looking back, I think I wasn't completely unaware."

"You knew what you were doing?" I whispered.

"It's hard to explain. That night you left me, my feet started to become numb from the cold pavement. Then, my body… it just kind of took over. I was in a fog and I was only vaguely aware of what I was doing. Like being drunk, or high from some narcotic. I couldn't control it, and I was only somewhat aware of what I was doing. I was in such mental pain from that night, I believe my body did what it has been conditioned to do all these years."

"What do you mean, conditioned?"

"Well, remember when you asked me about this and these?" He pointed to his bicep and the back of his hand. "It's very blurry, but I kind of remember doing it. I thought they were dreams, but now I think it's like the guilt manifests itself into an action. And all these others, on my arms, from long ago, same circumstance. When I look at these cuts, they conjure up such overwhelming feelings of guilt. I don't just wear long sleeves to hide them from others, but to hide them from myself."

"And now you know why. Subconsciously, you believe that you're guilty for what happened to your sister, your mother."

"Makes sense, now."

"Okay, Tom." And I handed his shirt back to him. He nodded once and put it back on.

"But, Elizabeth cut your face?"

"What else has she done to me? I feel her now. Now that April has honed into this channel, I can feel her lurking." His head twitched and I got goose bumps.

We sat quietly for a few minutes, then I asked, "What about the journal?"

He shook his head and looked right into my eyes. " The first time I saw that book was in Scotland. Thomas planted that copy for you to see it, I'm sure of it."

I narrowed my eyes and nodded my head. "I believe you. But, since that is the case, why does he have it?" Tom cocked his head and then widened his eyes.

***

Tom and I stayed up late, me, crossed legged on the guest bed with my laptop and Tom at his desk. We scoured the Internet on our respective computers, matching the murders of Phineas's journal to current hate crimes directed at prostitutes and homosexuals. Many of them weren't too hard to find. Most of the dates placed Tom on his own, but one, the one clue that we were fervently looking for, proved Tom's innocence.

He read, "Christine Reynolds, a prostitute in the Docklands, was found propped up against dumpsters in an alley. Forensics determined that the woman was not murdered at the scene, but sometime earlier that same day, the killer had likely lured her to somewhere secluded where the crime would have been committed, and then brought the dead body to the alley. There was no blood surrounding her on the ground or anywhere near the scene of the crime. Her left breast had been removed, and her body was drained of fluids." Tom paused and lifted the open journal from the desk as he turned toward me. "This matches the journal excerpt: '*Walking behind the girl, I grabbed her by the hair and forcibly yanked her head back. Crack. Mmmmm. The sound of her neck snapping back. I took hold of her chin and the back of her head in a firm caress with my hands, and I twisted sharp and fast. That was the moment her breathing stopped. I laughed at the surprised expression on her face. I took her back to my place and used the implement I was so curious about. A simple metal piece with sharp ends, used as a torture devise, to tear apart a woman's breast. I should have kept her alive first to watch her squirm, but alas, maybe the next one. So, I…*'"

"Okay, Tom, I get the picture. When did this one on the net happen?"

"Em, Wednesday, October 6."

Tom turned his head and looked at me over his shoulder and half smirked. "We were in Annapolis."

I nodded. "We sure were."

"Relieved?"

"I believed you. But, to be honest, yeah," I admitted. "Are you relieved?"

"Actually, no. Because this means…."

"This means your father did it or hired someone to do it. Or someone else, somehow, got a copy of the journal."

He turned fully, sitting with his chest to the back of the chair, his legs straddling the seat, gripping the top of the chair with his hands. "But, how could it be Thomas? He's got emphysema. I've seen the medical bills. You've seen him."

"Look, Tom, I'm pretty convinced right now that your father is the most manipulative, evil person I've ever met. You were right. He told me a lot of truths to cast doubt, but they were only partial truths."

Tom closed his eyes and I saw his jaw twitch.

"Well, now, what do we do? We have to go to the police, bring this journal to them, tell them."

Tom shook his head. "I want to confront him first. I want to catch him in his lies."

"Tom! He's possibly a serial killer or at least an accomplice to one. You can't confront him!"

"Look, we've figured out one thing, right? But, Elizabeth is still haunting me. I've got to find out what she wants. I've got to get her out of my head. I don't think that's going to be possible with the police involved. Not just yet. We'll see April first and then we'll plan."

I thought this was a bad, very bad idea.

***

I awoke the next day in Tom's arms. His white oxford was on, wet with my sweat. He was breathing evenly. I looked at the clock, 1:00 PM. We went to bed so late, it's no wonder. It was Sunday afternoon, and the bright sun was filling the room with an almost ethereal glow. Fitting, in a way. I stared up at the ceiling thinking about last night, trying to sort it all out. I was terrified of what might happen with Thomas. I just wanted to get him arrested.

We had taken Mango out at 4:00 AM so he wouldn't wake us up too early, but he didn't want us to sleep any longer. Tom stirred and opened his eyes when Mango licked his face. He pushed him away gently and told him he would take him out in a minute. He squeezed me and kissed the top of my head, then got out of bed and silently went into the bathroom. I heard the shower start.

About 10 minutes later, I heard Tom shouting my name. I hopped off the bed and opened the door to the bathroom. Tom, with a white towel wrapped around his waist, was leaning with his hands on the sink staring into the mirror.

"I remember," he said, quietly.

He turned to me, frightened, and grasped my shoulders. "When I was a child, what he did." He released his light grip and walked out of the bathroom, over to the closet, and started to dress.

"Sit down, please." He said as he came out in grey skinny jeans and a pale blue button down shirt, untucked. I sat on the bed, he across from me on the lounge chair, leaning forward, elbows to knees, staring out the window.

"He used to make me watch. There is a room. There's a room in the basement of his house where he did things, such utterly unspeakable things, to women. He used to bind my hands together and tie them to a pipe on the wall so I couldn't leave. If I started to fall asleep, he would splash cold water in my face to keep me alert. He wanted me to pay attention so he could teach me. He would rape them, Anna. First, rape them, then torture them and then kill them. He would dissect them, after. And he made me watch. If he saw me look away, he would slap me until I watched." His voice rasped.

Clutching the blanket tightly, I asked in a quivering voice, "How old were you?"

"It varied, but it started as early as five, I think." He turned to look at me. "That's why the crimes in the journal seemed so familiar. The ones we connected to the early 1990s, those were the ones that I couldn't shake. And that's why; I was witness to them. And that room, Anna. He would leave me there when he took the women away. I didn't know what he did with the bodies, but obviously, he took them to an alley or some place. But, he left me in that room with the stench of death lingering. He kept me tied up so I couldn't leave, couldn't use the chamber pot he had left in there. And then when he came back, he would beat me because the room smelled of piss, mine.

"Sometimes, he would take me with him. He didn't always bring the women back. No, he lurked in the shadows with me next to him, explaining how to do it—how to commit the deed without being seen or caught. He told me that Phineas used to take him and teach him and that it was important to honor Phineas and that I needed to learn and continue this tradition. And sometimes he would just slit their throats. And I… did… nothing. Elizabeth is right. I am a coward. I should have killed him when I had the chance." Shame and despair crossed his face.

I got off the bed and stood in front of him. "Tom, April is going to be here in a few hours. We are going to do one more session and then go to the police. We are going to figure out the best way to do it so you don't get in trouble for anything."

***

After a day of fret and worry, we had a quick dinner, and then April came by. She had an emergency with another client and apologized for being so late.

We told her everything, but she didn't seem too surprised. She knew that book was evil and knew it was somehow tied to Tom. She was anxious to get to the crux of Elizabeth's involvement, however. We wanted more information before going to the police; besides the journal and Tom's recollections, we had no real proof, yet.

"Alright, we are going to do the same procedure as yesterday. Everything needs to be quiet so I may concentrate."

I got up off the sofa and took Mango to the bedroom, leaving him with a chewy bone, knowing he would gnaw on it for hours if we let him.

I put on the rain sounds, closed the drapes and dimmed the light. April's breathing started to deepen, and deepen, as she rocked back and forth, her arms across her chest, hugging her shoulders. Tom sat across from her on the sofa, next to me, staring straight at her. We both waited for the change to occur. And then it happened. Elizabeth's eyes popped open and she smiled wickedly at Tom.

"Here we are again, little brother. I'm getting a little tired of this. Tired of you!"

"I need some answers, Elizabeth."

"Fine. What?"

"What do you want from me? I want you out of my head, do you understand?" Tom said with much more of a commanding voice than he exhibited yesterday.

She took a breath and shook her head. "Oh, Tom, Tom, Tom. You really don't know what I want from you? You really have no recollection of all the things you've already been doing for me? Do you know how easy it is to get into your head in the first place? You are so fucking easy to manipulate." Her eyes blazed with hatred as she leaned forward.

"No, I don't know what you are talking about!"

Elizabeth sat back casually and laughed, maniacally. Then she began, "Well, first, I've used your body—I mean, I missed out on the whole sex thing. But, it only happened a few times, mind you." She laughed again, "A couple years ago, I brought a bloke home to Father's house. We were in the area, he wasn't home at the time, and so, we went up to my old bedroom. Of course you don't remember, but, he came home and found us and the look on his face was priceless! And then, remember a month ago? In the alley? We only were able to snog with the fellow because we were interrupted."

"The Rugby cap and black rimmed glasses," I whispered. It was Tom that night, but it wasn't. "April" turned toward me and gave me the scariest look I had ever seen, making me shrink back into the cushion. Tom's white face became whiter; his eye started to tick. Directing her gaze back at Tom, she continued.

"And second, my thick, thick, pretentious righteous dear brother, let me ask you something. Don't you think it's odd that when you started telling those ghost stories, an avenging angel came down to rid London of its evil doers? You gave me an in, Tom. Of course, when you were a teenager, I was able to push you a little, but there wasn't much point. You were a scrawny little imp. You're all grown up now, little brother, and the haunted houses allowed me to completely get in. They were my portal to get to you. To give you names and addresses, and once I got in, it got easier and easier. I didn't really need the haunts anymore. You see, dear brother, a part of you wants me in there. A part of you wants to avenge what Father did to us, to me, to Mum, to those poor men and women. You allow me in whether you want to admit it or not. It's fun maiming all those… those vile people who prey on the innocent, isn't it? You know, sometimes when I push a name on you and push you to the address and push you to grab the swine, you take over, Tom. The relentless beatings you administer, sometimes I just sit back and watch you go." A crazed smile erupted on her face.

The room began to spin as a wave of nausea overtook me. I had to breathe, breathe without a sound, as I didn't dare interrupt. I could only imagine what Tom was feeling. The realization, the horror of what Elizabeth was making him do. My breast bone felt like a sub-woofer as my heart slammed against it, quickening its pace. The whole scenario was ludicrous, but this was my reality—my original suspicions were correct—almost.

Tom started shaking his head, "No… no… NO! I wouldn't harm people like that. That's not me!"

She clapped her hands together, "Oh now, isn't it, dear Tom? You've got it in you. How could you not with the abuse you withstood, what you were made to watch? You think you or anyone else could come out of that unscathed? I mean, you killed me, after all. That's the first I saw you have some kind of backbone."

Tom tried to speak; tried to defend himself. His voice started to rise, until Elizabeth clapped her hands loudly and told him to shut it. She went on with her accusations and vitriol.

"You see, Tom, another way I'm so easily able to slip into your mind… your guilt. Your guilt for not protecting me or Mum, your guilt for killing me, your guilt for not coming out from under the sink when Mum called you. Maybe she wouldn't have committed suicide if you had come out."

Tom closed his eyes and shook his head violently and then stared straight into hers, his words quivering. "Elizabeth, I am deeply sorry. I am sorry for not protecting you. I am sorry I was so weak. But, Thomas was too powerful, too strong. I was so frightened of him. You have every right to be angry. However, none of this gives you the right to use me the way you have. I am not going to allow it anymore."

Elizabeth laughed, horribly; slapping his bad knee, making him wince. "Tom, you can get all the mediums you want! I can get into you when I want, plain and simple. But, I'll make a deal with you, dear brother. I'll leave you alone, forever, but you have to take care of our father. I want him dead!"

"NO! Elizabeth, that won't happen. We're going to the police. He's going to be locked up." Tom said, sternly.

She shook her head, vigorously. "Uh uh, nope. That won't do. I want him dead. But, you see, Tom, I could push you to do it." She stood up, then bent over, placing her hands on each of Tom's legs, leaning right into his face. "I have come close a couple of times, but I want YOU to do it. I want you to protect me, Tom. For once, YOU protect ME! And then you can fuck Anna in peace and get on with your life and finally, I'll be at peace." She pushed off of him and stood straight up. She then held her hands together as if she were praying or begging, almost.

"Tom, you have the skills! Dear Father made you watch, remember? Did you know Phineas taught him how to kill, took him right under his wing? But, you, you wouldn't participate, which made him even madder and more abusive toward you." She then started to pace back and forth in front of us. "But, you at least know how to slip in and out of the shadows, just like the way Phineas taught our father. You are a shadow when you need to be. I've made you famous, like a superhero. This vigilantism? It's all led up to the ultimate baddie. Our father."

Tom, who had been trying to keep his composure this whole time, couldn't hold it in much more. I saw his face break, his breathing quicken, his eyes blink, fervently. I knew he needed some release. This was all too much for him, for all of us.

Elizabeth crouched in front of Tom, her chin hovering above his knees. She grabbed both of his hands tightly and quietly coaxed, "Don't you want to do it, Tom? Just a little bit, yeah? Wouldn't you like to burn him like he burned you? Make him piss in his pants? I know you have it in you, Tom." She started to squeeze his hands, digging her nails into his flesh. Tom didn't move. "But no matter, I will push and push until you kill Father or you get caught. And if you're caught, how sad it would be for Anna. She loves you Tom, God knows why, but she does. I feel her. I felt her the first time you met her. And somehow, she felt my WRATH."

And then, she was gone. The whole room was silent, just a faint gnawing sound coming from the guest bedroom and the soft sounds of the rain. April took a number of deep breaths, let go of Tom's trembling hands, and stood up. Pinching the bridge of her nose, she opened her kind eyes and then sat down next to Tom, who was staring down at the indentations in his hands. She shook her head, licked her lips and stroked Tom's shoulder.

"Are you going to turn me in?" Tom asked April in a small voice.

"Good God, no Tom! You are not the Vigilante. Your sister is. The first time I touched you, I felt a jolt. I knew something was amiss, but I couldn't pinpoint it. Now we know."

"I need to turn myself in! Before I harm anybody else." He looked straight at me.

"Stop saying 'you', Tom! You are not going to go the fucking police and ruin my life, you understand me?!" I was shrieking at him. I couldn't believe what he was saying. "I mean, seriously, what are you going to say? My dead sister made me do it?"

Tom didn't know what to say. He sat, there, shocked.

"This is what we are going to do," April cut in. "You two are going to get some rest. But I am going to deliver the journal to the police and tell them that I had a premonition when I touched it. That I saw your father doing these crimes. That you had given me the journal after finding it in your father's house. We are not going to mention anything about the Vigilante. I have a good rapport with Scotland Yard. They'll believe me; they always do. Do you understand me, Tom?"

He didn't answer.

I retrieved the journal and handed it to April. She put her arm around Tom's shoulder in a very motherly way and said, "Knowledge is power. Now we know. Now we know everything. Things are going to get better, maybe not right away, but they will. I can see it." She patted Tom's knee, stood up and bid us goodbye. She instructed that she would be in touch once she talked to her contacts at Scotland Yard. I followed her to the door.

"Keep him here. Keep him safe, Anna. Maybe call a friend to help?"

I nodded slowly. She gave me a sympathetic hug and then left. I stared at the door, scared to turn around.

"Anna?" Tom rasped. "Anna, I think you should go. Please, take Mango and go to Jamie's."

"No, I'm not going anywhere. I'm staying right here with you," I said, meekly, as I turned around to face him.

He looked spent, so defeated and hopeless. I stepped back into the living room where he sat on the modern white sofa.

"Please, don't argue with me on this, I'm worried about your safety. I can't guarantee anything."

"No."

He started to raise his voice a little and his jaw contracted as he stared up at me. "Goddammit, Anna, this is not a request."

"No."

He stood up and grasped my shoulders, glaring right into my eyes. "What do I need to do to get you to leave? Hurt you? Do you want me to do that? Because if you stay, that could happen. I don't know how much control I have anymore, as if I ever had any in the first place. And I couldn't live with myself if I laid a hand on you. Do you understand that?"

"You can say or do whatever you want. I'm not leaving."

Resigned, he dropped his hands and his gaze and then walked into the kitchen. Opening the refrigerator, he grabbed a bottle of water then took a seat back on the lounge chair.

I took a chance, turned off the light, and sat on his lap. He didn't touch me at first, he just sat staring at nothing in the darkened room.

I rested my head on his shoulder and breathed him in... sweat mixed with cologne. Finally, he put the water down, but still didn't respond, still said nothing. I turned toward him, straddling his legs and kissed his mouth. Pulling back slowly, I focused on the outline of his face in the dark, trying to get a read on him. Then, as if a switch flicked, he grasped my face and kissed me, ramming his tongue into my mouth. Hugging my hips, he stood up as I wrapped my legs around his waist. He carried me to the sofa and dropped me down onto it. I heard him start to unbuckle his belt and then he tore at my jean's button fly. All the events of today and yesterday, the insane reality, poured out of him, poured out of us. I let him take it out on me, let him use me. All the pain, anguish, foreboding he was feeling, I took it. Tom was rough, but not to the point of really hurting me, just intense. It was one of the most exhilarating, yet incredibly sad experiences I'd ever had with a man. Sweating, breathing hard and exhausted, we lay on that sofa, his arms wrapped around me tightly, saying nothing, just basking in each other's here and now. Here and now was all I could deal with. I didn't know what tomorrow was going to bring. I kept thinking this was the end of us, the last night together. This feeling of dread and foreboding was hard to shake. My thoughts eventually knocked me into sweet oblivion and I fell deeply asleep.

***

— *1:30 AM*

"Ouch." The side of my face throbbed from hitting the hardwood floor next to the sofa. Tom was sleeping soundly, taking up all the space--no wonder I fell. Shaking off the pain, I stood up and felt my way into the kitchen to pour myself a glass of water. Not wanting to disturb Tom, I felt my way back into the den, closed the door, and then turned on the light. Flipping on the computer and stretching, I took a seat, typed in the password Paisley, and put on *So Who's Paranoid*. I kept it low.

I searched again for the two assaults that proved Tom not to be the Vigilante. My thoughts were a little clearer than earlier, logic and skepticism seeping back into my mind. I had to know if this channeling was real, if Tom was actually talking to his dead sister or all this was just bullshit—some weird set of crazy coincidences and wild imaginations. Pulling up the story on the priest, the night I had followed Tom, I scrutinized the whole article. And then I saw the time. 2300. 2300!? Wait, I thought it was 9:00 PM, which would have been 2100.

Oh God, I hate this fucking 24-hour clock! But, now I was sure it was Tom I had followed, or at least his body, if I believed all the crazy shit April was saying. Would he have had time to get to the priest? Yes. He was with the guy at the bar around 9:30 or 10:00, and I didn't get home until around 1:00 AM. That gave him plenty of time to assault the priest.

Taking a long sip of water, I searched for the story on the vigilante my mom had told me about in Annapolis. There certainly was an assault, just as my mother had described. The report came out in December, saying that the attack happened in early October, but didn't get reported until the victim tracked down his estranged wife and son in Virginia. Apparently, he accused them of hiring someone to attack him, and he threatened his wife with a crowbar. The wife, in turn, called the police and the whole story broke. The attacker was never found, only described as a tall person, with a black coat, wielding a baseball bat. The man succeeded in cutting the attacker's side, but after, he said that he was knocked out cold and his knife was missing. I sat back in the chair, shaking my head.

And then I thought about the baseball cap, the glasses, the black mask that the Vigilante wore. Where did he keep it all? The flat was organized beyond belief. Also, Tom didn't have that much stuff, only what he needed. So the articles, if in the flat, could only be in a couple of places. I went to the closet and turned on the light. Nothing. He really had cleaned it out since my parent's visit. Getting on all fours, I peered under the bed and then under the dresser—not even a speck of dust. I then walked into the closet in the bedroom, the one we now shared. I knew nothing was on my side, so I crouched down and looked under Tom's clothes. Once again, nothing, just shoes arranged in tidy rows. Rocking back onto my butt, stretching my neck, I spied something on the ceiling in the far corner, above the shelf where his clothes hung. A small door—probably access to the attic. Walking out of the closet, down the hall and into the kitchen, I quietly grabbed a step stool. As I started back down the hall, I hesitated as I heard Tom breathing deeply.

Back in the closet, I stepped onto the first step and then climbed to the highest tread and pushed on the little door. I was too short to actually see, but I was able to reach with my hands to feel around, and my hands found something. I reached behind it the best I could and pulled it out into the small opening. Gingerly, I crept back down the steps with the box under my arm and then sat on the closet floor. I took a deep breath and then opened the worn shoebox lid. Staring at me were black rimmed glasses—a close copy to his reading glasses, an England Rugby cap, black leather gloves, and a black ski mask.

All cried out, I couldn't shed a tear. I just stared at the contents in the box. If this were a horror movie or one of Tom's stories, I would have loved it, eaten it up, been intrigued, the fantasy of it turning me on. I probably even would have had a major crush on the main character—tortured soul, incredibly attractive puppet. But I was living it. And in fact, I did love the main character, but I wouldn't wish this reality on anyone, certainly not myself. I stood up in a daze, crawled into bed and under the covers. As I tried to sleep, my head swam with the things I knew Tom had done. Even if Elizabeth drove him to it, Tom was in there somewhere, allowing it to happen. Taking a bat to someone's head, knocking out teeth, shoving a pipe up someone's ass, methodically smashing toes and knees with a hammer. Imagining it all, picturing Tom doing all this, I wanted to throw up. Instead, I took a number of deep breaths and kept repeating to myself over and over again—it was Elizabeth, not Tom.

***

I awoke with a searing pain in my jaw. Sitting up, I threw the covers off me and ran into the living room while rubbing my jaw. He wasn't on the sofa. I looked in the kitchen, ran back to the bedroom, the bathroom, the guest room, the guest bathroom, no Tom. I then heard whimpering. I quickly ran to the foyer and saw Mango staring at the door.

The ache in my jaw ceased, but the realization of what it meant roared toward me like a freight train. Elizabeth was going to strike someone. The time was 2:45 AM. I had to find Tom.

CHAPTER 29

Not remembering how he got there, but knowing how it happened, Tom tried to make sense of his surroundings. Despite the mask the man was wearing, despite that he had no oxygen tank with him and was not endlessly coughing, and despite Tom's confused state of mind, Tom recognized his father on a very dark, relatively deserted street in Essex. Thomas had been stalking a prostitute. Elizabeth took Tom there and elbowed Thomas hard in the jaw, but then she disappeared, leaving a stunned and very confused Tom staring into the face of his would-be victim. But, he froze. He was disoriented.

The last thing Tom remembered was falling asleep on the sofa with Anna in his arms. This wasn't Tom. Tom wasn't violent, wasn't a killer; he was a man who just wanted to marry his beloved, walk his dog, and live in peace. He just wanted to escape his demons and live a normal life devoid of harsh memories, abuse, guilt, and death. He looked at his father, who staggered to get up. Thomas took off the mask and stared at his son. They locked eyes briefly, but Tom looked away, giving Thomas the opportunity to slam a rock he had picked up from the ground into Tom's forehead. Tom saw a blinding white light and then nothing at all.

Thomas watched, pleased with himself, as his son fell hard onto the ground. Swiftly, he grabbed Tom under his arms and pulled him down the dark street. Thomas had little trouble getting his son in the car; adept from the practice of moving many bodies before. He had to think about his next move. All the half-truths he had given Anna to get her to leave, the planted journal she found with Tom's name all over it, didn't chase her away. He actually liked the girl, but he'd have to deal with her. He was not going to allow Tom to live the life he himself should have had. Money, a wife, a proper life.

He transported Tom back to his house, in through the door, and down the steps. His jaw still hurt, but that's a small price to pay. Tom's Chuck Taylors bounced down each step as Thomas pulled him down, down, down to the basement room.

***

Tom, bleary eyed, awoke. Focusing as best he could with the throbbing pain in his head, he looked around at the dank room. Propped up against the corner wall, shivering, he felt the cold, hard floor through his jeans. His wrists were bound behind his neck, tied tightly to a pipe. His shoes and socks were gone. As his mind started to clear, more memories resurfaced. He knew this place, knew it all too well. He saw the broken chamber pot in the other corner. He saw scratches on the wall that he put there as a child. He saw the bed, the filthy mattress that his father's victims had been laid upon. Sometimes where he himself had slept. With the smell of death still lingering in the air, Tom's stomach began to roll in revulsion.

Then, he heard a noise, a click. Then a turn of a knob. A door opening. The sound was the same he had heard watching so many horror movies with Anna. How ironic.

"Look who's up."

"What have you done?" Tom slurred, attempting to keep his wits about him, shifting his body. His shoulders burned from the awkward position of his arms.

Thomas stood over Tom, straddling his legs. The alpha male stared at his pup. Stared him down until Tom had to avert his eyes. Only then did Thomas speak.

"Oh my dear son. What haven't I done? You were so damn easy to play. Look, I'm as strong as an ox. I don't have emphysema. I faked it, just to get you over here. I faked my medical bills, bought me an empty oxygen tank. And you fell for it all you pitiful boy. You paid my bills, took care of your poor helpless old man. I knew you wouldn't come back if I didn't play the victim. I know you better than anyone."

Thomas's voice trailed off into a false sympathetic rasp, "Your guilt drives you, boy."

"You're really not sick." Tom shook his head, trying his best to stay focused.

Thomas smiled and laughed, "No. Not at all."

Tom struggled to get out of the knot, but it only got tighter, the rope burning his wrists.

"Sorry, lad, but those knots are going to dig into your skin if you keep moving. I'll untie them in a bit, maybe let you use the chamber pot. Ah, but maybe I won't."

"Why are you doing this?"

"Oh, lots of reasons. But the most important reason is that you, my boy, are A FUCKING PUSSY!" Thomas spat, as he leaned over into Tom's face. Tom winced as he felt Thomas's fury invade every cell in his body. He braced himself for the blow he knew was coming. But instead, Thomas stood up and paced.

"When you were born, I was over the moon! A son, a son to carry on my grandfather's legacy, my legacy! It's in our blood, lad. My dear grandfather taught me well. Taught me how to rid the earth of the scum that pollutes our streets. Scum like you, you fucking faggot!" He pointed, angrily, in Tom's direction. "You'd never take part in any of the fun, the family tradition. As hard as I tried, no matter what I did to you, how hard I punished you, you refused. You just watched, weeping, pleading with me not to hurt them."

Thomas then crouched down so he was even with Tom's shocked face. Tom tried to look away, but Thomas grabbed him firmly by the chin, digging his pudgy fingers into Tom's flesh, forcing Tom to look into his eyes. Thomas leaned in, blowing his stale cigarette breath into Tom's face and said in a guttural voice, "And then, of course, there's always the sweet revenge for you taking my daughter from me. My wife as well."

"You raped your daughter and your wife, you bloody swine!" Tom seethed as he looked straight into his father's eyes, grimacing from the pain in his wrists and head.

Thomas ignored him, released his grip, and continued, "And I think about all the money I'll receive as being Trevor's only living heir, the money that should have gone to me anyway. You're not married yet, so Anna won't see any of it. In fact, Anna's going to be out of the picture soon, anyway."

Tom narrowed his eyes and set his jaw; adrenaline rushed through his bloodstream. With no hesitation, he yanked both his knees right into Thomas's crotch. The blow landed perfectly causing Thomas to fall to the side and howl out in pain. Tom continued to kick at his father with all the strength he could muster, while his shoulders and neck were screaming at him to stop. But, it was to no further avail, as Thomas rolled just outside of Tom's reach.

"You fucking bastard, if you touch her, I'll kill you!" Tom yelled, trying as hard as he could to get out of the unrelenting knots. After a minute, Thomas started to regain his strength, got to one knee, then pushed up to both feet. He stared down at Tom, his eyes smoldering with hate, but then, that grin… that sinister grin that Tom knew so well, overtook his father's smug face.

Thomas slid off his belt, slowly. "I'm proud of you son. You finally got me. But, a son who disrespects his father, well, you know what happens."

Still out of reach of Tom's feet, Thomas continued to speak, slowly, quietly, "Do you remember? Do you remember this room? Long days and nights in here? The filthy paisley bear was your only friend. Do you remember wanting your mum, but she was gone? And I'm sure you remember this," Thomas said dangling his belt in front of him. "I've been wanting to do this for so long. What you've turned into? A pretentious, little prig. Now let's see if we can reopen some of those scars, shall we?"

***

— *2:50 AM*

I was frantic as I got in the cab, directing the driver to Thomas's house.

***

Tom heard first a whirring and then a loud crack as the folded belt hit him squarely across his right cheek. His head violently turned to the left as he cried out. A second strike hit him across the other cheek, amplifying the throbbing in his head. Thomas quickly wound the belt around his knuckles, reeled his arm back and slammed Tom squarely in his nose, then mouth, then cheek, then eyes, then mouth again. Warm blood filled Tom's mouth and throat causing him to choke and cough, splattering blood symmetrically on his father's face. Thomas laughed. He wiped his face with the tips of his fingers and tasted his son's blood. The heavy meaning behind that action brought Tom to tears. He knew he was going to die. He knew he wasn't going to see Anna again. Flitting in and out of consciousness, he pictured her. He held onto to the image of her until he passed out. Then, three hard slaps across his face startled him back awake.

The pummeling didn't stop. Thomas's rage from years and years of hating and resenting his son reached meltdown and violently exploded. Relentlessly, he kicked Tom with steel tipped boots, bruising, breaking, cracking his son's ribs. He giddily stomped on Tom's knee, the knee he had struck with a baseball bat a couple weeks ago. Tom gasped and wheezed, trying to suck in air, but he only inhaled more blood, causing him to cough and sputter even more, but all the while, through the pain, through the dread, he pictured Anna.

Thomas, breathing heavily from working over his son, took a small break to admire his accomplishment. Bloody, broken, and swollen, Tom's body was still. Thomas knew he wasn't dead yet, as every so often, Tom would twitch. Thomas walked over to the door, opened it, and lightly closed it behind him.

In the silent room, barely awake and barely alive, Tom held onto the image of Anna holding Mango for the first time, Anna accepting his proposal, Anna getting lost in her music. He started to feel bliss in his barely conscious state, until freezing cold water doused his face. He opened his swollen eyes as much as he could, seeing a blurry image of his father putting down the glass and walking over to the corner, grabbing something or somethings. He thought he saw his father walk back towards him, dangling a rusty metal ring from a chain. Then, he felt hard, sharp metal close around his neck.

Through the ringing in his ears, Tom heard his father speak. "You like what you bought me? So many instruments of torture to be found on Amazon. My grandfather had to make his devices, but it's so much easier today. They are a bit expensive, but you could afford it." Thomas proceeded to fasten a twelve-inch metal sheath with small spikes on the inside, around each of Tom's knees. The iron maiden bit through Tom's jeans and into his skin. He was paralyzed, as he knew if he moved, the teeth from the contraption would sink deeper into his skin.

"Now, let's see how much restraint you have. I wouldn't move if I were you," his father warned.

Thomas casually walked over to Tom's left and removed the riding crop that was hanging on the wall. He cocked his arm back and Tom, once again, felt the wrath of his father and great-grandfather. The soles of his feet burst wide open, red pouring out onto the ground as the riding crop lashed out over and over again. All the muscle's in Tom's body contracted, a feeble attempt to keep from moving. The piranha around his legs kept biting him and biting him, tearing at his flesh, as the snake tore apart his feet.

When Thomas was satisfied that his son was too weak to do anything, he unfastened the blood-stained small iron maiden and untied Tom's arms. Tom was then yanked by the chain and ring attached to his neck, causing him to crash heavily onto the concrete, face first. Tom awoke. Clawing at the ground and trying desperately to breathe, Tom felt his shirt split open, exposing his bare, scarred back. He heard laughing as he felt the lash of leather straps rain down over and over on his back, bum, and legs. Fresh lines of red crisscrossed over the white raised scars. Blood trickled down, down, onto the ground. Tom was too weak, too spent to fight back. He thought he was screaming, but in reality, only whimpers were audible. He was slightly relieved when he thought his punishment had stopped, but then the unspeakable happened.

He heard the striking of a match, the puff of a cigarette, and then felt the small downward tug on the waistband of his tattered jeans. He was back in his room, right after Robbie had left, his father sitting on his legs, leaning into him, humming and painting his masterpiece. Knowing what was coming, Tom just about passed out again, but right before he did, he felt the small buzz in his head disappear completely. Elizabeth was gone. He had failed her, yet again.

***

Tom was in a dreamlike state. Shock had set in. The pain was unbearable. Old scars violently opened. New burns traced onto the old ones. New scars to further mar his body, his mind. When he tried to move, his body would scream so loud it was deafening, but somehow, he found a small glimmer of strength. Somewhere deep in his consciousness. He tried to grasp it, but it was like the horizon, impossible to reach. His brain told his body to crawl to the door, but he couldn't move. Then the voices started:

"I told you to kill him, remember? If you had just killed him, you wouldn't be dying yourself." The voice repeated, over and over, in his head. Through the voice, he tried to concentrate; tried to breathe, but it didn't help, for he started to hallucinate.

CHAPTER 30

Scrambling from the cab before it even fully stopped, I sprinted into the unlocked house and started screaming for Tom. I was so tunnel-visioned that I didn't even see Thomas until I felt his meaty hand grasp my arm and sling me to the ground. He grabbed a fistful of hair and dragged me to the basement steps, hurling me down with a swing of his powerful arm. Before tumbling the whole way and breaking my neck, I was able to grab onto the banister with one hand. I looked up, finding Thomas slowly walking down the steps toward me, whistling some song. I quickly ran down the rest of the way to the dimly lit basement. I could scarcely see, but I followed the scent of horror to a door. I felt for a knob, but before I found it an elephant slammed into me from behind and crushed me against the wall.

"You sure you want to go through that door? You might never come out," Thomas warned. Then, I almost heaved when I felt a slimy slug climbing up the back of my neck, Thomas's tongue. As he licked me, he exhaled stale cigarette smoke into my ear as he whispered how much fun we were going to have. He then opened the door and flung me into the room.

***

Tom lay on his bed. He thought he might be catching an ailment because he was shivering. But, he also felt warm. Warm liquid was covering his body. 'Oh,' he thought, 'I'm in the bath. I'm taking a bath.' He then smelled smoke. He worried there was a fire, until he saw Anna come through the bathroom door in a haze of smoke. It's just smoke from Anna's cigarette. But wait, Anna doesn't smoke.

***

Tom was lying in a heap on the ground. There was so much blood on his face and body, illuminated by the small lamp that emitted a ghostly glow into the room. I yanked off my Ministry shirt, leaving me cold in a tank top. Gently wiping his face, sopping up the blood and snot, I was able to hear faint breathing. His beautiful face was barely recognizable as there was so much blood. His eyes and cheek were swollen, his lips red and puffy, his nose askew. Blood had filled up in his mouth and was dripping onto the floor. His back was mottled with angry welts and bloody gashes, torn up and exposed. One leg was contorted at an odd angle. I took the rag to his feet... the gashes like hash tags. I tried to keep it together, tried to control myself, but I couldn't keep it in. The smell and reality of Tom's blood filled my senses as I crawled over to the corner of the room and threw up.

While waiting for the cab, I had called April and left an urgent message. I knew she was going to the police and I hoped she was having success, hoping they would get here in time. I called Seamus, but also had to leave a message. Why I didn't think to call the police myself was beyond me. I was so panicked; I wasn't thinking straight, wasn't thinking at all. Just desperately reacting. Why did I figure I could come over to a serial killer's house and just take care of things? I walked right into the danger and instead of saving Tom, I was killing him and possibly myself. Stupid, stupid!

After wiping my mouth with my wrist, I crawled back over to him. If I tried to stand, I knew I would fall right over, for I felt as if all my muscles had atrophied

"Tom, honey, please wake up." I cried, "Please, please, stay with me here." I started sobbing.

"Anna?" It was barely audible.

I gulped. "Tom, I'm here."

His whispered voice had a lisp. "I've failed, failed everyone. I'm so sorry." The red drips from his mouth became a downpour, so I held the already blood-soaked rag of a T-shirt to his mouth.

He gently placed his hand on mine. "Elizabeth's gone." Tom tried to speak more words, but I couldn't make out what he was saying.

The door burst open wide. Thomas stood in the frame, gloves on and a knife in his hand. He ordered me to the bed, but I refused, so he grabbed Tom by the hair; he yanked his head back hard and put the knife to his throat. Tom uttered a small noise.

"Do it, or he's dead."

The adrenaline shot through me like a bullet as I scrambled to my feet and hurried over to the stained, mildewed mattress. I opened my mouth to scream, but nothing came out. Instead, Tom, like a ventriloquist screamed for me, loud enough for the walls to cave in. Thomas had stabbed the knife into Tom's left foot. A huge wave of vertigo crashed over me as Thomas turned the knife like a screw, further into Tom's foot. I stared in horror as Thomas stood up, leaving the knife embedded in Tom's mangled foot. Primal sounds, like a dying animal's, were coming from Tom's throat.

"Anna, I've been hoping for this moment. You're really not my type, but you'll do. You are a bit fetching, and besides, this is really for Tom. He… prefers… to watch."

I was terrified. I tried reasoning with him. "Thomas, look, what do you want from us? Just let us go, let us be. This is your son, Thomas! Haven't you harmed him enough in this life?" The quiver in my voice made it sound almost unrecognizable to me.

"Oh, shut it! That pile of shit lying on the floor is no son of mine. He's a faggot, he's an officious git, he's a disappointment! My grandfather would be rolling in his grave if he knew what my offspring had become. But no more, Anna, no more play acting, no more pretending. He's done for, and fucking you is just the icing on the cake. That's the last thing he'll see before I burn his eyes out!"

"Okay Thomas. Do what you want to me, but leave him alone, you've done enough! I won't struggle if you leave him be."

"Maybe I like the struggle, girl." And with that, he pounced on top of me. He knocked me down so I was on my back on the mattress. He straddled my legs, threw his cigarette butt on the ground and started tearing at my tank top. He exposed my bra and then my breasts. He paused for a second and then licked his disgusting lips and plunged his teeth into my neck. I screamed out, tried to fight, punch at him, but to no avail. I heard Tom screaming my name in the background. Thomas slapped my face repeatedly, then undid his pants and started to undo mine.

This isn't happening. This can't be happening.

But, then,… but then something changed. Something started to buzz in my head, some kind of vibration until it overtook my consciousness. I was vaguely aware, but not quite. My arms reeled back and my fingernails scratched at his eyes. Did I do that or was it a dream? Everything was so foggy, I started to forget who I was, even my name. And then, I saw my attacker recoil, teetering upright like a roller coaster at the top of the hill. Then, slowly he started to fall forward onto me, the roller coaster barreling down the hill. His weight was suffocating and I couldn't get him off me. That's when I came around. That's when the buzz stopped, left me. I looked to my left. Tom was there, hovering over us, barely able to stand, my bloody shirt wrapped around the hilt of the knife in his right hand. Blood mixed with blood on that knife. Focusing my eyes behind Tom, I saw a faint figure. No, two figures. Two females, one young, one older, but definitely there, and familiar. And then, they were gone. Tom crumbled to the ground, dropping the knife. I heard it ping as it hit the ground.

Trapped under the heft of Thomas's slack body, I pushed and pushed pointlessly. His weight was crushing and I didn't know how much longer I could bear it. But then I heard my name, Tom's name. I screamed to the voices, yelled as much as I could with the elephant on my chest. I heard a creak and then a bang. Seamus came into view, followed by two policemen, Jamie, and April. The three men pulled Thomas off me while I gasped and gasped until Jamie started hugging me, instructing me to calm my breath. April pulled her sweater off and draped it over my bare skin while Jamie rocked me back and forth, stroking my hair as I cried relentlessly, wetting her shirt. More men came in, EMTs loading two bodies onto gurneys. They brought one for me, but I didn't want to let go of Jamie, didn't want to see what I dreaded most. And then I heard a voice while my face was buried into Jamie's soft chest.

"This one's dead."

CHAPTER 31

— *Five days later*

I walked with Mango down Harley street, taking in the beautiful doors and entryways that decorated my street. He did what he had to do on his favorite tree, then pulled me into Regent's Park. I released him, not worried he would run off, and threw the ball. He would catch it, bring it to me, and then hang onto it. Tom had never been able to get him to drop it, but I would try to train him now.

After a bit, we walked back to the flat and I ran Mango up the steps to the front door. I fed him, gave him water, and walked down to the guest bedroom. I looked at the paisley bear, staring at me from the pillow. I started to tear up again, so I put him on the top shelf of the closet. Taking inventory of the room, I started to straighten it up a bit. I had been sleeping in there. I couldn't bring myself to sleep in my room, not yet. Things were still too raw. I went back to the kitchen and cleaned the dishes. The place looked pretty good. I looked over at the answering machine, saw the blinking "1" and clicked on the message. Trevor.

I started to cry. Cry for the hundredth time this week. I bent down and gave Mango a big hug and then left the flat. I decided to run this time. I didn't want to take a cab or the tube, I just wanted to run, get some air in my lungs. For the first time, in a long while, I felt that today was going to be good, The Damned song "There'll Come a Day" filled my head.

I stopped in front of the hospital and walked inside and then up the steps, two at a time. I talked to the nurse who I had been in contact with most of the week. He led me to Tom's room. When I opened the door, Trevor came over to me with tears in his eyes, gave me a huge hug, and left the room.

And there was Tom.

He smiled when he saw me, tears rolling down his face. Shiny braces were affixed to three of his upper teeth, left of center, including one of his vampire teeth. His eyes were badly bruised, but at least his bandaged, broken nose was centered on his face. Lacerations were drawn all over his face and arms. I pictured what the bottom of his feet and the rest of his body must look like. But, he was starting to heal. His left foot was bandaged from the surgery that hopefully succeeded in repairing the muscles and nerves severed from the stab wound. His left knee was in a brace. But, to me, he looked amazing. He was awake, he was smiling, and his eyes, as Caribbean blue-green as ever, looked at me with such love and relief, I nearly broke down.

"Hi, love," he said as I walked over to him. All I wanted to do was crawl into his bed and hold him, but I was afraid I would hurt him. I did it anyway. He gasped a little, but relaxed into me.

When I sat back up, he wiped away his tears with the back of his hand and said with a slight lisp, "I must look ghastly."

I smiled, remembering, "Um, let's just call it rugged. I think you look beautiful."

"Are you okay, love? Did he harm you?"

"No, just a little gash on my neck, but really nothing. We can talk about that later, okay?"

I got up from the bed and pulled the guest chair over. Gingerly, touching his arm, I said quietly, "I thought I lost you, Tom. I thought you weren't going to make it." I began to well up. "Trevor, Seamus, and Jamie have been taking turns with me sitting vigil or helping me with Mango while I was here. April, Holly, Andrea, and Jack came over a number of times as well. You've got a lot of love surrounding you."

Tom smiled again with a slight nod.

"Did the doctor say anything to you yet?" I asked, wondering how many procedures, how many days of recovery it would be until he could come home.

"A little. She'll be back in a bit, but told me it was touch and go. They were able to re-inflate my lung and get me a transfusion quickly enough before it caused any permanent damage."

"Are you in pain right now?"

"Em, I'm on a lot of pain killers. This morphine is a Godsend. I tell you, though, I now can empathize with teenagers having to wear braces. They are not comfortable."

The doctor walked in. A woman in her late forties, I presume, with mousy brown hair, but a kind round face. I introduced myself and sat back down. I hadn't met her before, but I knew there was a team who had worked on Tom.

"Well, we're very happy to see Tom awake. He's got a feisty spirit in there."

Tom and I exchanged a look.

"It's going to be a long road to recovery, however." The doctor pulled up a chair and started to explain. "I'm not one to sugar coat, so I'll get right to it. Tom had internal bleeding, broken ribs, a punctured lung, a concussion, and a lot of blood loss. We are pleased with the progress on the internal injuries. I do think the surgeries on his knee and foot will prove to be successful. With some PT, he should be able to regain use of his foot and knee. He has multiple, multiple lacerations and bruises all over his body. These will heal in time, although there will be some scarring, I'm afraid. There are some elective procedures to help with that, however. You might want to consider that after the more serious issues are past." She said, sympathetically, turning to Tom.

"With the plastic surgery on your nose, it should heal pretty well, but we'll have to see when the bandages come off. You may need more than the one surgery you've already had. We had to get it set right so you'd be able to breathe through it okay. The braces on your teeth will come off in a couple weeks once the teeth hopefully hold. They were hanging on by threads. The team, however, is optimistic you'll fully recover, eventually." Tom had a mountain to climb, but he was alive, and that was the important thing.

Psychologically, the healing process may take even longer, for both of us. But, I know we'll persevere.

"I know you must have a lot of questions and a lot to process, but I am about to go into an emergency surgery. I'll come back later, however. Try to relax and know that things will get better," the doctor said. She left the room, quickly.

I took Tom's right hand. It was the only place that I was sure I could touch that didn't hurt.

"And... Thomas?" He frowned.

I closed my eyes and shook my head. Tom just nodded and remained silent, in deep thought, but shed no tear. He gave himself a little more morphine from the drip and eventually drifted off to sleep. I watched him for quite some time, watching his chest slowly rise up and down.

After a bit, I switched on the TV, wanting to see if there were any more reports. Of course, it was all over the news. They were repeating a press conference I had missed earlier:

"We have solved the mystery of the serial killer who was responsible for the recent murders of numerous men and women. The women were targeted by this serial killer because they were prostitutes, the men, homosexuals. The suspect, now deceased, was the grandson of the notorious Phineas Hall, responsible for the murders of over thirty women and twelve men in the 1960s. Mr. Hall followed in his grandfather's footsteps and copied his methods of killing. We believe the suspect was also responsible for the murders of twelve more women and three men in the early 1990s. The methods used were carbon copies of his grandfather's, including the use of torture devices used long ago.

"Three days ago, Thomas Hall was found dead in a small basement room of his house, a stab wound to his kidney. In that basement room, Thomas Hall's son, Tom Hall, and Tom's fiancée, Anna Pearson, were rescued after being held captive by Hall, Sr. Ms. Pearson had minimal physical injuries, however, the young Mr. Hall was taken to Hospital and is listed in critical, but stable condition. I will take a few questions."

"Why were the two victims held captive?"

"That is still under investigation. Next?"

"Who killed Thomas Hall?"

"That is also still under investigation, however, one of the captors witnessed a very tall female wearing a mask come into the basement room and stab Hall, Sr. Our witness claims she left immediately."

"Was this the Vigilante?"

"That is still under investigation, and as far as we know, unrelated to this case."

A broad smile crossed my lips.

EPILOGUE

Tom has been back from the hospital now, for a number of months. His injuries are healing, although his long, smooth stride has turned into a long, smooth limp. Many of the scars on his body will always be there, but with time they will fade, like the memories. The plastic surgeon performed miracles to restore his face; it looks exactly as it did before, besides some light scarring. His physical therapist says his limp should vanish over time. Mentally, Tom has been seeing April on an ongoing basis. He is learning to deal with his guilt and post-traumatic stress he endured from his past and recent abuses. However, he still has nightmares where he wakes up terrified and sometimes disoriented, but I'm always there to calm him down and bring him back to reality.

It took a while to convince him to not go to the police and turn himself in as the Vigilante and for killing his father. But we were persistent. Seamus repeatedly threatened him with bodily harm, April persuaded in her gentle way, and I led the charge with my argumentative determination. Tom finally acknowledges that he had no control over his actions, except for killing his father to save me, and that going to the police would only ruin his life and mine for no reason—and Seamus's life, of course. Tom, however, has given large sums of money to organizations that help abused women and children.

The blackouts have ceased, the cutting has ceased, and there have been no more reports of vigilantism on the news. We were, however, sensationalized in the media, and reporters camped out at our front door for a bit. Eventually, they started to leave us alone and went onto the next crazy story. Business at the ghost tour has never been better. Jamie isn't the only one with a crush on Tom.

We resumed the wedding plans, but moved the date. I don't know what challenges we will have in the future, but I believe the worst is in the past. At least I hope, I mean, how could anything be worse than what we endured?

And me? I've not had any more episodes. April explained there was some kind of supernatural connection between me and Elizabeth. That maybe Eloise, in her own way, was trying to save Tom from his sister, from his father. That she gave me the strength to defend myself against Thomas during the attack. That she created some sort of link between me and Elizabeth. This would, at least, explain the severe pain I felt from Elizabeth's brutal attacks and the dreams of the lady I had. I looked at old pictures of Eloise and Elizabeth when we cleaned out Thomas's house. I couldn't be certain, but Eloise sure looked like the lady in my dreams. The pictures I scrutinized sure looked like the woman and teenager in the wisps who were behind Tom in the basement. I couldn't be positive, but April believes it was them and I sure trust April. But, if there's one thing I learned, things aren't always as they seem, nor are they easily explained.

And that night, the night I thought was the beginning of the end? As usual, I thought wrong. It was the beginning of a new beginning. The only graphic tee shirts that will fit me now are the oversized ones… at least until October.

ABOUT THE AUTHOR

Janice E.C. Coleman is a first-time novelist with
a love for the paranormal and anything Halloween.
One night on a ghost tour, she stared up at a
haunted house's window, and the idea for
Night Walker began to take shape.

Janice lives with her husband, daughter, and
two rescue dogs in Annapolis, Maryland.

COLOPHON

The chapters of this book are
set in Garamond 11 point type.
The front cover and title page are set in
Philosopher, an open-licensed font
designed by Jovanny Lemonad.
The back cover uses Caslon.

Made in the USA
Columbia, SC
04 April 2018